The Wrong Sword

Ted Rabinowitz

Aigrefin Press

The Wrong Sword

Published in the United States of America
Cover Design: David Fymbo

ISBN: 0692500898
ISBN-13: 978-0692500897

DEDICATION

For my grandfather, Mort Bilenker, the first
storyteller in our family. *Alahv ha-shalom.*

CONTENTS

ACKNOWLEDGMENTS

Nobody does anything well without help; despite the image of the lonely author in the garret, writers are no exception.

First, my mom, my dad, and my brothers Alan and Lon (one by blood, one by time served in the trenches). Then there's the rest of the extended Rabinowitz clan, from California to the New York islands. Such an accomplished tribe!

The good folks at the Fire Rose Writers Lounge and the Secret Rose Theatre—Kaz Matamura, Mike Rademaekers, and "Pea" Chiba—who displayed superhuman patience with a cranky unpublished author. If you're in Los Angeles, check them out.

Then the team that stood watch at the first birth of *TWS*, when it was published by Musa, before its current indie incarnation: Michael Carr, my agent; Matt Teel, who edited that first version; Coreen Montagna, who provided line-editing and interior book design; and finally Daniel Lu, who proofread the hardcopy edition.

Thank you all.

1. THE PREVIOUS OWNER

The king stumbled down the tunnel, trailing blood. He had ridden for three days without stopping, and he could barely stand. His queen was dead. So were his sorcerer, and his best friend, and most of his capital city. His own son was hunting him, with traitors and foreign mercenaries. His dreams of uniting the land again under one *pax*, one law, were dead as Alexander.

Sometimes, it sucked to be the king.

As he dragged himself forward, his sword whined and muttered, begging him not to sheathe it, to wield it once again for justice. Of course, it was the sword that had gotten him into this mess in the first place. It had taken him out of the stables, made him king, given him the power to do any bloody stupid thing he liked. A giant circular table! A Perilous Seat that only the pure could sit in! A Britannia-wide manhunt for a four-hundred-year-old cup! What had he been thinking?

And the sword was still making it hard for him. The prince, his appalling son, had enough pure meanness to force the sword into obedience, no matter how the sword itself felt about it. That was the one thing the king could not allow. So instead of expiring peacefully on a couch of

1

shimmering samite, surrounded by weeping damosels, he was limping down a Welsh burial mound, leaking fluids, hoping desperately that he'd get there before—

"Hello, Your Highness."

It was Hwyll son of Kaw, a nasty piece of work who loved knives and hated soap. The king had disliked Hwyll even before the knight had gone all Ostrogoth and woven those shark's teeth into his beard. And behind Hwyll, filling the rocky shore between the tunnel mouth and the lake, were a dozen private military contractors. Saxons, by the look of them.

"Why, Hwyll, what are you doing down here? Come for the waters?"

"Hand it over, Your Highness." Hwyll extended his hand.

The king smiled to himself. His son might have a spirit strong enough to master the sword, but Hwyll? The knight was a dead man, and he didn't even know it.

"You want it? Here!" The king tossed the sword into the air. Hwyll caught it, hilt-first.

And screamed.

He staggered backward, then shook the sword as though it were red-hot grease clinging to his skin. He screamed again, fell to his knees, and with a final whimper, shoved it point-first into the cavern floor. The blade cut into the bedrock like cheese, sparks flying everywhere, squealing against the stone.

Hwyll collapsed, twitching. The Saxons backed away, making witch signs and muttering charms. *Bloody pagans.*

The king limped to the sword and grabbed the hilt. Strength poured into him, and he pulled it effortlessly from the stone. He twirled it casually in front of himself, once, twice.

"Right, then," said Arthur, for the very last time. "Who's next?"

2. EIGHT HUNDRED YEARS LATER – TUESDAY

It was a bright, breezy morning on the Rue St. Germain, and five or six knights were getting their post-Matins exercise by abusing random townsfolk. Henry had been on his way to meet a promising new friend when he spotted the knights, but seeing the flower of chivalry about to single out a young dairymaid for some serious harassment, he knew at once he had to meet these bold cavaliers and share the good word.

"Hallelujah! Hallelujah! Praise *le bon Dieu* and Our Lady of Paris! I have found it!" Henry stumbled into the street and fell to his knees in front of the knights. His teenaged face was a mask of well-practiced joy.

Caught up short, the knights stumbled to a halt, their swords snaking between their legs. The dairymaid fled. The leader of the knights, a tall, bony thug with big hands and long black mustachios, jerked Henry upright by his robe.

"What? What have you found?"

"Why, the—" Henry stopped, as if he had just remembered to keep his mouth shut. "Oh...uh. Nothing.

3

Just a relic for our monastery. Got to be going, thanks for stopping by—"

The knight grabbed Henry's shoulder. His hand felt like a cobblestone. "I don't like monks," he said, to no one in particular. "They think they're better than honest knights."

"But—"

"And I especially don't like pimple-faced smartasses, and you look like one to me."

Got that in one. But Henry didn't have time to smirk, because the knight lifted him into the air and shook him like a rattle.

"What did you find, you scabby little novice?"

"The sword! The sword! I found the Great Sword, Your Highness!"

The knight dropped him to the ground. "Show me."

When they got to the smithy, the knights made a point of filling up the place, bumping into things, pawing and dropping the merchandise. Henry had seen this trick before, but for real intimidation, you needed a shop filled with breakables, not a tent selling ironwork—it isn't easy to shatter a horseshoe. These guys were thick, even for Normans.

"Shopkeeper. Shopkeeper! Show yourself!"

The rear flap opened. A Turk entered, wrinkled and exotic, with a pointed beard and a big green turban. "How may I help the noble sir?"

The knight, Brissac, shoved Henry to the counter. "I want to see the sword of Charlemagne."

The Turk whirled on Henry. "You told him! I mean… me very sorry, monsieur, but me no have sword—"

Brissac pushed Henry aside and leered at the merchant. *Jesu,* thought Henry. *Does this guy have* one *expression that isn't nasty?*

"Show me Joyeuse, or I will see your anvil sunk five fathoms in the Seine."

The Turk held up his hands in surrender. Then,

reaching under the counter, he unwrapped a cloth bundle and laid out its contents.

In the dim light of the booth, it seemed to glow. Broad at the haft, pointed at the tip, its pommel a single ruby, it was every inch a broadsword of the ancient Franks. Even Henry had to admit that it looked good. Brissac sank to his knees, tears in his eyes.

"Aye..." His voice was a whisper.

The other knights gathered around. "It is Joyeuse." One of them pointed to the haft. "Look, there's Charlemagne's crest, etched in the blade."

"*Dieu et mon droit,*" another nodded.

"The prince will love this."

The Turk reached for the sword, but Brissac was there first.

"Not so fast. What price did you give the monk?"

"My Lord—"

"What price?"

"Two hundred *livres.*"

Brissac nodded. "I will pay you one hundred."

"But—"

Brissac leaned in. "Or would you rather I told my prince that Joyeuse, the sword that united all Christendom under Charlemagne, is in the hands of an infidel?"

The Turk wilted. "Very well."

"No!" Henry yelled. "You promised—"

"What can I do?" The Turk shrugged and turned away.

Brissac nodded at one of his men, who dropped a purse on the counter. Brissac took the sword, and the knights left. *One plantagenet, two plantagenet, three plantagenet...*Henry counted to twenty, then peeked through the door-flap. "They're gone."

"The Turk" carefully peeled off his beard and mustache, revealing Alfie's wizened Welsh face, split by the biggest grin in Paris. "A hundred *livres.*"

Henry nodded. "A hundred *livres.*"

Alfie's eyes were wide. "A *hundred livres.*"

Henry snorted. "A hundred *livres!*"

"A hundred *livres!*" Alfie was laughing helplessly now.

"A HUNDRED *LIVRES!*" Henry threw his arms wide.

"YEEEHHAAAAAAA!"

They locked arms and danced.

3. A SWORD OF THE NINE

Henry raced down the Rue Mareväl, the stash of silver *testons* and *dixaines* carefully distributed in six different pouches under his braies and tunic. And that was just the change from two of Brissac's gold pieces. A hundred *livres!* They could live like kings. Spanish oranges twice a week, pheasant for feasts and mutton for mainstays, chops and tripe and bacon and pies...and girls.

Henry grinned. Being fatherless, guildless, and just a hop from the gallows hadn't exactly helped him to impress girls in the past, but that was about to change. With even one more of those gold *écus*, he could become a legend. New tunic, new hose, rent a horse, show up at the hayings next week. Jesu, he could *buy* a horse. Why not? *Ever see a real Parisian before, ma belle? That's right. We do things differently in the big city.* But first, he had to run some errands.

The chaos of colleges, lecture halls, and *scriptoria* that was the University of Paris had grown up around the Abbé St. Genevieve like the mushrooms that sprout on trees after the rain. There were dozens of booksellers, but even with the new wealth, Henry wasn't rich enough to buy a book. Not yet. But he had the next best thing.

A right onto the paved Boulevard St. Michel, a left into

the muck of the Rue St. Severin, and he was cutting through the courtyard of Severin's church into the chapter house, where Tomas of Padua was delivering his weekly theology lecture.

The Paduan was popular, and the *oratorium* was packed. Half the students had stolen chairs from the chapter house, more were leaning on walls or staffs, and a few were literally hanging from the rafters, dribbling wine on their comrades below. Even in a cosmopolitan mob like this one, Henry noticed, the students tended to divide up by dialect—the *Allemani* from across the Rhine sitting in the front, having arrived punctually at the hour of Prime: the *Romani* and *Britannii* perching where they could, and the *Francii* lounging around casually as if they owned the place.

"The disputed question is on the nature of Original Sin. *Sic* or *Non?*"

As the students roared out Biblical quotations for and against, Henry squeezed his way through the mob, getting some angry jabs in return, until he spotted a student he recognized.

"*Ave, filius Golias,*" said Henry. The other goliard raised his hand.

"*Ave, frater,*" he replied.

Henry switched from Church Latin to Paris French. "Where's the Worm?"

"He sold a copy of Aristotle yesterday. Follow your nose."

Henry breathed deep. Above the smells of wine breath and unwashed bodies, he caught the scent of cloves. He followed it through the crowd, out the far door, and into the cloistered walk where the Worm did his business.

Short and pimpled, Pieter of Flores (AKA Petronius Vermiis, AKA Pete the Worm) was convinced he was St. Valentine's personal representative to the women of Paris. He clearly had made a sale yesterday, because today he was wearing a red silk *bliaut* and enough clove oil to stun a horse.

"No chapbooks!" The Worm waved back a student who was pressing close with a sheaf of scribbled parchment. "I don't need class notes. Get me something illuminated, and we'll talk." The student slumped. The Worm leaned in close. "You're a brother at St. Barnabas. They've got a great library. Just...look around some time." Then the Worm spotted Henry and shooed the other schoolmen away.

"Not too busy?" Henry smiled.

"The usual?"

"Yeah."

"Two *sous*."

"Since when?"

"Since Joris of Bruges saw you changing gold coins for silver."

Henry's gut twinged. It was never good news when people knew your business. He promised himself to be more careful next time. As casually as he could, he counted out two of the new *testons*, and they haggled over the value of the coins until Henry threw in a few *deniers du louis* to make up the difference. The Worm led him out of the cloister and into the warren of dormers behind the chapter house.

The Worm was the biggest...freelance librarian...in Paris. Of course, he rarely kept more than one or two books on hand at a time, but he could procure a copy of *The Four Books of Sentences* or *The Matter of Britain* in a day— Aristotle or Augustine in two.

They scrambled up the stairs to the wide garret that the Worm used as his base of operations. He pried up a floorboard and handed the book underneath to Henry.

"There you go. *Ave filius Golias.*"

The Worm left, and Henry opened the book. The folio was huge and bound in oak, and chained to the joist underneath the floor. That was no surprise, of course; one stolen folio could feed a large family for a year, if you could find a buyer. *The Treatise on Knightly Prowess*, by one Gervasius Florentium. Probably a fake name—especially since the book was written in Saxon, not French or Latin—but the information was good. Good so far, anyway.

Quickly, Henry thumbed past the labyrinth design on the frontispiece and the descriptions of ancient armor, ancient horsemanship, forms of address, to the meat of the book—the weapons. Gervasius, whoever he had been, was some sort of eccentric: a learned man who didn't use Latin, a scholar who apparently cared nothing for law, Aristotle or even theology, but only for history—the history of arms.

Henry had no idea where the Worm had found the book, and he didn't ask. It didn't matter: Thanks to Gervasius' descriptions and drawings, six "Joyeuses" were floating around Paris. Now it was time to give Charlemagne a rest and see what other famous swords he could provide to gullible tourney enthusiasts.

Henry passed over Greek *kuthrai* and Viking broadswords, Scottish claymores and English pikes, until he found what he was looking for: the swords of the Tale of the Nine. Nine legendary weapons forged for the heroes of the great nations of history. It was amazing the hold this story had on the castle-building classes. Well, if they wanted magic, Henry would be happy to provide it. He leafed past Charlemagne and Joyeuse and went on to the more exotic members of the Nine. There was Arpé, the sword of Alexander, said to have been passed down from Perseus and to have slain the Medusa; the sword of David, lost in the destruction of Jerusalem; and there—

A Roman cavalry *spatha*. Slender, unadorned, with a cup of a hilt—just the weapon for St. Constantine, Emperor of Rome, benefactor of the Church, patron saint of knights and horsemanship. Now that he thought about it, it might even have a piece of the True Cross in the hilt. Of course, it was plain, and rather small...but Valdemar Smith could tart it up a bit, make it more exciting. Yeah, this was the one.

Henry dug a scrap of parchment and a stick of charcoal out of his scrip, sketched the *spatha*, jotted down all the information, and returned Gervasius to his niche under the floor. St. Constantine would ride again, with a little help from Henry.

The Paris smiths were clustered next to the fullers, an arrangement that kept the noise and stink where it belonged, in the eyes of the city fathers—off the Right Bank and the Île de la Cité, and firmly established among the students, vagabonds, and thieves of the Latin Quarter.

Henry didn't care. It made his trip that much shorter. He walked past the open door to Valdemar's smithy and waited in the alley. A few moments later, Valdemar's apprentice left. Once the prentice was completely out of sight, Henry entered.

"As promised, one *livre* in silver." Henry pulled out a pouch and dropped it on the counter. Valdemar—big, sullen, with muscles out to his ears—made it disappear.

"And we have a new job." Henry slid the parchment across the counter. Valdemar picked it up and looked at the drawings. "It's called a *spatha*. We need it three feet long, and you'll have to make it—I don't know—more pretty, I guess. It's not too impressive, but it's what St. Constantine used, so—"

Valdemar dropped the parchment. "Five *livres*."

"What?"

"The deal's changed. Five *livres* for this...*spadda*."

Henry chewed on that for a moment. "So you heard about the sale too."

"Aye. So did my strikers. And my grinder. And the man who does the hilts."

"You know it was an accident. We never expected a hundred *livres*, and we'll never get that again. We're lucky if we get ten. Five *livres* could mean almost our whole take for the *spatha*."

"It's not about the money, boy. It's about the risk."

Henry smiled and spread his hands. "Help me out, Vee. Where's the risk?"

"You just cheated Prince Geoffrey's men out of a fortune. You don't think there's a risk?"

"Prince?"

"Geoffrey of Brittany. He's staying with King Philip. And if there's risk to you, there's risk to me as soon as they catch you, break you, and find out who made the swords for you."

"Geoffrey...Geoffrey Plantagenet?" Henry couldn't breathe. His mouth felt like it was stuffed with dust.

"You didn't know?"

Henry flew out of Valdemar's shop, back to the Rue St. Germain. By the time he got there, night had fallen, and Alfie's tent had vanished.

4. FUN IN THE CELLARS

Henry's heart slammed against his ribs as he sprinted across the Plâce Royaume, searching right and left for Alfie. The mercers were breaking down their booths, the fishmongers and grocers were long gone, the tinkers—
Wait.

Henry breathed deep. Alfie must have already packed the tent, using his usual band of street kids. It was just common sense, never stay on the same pitch once you've made the sale. Which meant that Alfie would be waiting for him with the rest of the gold at the Cellars.

Had to be.

Fifty feet under the Île de la Cité, deep below the streets of Paris, the Cellars was holding its traditional Tuesday night fester. It didn't differ much from the Wednesday, Thursday, Friday, or Saturday binges in terms of noise, stink, or crooked gambling, but it was more lively than Sunday nights, when most of the participants were still a little subdued after Mass.

Alfie claimed that the Cellars had been there longer than the city itself, and Henry believed it: He'd seen Latin tags left by the legions, carved into the bedrock behind the wine casks...proof that if you provided sleazy entertainment, your business could last a thousand years.

Henry found the dim courtyard a few streets north and west of the half-built cathedral of Notre Dame, and took the stairs that led to the narrow alley that ran past the river's edge. It wound deeper and deeper until the walls around him met overhead and he was heading down into the earth, past foundation stones and buttress timbers and living rock. And there it was, noise and light coming up from the bottom of the stairs. He entered.

It was a huge cave, expanded and smoothed out by some former owner. Henry handed the door guard a *dixaine* and descended the stairs that ran down the wall to the floor forty feet below.

Torchlight and smoke, stench and noise. Two musicians at the far end were playing Bertran de Born's latest peasant-bashing *sirventes*. There were dozens of boards—thirty-foot long tables on trestles—and they were packed with the scum of Paris: thieves, runaway serfs, grad students.

"There he is! Three cheers for the greatest rebel in Paris!"

The music stopped. Everyone turned and got a good long look at him. *Terrific.* He whipped his *chaperon* over his head as the applause rang through the hall and scuttled to the bottom, where Mattie was waiting for him. Of course.

"You were incredible! A hundred *livres!* Everyone's talking about it!" Mattie was pale and slender. A little taller than Henry, he looked even younger, with delicate features and reddish-brown hair. His big eyes were glowing with hero worship.

"Is everyone talking about it because you told them?"

"Well, sure, don't you—"

"Great. Now it'll be even easier for him to find us."

Mattie's face dropped instantly. "I…I didn't think—"

Henry handed Mattie some money. "Forget it. Just get us some wine and bread." Mattie took it and left.

Henry spotted Alfie and sat down. "Geoffrey

Plantagenet, Alfie."

Alfie nodded sadly. "I know. That tall one, the Norman who put his hands on you, it seems he's Geoffrey's right-hand man." Even though it looked like they had no secrets left to keep, they still spoke the Welsh Alfie had taught him years ago.

"What do we do?"

Alfie sighed and fiddled with his cup. "Richard and Saladin go out riding one day," he said. "Suddenly, they're surrounded by Moors. Richard turns to Saladin and says 'Saladin, Saladin, what do we do?' And Saladin turns to him and says 'What do you mean *we*, infidel?'" Henry chuckled, even though Alfie had told him the joke a dozen times.

"Henry, lad, you're the one in danger. They saw your face. I'm just a 'Turk.' Maybe they'll find me, maybe they won't—there's been swindlers 'pulling the Turk' in Paris since St. Louis' time. But you—"

Henry nodded. "I'm the target."

"Aye." Alfie put his hand on Henry's arm. "Don't worry. We knew this would come some day, didn't we?"

No, we didn't, thought Henry. *I thought I could finally stop running.*

Mattie arrived with a jug and a loaf. "For the heroes of the revolution." Henry grabbed the bread; he was starved.

Mattie leaned down. "Listen. I could help with the next one. I know how to fight the feudal power structure."

"'Fight the power structure'? Have you been hanging out at the university again?"

"You need me. I understand the dominant privilege of your enemies."

Henry stood up. "Tell you what." He picked up a broom. "If you want to help, all you have to do is stop me." He snaked the broom around, and the point tapped Mattie on the shoulder, the arm, the stomach.

"That's a sword poking at you, villein." *Tap. Tap.* "What do you do?"

"I fight!" Mattie swung at the broom—but the broom wasn't there. A tap on the head. A tap on the arm. Mattie swung wildly again, and again.

"Oh yeah, peasant? Where's your fight? I have the reach on you. I have you at my mercy." Now the taps were pokes. Then jabs.

"You—" And then Henry sent a jab straight into Mattie's chest, hard. Mattie went sprawling on the floor. Henry leaned down. "I'm a knight. I have a sword. I've trained for years. I can touch you any time I want."

Mattie's mouth opened and closed again. Feeling ashamed, Henry shoved his face into Mattie's. "Stay down, Mattie. Stay down and live."

Mattie got up, trembling. "You REEK!" He ran off.

Alfie watched him go. "A little rough on the kid, maybe?"

Yeah. Henry looked down. "Well, what if he tried to attack a real knight? I'm saving his life." He pushed away his guilty feelings and drank some wine—the St. Wandrille special, watered and sour, one step above drinking from the Seine. "Oh, I don't know. He just gets under my skin."

Alfie hesitated for a moment, as if about to say something, and then shrugged. "Laddie, I know a man in Brest, a sailor. He can take you over the English Water, or south across the bay to Léon, or even the Inner Sea."

Henry grinned. "Just for the fun of it?"

Alfie nodded. "Aye, but the two *livres* you'll give him will probably help. In a year or two, someone will kill Geoffrey, and you'll be able to come back."

"Sure they will, Alfie."

Alfie raised a finger. "One thing I learned in the rebellion, laddie. Men like Geoffrey come and go. They reach too high, and someone cuts them down. But the poor and the wronged—those are forever." Alfie took another drink. "Enough philosophy. If I'm not here when you get back—"

"Of course you'll be here."

"If I'm not, Valdemar will be, and he'll hold the rest of your cut for you."

"Really?"

"He likes you, laddie. Don't know why. But he'll take ten percent. Or you could have the whole cut now."

Alfie reached inside his tunic. Henry stopped him. "Can you see me traveling with that much money? Give it to Valdemar."

Alfie snaked some coins into Henry's hand. "Well, take these for the road, then." Henry glanced down—five *écus*. A fortune, but he felt no joy now. "Go to Brest, and ask for Paul le Galois. He'll answer to 'Pwyll' when you meet him."

"Well, if I'm going, tell me…how did a Welshman get a name like 'Aelfred,' anyway?"

Alfie laughed. Henry hesitated, then hugged Alfie. "Be smart, old man."

Alfie nodded. "Take the back way."

Henry walked to the rear, past the trestle tables and the kegs lining the wall, to the giant fireplace whose flue vented forty feet through the rock. There was a path through the fireplace, around the fire itself, to a rear exit. It wasn't secret, exactly, but it would make anyone following him easy to spot.

Up the back stairs and out on the street. The coast seemed clear. Then he heard it: the faintest rasp of steel on stone, as if by a sword accidentally scraping against a wall.

Oh, Jesu. Henry tucked in his head and ran. Behind him he heard the clatter of hard boots against cobblestones, and the jingle of chain mail—these morons were actually wearing armor. *Thank you, St. Dismas, patron of thieves!* With that noise, he could know just how close they were—*too close* was the answer right now. He picked up the pace.

There were two bridges off the Île de la Cité, and only one that would take him back to the Latin Quarter. Henry pounded for the other, the Pont l'Evecque, hoping against hope that Prince Geoffrey didn't have enough men to cover both.

He could tell from the sounds behind him that he was gaining. He turned a corner and the bridge appeared, shining in the moonlight, broad and empty. *Thank you, thank you, thank you.*

And then he was on the bridge. Behind him came the knights, but ahead of him—

A troop on horseback.

Henry spun toward the river, but before he could get to the edge of the bridge, a knight on horse grabbed him. The last thing he saw was the moon on the water.

5. INTERVIEW WITH A PLANTAGENET

Henry wiggled a little to the right, a little to the left. No give. The chains held him fast. You didn't usually see that kind of workmanship from a prison blacksmith. But then, this was Paris; he wasn't playing the provinces anymore.

The black door swung open, and the prisoners groaned in the sudden daylight. Henry squinted. He could just make out two figures—

"Henri de la Ville-Perdu!"

Damn. All of the sudden, the filthy dungeon seemed positively cozy…at least compared to whatever was coming next.

"There he is." The bailiffs hauled him to his feet. "Up you come." One of them actually looked at Henry with a little sympathy, and Henry felt his guts go loose with fear.

They didn't go down to the torturer's cells, as Henry had been afraid they would. He had a few really bad moments when they took him out into the main courtyard, but they passed the headsman's block too, and entered the central keep.

There were tapestries everywhere, even on the floor. The bailiffs walked over them like they were straw. There were also servants, lots of them, all in velvet and cloth of

19

gold. *Trés* fancy. The prince himself must be in residence. A personal audience with Geoffrey of Brittany. What an honor.

* * * *

"Kneel, pig!" A rap to the calves, another to the shoulders, and he was down on his knees, looking up. It was very efficient. Henry glanced at the one doing the shoving—of course. "Brissac, buddy! How's the sword working out for yo—" This time, the blow knocked him to the ground. Brissac towered over him, blade half out of his scabbard.

"Stop." The man sitting in front of them raised a hand.

"But, My Lord—"

"Leave us, Edmond." For a moment, Brissac seemed about to argue. Then he bowed and left. The man returned to his consideration of Henry, studying him like a horse that might just serve. Henry returned the favor. He saw a solid, well-muscled man in his late twenties. A neat beard covered a scar that ran from cheek to jaw; his hands showed the swordsman's callus on the palm and the bridge of the thumb. Geoffrey's brother Richard was supposed to be the giant in the Plantagenet family, a tower of war—but Geoffrey was no seven-stone weakling.

"Rise, boy."

Henry got to his feet, but slowly. If beating prisoners was his job, Brissac was clearly a man who loved his work. "You are Geoffrey Plantagenet."

"Try 'Your Lordship.'" Geoffrey smiled. "You will live longer that way, I guarantee it."

"May I sit…Your Lordship? It's been a week in your dungeons…I think."

"By all means." Geoffrey indicated no other chairs. After looking around, Henry seated himself tailor-fashion on the carpet.

Geoffrey poured himself some wine. "And of course, they are not *my* dungeons. They are the municipal prisons of Paris, under the control of our right trusty and well-beloved cousin Philip, by the grace of God King of France and Count of the City. Good thing he didn't put you in there, eh?"

Henry kept his smile firmly in place. King Philip was supposed to be relatively sane and even occasionally merciful—although the Plantagenets had certainly lowered the bar in both departments. Geoffrey was telling him that, just or not, Philip had nothing to do with this "arrest." Henry could disappear at any moment, and the only persons who would know or care would be an antique Welshman, a phlegmatic blacksmith, and a tavern sweep with an overheated brain.

"My Lord, surely a prince of your station—"

"Spare me." Geoffrey rummaged through a desk and pulled out a writing tablet. "Let's see. The ninth of November of last year, a Frankish broadsword to one Etienne of Anjou, seven *livres*. The twelfth of December of last year, a Frankish broadsword to one Gaspar the Bold, eleven *livres*."

"Are you sure that doesn't say *'libres'*? I borrow books all the time, and if I forgot one or two—"

"Ah, yes. *'libre,' 'livre.'* A pun. Very funny. In fact, my agent has it written down here—'thinks himself clever.' See?" Geoffrey pointed at the *tabula*. "Frankish broadsword, Frankish broadsword, Frankish broadsword…oh, wait, this one's a spear. A Roman spear that just might be the Spear of Destiny, perhaps?"

Henry tried to hide his surprise. This guy was good.

Geoffrey closed the tablet and tossed it aside. "Did you rob a grave?"

"A grave with six perfectly preserved swords?"

Geoffrey smiled. "I only mentioned five."

"Let's see you keep count after a week in your dungeons."

"Two days. How did you know about the sword?"

Was this a trick? Some way to get him to confess and pack him off to the headsman? Henry needed a moment to think. A faint might be useful right about now…Henry went limp. His eyes drifted down—

Thunk. The prince had barely moved. He'd just…flickered a moment, and Valdemar's broadsword was embedded six inches deep in the wooden beam next to Henry's ear. The *twang* of the blade stirred in Henry's brain like the buzz of a mosquito, and choked the breath in his throat.

Without a pause, without even a change in his breathing, Geoffrey was an inch from Henry, his face a mask. "My time is precious. Answer my questions, and you will see tomorrow. Do you understand? Say 'yes, My Lord.'"

"Yes, My Lord."

Geoffrey didn't move. Henry was eye to eye with him now. In each pupil he could see a tiny spark, a little flame of royal arrogance, stoked and fed until it was a giant bonfire of pure crazy.

"How did you get the swords?"

"When one is able to read, My Lord, the past is open. I found a book that described the weapons of old."

Henry stopped. He didn't want to prompt Geoffrey to ask about the smith he'd needed to make the swords, or the money he'd needed to pay the smith. But the questions seemed inevitable. Henry held his breath—

"So you can read."

That was a surprise. Not that he was complaining, but why did Geoffrey care if he could read? "Yes, My Lord."

"This book, it was in Latin?"

"No, My Lord. Saxon. One of the tongues of *l'Angleterre.*"

"I'm moderately familiar with it." Geoffrey's tone was dry enough to parch a swamp. Of course. The Plantagenets were Angevin French, but it was holding the English throne that made them royalty.

"And you can read Saxon, and Latin, and…what else?"

"I—" But now the shock and hunger caught up with

Henry, and he slumped in earnest. Geoffrey sighed in irritation. "Oh, damn it, take a chair, take some wine. I won't kill you." He clapped his hands. Servants appeared with a chair, wine, and food. They seated Henry, handed him a cup, and withdrew. "Drink. Eat."

Henry grabbed at the meat and felt strength flowing back into him. Geoffrey put his hand on Henry's.

"Slower, or you'll vomit it all back up. Chew. Take a moment."

With an effort, Henry slowed down. Geoffrey sat back in his chair.

"You read Latin and Saxon. That's good. We Plantagenets respect learning. What other languages do you have?"

"I can make do in Welsh. And Breton and Norman, of course."

"That's right, you're a Breton. One of my subjects, in fact. And you've studied weapons…from a book."

Henry shrugged. "I know a claymore from a pike."

Geoffrey smiled. Even with the knives and threats, Henry was rocked by that smile. This guy had charisma, in spades. *His men would follow him anywhere, I bet. A whole army of jerks. Let's be very, very careful.*

Geoffrey paced to the window. "Then you know the fascination, the power the sword holds in the minds of men." Henry said nothing. "Pikes have broken cavalry. Greek fire has destroyed fleets. We knights choose the lance as our most powerful weapon. And yet it is the sword, even now, that compels the hearts of men. We tell tales of the Nine Great Swords. Charlemagne's. Roland's. They have become…" Geoffrey thought for a moment. "…weapons of the mind. Standards. They say Saladin retreated to Damascus when Richard captured Mahomet's sword from him."

"And here I thought it was the plague."

Geoffrey smiled again. "Peasants. You have no heart, and you wonder why we despise you." It was interesting—

the smile stayed charming, no matter what Geoffrey was saying. Something to remember.

"I need a sword, a special sword, to inspire men. I need a standard."

The light dawned. Henry had to admire the scheme. "Ah. Say no more, My Lord. Name the king, and I will have the sword ready for you by next month at the latest. Of course, there will be expenses—"

"No." Geoffrey's voice was winter-cold. Henry realized he had just skated back toward the headsman; he shut his mouth. "I need no forgery from you. I need the veritable sword. I have a map, I have clues, I have a trail. I need you to read the clues, riddle them out, and then to find the sword and prove it true."

Henry's heart sank. A sword, a map, a quest...it sounded like a fable from Geoffrey of Monmouth, or Chretien de Troyes. "And which...which sword is this, My Lord?"

"The one they call Cut Steel. The sword of Arthur, another lord of the Bretons. Excalibur."

Of course. "Uh...perhaps, since you've spent most of your life on the Continent...My Lord...you didn't know that Excalibur is...just a legend?"

And here came the smile. "Then you're in trouble. Aren't you?"

6. NORTH BY NORTHWEST

The rain drifted into the courtyard, a gray mist that beaded on wool and fur, and hardened shoe leather into blistering discomfort. Henry tried to ignore it and focus on what he needed to do. You'd think he'd be used to travel by now. He had covered more miles in sixteen years than most people saw in a lifetime. Ever since his hometown of Sanbruc had earned the title of "the lost village," he had been constantly on the road, from Brittany to London to Cornwall to Paris, all thanks to the Plantagenet family's Rampaging Knights Urban Renewal Program.

But as he stood in the damp courtyard, watching the supplies being lashed to the mules, Henry felt the tears well up behind his eyes. When he'd finally come to Paris and hooked up with Alfie and Valdemar and the rest of the goliards, it looked like he'd found a place where he could stop running for a minute and get in out of the cold. But here he was, on the road again, this time tied to a mule to travel north to Calais, and from there across the water to Gwynedd in the dead of winter...It wasn't fair. And just like everything else in his life, it was the fault of jerks with swords.

Henry tried to get control of himself and looked

25

around the courtyard. It was filled with market stalls. He realized with a rush of horror that one of the vendors had a Welsh accent. And another had muscles out to his ears. *Alfie and Valdemar. What are they doing? Are they crazy?*

"You have the money and the supplies. Go fast and quiet until you're on Welsh soil, out of reach of John and Philip." Geoffrey glanced at Henry, tied up by the mules, and turned back to Brissac. "And remember, Edmond, the boy is a resource. I don't want him dying on you before you find the weapon."

"It will be…hard, Lord. He is insolent."

Geoffrey laughed. "Yeah, he gets right under your skin, doesn't he?" Then he raised a finger. That was all he did, and yet Brissac was riveted. Brissac knew with a solemn joy that, penniless and dressed in rags, Geoffrey would still have been his master. "But you know what's at stake."

"One king. One country. One law."

"Keep that in mind, when our little friend irritates you. Think what could happen, if John finds the sword before us. Or Philip. Or Uncle Raymond, God forbid. Even I'm afraid of that one."

Brissac looked pained. "But, Lord, surely a knight would—"

"How many good knights have we sent already to the Chapel Perilous?"

"Twelve, Lord."

Geoffrey nodded. "Did any succeed, any that I was unaware of?"

Brissac said nothing.

"Where honor fails, low cunning may succeed." Geoffrey studied Henry, sizing him up. "This one has a gift for survival. He has lived for ten years without father or mother, place or guild. Can you say as much?" Brissac shook his head. Geoffrey continued. "He can read Welsh and Latin. *The Book of Four Branches* tells us Arthur was a Roman and a Celt. Any chronicles he left, any hints or riddles, will be in those tongues. And the boy knows weapons." Geoffrey smiled. "Well enough to fool you, at any rate."

Brissac ground his teeth.

Geoffrey smiled even wider, and stretched. "And if he dies, who's to care?"

＊＊＊＊

Henry tugged at his ropes. The cords were hemp. That was good, even though they scratched like cats' claws—hemp was stiff and brittle. It didn't have the flex and give of good wool rope. So there was a lot of room for Henry to work with...

The first coil popped off his wrists. Henry kept his back to the wall and concentrated on looking depressed. His guard kept working on the radish he'd been gnawing since breakfast.

The second knot was loose. At this point, an amateur would have just dropped the ropes and bolted, but Henry kept the ropes on and scanned the courtyard. The entrance was filled with men-at-arms. No good. The walls were too high to scale. The stairs up to the battlements and the keep were in the rear, behind Geoffrey and Brissac, but also behind dozens of market stalls. Yeah. That was the way. If he got out himself, he could forestall whatever idiot plan Alfie and Valdemar had cooked up. So welcome to the Château de Paris—fortress, dungeon, home to visiting dignitaries, and playground of the agile and terrified. Just let Geoffrey the Jerk and Sir Jerk de Brissac move a little to the left...

"Henry. My boy." Geoffrey's hand landed on his shoulder. "Let's take a look at the food. I'll get you something sweet for the trip. Some raisins. You like raisins, don't you?"

Geoffrey took Henry's arm and led him toward the stalls. Henry desperately fiddled with his ropes to keep them from slipping off—even without the knots, Geoffrey's grip was like steel, and Henry didn't want him finding out too soon.

They wandered from cart to cart, getting closer and closer to Valdemar's. Henry started to sweat. And there they were, facing Valdemar in disguise across a mound of onions.

Geoffrey picked up an onion, examined it. "Hmmm. This produce looks none too fresh. Peddler, come here."

Valdemar came around the cart. Henry saw Valdemar's hand moving inside his cloak. *No, no, no!*

"This produce is rotten. Take a look." And before Valdemar could move, Geoffrey had leaped up, grabbed his head, and slammed it into the cart's iron wheel. In an instant, he had knocked the giant smith unconscious to the ground, and taken the knife from his belt.

"Did you think me a fool? Did you think you could escape?" The knife was at Henry's throat now, pressing hard enough to draw a trickle of blood. "Look around you, boy. Look at the walls."

Henry looked up. The Swiss crossbowmen had their weapons cocked, aimed at—

There was Alfie, and there was Gerard, and there were Clothilde and Stephen and Guillaume…dear Jesu, there was Mattie, too. And all of them were looking at the business ends of crossbows.

"Please…"

"I am fighting for the future, Henry. I am fighting for a new Empire of the West. I will not let anything interfere with that. Do you understand?"

"Yes."

Geoffrey held up his hand. The Swiss lowered their crossbows. "Leave." Alfie hesitated. Geoffrey pressed the knife harder into Henry's neck. Alfie left with the others.

Geoffrey released Henry. "You will remember this, I hope."

Henry looked Geoffrey in the eyes, careful to keep his face blank. "I'll remember that you take hostages."

"Good."

7. ABBEY ROAD

Gray sky, white ground, black trees. Sound muffled by snow, until all you heard was your own breathing, and all you felt was the cold, sharp in your ears and your nose, dull in your boots and leggings.

Or, if you were tied to a mule on your back, wearing nothing but your tunic and drawers, cold everywhere and pain in everything. Henry tried to clear his throat and keep moving, even if that amounted to no more than shivering inside his manacles.

They had long ago left England behind. Now they traveled through a dismal waste, thick forests broken by ruins that were ancient before the Romans, standing stones that gave no shelter, roads that vanished under bridges leading nowhere. It was all pretty eldritch. Henry knew it from Alfie's tales—the *borth Annwn*, the Door to the Land of Shadow. A stone cairn appeared through the snow, wiped clean by the wind. Brissac turned in his saddle. "There it is. How are you, thief? Comfortable?"

Henry tried to control his chattering teeth, without much success. "C-Couldn't be better. How's the body odor? Taken a bath yet?"

The Swiss mercenaries laughed. Brissac wheeled on

Henry, his sword drawn—

"Ah-ah-ah! You k-kill me, wh-what will Geoffrey say?"

Brissac turned away, but Hauptmann, captain of the Swiss, rode up to Henry and examined him.

"*Ritter*...he could die. Let us cover him."

"The tower is near enough. Cover him then."

To be fair, Brissac hadn't shackled Henry until *after* he'd tried to escape. But they had just landed in Southampton; Brissac was still seasick; Henry could speak the local dialect, while the Swiss were practically mute; and by then, Alfie and the others would have vanished to where Geoffrey couldn't find them.

Really, it had been too good an opportunity to ignore.

But as Henry had leaned over the inn's stable roof and gently lowered himself to the ground, crossbow bolts had hissed out of the darkness, aimed so well they had pinned his clothes to the wall behind him without even drawing blood. He had been trussed up like a chicken in his own braies—

"There it is."

Henry craned his neck to see. *Wow.* It was a genuine, honest-to-goodness Dark Tower.

Black and ancient, it rose above the pines like a castle guarding a border. Beyond it the land opened out in a wide valley, shrouded in fog, indistinct except for the top of the Glastonbury Tor, a terraced hill poking out of the sea of mist. The road zigzagged up the slope and then cut through a dark wood, vanishing into shadow long before it reached the tower.

"The Chapel Perilous." Brissac leaned down and spoke in Henry's ear. "The key to Excalibur's resting place. Twelve good knights have entered, never to return. My Lord Geoffrey thinks you may solve the riddle where they did not." Brissac squinted up at the high black walls. "I think he is an optimist." He turned to the Swiss. "Take him down. We camp here tonight."

Hauptmann and Weiss lifted Henry gently off the mule.

While the other mercenaries made camp and built a fire, Hauptmann covered Henry with a cloak and handed him a wineskin.

As Henry drank, one of the younger, eager-beaver mercenaries asked Hauptmann something in German. Henry could make out the words "two watches" and "moonrise."

The other mercenaries shuddered. "We do not walk that road by night," said Hauptmann.

Brissac grabbed Henry's wineskin and tossed him a bedroll. "Sleep," said Brissac. "Tomorrow we see if you're better than a knight."

Henry was awakened early the next morning by the sound of Brissac and Hauptmann, praying. The Swiss knelt beside them, heads bowed. The Latin muttering rose to an earnest *"Defende nos in proelio, contra nequitiam et insidias diaboli esto praesidium!"* and ended with an impassioned "Amen!" The men stood and broke camp in silence.

Hauptmann hoisted Henry onto the mule and struck off his chains.

"Today you ride free," said Hauptmann. Henry gulped. *Whoopee.*

The path sloped up perfectly level, without rut or break—Caesar-smooth, they'd have said in Sanbruc. It was a flywalk, so narrow there would be no room to step aside for anyone coming down. With each turn, the empty space to the right and left became more impressive. The men were silent, focused on keeping the horses calm, staying away from the edge. By noon, they reached the summit—a wide, empty road lined by trees.

From each tree, too high to reach, hung a dead knight. There was a faint clatter as armor jostled against armor in the wind.

"The Boulevard of Souls," whispered Hauptmann.

"They're just suits of armor," said Brissac. "They're empty."

"You say!"

Henry licked his lips and stared. The helmets were sealed shut. No flesh was visible. The armor could be empty…or it could be corpses dangling from those hemp ropes, under the bare trees. He felt a trickle of cold sweat down his back.

"Shut up!" said Brissac. "Any cowards, flee now."

No one moved. Brissac mounted his horse and trotted forward. The others followed.

Half a mile on, Brissac slowed and stared upward.

"What is it?" asked Henry.

The knight stared at a painted shield dangling from one low branch. "Three herons *azure* on a field *argent*. Pierre d'Anjou. He saved my life at Poitiers." They rode the rest of the way in silence.

The boulevard widened into a plaza, and they came at last to the Chapel Perilous.

The battlements floated high above, blotting out the sun. The walls emerged seamless from the ground, as if the tower had grown like a tree from the living rock. Big stone carvings dotted the square in front of the entrance: a pillar, a sphere, a set of stairs that ended in mid-air. Chiseled into the flagstones were diagrams that could have come from Ptolemy, and images of hooded men carrying unguessable devices. On the front step was carved a seven-circuit labyrinth.

Brissac and the others didn't even set foot on the pavement, stopping their horses well short of the open square. Henry walked onto the plaza and examined the pillar. Small, irregular holes pierced the top like the sights on an arbalest. One faced south-southeast; beneath it a symbol had been chiseled off the stone, and the only thing left was the legend "MMCLVII." Henry looked through. All he saw was a notch in the far mountains.

"You have twenty-eight days." Brissac signaled the Swiss, who began to make camp.

"Exactly?" Henry returned from the pillar. "Or did you just pick the number out of a hat?"

"That's the number of days from when you go in to when your body appears on a tree outside."

"Oh." Henry stared at the black walls. His heart couldn't sink; it was already in his boots.

"All right, boy." Brissac put his hand on Henry's back. "In you go."

"Wait!" Hauptmann stepped up. "*Ritter*, allow him at least some way to defend himself."

Brissac stared at Hauptmann, as if amazed at the insolence; then he looked at the faces of the other Swiss, who had gathered behind their sergeant.

"Fine, then," he said. "Give him a blade, for all the good it will do."

Hauptmann took off his short sword and buckled it around Henry's waist. That broke the dam. Before Henry knew it, they had loaded him down with a helmet, two dirks, a shield, three slings, a knife—"For eating with," said Haer.

Henry turned to face the tower. Behind him he heard the ratcheting *click* of crossbows being cocked—in case he changed his mind. His back itching like mad, he strode out across the flagstones. The Swiss followed him a few yards in, crossbows ready. Then they stopped, and Henry walked on alone.

The square stretched out forever. Henry felt like an ant on a table. To his right and left he passed objects that were somewhere between statues and buildings—a ball on a cable swinging from a stone frame; a wide, shallow bowl carved with cryptic shapes; a series of gears laid flat into the paving stones. Finally, Henry arrived at the gates.

There were no gates.

It was an opening twelve feet high. Nine men could have walked in abreast. Clouds of fog rolled out of the gap to swirl around Henry's feet. He edged closer.

There was no floor.

Blocking the entry from wall to wall was a pit with sides as smooth as glass. Mist poured over the stone lip on the opposite end and hid the bottom from view. Henry turned back toward the Swiss, opened his mouth, and closed it again. If they had seen how the other knights had gotten across, they would have told him.

He sat down, dangling his legs over the edge. The other side was hidden in the mist. Could he jump? A blind jump into the nothing? *No, thanks.* Use a rope and a grappling hook? Was there anything to grab onto on the other side? Would Brissac even have thought to bring them?

Henry shifted uncomfortably and stood up. He had been sitting on more of the stone carvings. They were a series of six panels, starting with a naked man walking toward a—

No. Henry looked away from the walls, back across the plaza. The panels were meant to be seen by someone walking toward the gate, not away. He was looking at the last one first. He stepped out, and began again.

Looked at properly, the panels were actually the homiest things Henry had seen since Paris. They were just a typical "Stages of Man" carving, like the ones they had on the altarpiece at St. Germain. This one was the life of a knight. The first panel was a noble birth; then a child at play; then a page with a cup, then a knight with a sword, then a king with a crown and scepter. The last panel before the pit was Death—the soul of the knight leaving its body and all its worldly possessions behind it in a heap as it passed through the Gates of Peace.

Oh.

Henry unbuckled Hauptmann's blade and tossed it into the pit. After a few seconds, he heard the *clank* as it hit the bottom. The other weapons followed. Slowly, the mist cleared from the entrance.

For the first time, Henry was able to see a bridge over the pit, the same shade of gray as the mist and the stone. *No railing, of course.* He knelt down and felt the bridge. *Narrow and slippery.* Henry sighed. Better not take any chances.

Unarmed, on his hands and knees, he crossed the bridge into the chapel.

8. THE CHAPEL PERILOUS

Light flashed through the Chapel Perilous, scattering rainbow-fringed sunbeams into the hallways and cells. Henry pulled the blanket over his face and squeezed his eyes shut, but it was useless. There was no way to drift back to sleep. It was like this every sunrise. At midday, there was a deep, unfathomable *booming* sound, and at sunset, the dying wind blew a single vast organ note throughout the keep.

The chapel was a mystery of water and air, light and stone. Henry walked every day through signs and wonders.

He hated it.

He'd also decided that he hated the chapel's monks, who weren't the friendliest bunch you'd hope to meet. One of them had been waiting on the other side of the bridge when he crossed, a big man with a scar that reached from his tonsure to his chin. He helped Henry to his feet. When Henry said, "Thanks," the monk said nothing, just stood there.

Henry knew about the Rule of Silence. One desperate winter he had taken shelter with a bunch of Carthusians near Montrieux, bringing them food in their cells and emptying their chamber pots in exchange for not dying of starvation and exposure. He'd been grateful to be alive, but as soon as the snow melted, he had fled to Paris, where he didn't stop talking for three days.

So he knew that even the Silent had ways of getting their point across if they had to, a whole language of signs, if you were really chatty. Henry waited, and after a moment, Scarface turned and walked up the wide, mist-covered steps, slowly enough for Henry to follow.

The steps ended in a high, arching corridor that dwindled into the distance. It was bright with sunlight, but Henry couldn't see any windows. When he stepped inside, he gasped.

Every inch of the walls and floor was covered with carvings, more crowded with pictures than a book of hours. Here were nine pagan gods, Helios in the center, holding court in an oval coliseum; over there were the numerals from I to X, set equal to a cluster of characters Henry did not recognize; below his feet, what might have been stars mapped out a constellation unseen in any skies he knew.

He heard a soft shuffling sound, and from a corridor on his left came a troop of monks, dressed in white, each with a stone brooch pinned to one shoulder. They crossed in front of him, turned left, and proceeded down the corridor without a glance back.

The scarred monk didn't stop; after a moment to gape, Henry scuttled forward to keep up. They passed corridors on left and right, and crossed the chapel's dining hall, where a few monks, wearing black tunics embroidered with the sign of a cauldron, scrubbed the floor and cleared tables.

Finally, the monk led Henry to a cell that held a cot, a table, a loaf of bread, and a candle. Henry shrugged off his cloak and sat down, his mind whirling. Scarface turned to go.

"Wait!"

Scarface stopped. Henry groped for his next question,

remembering to frame it in Latin. *Why bother? Even if he does understand, it's not like he's going to answer.*

"So...Excalibur. You know where it is?" *That's it! Ya gotta be subtle!*

Scarface didn't respond. *Well, at least he didn't leave,* thought Henry. *I'll take that as a "yes."*

"How do I find it?"

Again, nothing from Brother Silent.

Okay, let's try the big question. "Do I really have a month?"

The monk glanced at a figure chiseled into the wall of the cell. Henry examined it. Two ovals, a larger and a smaller, touched at one point and were divided into hundreds of sections. A tiny bead of sunlight shone through a hole in the ceiling and illuminated one of the sections at the top of the design.

*Hundreds of sections...*Henry made a quick estimate. There were more than three hundred divisions. *Want to bet it's three hundred and sixty-five divisions, one for each day of the year?* The ovals were a sun calendar. And twenty-eight notches away from that sunbeam was a small stone marker. Four weeks from today, he'd be hanging on the tree.

"So...can you take me to the books?"

The monk turned in the doorway and waited. Henry grinned. *That would be a "yes."*

* * * *

The doors opened, and for once Henry had nothing to say.

The library was enormous, bigger even than the one at St. Benedict's in Paris. Like the rest of the abbey, every inch of stone wall was covered with carvings—but here the most important stones were the slender columns that supported enormous panes of leaded glass, letting in an ocean of winter sunlight. It was dry as a bone, and clean, free of the smells of rats and rotting parchment that were the terror of most *bibliothecae*. Beautifully carved tables supported rows of graceful writing stations.

The stacks ran down the middle of the hall, arranged by subject, language, and author. They were even decorated by topic: a statue of St. Catherine presided over the legal works, St. Jerome over the histories, St. Cosmas and St. Damian over the *materia medica*.

Well...time to get to work. Brissac had given Henry a scroll from Geoffrey. Now Henry sat down and broke the seal. It was a list, in elegant handwriting, of all the sources Geoffrey had used to search for Excalibur: Robert Boron, Geoffrey of Monmouth, the *Annales Cambriae*...

A list of failures. Henry tossed it aside. Geoffrey hadn't found the sword—so the sources he had used were worthless. That left the sources the prince had heard about but never found, and the ones, if any, he had never even thought of. But the grandmothers in Henry's village had been telling "Arthur tales" for hundreds of years before the Normans had adopted Arthur as their own—so if Arthur had ever existed, he'd been a Brython, a Celt, like Alfie and Henry, and he had fought the Saxons. That meant the best sources would be in Welsh, Saxon, and British Latin. Henry found the shelves decorated with the image of St. David of Wales, and started to read.

Within minutes, he had filled up his first writing tablet with notes and moved on to another. Each *lai* or *chanson* mentioned an older one; each chronicle referred to a second, or third, or fourth. Henry filled first one, then two, then four wax tablets with the names of new scrolls to examine. When he reached the end of the sixth *tabula*, he gave up and just started pulling scrolls from the shelves.

The days raced past, and Henry lost himself in a maze of clues and sources.

There is a grave for March, a grave for Gwythur,

A grave for Gwgawn Red-sword;

The world's wonder a grave for Arthur.

The Red Book of Hergest. The White Book of Rhydderch. The Black Book of Carmarthen. Strange bardic three-line verses, hints and riddles, scribbled out in the *ll*s, *wy*s, *dd*s, and *ch*s that made Old Welsh the terror of anyone with a speech impediment.

Three Worthies of Britain,
Cai the Fair and Gwalchgaur, Pryderi the Fearless;
Not one a match for Arthur.

There were stories upon stories. Stories within stories. The characters stayed the same, but their actions changed from version to version, like details in a dream. Arthur left Britain to fight the Emperor Lucius, and died far from home. Or Arthur defeated the Hun Attila, saved Lucius, and ruled in Rome as Lucius' heir, the Emperor Maximus. Arthur was childless, or he fought his son Medrawd and they died in each other's arms. Arthur had a queen, Gwynhafr; or Arthur had a different queen, also named Gwynhafr; or he had another queen, different from the first two, but still named Gwynhafr. Arthur's sister was the Morrigu; Arthur's wife was the Morrigu; the Morrigu was the mother of Arthur's son.

And the sword: It was Caliburn and Cadvaladych; it was found in a stone or it rose from a lake; it was finally thrown into Dozemary Pool, or the river Severn, or the lake of Llyn Lydau.

If the sword had been thrown into any of them, Henry was out of luck. There was no way they'd ever retrieve it, but Brissac would drag them across the Welsh hilltops in the dead of winter to give it a try anyway. Of course, even Wales in winter was better than hanging on a tree.

Not that it matters, Henry reminded himself. Because he was not going to wait like a lamb for the slaughter, thank you very much. It had been a week. Henry looked out the window. Once again, the sun was at its height. Once again, something *boomed* in the chambers below, to announce the hour of Sext. Henry stood, stretched, and grabbed a handful of candles, a flint, and a knife. Once again, it was time for Plan B.

In the seven days he'd been here, Henry had made a

point of learning everything he could about the layout of the Chapel…and its exits. Not that he'd found any of those yet. So far, Scarface had managed to herd him away from anything that looked interesting. But one of the things the brother couldn't hide was the procession of monks for prayer.

The monks were one more of the chapel's puzzles. Judging by the robes, with their crosses, stones, and other knickknacks, there were at least half a dozen different monastic orders sharing the chapel, all of them Silent. It was an arrangement Henry had never seen before—not that he'd ever seen any of these orders before, either. When the time came for prayer, each group traced a different route to a different room. As far as he could tell, it was never the same room twice. Henry had found that if he tagged along with one of the groups, he was safe from Brother Scarface, who usually marched with his own order. It was only when Henry struck off on his own, before or after prayer, that he ran the risk of being caught and dragged back to the library. But the midday gong marked one of the longer prayer sessions, long enough for Henry to do some serious scouting.

So as the Brothers of the Boat (dull blue robes, medium tonsures, boat insignia) chanted their *Kyrie* past the library, Henry joined ranks with them and strolled down the corridor. After a few hundred yards, they encountered the Brothers of the Book (black and white robes, wide tonsures, image of a book on the right sleeve) and Henry jumped processions. That took him down two flights of stairs and deeper inside the tower.

Four processions later, and Henry was as deep as he'd ever gone—by his own count, at least three floors below the central courtyard. The last of the monks had entered their prayer rooms, and the hallway stretched out before him. Even without windows, sunlight played on the walls and floors. Where was it coming from? Henry ran a nervous hand over the candles in his pouch and started walking.

He kept time in his head and by counting his footsteps. The noon liturgy lasted to a count of about two thousand. If he wanted to stay safe, he needed to turn back by fifteen hundred at the latest. Every few yards, he'd scrape a candle high on the wall to mark a trail back. Each door he came to, he tugged open if he could. He found storage rooms, sleeping cells, and…other things.

One vast room was nothing but friezes—wall carvings of different buildings and cities. There were the Pyramids. There was the Giants' Dance, the Stonehenge of Salisbury. There was an island city, ringed by canals. On the floor was what seemed to be a giant map, with points of interest indicated by gold stars.

The next room over was empty, but it burned with sunlight. Was this the source of the light in the halls? Hmm…he still had a little time before he had to get back. And there weren't any stairways leading down and out from this hallway…Henry entered for a closer look.

The light blazed. The heat seared his skin. His clothes were burning. He was blind! *He was on fire!*

A hand yanked Henry out of the inferno, threw him to the ground and rolled him over, beating at the flames with the folds of his robe. Finally the heat subsided, and Henry risked opening his eyes again.

"*Ave,* Brother," said Henry. "So, uh…this *isn't* the way to the garderobe, then?"

Scarface yanked him to his feet and frog-marched him back upstairs.

With green and purple afterimages playing across Henry's eyeballs, and his reddened skin peeling like a snake's, they returned to the library, where Scarface stood watch over Henry for the rest of the day. Henry didn't bother to tell Scarface that it wasn't necessary. He had learned his lesson thoroughly: Following "Plan A" might be boring, but at least you wouldn't burst into flames.

The sun fell, and rose, and fell again. Chastened, Henry

threw himself into the research. He huddled in the library, leaving only for the privy and for the bread he got from the dining hall, then diving back into the books. The days raced past—three, five, another week. Henry was deep into a Latin account of a general named Ambrosius when he came to with a start.

Something was wrong.

He stamped the pins and needles from his feet and stood up. He'd been at it all night, making a serious dent in the monastery's candle supply. Now it was long past Matins, and his breath glowed in a sunbeam as he tried to warm his frozen hands. He wondered what Mattie would have made of all this—some "hero of the revolution" he was, dying of frostbite and loneliness in a far northern library, working for The Man.

His mouth tasted like the Seine at low tide, and even his patchy beard was starting to itch. Sixteen days. He was getting closer. He had to be. He had read almost all of the scrolls in the Welsh collection. If he couldn't find Excalibur in what was left—

Something was wrong. Frostbite and loneliness...

Henry gasped in dismay. How could he have missed it? *He was alone.*

But a library like this, filled with books and well designed, should have been packed with monks. A normal monastery used its *scriptorium* from sunrise to sunset. Even if the books weren't meant to circulate, there would still be monks studying them, or making copies to sell or to keep safe...

Unless the books weren't important.

The library was a set-up.

Which meant that the answer to the riddle of Excalibur was elsewhere—wherever the monks were, wherever they tried to stop him from going. Henry glanced down at his notes, at the scrolls. Sixteen days. He had wasted sixteen whole days. In less than two weeks, he would be hanging from a tree!

Stop it. Panic would get him nowhere. He had to think. *Okay. First, assume that the answer* is *here in the chapel. Because if it isn't, I'm dead.* Henry started to pace, past the useless books, past the windows. The map room—the room with the friezes. It was important. He was sure of it. But why?

He thought about the carvings, picturing them again in his mind. Stonehenge. There had been something about that picture of Stonehenge…His eyes popped open. Stonehenge had been a ruin for time out of mind—but the carving had shown it complete, and with more pillars and altar stones and details than Henry had ever heard anyone mention.

The sculptor had seen Stonehenge when it was new.

The two great pyramids were shown without the Sphinx. Because the frieze was carved before the Sphinx was built?

Henry felt the age of the Chapel press down on him like a lead weight. Before the Normans. Before the Romans, before Jesu himself…

The Chapel Builders must have known what happened to books over the centuries. They must have seen the libraries of Alexandria and Rome go up in flames. One spark from a conqueror's torch, and the great books were nothing more than kindling for a bonfire. And the Builders wanted their knowledge to last.

So they had carved it in stone. Stone wouldn't burn, wouldn't rot, wouldn't be stolen by some freelance librarian with a taste for clove oil. It would last the ages, for those with eyes to see. The books were in this room, but the *real* library was all around him, carved into the Chapel's walls.

Somewhere in this giant archive was the answer he was looking for. But where? If each carving represented a bit of information, how did you find what you needed, let alone find it in the right order? It was like the problem you faced with any book. The letters were run together without spaces, so it was up to you to sound them out and find the words buried in the alphabet. You used your finger and your voice, so the actual text was like a partnership between the book and the one who read it.

The Brothers of the Cauldron walked past, on their way to afternoon prayers. Henry wondered idly which room they would choose for their prayers this time. Which room—

I am brilliant! BRILLIANT! Second time today!

Henry left the library and followed the monks. After marching a few hundred feet down the corridor, they turned right and entered a large room facing west. If Henry were right, a carving in this room would tell him everything he had ever wanted to know about pots, grails, cauldrons, and *kraters*. He looked around.

Illuminated by the day's last light, the room's friezes seemed to glow. Carved over the lintel of the door, the largest frieze in the room showed a dozen men gathered around a richly decorated cauldron, burying it in the earth.

＊＊＊＊

The next day Henry was up before dawn. Choosing which brothers to follow had been easy. The only ones who seemed close to what Henry was looking for were Scarface's monks, and that was only if the symbol Henry had assumed was a cross was actually…a sword.

The sky brightened. As the sun rose over the horizon, light flashed through the Chapel halls, just as it had for the past two weeks, and the monks began their chanting. Henry waited until Scarface and his order walked past, and then fell into line.

The *oratorium* for Lauds was a wide, open room facing east, with only a low stone wall to keep you from taking your last step over the edge. As the monks began to sing the *Benedictus*, the rising sun played over the carvings, highlighting the images of a king, his armies…and his sword. Henry grinned. *Thank you, St. Dismas, I'm going to live!*

The Brothers of the Sword prayed five more times before the sun set, each time in a room featuring the exploits of a hero with a sword. Whether the hero was Arthur, Henry couldn't tell. To be honest, he didn't care. It was Excalibur, not Arthur, that would save his life. So Henry scanned the walls for clues, and gradually assembled a story: A sword was carried across the sea from…a giant island? Avalon? A ringed city? It didn't matter. The sword was placed in a stone in a lake, a cave. A hero drew it forth. With it, he led a band of warriors and established a *pax*. There was a great castle, a source of order and justice in the land. A final battle…

But here the carvings let him down. They showed the battle in detail: a fight between father and son, betrayal, the hero's return to the Otherworld. They showed the sword restored to the stone. But they didn't show *where*.

Well, there was still the Compline prayer. He didn't particularly want to get up at midnight, but if that prayer service held the answer, that's where he would go.

As the Vespers service broke up, Henry noticed Scarface and a few of the other monks glancing at him. He had a hunch that the brothers would be passing by his cell that night.

9. THE LAST ROOM

Candles, flint, knife, rope, *tabula*, and stylus. Henry was as ready as he'd ever be. The hour candle by the bed had burned down to midnight; the brothers would be coming at any moment.

Henry heard the slap of sandals on rock, saw torchlight, and Scarface and the brothers appeared. This time, they didn't chant or sway past. They waited until Henry joined them, and began the march.

Down twisting staircases. Through long halls covered with older, stranger carvings than any he'd yet seen. Past mysterious wells. The torchlight threw shadows on the walls and played across devices he couldn't even guess at. Henry kept track of every twist and turn, determined to remember his way back if he had to.

Whatever warmth there was in the rest of the keep wasn't here. The air grew colder and colder as they dropped, until their breath steamed out of their mouths and chunks of ice gleamed in the fonts of holy water.

Finally, they arrived at a smooth granite door, twelve feet high, carved with the sign of the labyrinth. It must have weighed tons, but it swung open silently when Scarface touched it with one hand. They entered, mounting their torches on brackets in the walls.

This room was unlike the others. No carvings, no maps, no machines. Plain and barren except for the door—and two suits of armor, complete with swords, facing each other from opposite sides of the room.

Oh, no. They want me to fight somebody. Henry gulped. It wasn't fair! He'd been so clever! But in the end, it always seemed to come down to swords.

Henry sagged to the ground in despair. "You want me to do this now? Die in the middle of the night?"

For once, Scarface hesitated. He stared at Henry for a moment, and then glanced at the other monks. Taking Henry's tablet, he scrawled a picture of the sun, and the Roman numeral *II*. And then the monks filed out, leaving Henry alone, staring up at the suits of armor.

II meant the hour of Prime—he'd have until daybreak. If there were anything to do, he had to do it in the next few hours.

* * * *

The monks returned at dawn. If anything, it was even colder now than it had been at midnight. Henry stood carefully and slowly, ever so slowly, put on the helmet, the mail shirt, and the sword. Across the room, he saw Scarface doing the same. One part of his mind, detached from the situation, noted *modern falchion, cheap Norman design, half a* livre *at best.* Soon, all too soon, Scarface was ready. He turned to Henry, and made the sign of the Cross.

Henry screamed. "STOP THAT SHIT, YOU SON OF A BITCH! IF YOU'RE GOING TO KILL ME, THEN DO IT!"

The monk's face darkened. Henry didn't stop.

"Baisez mon cul, cochon! Kiss my ass! Take your honor and stick it where—" There was one thing to be said about a life on the road—it gave you a rich vocabulary. Henry used every last bit of it.

At first, Scarface did nothing, waiting for Henry's tirade

to wind down. But it didn't. As Henry warmed to his topic, he became more and more inventive.

Scarface's control began to crack.

Insults about the monk's courage, ancestors, personal habits, and virility added wood to the bonfire without igniting it, but when Henry started in on Scarface's mother, the monk finally lost it.

White-faced and furious, Scarface charged forward, his sword raised high.

Still six feet across the room, the monk's legs flew out from under him, and he hit the floor with an enormous, undignified crash.

Henry tiptoed forward as quickly as he could. He had to be careful, though. He had to watch out for the trails of slick ice that crisscrossed the room. They had formed in the night, after Henry had crept out of the room to a font, drawn three buckets of icy well water, and poured them all over the frosty floor.

Really, somebody should have kept better watch. The brothers were clearly getting sloppy.

Sidestepping the last ice slick, Henry kicked Scarface's sword away and backed off. He heard a clicking sound behind him and turned. One of the other monks—the one he'd privately named Too-Big—had picked up Scarface's sword and sheathed it.

Slowly, Scarface got to his feet and met Henry's eyes. For the first time since Henry had met him, Scarface grinned wide and pointed to the far wall. Henry turned to look.

A line of shadow appeared at the top of the wall, racing to the bottom to define two doors swinging open. Beyond was an empty chamber with a window that framed Glastonbury Tor.

Henry walked into the room. There were no pictures, no friezes. Just a single verse in Welsh above the window:

Three signs to the sword of kings:
An island of glass, and a lake under stone,

And a voice without cease.

The "voice without cease" didn't make much sense, but the rest was more promising. The "island of glass" was Ynas Wytryn, entrance to the Otherworld, and the sword might have accompanied Arthur on his final voyage there. If he could just find that…

Oh, no. It can't be that easy.

Glastonbury Vale was filled with fog. The sun streamed across the white haze, through which Glastonbury Tor poked like an island in the middle of the sea. Coated with snow and hoarfrost, the mountain gleamed above the waves of mist, like an island made of glass.

10. THE SWORD IN THE STONE

Henry poled the wide, flat-bottomed barge across the foggy swamp of Glastonbury Vale to the tor beyond.

The ferry had been waiting for him at the Chapel's dock when he'd gotten out. About halfway across, he had considered ditching Glastonbury Tor entirely and just poling like crazy for the far shore of the marshes. In the end, he'd decided not to. After all he'd been through, he had to see if Excalibur was really there. And if the sword actually did exist, it might give him some leverage with Brissac. And anyway, it was dead winter, and he didn't have a horse, a purse, or a speck of food, so his fleeing choices were actually a bit limited.

The barge landed with a gentle *thump*, and Henry got out. The dock led to a smooth, well-made road that curved around the tor to the right. Henry smiled and walked around the bend.

"Congratulations, boy."

His heart skipped a beat. It was Brissac, smiling his nastiest smile, and the Swiss, who looked a little more welcoming—was Haer giving him a thumbs-up?

"How…how did—"

"We've kept watch on the Chapel from all sides. We

saw you leave, and we picked our way across the swamp to meet you. You owe Weiss a new pair of boots, by the way." Brissac turned to survey the tor. "So—it's here, the sword? Or was this just some half-baked escape attempt?"

"If it's anywhere, it's here."

Brissac glanced at him sidelong. "Eh. I wouldn't have expected it. Good work, boy." He tossed a staff at Henry. "Now get moving."

* * * *

Out in the snow, exposed on the hillside, Henry led the way with the staff, pounding the ground every three or four steps. The temperature had risen since morning, turning the dry powder into icy slush. Brissac and the Swiss followed, bewildered and getting angrier as the snow melted to water and seeped into their boots.

"Why are we here?"

Henry shook off Brissac's hand and kept going. "'Isle of Glass,' remember?"

"Yes, yes. But the entrance is obviously in the ruins at the top of the hill—"

"Really?" Henry turned and pointed to the mound. "Remind me. Didn't I tell you about 'the lake under stone'? About the cave?"

"Yes—"

"And where do you enter a cave? From the roof? Or from a passage to the floor?"

Brissac clammed up.

"We've been all around the tor. If I'm right, the entrance should be—" Henry banged the ground with his staff. After a moment, he was rewarded with a hollow, booming *thonk*.

"—there."

Two hours later, they had removed the snow and ice and broken through the frozen soil. The snow melt had raised the sharp smell of wet earth. The trench was already several feet deep into the side of the hill when one of the mercenaries hit buried stone with a *clank*. "I see something," said Hauptmann.

It was a door of gray rock, carved in infinite detail with looping whorls and knots and crosses. Across the top was an inscription: *Hic iacet sepultus inclitus rex Arturius in insula Avalonia.*

"What does it say?" Brissac crowded close, staring at the door, his hostility forgotten.

"Here is the grave of Arthur, king in the isle of Avalon." Despite himself, Henry felt the hairs rise on the back of his neck.

A new voice spoke. "You may not enter."

Henry turned. The monks of the Chapel surrounded them on all sides. No noise, no sound. They had just appeared like magic. How did they do that?

Brother Scarface walked forward, staff in hand, and took up a spot between Brissac and the door.

Brissac's jaw dropped. "Pierre!?"

Scarface smiled. "Hello, Edmond."

Brissac raced forward and hugged the monk. Henry was amazed. It was the first time he'd seen the knight show affection for...well, for anything.

After a moment, Brissac released Scarface—Pierre—and stepped back. "We thought you dead!"

"I am dead to my old life, Edmond." Pierre pointed to the other monks. "So are they."

"What...what happened?"

"We came seeking the sword. We failed the test, and took holy vows to protect it, instead."

"You failed? And *that* succeeded?" Brissac pointed at Henry with disbelief.

"So far." Pierre nodded. "Of course, the most important tests are still to come."

"You failed, but you lived." Henry kicked at the snow in frustration. "Gee, *fra*, thanks for telling me."

Pierre glanced at Henry. "Some people do die."

Henry shivered.

Brissac stared at Henry for a moment, and then got

back to more important business. "But, Pierre, this is wonderful news. You can come with us when we bring the sword to Prince Geoffrey. He'll reward you with—"

Pierre shook his head. "Geoffrey cannot have Excalibur."

Brissac grinned as though he couldn't believe what he was hearing. "Nonsense, Pierre. He wants to unite the West. You know that. What more noble cause could there be?"

"None." Pierre nodded. "But Geoffrey is not the man."

"Of course he is." Brissac's voice had lost its sparkle. "You swore an oath to him for that very reason."

"Then where is he? Is this not his quest?" Pierre waited for Brissac to respond. "No answer? Silence? For the love we shared in arms, Edmond, I will make you this offer. If Geoffrey truly wants Excalibur to unite Christendom, let him stand before me and ask."

Brissac growled. "My lord has better things to do than chop logic in a swamp with a failed knight."

"Indeed." Pierre nodded wearily.

Brissac's knees flexed into a crouch. His hands dangled loose at his sides. "Pierre, you're a holy man now. Don't make me kill you."

Henry stepped between Brissac and Pierre. "Look. We can fix—"

Brissac shoved Henry out of the way and stood directly in front of Pierre. "Stand aside."

Pierre's hand tightened on his staff. "No."

Without breaking Pierre's gaze, Brissac yelled, "Hauptmann!" And there was the *click-click* of crossbows being cocked.

"You monks have staves, Pierre. Maybe swords. For all I know, you're armored like turtles under those robes. But do you really think you stand a chance against Swiss crossbows? Does your oath command you to die for no reason?"

Henry looked around. The Swiss outnumbered the monks two to one, and all of them had their weapons out. They didn't look happy about their targets, but they didn't look like they were going to disobey, either. "For a noble knight, you sure like killing from a distance."

Brissac nodded, never taking his eyes from Scarface. "You I will kill with my bare hands, I promise." He returned his attention to the monk. "Must I prove that I'm willing to shoot?"

Scarface looked deep into Brissac's eyes, and clearly didn't like what he saw. "No," he said, his voicing dripping with contempt. "I believe you...*knight*."

"Then drop your weapons and sit on your hands."

The monks sat. Brissac turned to Henry. "In you go."

"What? Wait—" But two of the Swiss grabbed him by the arms, while another two opened the door.

"NO!" Henry screamed, but it was too late. The terrible *thud* of stone hitting stone echoed down the tunnel like the Last Trump. The door was shut fast. Brissac had trapped him under the hill. He was buried like the dead.

Henry shook himself. *Don't think like that.* It was just a barrow, a mound. There was a way in, so there was a way out...maybe more than one. They'd thrown a torch and a staff in with him. Henry took out his flints and lit the torch. The light showed a tunnel running arrow-straight into the earth. The walls were carved with more of the knots and fretwork he'd seen on the door. It was actually warmer than outside. At this rate, he was doing better than Brissac and the Swiss.

Feeling calmer, Henry started down the tunnel. Then he saw the brown splashes on the floor. *Dried blood.* He took a deep breath and kept going.

He tripped over the first skeleton about twenty feet down the tunnel. The bones collapsed into dust. The armor that had held the bones was rusted to the ground, and no modern knight would have worn it—a helmet with a crest; greaves and cuirass; arm guards.

Henry felt old fears rise up and choke him. The Chapel had been scary—mysterious and deadly. But this…this wasn't deadly. It was just dead, death itself. The stories he'd heard from his grandmother and Alfie—the things that waited under the mounds and behind the standing stones, the pale maidens with teeth like daggers, the ancient darkness, the cruel, beautiful fair folk, the dreams walking toward daylight—

Henry crouched down and hugged his knees. *No. Dead is dead. "Otherworld" means "dead and gone," nothing more.* After a moment, he stood. *All right. Just some old bones. Let's go.* He gathered his courage, held up the torch, and went on.

Soon he passed another skeleton, and a third. The armor was always broken. Bronze and iron were sliced like cheese. Henry swallowed the lump in his throat. Each step took him closer to whatever had done this; each step seemed to echo through the tunnel. Finally, he stopped and took off his boots. Barefoot and quiet, it was easier to go on.

The tunnel opened out into a vast stone cavern, lit by a crack in the stone roof. And in front of him—

An army of the dead.

Skeleton upon skeleton in broken armor, facing forward, tumbled down. There had been a terrible fight here. All of the armor had the same insignia, a black crow on a red field. They had all been on the same side. Who had they been fighting?

Henry picked his way forward. Ahead of him, a sunbeam lanced through the roof onto an island in the middle of an underground lake. At the water's edge was one last skeleton. This one's armor was no better than the rest, but it had a different insignia—a gold dragon on crimson.

Henry looked around. One against dozens. This poor guy had fought alone, under the earth, all the way to the water's edge, totally outnumbered.

"I don't know who you were, brother, but you had

more guts than I ever will." Henry covered the skeleton with his cloak and made the sign of the Cross. "Rest in peace." He turned back to the lake.

Hmmm. In the lake, an island with a rock outcrop in the middle. On top of the outcrop, a squared-off block of stone. Stuck into the stone—

A sword. The blade gleamed in the sunlight, elegant and deadly. Henry stood for a moment, amazed. That was it. That was the sword, and he had found it. Not Geoffrey or Brissac or...or anyone.

Him.

He stuck a finger in the water. *Jesu, that's cold!* But there didn't seem to be any choice. He stripped, tossed his staff in the water, and jumped in.

Yikes! Henry thrashed through the icy water to the other side. He leaped out of the lake onto the shore, gasping for breath and slapping himself to get his blood moving.

He hopped around until parts of him stopped shrinking, and then picked his way up the outcrop. The climb was only a few minutes, and then he was facing the sword in the stone. There were letters on the slab. Henry clutched at his Latin, trying to interpret. *Hic gladius est dolor magna in natibus.* "This...sword...is a...big pain?" That couldn't be right.

Henry knew he had to pull the sword from the stone, but touching it felt...sacrilegious, like peeing into the holy water at St. Severin's. *Well, here goes.* He wrapped his hands around the hilt and pulled. Nothing. The sword was stuck like it was part of the stone. Henry pulled again, and a third time. No good.

So I'm not King Arthur. Big surprise. What if he just went back up the tunnel and told Brissac? Let him try his luck with the sword? Back on the surface, Brissac and his mercenaries were probably still in their stand-off with the Brotherhood. Somehow, Henry didn't think they'd appreciate an interruption just for the information that someone else had to get Excalibur. No, if he wanted to live, he'd have to come back up with every advantage he could get.

He tried to study the stone again, not as a terrified kid, but as a thief. Maybe the whole story had been a trick. That's how he would have done it, if he'd been Merlin—some mechanism inside the boulder, a clamp or a spike, holding the sword tight until just the right person, the one who knew the secret, came to pull it out.

The stone was big, three and half feet tall, the same wide. Limestone or marble. *Easy to carve,* thought Henry. Someone could have chiseled a secret lever, no problem. But no matter where he looked, no hidden catch, no grip, no trick panel. Solid as bedrock. Except…a little wobble.

Henry studied the base of the stone. It sat low, in a sort of bowl in the hilltop. But on one side, the bedrock had fractured, leaving a gap beneath. Off-balance, the stone rocked back and forth. If he could rock it far enough out of the bowl—

Am I actually going to do this? Henry didn't let himself hesitate. Instead, he found a rock for a fulcrum, jammed his staff under the stone as a lever, and heaved. The marble stone shifted off its base. Another heave, a third, and a fourth. The stone tipped over. Slowly at first, then faster and faster, the stone bounded down the slope, finally smashing to pieces on the rocky shore of the lake.

Untouched by the years, undamaged by the fall, Excalibur gleamed among the marble fragments, its edge catching the light from above. There were no jewels or fancy goldwork on the hilt, no engraving on the haft. Only its graceful lines and the steel of the blade, so flawless it looked like a strip of pure silver, suggested a weapon that was anything but ordinary. Henry climbed down and, holding his breath, picked it up.

The cave exploded with the sound of trumpets.

A heavenly choir began to sing.

A surge of power ran up the sword into Henry's hand.

A voice thundered through the cavern. "Whosoever Pulleth The Sword From Out The Stone, Is Rightwise Born King of All England."

Henry screamed and threw the sword into the lake.

Silence.

Henry whimpered. After a moment, he took his hands off his ears and stood up. "Who said that? Where are you? Where are the trumpets?"

Most people like the trumpets. They add a sense of drama.

The voice was female, aristocratic, a little finicky. But no one was there.

Henry looked down at the sword in the water. "You said that!"

An image appeared briefly in the water—the face of a pale, beautiful woman with silver hair and eyes. The voice rang in his head. *Of course I said that. What shall I call you? Sir? Prince? Are you king already?*

"Uh, no. 'Henry' is fine. Just 'Henry.'"

The voice was sympathetic. *Oh. I understand. It's all right. Some of my best bearers had humble origins. Why, Arthur himself began as a squire. Do you have a scabbard for me?*

"Uh, no. To be honest, I didn't expect this."

Humility. You didn't know if you'd be able to pull me from the stone. Hmmm…good. I like that. Well, aren't you going to pick me up?

Slowly, very slowly, Henry reached into the water and picked up Excalibur.

* * * *

Henry strolled up the hallway, back to the surface. After the skeletons by the lake and the ghostly face in the water, the corridor was practically homey—except for the legendary killing machine that Henry was holding. The one that was trying to make small talk.

So, tell me about yourself. What was your last sword like?

"Well…uh, it was a Frankish broadsword."

Was it pretty?

"Yes, but it…wasn't genuine."

That's so often true with the pretty ones. I can't tell you the trouble Roland had with Durandal. She wasn't that sharp, either.

Henry increased his walk to a jog.

Have you slain any dragons yet?

"No, no dragons. Very few dragons in Paris, actually. None."

What about ogres?

"No ogres. We have some law students."

Oh, they're no challenge. So how does a noble knight stay fit for battle now?

"I'm not really a noble knight. I'm more of a messenger who's supposed to take you to the noble knight."

If you'd asked him before he went underground, Henry would have sworn it was impossible for a sword to look shocked. But now he realized his mistake. It was something in the way the light reflected off the edge—

You're joking.

"Believe me, I wish I weren't."

But the stone, the clues, the lake—they're part of the quest. Do you mean to say that someone actually tried to...to hire it out?

"Well, if it helps, it's not how I would have done things."

The sword screeched to a halt, stopped in midair. Henry couldn't budge it. It was as if it had been quick-frozen into a lake of ice.

No. I am sorry. I will put up with many things—bad posture, poor storage, even irregular sharpening—but I will not be quested for like some cheap relic.

"But—"

Take me back to my stone, young man. Take me back this INSTANT.

"But, but—there isn't any stone anymore. It's smashed to pieces."

The very air in the tunnel vibrated with outrage. *You broke my STONE!?*

"I had to...to get you out..."

Maybe that was a clue, young man? That you weren't worthy?

That you needed to wait for someone else? Did that never occur to you?

This was insane. He was hundreds of miles from home, surrounded by homicidal maniacs, buried alive, and arguing with a sword. He tried to get a grip, and failed. "I didn't have a choice!" he yelled. "All those knights you like so much would have killed me if I hadn't come back with you!"

Another long pause. Was the sword...considering?

These men forced you?

Henry nodded. "Yeah. Tied me up, threatened my friends, the whole processional."

Well. Maybe it was a symptom of his departing sanity, but Henry felt he could almost see the sword nod its head. *Let's take a look at them, and see what there is to see. And stand up straight, for Heaven's sake. Slouching does no one any good.*

* * * *

Outside, the monks and most of the mercenaries were gone. It was just Brissac, with three of the Swiss, waiting for the sword.

"Where is everyone?"

Brissac stepped forward, waving away Henry's question. "Is that the sword?"

Henry nodded. "Oh, yes. It couldn't be anything else, believe me."

The snarl faded from Brissac's face, replaced by an expression of awe. "I didn't think it possible...Give it here."

Henry raised the sword, and Excalibur's voice rang in his head.

Don't do it. He's hiding something.

"How can you tell?"

Brissac glared at him. "How can I tell what? Who are you talking to?"

Excalibur spoke again, more urgently this time. *After two thousand years as the sword of heroes, I can smell treachery.*

Henry looked around. The ground was trampled into

mud. There were flecks of blood on the snow, and the Swiss looked…guilty. He needed time. He needed to stall. "All right, let me think."

"Think about what? Give it here!" Brissac stepped closer.

"Uh, just a moment. Let me get a scabbard for it. English winters are just…murder…on blades."

Henry turned to where they'd stored their equipment, next to a tumbled standing stone.

"NO!"

But Brissac was too late. Henry saw what the knight was trying to hide. Behind the boulder were the bodies of Scarface, the monks, and the rest of the Swiss. They were all dead.

"Jesu…"

Behind you!

Henry spun around just as Brissac lunged at him, sword out. Brissac's point caught him high on the shoulder before he stumbled backward.

And then the power was back. It spread from Excalibur through Henry's hand and arm, into his chest, down his legs, rooting him to the earth. He took three steps back, light on the balls of his feet, legs bent and right arm extended. The blade felt heavy but easy to move, a fearful engine, perfectly balanced.

Brissac nodded. "So you do know something about fighting. Good. Less to confess."

But Henry wasn't listening. Excalibur was there, in his head, thinking along with him. A glittering, murderous ghost, filled with edges, points and battle plans, rules and fury. It was like a head full of knives. Henry screamed.

It came out as a battle cry.

They charged together. Brissac made a feint to the head, another to the chest, and then an attack to the legs—

But Excalibur was there, at head height, and mid-chest, and thigh. And it met Brissac's sword, and disarmed him, and cut him low on the chest, slicing through the leather jerkin into the skin. Brissac's blade exploded out of his hand, and he fell to the ground, bleeding.

Excalibur faded from Henry's mind. Suddenly, it was just a scary magical sword again, and not a possessing demon. Henry stared at Excalibur, at Brissac, at the stunned Swiss.

"BOO!" he yelled. The Swiss took off, leaving Brissac clutching himself on the ground.

Henry knelt beside Brissac. "Why did you do it?"

Brissac licked his lips. "Geoffrey's orders. Keep secret...that he didn't come...himself. People must believe...in a quest...for the sword."

Henry rubbed his eyes. It made no sense. "You killed the monks for a lie?"

Brissac shook his head. "No. For a king. A king to...unite us. One land. One law. One king."

Crazy. These Normans were just crazy. Didn't they eat snails and frog legs? Brissac lay on his back, on the ground. Henry looked down. If he let Brissac run off...

Then Brissac would follow him. And wait. And some dark night when he didn't have a magic sword nearby, Brissac would kill him.

Henry had no choice. He swallowed hard. He had never killed a man before. He had spent his life running from men who had.

"Mercy. I yield." Brissac squeezed out the words like seeds from a grape.

Henry shook his head. For once, he had no snappy reply. He raised Excalibur—

Which froze in midair. Again.

No. He has yielded. We shall not strike.

"Look, I don't know how you did things in Camelot, but this is the real world—"

Brissac looked bewildered. "Who are you talking to?"

Henry ignored him. "—and it's a hundred miles to London, and even farther to Paris. If I don't kill him now, he'll sneak up and kill me. You want to belong to him?"

That is neither here nor there. He has sought mercy, and by the Code of Chivalry, you shall give it to him.

"If you're going to kill me, you could at least speak to me!" Brissac sounded frantic.

"Not now!" Henry turned back to the sword. "I am—"

You are a most inappropriate young man, but you shall not commit murder while you wield me.

Henry tugged. Excalibur was stuck fast in…in nothing at all. "Right. I'll just get another sword." After a struggle, he let go of Excalibur. The sword dropped point first into the frozen ground, and Henry grabbed a blade from the body of one of the mercenaries.

Stop!

This was scary. He could hear Excalibur even though he wasn't holding it. Never mind. *Concentrate.* He could do this. Henry held up the weapon. Brissac closed his eyes. Henry stood silent. Everything seemed clearer, brighter. There was a roaring in his ears. Henry breathed in. Could he do it? Kill a wounded man? Kill any man? Brissac would have done it, without a thought. *Blessed St. Nicholas, patron of children and thieves, help me. I'm just a kid.*

The moment stretched—longer, longer. Henry realized he was holding his breath, and he let it go. Slowly, he lowered the blade. "Get up. Run. Or I'll let Excalibur take you."

Brissac scrambled to his feet and limped down the track. Henry looked around, at the dead men, at the blood, at the magic sword stuck into the ground. Then he closed his eyes and threw up.

* * * *

Ten minutes later, he felt better…more numb, anyway. The wind was biting into him, and the wet snow was seeping back into his boots. He stared at the bodies, and at Excalibur, still point-first in the dirt. What a mess.

Well. At least you didn't butcher a helpless man. That's something, I suppose.

Henry wiped his mouth. "Shut up."

Mind your manners. Now pick me up and clean me.

Henry stood. "Riddle me this. What's got a big mouth, but no legs?"

What?

"You."

Henry grabbed a staff and turned toward the ferry.

What's that, Prince Geoffrey? You want all the lands of Christendom? Of course I can win them for you. I'm just sitting here, in a swamp, not doing anything...

Henry stopped. "I hate you."

When you clean me, be sure to get a chamois cloth, and to use smooth, vertical strokes.

Henry sighed, stooped, and picked up Excalibur.

11. A BOY AND HIS SWORD

"What do you mean, you won't take it back!?"

Yes, what do you mean?

Henry shifted on top of the horse. The monks were packing for him, while Too-Big—alias Brother Wulfgar—checked Henry's bandage. He looked sorry, but firm. It was a combination Henry had never seen before, and he didn't like it.

"You woke the sword. It is your destiny."

"Oh, you think I have a destiny." Henry smiled with relief. "Don't worry. I have it on good authority from dozens of monks, sheriffs, and antique sword collectors that I have absolutely no purpose in life whatsoever. I'm worthless. Giving me Excalibur is about as smart as wrapping St. Margaret in bacon and sending her off to hunt dragons."

Exactly. You're making uncommonly good sense.

Wulfgar shook his head. "Soon Geoffrey knows what happened here. We cannot stop his army."

"Prince John could. And he's your regent, too."

Wulfgar set a pin in the cloth. "John cannot stand against Geoffrey. And other things there are here to protect."

Henry winced in pain as Wulfgar tightened the bandage. "Damn it! Er, sorry. I should have killed Brissac when I had the chance."

Regret is the weakling's meat and drink.

"Mercy is not a mistake," said Wulfgar. "Do not despair. You found the sword for a reason."

"Yeah, so it could be a three-foot pain in my behind." Henry adjusted the bandage. "So what is the story with you guys? I mean, where did you come from? What else are you guarding? Are those really dead guys in the trees? What's with all the sculpture in the front plaza? Is there really an Avalon?"

As if he hadn't heard a word, Wulfgar rummaged in a box and handed Henry a small coin pouch. "Go to Constantinople, where the great princes of Christendom gather for crusade. Our chapter house is there. If there is no prince worthy of Excalibur, the masters of our order will help you."

Henry laughed weakly. "But…you can't be serious. I'd have to cross all of Europe." A trip like that could take a whole year, if you completed it at all—and that was if you were going with a band of armed knights. A lone traveler had about as much chance of getting to Constantinople as Alfie did of becoming Prince of Wales.

Oh, whine, whine, whine.

"Shut up, or I'll let Geoffrey have you," muttered Henry to the sword.

Wulfgar looked confused for a moment, but continued. "You are not alone. We guard more than the sword. When in danger, for your mother's sake, ask for aid as a stranger going to the East."

"But…I *am* a stranger, going to the East."

"So no problem." Wulfgar continued, "Maybe you even find someone who deserves the sword."

Henry smiled bitterly. "Trust me, no one deserves this sword."

* * * *

It had been four days since the slaughter at the Isle of Glass. Every night since, Henry had dreamed of Excalibur in battle, in his head again, thinking his thoughts, moving his limbs. He had thought that nothing could be worse than that moment. But traveling with the magic sword had proved him wrong.

One mile from the abbey:

Well, you are not an ideal candidate, but even the humblest clay may be molded. Now, there are certain rules you must obey—

"Oh, yeah?"

First, you shall bathe. Then—

"A *bath?* In the middle of *winter?*"

Sir Gawain bathed each midnight from Advent to Epiphany in the Pool of the Winter Queen. What frightens you is the thought of soap.

"Really? Well, I bathe once a month in the summer, whether I need it or not. And I don't care what you think you know about the human body, I'm not freezing bits off by swimming in December. What do you care anyway? You don't even have a nose!"

The quality of the wielder is a reflection on the sword. Next, you shall see a barber or chirurgeon at the first town, and have that awful scruff shaved off until you can grow a proper beard. And stop slouching—

Wait a minute. No wonder this sounded familiar—it was just like the arguments he had with Mattie. The brat would pick away relentlessly at some bit of trivia, until, just to make him go away, Henry would say—"You're right."

Eh? What?

"You're absolutely right. I do need a bath. As soon as I can find one, I promise I'll bathe."

Why not now?

"If I did, I would leave you unguarded on the river bank, where anyone might take you. Is that what you want?"

No…no…of course not. Very well, then.

Blessed silence. Maybe this could work. Henry started

to smile.

Of course, as my bearer, you must know my lineage.

"Excuse me?"

My lineage. Forged in the West by Weyland out of Wulcan. Borne by Ambrosius out of Bran. Foretold by Mathonwy in the Book of Three Starlings. Hidden by Myrddin for the clan of the Dragon. Pay attention. You will be graded.

Five miles from the abbey:

And tempered was I in the waters of Llydau—

"Right."

...and a splinter of the True Cross was melted into my blade.

"Really?"

That I would be a sword of mercy and peace.

"A sword...of peace."

Aye.

"And a splinter of the True Cross...the *wooden* True Cross...was *melted* into your blade."

Silence.

Maybe it was one of the nails from the True Cross.

"Sure. Let's go with that."

What do you mean?

Twenty miles from the abbey:

And Guinevere. Don't get me started about Guinevere. She never left Arthur alone with me if she could help it. Jealous, cold, petty— why are you poking at your ear like that?

"Just making sure that my brains aren't leaking out."

What?

"Nothing."

Thirty miles from the abbey—

* * * *

Long shadows raked the barren plain. The snow stretched out for miles, left and right, to the faintest hint of a line of trees in the distance. There was no sound, no wind. The sun was a red ember on the horizon. The only break was a crossroads ahead, next to a tree.

As Henry got closer, the tree started to look different. It was too short and too thick. There weren't many branches. Then he realized there weren't any branches.

Then he realized it wasn't a tree.

The creature was ten feet tall, warty and green, with lank matted hair and six-inch fingernails and a club the size of a table. Even its pinkies had muscles.

"I am the Ogre Marhault," it said, in a voice like a toad crossed with an avalanche.

Henry blinked. "Okay."

"None may pass the crossroads, save they defeat me. Many have tried! Many have died!"

Have no fear. We can defeat him.

And now he heard from Excalibur. Terrific.

"Of course we can. Um…so…" Henry faced the ogre. "You must be quite the menace to travelers."

"I have slaughtered thousands!"

"Odd. I'd have thought the monks would have mentioned you."

"Monks?" Underneath its warts and boils, the ogre's brow furrowed.

"Yeah. They know this neighborhood pretty well, they knew I was heading this way…So, you'd think they'd have mentioned an obstacle as formidable…and, frankly, as supernatural…as yourself."

"I will smash you!"

"Right. Could you wait a moment?" Henry glanced at the crossroads. The snow was unbroken.

Prepare yourself, said Excalibur. *I know you do not crave battle, but there is no reason to fear it.*

"No worries." Henry edged to the side of the road.

What are you doing?

"WHERE ARE YOU GOING, LITTLE MAN?"

"Well, see, I don't really need the crossroads that much. It's all yours. *Au revoir.*" And he stepped off the road into the field, leaving a track behind him in the unbroken snow.

Where are you going? Are you fleeing the scene of battle!? Turn back, you—

And then Henry woke up. There was no crossroads, no

ogre. His horse still dozed by the embers of the campfire, but the sound of hoof beats filled the clearing where they were camped. Henry crouched and peeked around the side of the boulder that shielded them from the road.

The air was freezing dry, and starlight coated the ground. Galloping past, not fifty yards from where he hid, came a troop of men on horseback. Ice crackled on their armor, and the stars shone on the lions of England.

Who are they?

"John's men," whispered Henry. "He's regent, and brother to Geoffrey."

Regent? No good king ever started as regent.

"He's slightly evil, yeah." Henry squinted, trying to get a better read on the men. Were they knights? Frisian mercenaries? "Oh, sweet Jesu."

There he was, gaunt and bringing up the rear, but still going like grim death—Brissac. "That tears it."

Why?

"John and Geoffrey hate each other. If Brissac is traveling with John's men, they've joined forces to hunt us down."

Fear not. Now that I am awake, you need but lay your hand on my pommel, and we shall make short work of them.

"Thanks for the offer. Just for now, let's see what we can do about escaping quietly instead." Henry wasn't about to admit that the only thing that scared him worse than Geoffrey was the thought of the sword in his head again, twitching his limbs like a puppeteer, thinking thoughts like razors. Instead, he woke his horse gently, making sure it made no noise, and stamped out the last of the fire. When the hoof beats finally receded into the north, he pointed the horse south and hoped for the best.

The next day, riding through a nameless hamlet, Henry got odd looks from the peasants. Maybe they'd never seen a horse before, or maybe they'd been told to keep watch, and offered a reward. He didn't stick around to find out.

Twice that afternoon, he plunged deep into the barren

winter forest. The first time was purely out of fear. The second time wasn't. He just barely avoided a troop of fast, serious-looking knights wearing the gold lions.

Take me in hand! Use me!

"I'm not worthy."

You could be.

"Let's save you for your true bearer."

* * * *

Someone was in his room.

Moonlight poured through the window, coating everything a ghostly silver. A figure moved toward the bed, a woman in white, her dark hair loose about her shoulders. Wild thoughts raced through Henry's mind. He was rigid with fear and anticipation—

The woman clasped her hands in front of her and kneeled by the side of the bed. With a mixture of disappointment and relief, Henry realized this was a plea for help, not a midnight assignation.

"I am Maryamne. My father was captured by bandits. I need a brave knight to rescue him!"

"Uh, uh—Let me make some light." The wick in the oil lamp was still smoldering; after a moment, he was able to coax it back to life. In the lamplight, Henry saw a beautiful woman, dressed modestly (too modestly, darn it) and well in silk and fur. She had a big ring, and a cap with a gold brim. Her eyes were damp with tears. Henry hauled himself upright in the bed and tried to gather his scrambled thoughts.

"Okay. Right. Well, don't worry."

"Yes?" Maryamne's eyes shone.

"It's not a problem. This county is crawling with Prince John's men. I'll help you find them." It was a risk, of course—the knights he found might be the ones looking for him. But they wouldn't be expecting him to travel with a woman, his horse was pretty fast, and he wasn't weighed down with armor...Yeah, he might be able to get away with it. He felt a little glow of virtue. "Inappropriate young man," eh? "Weakling?" He'd show Miss High and Pointy what was what.

"But, but—will not *you* help me?" Maryamne's eyes filled with tears again.

"I *am* helping you. Wait…you mean, you want me to fight a gang of bandits single-handed?"

"Of course."

"But I'm taking you to trained knights. This is their job. It's what they do."

"But do you not wield the sacred sword Ex—I mean, I saw your sword! You are a noble knight, surely?"

Suddenly, things were a little clearer. Henry studied Maryamne more closely. "How much ransom are they asking, these brigands?"

"What? Oh…a…a hundred marks of silver."

"Is that a real ruby on your bonnet? That's at least sixty marks right there."

"Are you suggesting I pay the ransom? Infamous!"

"Why? Don't you care about your father? Wouldn't you do anything to save him?"

"Of course—"

"And here I present you with two perfectly safe ways to rescue him, and they're not good enough for you? Why is that?"

"I—I—" Maryamne stood, furious. "You are beneath contempt!" And she stalked out of the room, slamming the door behind her.

Henry turned toward Excalibur, which was leaning in its scabbard next to the bed. "Well? Any comments from the court jester?"

What does it matter? You could have proved yourself worthy of me, and you failed.

"'Proved myself'? You mean, by drawing you in battle again? By letting you crawl up inside my skull?"

Of course.

"Not going to happen."

Excalibur paused for a moment. *This isn't over.*

"Yeah, well, we can bicker tomorrow." He pulled the quilt over his head—and woke up.

There was no bedroom. No quilt, no window, no oil lamp. He was in the stables, and his horse stamped and whinnied in its sleep. Henry readjusted the pile of straw he'd been using as a bed, and glared at Excalibur, strapped to the horse's saddle. The sword stayed quiet.

The next day, Henry rode out before the sun broke the horizon. As the sun rose higher, patrols became more frequent, and places to hide became more scarce. Once they reached Salisbury, Henry knew, things would get even worse—the long stretches of open, coverless road south of the Sarum plain would be a special terror. With each mile, the sword became more insistent, more demanding. Excalibur's idea of an escape plan was apparently a countywide killing spree.

Nonsense. Light exercise, nothing more.

And then things got really bad.

12. THE KNIGHT OF FASHION

They were two hours south of Salisbury, just at the crossroads, when Henry heard the hoof beats behind him. Dismounting, he led the horse off the road.

No. Not this time! Stay and fight, you coward!

"No, thank you."

There are only three of them! You can tell by the hoof beats!

"Well, that's two more than me, and three more than I want to face. Now, if you'll excuse me—"

No. By God and Arthur, you shall stand and fight!

Excalibur froze, sending Henry sprawling. The sword and his leg were rooted to the ground.

"What...are...you...DOING!?"

Those are knights. We are at a crossroads. Their leader shall challenge us to single combat, and I shall be able to judge his worth. And it will be good training for you. Hmm. Simple. Traditional. I like it.

"Of course you do! I'll be dead!"

Oh, honestly. You wield Excalibur. What could possibly go wrong?

Henry heaved at the sword, which lurched from the air with a frozen "pop," so that he stumbled back across the road, and then froze up again. He tried to pry the sword from his belt, and then to pull it from the scabbard and throw it away, and heaved himself to the ground instead.

Then the knights appeared around the bend.

Thirty of them.

"That's not three knights."

It sounded *like three knights.*

"That's not three knights!"

It's this cursed snow. It muffles sound.

"SEIZE THEM!" This from the knights' leader, a fashion plate in blue and red.

"IT'S NOT THREE KNIGHTS!"

I know, I know, sighed Excalibur. *Very well, you may advance to the rear.*

It took Henry a split-second to recognize that this was "retreat" in Excalibur-ese. Then he sprinted for the trees.

"KILL HIM!" yelled the Knight of Fashion. The knights charged off the road, but the ground was rough and still covered in snow. First one, then a second horse went down, and the knights dismounted and started to run instead.

This was what Henry had been counting on. Horseback on a road, he was a dead man. On foot, in a forest, chased by men in armor, he had a chance.

"Do you know this country? Did you study it while you were with Arthur? Or did you just spend all your time dreaming about murder?"

I know this land.

"I'm looking for something to break their line of sight. A place to hide, a cave—or hills and a river would be perfect."

Half a mile southeast you shall find a stone castle, strong and fortified, with plenty of...of hiding places. Beyond is the river Arduinus, that the Brythons call Ardwyn. It does not freeze in winter, and there is a ford nearby.

"Right." Henry had spent years in the open. He didn't make the mistake of charging ahead. Snow in the woods hid pits and roots that could sprain ankles and break bones. Instead, he hopped from bare root to clear rock, despite the sound of the knights getting closer and closer behind him.

Then he heard it—the first *thud*, and the muffled groan of someone who'd just put ten stone's worth of weight on a foot in a hole. Another man down. The rest would be slower now, slower than he was. Henry tightened his lips and kept going.

An hour later, the sounds of pursuit hadn't died away, but they hadn't gotten closer, either. Henry scrambled up a slope and arrived on a wide ridge covered in shattered rock, blocks of gray stone two or three times the length of a man.

Henry looked around. *"This* is your castle?"

Excalibur was silent for a moment. When it spoke, its voice was thin and distant. *It was. In the days of Arthur, it was…This was Caer Allawn, the keep of legions. It was a mighty…*Then the weapon seemed to collect itself. *Go to the right, past the granite boulder and the white standing stone.*

Henry scrambled past the boulder, and shuffled down into a dark wood, with twisted trees crowding close to the path. The path wound past a hill, then a ruined barrow, then through a broken archway that might have been part of a bridge, once. On the other side was a clearing. It was moderately eerie…but with Excalibur on your belt, eeriness was practically guaranteed wherever you went.

As I promised.

Henry slumped to the ground. In the distance, he could hear the shouts of the knights getting fainter.

You could still oppose them. They are divided now. You could emerge from hiding, challenging them to single combat one by one—

Henry tossed Excalibur against a boulder and unslung his bedroll. Spare clothes, flint and steel, a quilt. Nothing else. The food had all been in the horse's saddlebags.

"How far is it to Southampton on foot?"

Southampton? I know it not.

Henry racked his brains. Did the town have a Latin

name? Had Southampton even existed in Excalibur's time? "Um...Clausenium. How far to Clausenium, or to Isla Vectis?"

Five days. A week, perhaps. Why?

"No reason." A week without food.

He set up camp in a small cave and gathered firewood. As night fell, he stacked the wood to give him a long-burning fire, and sat staring into the flames.

This time, he was expecting it. He heard the wind rise. He turned, and there were three women of supernal beauty in the clearing. They were dressed in white and untouched by the cold.

"We are the Sisters of the Wyrd." The first one stepped forward, her blue eyes glowing, her black hair floating around her body. "We offer you the choice of heroes."

"Yes?" Henry's voice was hoarse, but it wasn't fear that was making it hard for him to speak. He was close enough to smell their perfume, a combination of myrrh and sandalwood. He couldn't think straight. Was that the second Sister's hair, brushing his cheek?

"If you wish to retain your honor, you must face the dragon; turn and flee, and you shall submit to us, and be lost forever—"

"Hmm. Dragon...or girls. Dragon...girls." Henry shrugged off his cloak. "Okay." He stepped forward—

STOP IT. STOP IT.

Excalibur's voice rang through the clearing. The Sisters seemed to hear it, and stepped away from Henry.

My apologies, Daughters of Themis. I should have known this would be pointless.

Silently, the Sisters drifted out of the clearing. Henry sat on a boulder, breathing hard, too worked up to even notice that his cloak was still in the snow.

Was that display just for my benefit, or would you truly have embraced them?

"I don't know."

Arthur knew better than to approach the Sisters. It would have meant your destruction.

"SHUT UP!" Henry snatched up Excalibur by the scabbard and hurled it into the clearing. He didn't want to talk. He wanted privacy, he wanted to be alone, he wanted women and wine and red meat, and none of that was going to happen. He grabbed a branch from a tree and started whacking everything in reach—the trees, the ground, the boulder, the cave walls—until he was exhausted.

He leaned against the tree, sweating and shivering, and caught his breath. Finally, he put his cloak back on and sat by the fire. He left Excalibur lying against the stone.

When did you guess?

"That you were responsible? Pretty fast." Henry's stomach was already starting to gripe; he chewed on a twig to still the pangs. "You go your whole life without even a spooky feeling, then you get one magic sword and it's all ogres, enchantresses, and midnight apparitions. It wasn't hard to figure out." He warmed his hands at the fire. "Plus, there was that whole focus on taking pointless risks—that's kind of your hallmark."

Every bearer of the sword must undergo three trials to prove his worth.

"I figured out the riddle of the Chapel! No one else did that!"

Congratulations. That proved your wit. But a king must also have bravery, compassion, purity...you failed them all.

"Are we going to have any more of this?"

No. You win. Any monsters you meet from here on are your problem alone. I had thought to awaken the qualities of knighthood in you. I'm sorry I wasted your time.

"Right, then." Despite everything, Henry felt a sneaking sense of...guilt. It was ridiculous. What did he have to feel guilty about? And what did it matter? Thanks to Excalibur, he would starve to death in the wild, if John's men didn't catch him first.

He shook it off and unrolled his blanket. "I'll see you in

the morning. If any dragons stop by, don't wake me."
  I shan't.

13. THE PARDONER'S TALE

One step, two step. One step, two step. *Ta gauche, ta gauche, ton droit, gauche, droit.*

You sang songs to keep yourself moving. For a while, the hunger had kept him alert. He had even caught a fish. But that had been two days ago, and he was drifting. Once you got sleepy, really sleepy, that was the end of things—and he was already far enough gone that he couldn't worry about it the way he would have a day ago.

Another step, another, and yet one more…

Wake up, Henry. Wake up! Wake up!

Henry's eyes snapped open. He was on a path between two snow-covered hills. He couldn't remember how he'd gotten there.

He shook his head, trying to clear the clouds. "Where…"

Half a day west of Sorbiodunum.

Henry mentally translated the place names. "But…but that's Salisbury! We needed Southampton…"

I have tried to wake you for hours now.

Henry slumped against a tree. They were deep in the empty south and west of the country, with no food and no horse, and there were no large towns—just a few tiny hamlets and country fiefs, where food was locked tight and strangers were guilty until proven innocent.

He rubbed his fingertips together. They were numb and pale. He stood up and walked a few yards. A few more. Then his knees buckled and he fell, face down in the snow. He was going to die.

Henry.

"Go away."

Henry, I can help.

"Too late."

No. There is a road nearby. A road of the legions. It had outlasted the Romans by Arthur's day, and it should be there still. It will take us straight to Clausenium or Portus Magnus or wherever we need to go, without break or hindrance.

"Can't stand."

Henry, I can sustain you until we find food. But you must let me in.

"Nice...try."

Henry, it is our only chance. I do not wish to be stranded here, at the mercy of the first footpad who comes along. Let me do this, and I will go no farther than giving you the strength you need to continue.

"You...won't be in my head..."

No.

"Swear on your soul."

I swear on my honor, which is more important.

Henry tried to think, to weigh his choices, but it was too late. He couldn't think clearly anymore, and even if he could, he couldn't see that he had any choices left. He would have to trust. "Do it. Do it!"

Place your hand upon me, and do not fear.

Henry breathed deep and clutched Excalibur's hilt. Cold and dark, like a brook in winter, strength flowed into him. His mind cleared, and it was his own.

The Caesar road is over that hill. Keep your hand on me, but do not delay—I cannot maintain this forever.

"Let's go, then." He got to his feet.

The hill was dry and brown, three times the height of a

man, but at least the wind had blown it clear of snow. In a few minutes, Henry had reached the crest and hiked down the other side to the Roman road.

Straight as a lance, wide as four men walking abreast, it cut through the countryside to the horizon. No roots broke its surface, no mud covered the fitted stones, there were no gaps where scavengers had pried up the paving blocks. Henry knelt down to touch it.

Have you never seen a relic of Empire?

"Sure. The aqueducts at Lyon. But no one has the money to maintain them."

This was built by the Romans at the height of their power. And even this is nothing compared to the works of the Men of the Western Isles. It was for the return of these works that Arthur raised his knights...for a pax *that bound together all peoples.*

"I thought it was for the Holy Grail."

The Sangréal...we found it, and lost it. It waits.

"Really? Where?"

We have little time.

"Right." Henry stepped onto the road, heading east.

Walking the road was like moving in a dream. No fear of bandits, no detours, no roadblocks or fallen trees. Fields and castles appeared in the distance, vanished again. Even the wind seemed quieter. Henry marched forward without hunger or fatigue, like a thing of metal himself.

Night fell, and Henry looked for a place to set up camp.

I would not advise it.

"What do you mean?"

Continue on instead. Trust me.

"Why?"

Excalibur hesitated. *Every man has...reserves in his body that he cannot touch, cannot use, except in the most dire emergencies. That is what we are using now, to reach Southampton.*

"And this means..."

If we do not reach food and shelter in time, you shall collapse. In fact, if you break your bond with me even now, you shall be in grave danger.

Henry swallowed. "You mean, I have to eat a sausage before I let go of you, or I'll die?"

Essentially…yes.

"Oh, I hate you. Hate, hate, hate."

Would you rather I allowed you to die on the road?

"I wouldn't have died if you hadn't alerted the knights and scared our horse away!"

I saved your life and all I hear is complaint!

The argument lasted all night and twenty miles. In the morning, they rounded a crest of hills, and in the farthest distance, Henry could make out the blue line of the sea. Ahead, the Roman road intersected a newer track that led southeast.

"That should take us to Southampton. Another half day, maybe, and then to sea."

The sooner, the better. We have little time left.

"Wait." Henry held his breath, listening. There it was, faint but growing…the sound of hooves. "Oh, no, no, no—" He looked around wildly. They were on a wide, gentle slope that ran down to the shore. It was completely open, with no snow and no cover. Hiking up his braies, he sprinted down the track.

"Any more tricks up your scabbard?"

"Tricks?" No. I have done all I can—until you actually meet these men. If you choose to stand, and not run, I can help you then.

"You got your wish. They're on horseback, and I've got no place to hide. Doesn't look like I have a choice."

Fear not. You shall have a glorious end.

"Terrific."

The hoof beats grew louder as he ran. Leaving the road to scramble up the rocky slope of a nearby hill, he saw the horseman ride out of the pass and turn east after him. It was a large band, flying two banners—the lions of England, and Geoffrey's personal insignia, a silver helmet on a blue field.

As the knights rode in closer, Henry noticed something

he'd missed before: Sir Fashion, the knight from the road, was leading them…and he wore a small gold crown. Sir Fashion had to be Prince John, and he was leading his own knights, with Brissac, Geoffrey's representative, bringing up the second team—what was left of the Swiss.

Henry thought about that as he reached the top of the hill.

That's it. Higher ground befits a hero.

"Oh, I'm not keeping you."

What? You would sell me for your miserable life? Have you no—

"Honor? No. A plan? Yes." Climbing a convenient boulder, Henry sat down on the top, tailor-fashion, with Excalibur lying on his lap.

He didn't have long to wait. In minutes, the knights had arrived at the base of the hill. It was too steep for the horses; they dismounted and climbed on foot, with John and Brissac in front.

"Give it up, boy," said Brissac.

Henry licked his lips, and looked past Brissac to Prince John. He saw a tall, languid young man with jet-black hair and a perfectly groomed beard. John wore blue and scarlet, and looked like he owned half of the world and held the mortgage on the rest. At first, he didn't resemble Geoffrey all that much. But then his eyes met Henry's, and Henry saw that little spark of arrogance, honed by royal family life into sheer insanity. No question, he was a Plantagenet.

"Sure, Eddy," said Henry. "Should I surrender it to you, or to Prince John?" Henry bowed from the waist. "Your Highness."

"Don't play games, boy. You've done well, but it's over now. Give me the sword, and you can go free. I promise."

"You shall give Us the sword and be free to go." Prince John stepped in front of Brissac. "We are the regent, and of the Blood Royal. Our Word may be trusted."

Henry hid his smile. "Of course." He held up Excalibur in its scabbard, and turned toward John. Brissac tried to get between Henry and John—only to find John's sword, a giant claymore, drawn and in the way.

"Kneel, Edmond de Brissac."

Brissac went down on one knee.

"Ah, good. You do remember your oath to our family. We thought you had forgotten it, and turned thief and traitor."

"No, Your Highness. I merely follow my lord's orders."

"We are your lord."

"I have sworn fealty to Prince Geoffrey, Your Highness."

"We are the Prince-Regent of England, not the Duke of Brittany. You shall obey Us."

"Your highness, I—"

The attack was like lightning. One moment, John was relaxed, standing, surrounded by retainers like a proper prince—the next, he was swinging the giant claymore one-handed like an arming sword. Brissac rolled away and bounced up on his feet, his own sword out. In a flash, John's men squared off against the Swiss. Steel rang against steel; blades cut at each other, at the open air, at an enemy's armor, or tunic, or flesh.

Henry took this as his cue to leave. He slid off the far side of the boulder and stumbled down the slope as fast as he could. *Hmmm,* he thought. *I might even be able to grab one of the horses.*

Excalibur shrieked. *Oh, despicable! Oh, vile! Fleeing the battle while good men fight!*

"Good men? Name one."

That is neither here nor there.

"And neither are we, with luck."

And his luck seemed to be holding. The two men left with the horses had run up to join the fight. If he could just circle around in time, he might be able to grab one horse and panic the rest.

Henry pelted down the slope, one hand on Excalibur,

praying under his breath to St. Dismas to get him to the horses and away before the soldiers realized what was happening.

He had gotten almost to the bottom when his foot turned on a rock. He went down hard, and Excalibur flew from his outstretched hand.

The bond with Excalibur was broken. The strength drained out of Henry's body. A ton of weight crashed down on him, and the ground reached up and smashed him in the head. He could barely move his eyes to follow the sword as it arched up and up, and then slowly, ever so slowly, turned point down and plunged earthward like a comet, to bury itself in the ground, with only its hilt sticking up. The world went black.

Henry. Wake up, Henry. Henry. Henry!

Henry opened his eyes. He could hear John's men yelling and whacking. And then Brissac's men. And then both. He fell asleep.

HENRY!

He opened his eyes again.

We may yet succeed. Take my hilt.

Henry lay there, limp as a corpse. Moving was hard, but wanting to move was even harder. He stretched out one arm, then the other. With infinite weariness, he lifted his body from the ground and crawled. Excalibur was barely a man's length away, but it seemed as far as Constantinople. He gulped thick breaths of air, hoping it would wake him up. Finally, he reached out and touched the sword.

Strength returned. He stood up and pulled Excalibur from the ground. He looked back at the knights—still fighting. Jogging to the horses, he scattered all but one and hopped on.

Congratulations, vile creature.

"What crawled up your scabbard? Annoyed I'm still alive?"

Your trick. Your low stratagem. It was shameless. It was base. It was—

"—clever?"

Yes, said Excalibur, in utter disgust.

Henry lowered his head and goaded the horse. They raced down the road, the waves getting closer and closer on their right as the path cut down the slope toward the sea. Desperate plans whirled through his head. He tried to remember if high or low tide was near, but he couldn't. Like all the children in his village, he'd been raised knowing the tides and currents for the whole year on both sides of the Channel. But that had been a long time ago, and besides, his village was dead.

Since he couldn't know when, or even if, the ships at dock would sail, he would probably have to hide until he could make his move, and pay through the nose when he did. He touched the tiny purse that the monks had given him. He had silver, enough to get him on a ship, but not enough to bring him back…assuming he lived to come back.

The horse topped a rise and there was Southampton spread out before them, from gatehouse to docks. Henry tapped the horse's flanks, and they descended toward the town.

14. OUT OF THE FRYING PAN

Southampton Free Port. Henry smiled. After relics, tombs, and otherworldly apparitions, Southampton was the splash of water that ends the dream, a reminder of the big, bright, ordinary world. The docks were still full of the yard-sailed cogs that had carried Bretons, Gauls, and Easterlings back and forth across the water for a hundred years. There were still the bales of furs, beads of amber, and bundles of finished cloth that had made the Baltic trade so profitable, and merchants from the Low Countries, the Hanseatic League, and points even farther North and East. The air was filled with the bustle of people closing deals, telling stories, jabbering away in two or three different languages, making a living from brains and drive, and not a noble in sight.

Why do you smile?

"I like Southampton. Don't you?"

It's no Tintagel.

Henry had sold the horse at a significant discount within minutes of getting inside the town walls, and taken the coins to an inn minutes after that. The place was seedy and run down, but its walls carried the marks of a dozen guilds, from the mercers to the boatwrights, and places like that usually didn't cooperate with the nobility if they could help it. He ate, drank, and crawled to his pallet to sleep, never once breaking his grip on the sword.

In the morning, he felt like death warmed over, but he could take his hand off Excalibur without fainting. The next two days were cold and wet; a freezing storm had blown in from the North Sea. Henry spent the time hidden in his garret, dozing, eating, and spying on the streets below, watching John's knights ride through the town. On the third day, the weather cleared.

So? What does the weather have to do with us?

"Now that the winds have died down, half a dozen ships will try to beat the next storm and set sail for Brittany. For all John knows, we could be on any one of them. I give them another day of looking for us here, and then they'll give up. Prince John doesn't strike me as the patient type."

You are quite adept...at hiding.

"Yeah, yeah."

The next day dawned clear, cool, and apparently John-free. Henry strapped on Excalibur and headed through the city's gates to the docks. He felt the terror of the last few days fading. All he had to do was sail to far Constantinople, find a hero, give him the sword, and let him slice Geoffrey (and John, and Brissac) into pork chops. And then privacy, no more nightmares, glorious peace and quiet. He could let Mattie yammer away about the revolution, while he and Alfie and Valdemar figured out some new cheat, something entirely unconnected to swords. Maybe real estate.

The odds of getting a ship weren't great, but after four or five hours up and down the wharves, Henry finally found the *Gorgonoki*, headed for Bordeaux, Bayonne, and points south. The ship was...eclectic. He recognized the prow of a Viking longboat, the lateen sails of an Araby trader he'd seen once in a drawing, and the big square back of a Saxon cog, not to mention about fifteen different types of wood scattered throughout the hull's planking.

I don't like this vessel.

"Of course you don't."

Is the sail supposed to have those mildew stains?

"Gives it character."

You almost stepped through a weak spot in the deck.

"Captain Dimiturglu says that'll be fixed tomorrow. A little tar, a little planking, good as new."

And what kind of name is "Gorgonoki" anyway? Where is this ship from?

"Switzerland."

Switzerland!?

Well, yes, it did sound suspicious, but Henry wasn't going to admit that to Excalibur. And whatever the sailors were speaking, it wasn't French, Italian, or German. Plus Captain Dimiturglu was a hugger, and Henry didn't like anyone who hugged strangers without an excuse…or a bath. But the *Gorgonoki* was the only ship heading south. Every other ship in the harbor was either a Channel hopper, or sailing north and east for the Baltic run. Rather than wait around for John or Brissac to return, Henry was inclined to set sail now and ask questions later. Besides, if worse came to absolute worst, he could always draw Excalibur—

Henry shook his head. He didn't want to think about that nightmare again. Knives behind his eyes and in his heart. The worst would really have to come for that to happen.

* * * *

The tide would go out around sunset, taking the *Gorgonoki* with it. Henry rose at dawn and walked to the main square in front of the gates leading to the harbor. Everything seemed fine—

"Uh-oh." Henry sidled quickly but casually into the shadow of an alley.

What is the problem? Too much sunlight burning your paws and tail?

91

"Hah-hah, I'm a rat, I get it." He peeked around the corner again. "No, there's just a lot of soldiers hanging out by the dock, poking their swords into barrels and hay wagons."

Even in Arthur's day, we sent soldiers to investigate pirates on the docks.

"Yeah, well, did Arthur go himself?"

What?

Because there was no doubt. The tall, hooded figure trying to look all mysterious and silent by the wharf was Prince John. And the "priest" trying to hide his mustachios in his cassock was Brissac.

Hmm. Inconvenient, but at least this will give you a chance to redeem yourself. Now, when attacking two opponents at once, audacity is—

"Wait." Henry watched the troops closely. A fur merchant tried to move his cart, and was subjected to a thorough search. A mercer found all his goods unloaded before he was given leave to board his ship. But a party of knights slouched on board their sailing cog with barely a glance from John's men.

"Huh." Another knight rode through the gates. And a few more. The soldiers ignored them. The first knight trotted to an inn with a stable attached and led his horse inside. Henry followed.

Henry, what are you doing?

"Getting us out of here."

Henry lingered outside the stables as the knight's squire undid the knight's armor, took his horse, and settled everything in its stall. The knight spent a few minutes yelling at the squire, and then went inside. The squire sipped moodily from a wineskin. Then he took a longer swig. Then a longer one. The squire's head drooped. He started to snore.

Don't you dare.

"Dare what?"

****

Impostor!

The sun was shining, the birds were singing, and Henry was trying hard not to fall on his face.

It wasn't easy. The armor he had…borrowed…was eighty pounds of dead weight and about as comfortable as the pillory. He was sure he'd missed at least two of the straps on his breastplate. Plus the horse was obviously used to being ridden by a sadist with a weight problem, because it was trotting all over the place like a six-foot high puppy. Judging by the scars on the poor beast's flanks, just about anyone was an improvement over its former master.

Outrageous, brazen pretender.

"What's your point?"

To steal a knight's armor. What more vile crime could you have committed?

"Oh, not using a fingerbowl, burning down a village, torturing a family to death for pearls and coral they don't have, it's all good."

Henry had trotted the horse through the streets at the far side of town, trying to get used to the new gear and transportation. It hadn't been a notable success.

Your time is coming, young man. You fool no one in your borrowed finery.

"You better hope I do, or you're spending the next fifty years as Geoffrey's pocket knife."

They trotted forward for a few streets in silence.

"Maybe I didn't understand. Do you want to be in the hands of a power-mad dictator?"

A few more streets.

"Maybe that's what makes you happy. Some dead peasants for breakfast, a little tyranny for lunch, and then a light snack of despotism right before bedtime. I wouldn't like it much, but maybe you fancy magic-sword types think it's the best thing since sliced serf—"

Enough!

Henry shut up.

Keep your weight off the saddle. Lean a little forward, and keep your knees bent.

"Thank you."

I don't know why I'm doing this.

Henry tried to lift himself off the saddle. He managed for about a hundred feet before the weight of the armor forced him back down.

"I did it. That was—what—almost a minute!"

Excalibur sighed.

They arrived at the gate. The line was even longer now, but Henry breathed a sigh of relief: He couldn't see Prince John or Brissac anywhere. Had they gotten bored? Taken a lunch break? No matter. Time to move.

Remember, you are a knight. You are entitled to go to the front. Back straight! Knees flexed! You're a knight, you worthless pig!

Henry nudged the horse with his knees, and they trotted forward. Riding in a steel shell was confusing. The armor started moving a few seconds after the horse did, and stopped a few seconds after it stopped. Henry had to catch himself by grabbing on to the saddle horn.

Two pikemen dashed in front of him, the butts of their weapons grounded in the dirt.

Henry tried to pitch his voice low and loud. "Who dares...to...uh...impede the progress of Sir..." Henry's mind went blank. Who was he? Real knights had all sorts of symbols and devices painted on their armor—the heraldry announced who you were, where you were from, and who had bought you Christmas presents when you were five.

Henry glanced at his shield and saw a hawk, a bunch of stripes, and something that looked like a constipated weasel, but he knew as much about the meaning of the images as he did about German cheesemaking. He could be anybody—

This is the device of the Sagramores of Milan, ancient even in my day.

"...Sir Sagramore of Milan?"

A knight trotted forward on his horse and glanced at

Henry without interest. "We are under the peace of Prince John of England, Sir Sagramore. Please disarm."

"You ask a knight to disarm? Monstrous!"

The knight sighed. "We ask only that you do not enter the Plantagenet empire equipped as for war, Sir Sagramore. Your helmet, please."

Henry said nothing. The moment stretched. The pikemen got antsy. They moved closer, eager looks in their eyes. Well, what did it matter if the prince and the jerk weren't here? Slowly, Henry reached up to remove his helmet, his heart pounding.

"I shall have words for Prince John when I see him."

The knight nodded, barely looking up from his writing tablet. "Indeed. Then you are in luck, Sir Sagramore. There the prince is now."

The knight pointed across the town square. Prince John was entering at the head of a squad of men-at-arms. The knight waved his hand. "Your Highness! Sir Sagramore of Milan wishes an audience with you!"

John turned to face them. From across the square, he locked eyes with Henry and smiled. It was the smile of a wolf. A wolf with rabies. Henry's chest tightened like a drum-skin.

"How do I get this nag to gallop?" muttered Henry.

You don't want to. This is a war horse, you could not control it at—

"Now."

I'm warning you—

"NOW!"

Quick, with your heels and yell, "Chargez!"

"CHARGEZ!"

The horse trumpeted, rose up on its hind legs, and wheeled around. Henry almost fell out of his saddle and clung desperately to the horse's neck. Confused, the horse started to gallop—straight back through the gates and into the town.

John turned to his men. "He dies, or you do!"

I told you so! shouted Excalibur. *You have no control! You are no knight!*

The streets whirled past on left and right, cobbles striking sparks from the horse's shoes, and the trees and awnings that made Southampton pretty threatened to decapitate Henry if he sat up at the wrong time.

"Yeah, great! Any other wonderful advice?" he shrieked, as he ducked under a tree.

Hold on.

"Thanks!"

Don't mention it.

And now John's men had pulled out onto the street behind them.

"Stop, thief!"

As soon as this horse stops, Johnny-boy, thought Henry. And now a flight of steps appeared. *Oh, no—*

Going down two flights of stone steps on a crazed charger is like riding a washtub down a waterfall. Henry held on for dear life as the horse leaped, skidded, neighed in panic, and scrambled down from cobblestone to cobblestone. Townsfolk jumped out of the way. Laundry and groceries went flying. Henry was sure people were making noise, but he couldn't hear anything above his own screams.

Whatever you do, don't throw up, said Excalibur.

Henry's stomach promptly started to churn. "I hate you."

And now they were racing down a wide arcade, with booths under the eaves. As his horse's breathing deepened, Henry decided it was time to lighten the load a little. First, the helmet.

"*Sacré!*" One of the soldiers went down, nailed on the *tête* by the helm of Sagramore. Now, a gauntlet—

"*Cochon!*" Henry was starting to get the hang of this. Now the other gauntlet. He kicked off a greave and spun the gorget behind him, leaving just the chest plate and the arm pieces.

They galloped through a fullers' courtyard, the stink from the cleaning vats clearly afflicting princely John more than Henry. Henry adjusted his bearings. If he remembered correctly, just a mile to the left was the church of St. Peter the Fisherman. If he could make it there—

They landed on the stones of the main square still in one piece. Ahead of Henry was the church, its doors wide. Sanctuary. Once he got in there, not even John would dare to touch him.

Henry kneed the horse. "GO!"

They charged across the square just as John and his goons appeared out of the alley. Off came the rest of the armor, and Henry and the horse galloped up the three broad, shallow steps to the open doors of the cathedral, and inside.

Cool. Dark. Peaceful. The horse came to a stop. Henry rolled out of the saddle and collapsed to the floor of the cathedral. He looked up. Five burly priests stared down at him.

"Sanctuary!" he gasped. "I claim...the right...of sanctuary."

The priests looked at him. Then they looked outside, where John's men were galloping closer and closer. Then they looked at each other. Then they edged away into the darkness.

"You jerks!" shouted Henry. "Just see if I donate to the building fund now!"

John's soldiers entered the door, blocking out the light. Henry went for the stairs. He dashed through the apse, past the priests who had been enjoying the show, and into the nave.

The light streaming through the stained-glass windows was a big hit with Excalibur.

This is glorious! Not even Camelot had such beauty!

"Great. The stairs?"

Oh. In the shadows next to the altar, in that large column. Can't you see them?

"Now I can."

Henry hadn't paid much attention to the cathedral when he'd been in Southampton with Brissac, but he knew three important facts: It was big. It had two or three separate rooftops equipped with nice, climbable flying buttresses. And its rear was very close to the houses of Underchurch, the neighborhood that had sprung up between the cathedral and the river.

Henry dashed for the column, with John no more than three yards behind. The stone stairs corkscrewed above, lit every ten feet or so by a tiny slit of daylight. Henry scrambled up, using his hands as much as his feet. The stairs were worn down in the center, slippery. Below him he could hear the soldiers. Closer. Closer.

And then he was up and out in the bell tower. The wind was blowing hard and cold, and it smelled of snow and the sea. Henry could see past the towers, out to the harbor, and east across the white and brown countryside. The bells hung in giant racks from their yokes in the ceiling. A priest stared at Henry, horrified.

"Bar the door!" yelled Henry. "Saracens!" He didn't wait to see if the priest actually believed that the hordes of Saladin had traveled two thousand miles to assault suburban England. He scrambled over to the lip of the tower and saw he'd miscalculated. The buttress was on the other side of the tower, past the door—and now John's men burst through, standing between Henry and his escape.

John pointed, and the soldiers spread out left and right to flank him. He made a few passes with his sword, and his men stalked forward.

The wall was behind Henry. John was in front of him. He was trapped. Unless—

Henry grabbed the bell rope and started to climb. The rope sagged under his weight. BING! The bell, a high B-flat by the sound of it, swung loudly in its yoke. The soldiers put their hands to their ears.

BONG! Henry climbed across the yoke mechanism, twenty feet above the soldiers, where he was sheltered from the full noise of the bells. DING! Unfortunately, the bells themselves were too high above the tower floor to actually hit any of them, but Henry rocked the ones he could, trying to generate as much painful clamor as possible. BING!

The soldiers spread out. BING-BONG-A-LONG BING! Henry circled, checking out the tower from up top...

There it was. The flying buttress leading down to the lower roof, just off the east side of the tower. BONG-BONG! Henry eased forward and tossed his knife behind him. It dropped with a clatter on the west wall, and the soldiers clustered around it. Henry dropped down, leaped over the low east wall, and crawled onto the ledge. Only ten feet down to that tiny, tiny buttress—

"Could you help me out here, Excalibur? Tighten my grip, or something?"

You'd like some advice on dueling against masonry? A little information on sword-strokes specially designed to attack architecture?

"All right, all right. " He let go, and dropped.

"There he is!"

For a sickening moment, Henry's feet threatened to shoot out from under him. Then he got control, and inched out along the buttress toward the tiled roof that covered the nave. He didn't look back, but he listened for the muffled thuds that would mean he was being followed onto the buttress. One foot, five feet, ten feet—nothing. Twenty feet, he was at the roof's edge, and no one had followed. Smart—the spider's walk of the buttress was no place for a man in armor. Henry chanced a look back. Johnny was shouting at the troops. Now they were dashing back down the stairs. Trying to head him off, no doubt.

Henry leaped down to the roof, and raced across the

tiles to far end of the church. There were more buttresses, at least five of which overlooked the roofs of houses. Eeny, meeny, miny—

—moe.

Henry jumped onto a house-top, and then across the street to another roof. He was in Underchurch now, a warren of buildings and alleys. The houses leaned out over the streets (so the folks on the top floors could dump their slops more easily on the folks below) and the roofs almost met in the middle.

The roofs were a little world of their own, filled even in winter with pigeon coops, barrels of dried fish and pickled vegetables, cloth and lumber and rope. Henry leaped from roof to roof, finally knowing where he had to go. Three blocks south and east, and he was on a warehouse overlooking the church plaza, sharing the wood coping with a vat of onions and a dozen barrels of slowly salting cod. He squinted at the plaza. He was in luck—John had taken the bait. He could see the men running through the maze of alleys, trying to catch him on the ground.

What are you doing?

"Doubling back."

He worked his way back across the roofs to the cathedral. His luck held—his horse was still there, snapping and rearing, holding at bay a dozen up-and-coming young entrepreneurs who clearly wanted it for themselves. One flourish of Excalibur, and they were flying down the alleys. The horse trotted to him like a puppy. Henry grabbed the reins, hitched himself onto the saddle, and rode toward the gates.

One block, fine. Two blocks. Three, and he heard the sound of hoof beats and running feet. Four, and the gates were in sight. Five, and he was galloping onto the dock, and John and—yes, it was Brissac—were right behind him.

And there it was, the ship about to raise anchor. Henry dug in his heels, and the horse whinnied and raced forward. It leaped onto the deck as they raised the gangplank and the tide took them out, away from the dock, the wharf, and the gates.

As the *Gorgonoki* drifted south, faster and faster, Henry crawled up into the rigging. There they were, one parti-colored figure and one with long black mustaches, standing furious on the wharf.

"So long, Prince Jerk!" yelled Henry. "Give my regards to your jerk brother!" And with that, they were around the last bend, headed for the open sea.

15. NOT CONSTANTINOPLE

"There to go for you. Constantinople."

"That's not Constantinople. That's Bordeaux."

"No, is Constantinople."

"Look, I know Constantinople when I see it, and that's not Constantinople."

They were standing on the deck of the *Gorgonoki*, Henry and Captain Dimiturglu, staring at the city that was definitely not Constantinople.

"How for you to say is not Constantinople!?"

"For one thing, Constantinople is on the sea, and this is a river."

"But this just river side of Constantinople. How you know other side not sea side?"

"Because this is the *Garonne* river. That city would have to stretch for fifteen hundred miles for the other side to be the sea."

"Look is there." Dimiturglu pointed. "Church of St. Sophia."

"That's a warehouse."

"There is Golden Horn."

"Barge dock."

"Straits of Bosporus."

"Drainage ditch. Do you really think you can get away with this?"

Captain Dimiturglu draped a friendly arm around Henry's shoulder. "Crazy visions you got. Come with me to barber, we bleed you, you see right, everything good. I buy for you first leech."

Henry shook himself loose and stepped back. "We're two thousand miles by sea from Constantinople. Sail me there, or give me my money back."

At this, Dimiturglu hung his head, and then glanced back at the other crewmembers.

Henry rubbed his forehead. "You don't have my money, do you?"

Dimiturglu smiled, embarrassed. "You know, in Nantes, we go drinking? There is these girls, and they—"

"You partied my money away, and you didn't even invite me."

Now the sailors really did look ashamed. One of them slapped Dimiturglu upside the head and babbled in Whatever-ese. Dimiturglu nodded sadly. "Semikodomir says you right. We should to invite you. We break Code of Guy." Then he brightened. "But is okay! You like Bordeaux. Fun town. Lots of girls! Right, boys?" The sailors nodded. Dimiturglu elbowed Henry in the ribs. "And the Queen, the Queen of England herself." He whistled and sketched an hourglass shape with his hands. "Here is Court of Love, boy. In Bordeaux, all about love. And sometimes killing with swords. But mostly love."

They deposited him on the wharf. "No hard feelings, eh?" Dimiturglu hugged him again. "Anyway, is no ship go take you Constantinople except those crazy Vikings. This as far as you go. You good boy. Use Captain Dimi's name, people give you discounts. Good speed."

Henry kept his mouth shut and his face glum until the captain was back on his ship. Then Henry turned and strolled down the wharf, fast but casual.

Are you going to let that little troll get away with that?

"It's fine."

NO! It is not! Draw me! Go back for Justice!

"During that last hug, I cut his purse. We've got enough Justice to last two months, I think." They got off the wharf and headed into town.

On the voyage south, the cold weather had broken, and now spring was blowing through Bordeaux with the smell of new greenery, wet, black earth, and the last of winter's provisions being opened—raisins and dried apples, old beer, cakes of figs and hard bread softened in wine. Between the spring breeze and the city's southern latitude, the day was positively warm. Henry threw back his hood and turned his face to the sun.

He bought a couple of dried figs from a peddler. They were new to him; the fruit usually didn't get as far north as Paris. "Tasty," he said, chewing.

Keep your mouth closed.

Henry shut his mouth and looked around. It sort of looked like the captain was right—this *was* the City of Love. The merchandise on display was flowers, trinkets, and sweets; the streets were packed with happy couples, young and old; bright red hearts and blue forget-me-nots fluttered on banners from every window and rooftop; the women seemed to think that anything less than three colors in their dresses was immodest; and there were more public displays of affection per yard here than there were per mile in Paris. Billing, cooing, kissing and hugging were everywhere. Henry was embarrassed and jealous at the same time.

"Oh, no," he said.

Now what?

They had arrived at the main street. The old town wall was hidden from view by a mob of pale, skinny youths with over-spangled lutes and slicked-back hair.

"Troubadours. I hate troubadours."

Troubadours?

"Jerks with lutes. Bertran de Born wannabes."

Oh. Musicians. *In Camelot, they had to sleep outside the city walls.*

"Really. Tell me more."

The musicians had grabbed all the sunny street corners and church steps, and were yodeling away about their lady-loves in nasal Provençal, a dialect of French that even the French found annoying.

"Were the world all mine,
From the sea to the Rhine,
All, I'd give it all,
For the Queen of England in my arms."

Of course, the girls were eating it up. "I totally chose the wrong career," said Henry.

What?

"Nothing, nothing."

Well, at least they weren't singing about stringing up the serfs, Bertran's speciality. And as Henry and Excalibur walked north, there was more entertaining entertainment available: jugglers, fire-eaters, dancing monkeys, even some Italian thing with actors in masks—all good, clean fun, especially when the monkeys got upset and started throwing their poo.

Enough of this. That captain and his boat have surely left by now. Let us return to the docks and book passage to Constantinople.

"Tell me. Did you notice any ships that looked like they were headed to Constantinople—you know, big ships with enough ballast and sail to go around the Pillars of Hercules in winter and enter the Inland Sea?"

I am no expert on sailing ships. I am a sword.

"Well, I didn't see any. All the ships I saw were fishing boats. We're stuck here until the right ship comes in…unless you think it's smart for us to climb through the Alps in March. Does that sound smart to you?"

You sound *smart. Too smart by half.*

"The weather's changing. We could get the right ship any day. I promise, we'll go back to the docks first thing tomorrow, and every day until we find a ship. And if we find a good caravan going up the Garonne and over the mountains, I'll…I'll seriously consider it. All right?"

I can always call back the ogre.

"Good, I'm glad you're being reasonable about this."

Keeping track of the streets in his head, Henry followed the line of vendors' wagons north and east until they arrived at a market set among the pillars of a vast marble ruin.

"Look familiar?" Henry asked.

No, the city is new to me. But this building must have been a temple of the legions—look, there are the Roman eagles on the pillars.

Henry shrugged and paced through the colonnade past the vendors. After gathering a few odd looks, he drew his cloak down over Excalibur—evidently, there weren't too many scrawny young clerks carrying knightly swords in Bordeaux.

He climbed on top of a limestone block to get a better view of the ruins. Something was bothering him, gnawing at the back of his mind. Something about the way the pillars were arranged—

"—a most sorry vagabond, traveling sometimes as a monk-novice, but carrying an antique sword. A youth of middling height, hair brown, eyes green, a scar across his chin, answering to the name of Henry of Sanbruc, or Henri de la Ville-Perdu—"

It was a dapper knight in Geoffrey's livery, perched on a broken pillar, reading from a scroll in Norman French. He paused for a moment, and a clerk repeated the description in Provençal. Then the knight snapped his fingers, and the clerk unrolled a scroll and displayed it to the crowd. It was a drawing of Henry, accurate down to his haircut…if you ignored the unicorn, herald angel and pear tree the illuminator had thrown in for good measure.

Henry swallowed an urge to bolt. The last thing you wanted to do when you were a fugitive was to draw attention. If you were going to leave, fast but casual was the key. If there were anywhere to run to, that is…

Henry glanced up at the walls of the ruin—pikemen in blue and silver paced the temple outskirts.

"Hmm. Not good."

Why?

"Uh…Do you see the guards? The weapons?"

But you're a thief. Why don't you just appeal to the thieves' guild to spirit us past?

"Thieves' guild?"

Of course. Daring rogues, gentlemen of the highway, Robin's Merry Men. Everyone knows you have a guild, and even a king, corrupt as he may be. And its tentacles reach everywhere, from London to Rome to Jerusalem itself. The minstrels at Camelot sang about it all the time.

"Really."

Now, I must make clear that I don't approve of this, but sometimes even I must choose the lesser of two evils—

Henry sighed. The one time the sword was willing to compromise, and it was with an entirely mythical organization. He edged around the crowd, moving from pillar to pillar, scanning the square for some place where he could wait, watch, and make a plan that didn't require the all-powerful, mythical thieves' guild to come and rescue him. He didn't see anything offhand.

An old Florentine was standing at the far end, ignoring the speech and running a quick-moving little shell game. Henry drifted closer. The shell game was a classic, the first rig that Alfie had taught him—three extra-large walnut shells and a tiny dried pea. The mark tried to guess which shell held the pea after the *tricheur* shuffled the walnuts. Of course, the pea was never under the mark's walnut. A really good shell man, like Alfie, could make the pea jump from walnut to walnut like St. Vitus hopping to Calabria. A thing of beauty, it was…

What's wrong?

"Oh, I'm just getting sentimental." Henry knuckled a little water from his eye. "Don't worry about it."

"I say the shell is...there." The player, a big, muscular man with a beard, pointed to the middle shell. The Florentine picked it up, revealing the pea.

"Money, money, money!" yelled the Florentine. He paid Muscles, who was, of course, the Florentine's shill. The rest of the audience crowded close, shouting to put their money down. Henry elbowed his way quietly toward the table.

What are you doing? You know this is a mere cheat.

"The old guy probably knows the ins and outs. We want an out, right?"

He stepped up to the Florentine's table. "Not too bad, grandfather," he said quietly, "But any rogue could spot the pea falling in your lap."

The Florentine nodded. "But he might miss something else, young master."

"Really? What could—"

"Behind you and to your right, an agent of Prince Geoffrey, who marked your description when you entered the square." The voice was quiet, serious. Welsh.

"Alfie?"

Alfie nodded very slightly under his Italian hat. "Valdemar is passing behind you. When he comes to your left, hand off the blade. Then win a few rounds and stalk off with your cloak thrown back so the liegeman can see you're not carrying a sword. Understand?"

"Aye." Henry touched Excalibur's hilt. "You heard—"

You know this man? You trust him?

"With my life."

Very well. His servant may hold me...for now.

Muscles—Valdemar, of course—came up behind Henry, one hand held low. Henry slipped off his buckle, and Excalibur's scabbard dropped into Valdemar's hand. The smith walked off, the sword just one long object in the bundle of planks and barrel staves he carried.

"I'll have a go at this game," said Henry loudly. "It seems simple and profitable!"

Alfie shuffled the shells, and Henry played until Alfie glanced behind him and nodded that the coast was clear. Henry turned to the crowd and held up his winnings.

"This old Italian is a fool," yelled Henry. "Win your money while he's still breathing!"

Behind him, Alfie whispered, "In front of the Church of St. André, at noon."

Henry nodded and left Alfie to his work.

Hustling through the alleys to Alfie's rendezvous, Henry was disgusted with himself. Now that he knew what was going on, the signs of Geoffrey's presence were everywhere. The prince's insignia was up on the gates to the old town. Sprinkled among the brightly colored *Bordelais* were hard young men dressed in dark clothes and walking like they had long metal sticks dangling under their cloaks. They spoke Swiss German or the northern dialects, instead of Bordeaux's Provençal.

He should have noticed it all as soon as he entered the city. No question, arguing with Excalibur all the time was destroying his concentration. He turned the corner and entered the plaza.

It was clear why Alfie had chosen this square: Wedged between the Queen's castle and the Cathedral of St. André, it was packed with goliards, who loved princesses and queens, but not their male relatives. Queen Eleanor's colors were everywhere, and the swordsmen all spoke the *langue d'oc*. Henry drew a deep breath and relaxed. A little while later, he was flanked by Alfie and Valdemar, with wineskins and a magic sword.

Valdemar handed Excalibur back to Henry. "I tried to draw it, but the blade must be rusted to the sheath. I could fix that."

Henry buckled Excalibur back on. "No, the scabbard just sticks sometimes. See?" He pulled the blade out to demonstrate.

Tell your friend to wash his hands more often.

"Hello to you, too," Henry muttered.

They divvied up the wineskins and took shelter under one of the oaks that dotted the Geoffrey-free plaza. Henry leaned against the trunk and sipped from his skin. The wine was delicious. "So what are you doing here?"

"We're here for the wedding."

"What—"

"Geoffrey and the Princess of Navarre, his cousin. You know, a smart man of the people can make a mint off a royal wedding, lad. It's the one time the land-crazy oppressors unpucker and start spending. Wedding gifts, wedding purses, wedding drinking and fights and gambling…"

"No, I mean how did you get here?"

Alfie shrugged. "Geoffrey is snapping up domains right and left. Didn't you hear? Once you were gone, he left Paris to attack the County of Blois."

Valdemar nodded. "Aye. Chartres, Orleans, and Le Mans are all his."

"And with you and Geoffrey gone, it was easy enough for us to bribe the gaolers and get out."

"What about Mattie? He got himself involved in that rescue plot of yours—real clever, by the way. It took Geoffrey, what, ten whole minutes to figure it out—"

Alfie and Valdemar shared a look. "Mattie's fine," said Valdemar. "But you owe us two *livres* for the bribes, and another two for my anvil."

"Take it out of my share."

"Can't."

Henry's jaw dropped. "It's gone already?"

"Not our fault," said Valdemar, defensively. "Not this time, anyway."

"Aye," nodded Alfie. "We deposited it with Judah of Leon. Then King Philip 'nationalized' all the goldsmiths who weren't protected by Mother Church."

"'Nationalized'?"

"Stole with lawyers," said Valdemar. "It was Geoffrey's idea."

Henry chewed that over. From poor to rich to fugitive to poor again. "Stinks to be us."

"Stinks to be Judah," said Valdemar. "He's got family."

Henry stood up. "Oh, well. We'll get to Constantinople somehow." Alfie and Valdemar stared at each other, then at him. Henry sighed. "Uh…let's get some lunch, and I'll explain."

As he said it, people started to stream past them toward a platform at the southwest corner. The plaza erupted in cheers.

"The Maid." Valdemar nudged Henry. "This should be good."

"The who?"

Alfie explained. "The Maid of Aquitaine. She's a girl who makes speeches in the square. The bishop tried to stop her, but the students and troubadours love it. She's their mascot."

"A girl?"

Valdemar nodded. "In man's clothes." He smiled. "Pretty, too."

Alfie and Valdemar traded grins, leaving Henry puzzled and a little annoyed. They strolled through the crowd.

"What's the platform for?" asked Henry.

"You know, royal decrees, church services, executions…" Alfie shrugged. "Show business."

With Valdemar ahead of them, they had no trouble making it to the front row. The Maid was in full swing.

"…and now, this wedding. This *royal* wedding if you please, where an innocent girl is bartered off to the highest bidder, like a prize cow to a farmer!"

She got a fair amount of applause for that—mostly, Henry noticed, from women, and from men with women standing next to them.

"Sing it, sister!"

"Power to the peasants!"

"A woman is no one's property! She can love whom she likes!" This time, the cheers came more from the raunchy looking University students.

"Ipse dixit, inamorata!"

"Amor vincit omnia!"

Henry couldn't take his eyes off her. She was beautiful, even in hose (*especially* in hose, thought the earthier part of his mind) but she was also hauntingly familiar. Henry was sure he knew her—knew the chestnut hair, the strong, pale features, the big brown eyes that glowed with purpose—

"Grab him!" Alfie and Valdemar caught Henry on each side as he sagged in shock.

It was Mattie the tavern boy.

I should have known, thought Henry, in a daze. *He always smelled good.* SHE *always smelled good. And I never saw him,* HER, *taking a whiz.* But Mattie had seen him using the privy at the Cellars. Dozens of times. Henry groaned. "Let's get out of here."

Alfie shook his head. "Nahh. She's just getting warmed up. She's got style, this one. Reminds me of old Tom Becket, back in the day."

Valdemar grinned. "What's the matter, boy? We told you she was *fine*."

Henry hid his face in his hands, but not fast enough to keep Mattie from seeing him. Her whole face lit up.

"HENRY! HENRY!" She waved with both hands and dived off the platform. The students caught her and handed her off, one to the next, until she stood in front of him and hugged him tight. The crowd cheered.

"How are you? Where were you? How did you get here? Where did you get that sword? How did you find us?"

"Uh…Mattie. You…look good." Henry coughed, and shifted from one foot to the other. His face burned. "So…you're a woman. That's…uh…great."

What do you mean, "So you're a woman?"

"I'll tell you later."

Mattie nodded. "Yeah. And you, you…talk to yourself. Are you all right?"

"It's a long story."

"Good. We can trade."

She looped her arm through his. Henry looked around. Somehow, Alfie and Valdemar had disappeared, and everyone else in the crowd was staring. Staring nicely, but staring.

"Come on, let's get some food."

16. UPTOWN GIRL

"I still can't believe it, lad." Alfie stared at the scabbard and lowered his voice. "That's the real, the veritable Excalibur?"

Henry nodded. He didn't say anything. Mattie was sitting next to him, and despite the male clothing, she'd somehow dug up enough money to buy perfume. The scent of rose attar had crawled up Henry's nose and was hammering at his brain. He still couldn't believe it. It was obvious. It was *so* obvious. How could he not have seen it?

Well, it had been half a year. She'd lost that pasty underground complexion that came from working in the Cellars. Her hair was longer, not shorn close to the skull in a student crop. She'd never giggled, or acted…girly…in the Cellars, not that she did now. And she seemed to have grown, several inches, around the, the…and around the— he closed his eyes.

They were sitting at a table under an awning, watching the bustle in the plaza. A contingent of knights from four different counties had gathered to sing of Queen Eleanor's beauty and virtue. The Queen herself was nowhere to be found, but apparently that was a good thing—the farther away and more impossible the object of your affections, the better, as far as the Laws of Courtly Love were concerned. Of course, that meant everyone else had to suffer through the crooning, while Her Royal Instigatorship got off scot-free, but it's the thought that counts. Mattie seemed to like the singing, anyway. She was smiling.

As Valdemar smeared goat cheese on a chunk of bread, Alfie scrutinized Excalibur, careful not to touch it. "There's an angle here, lad. Exhibitions, maybe. Miracle shows. A traveling circus. You know, something educational. I have this glowing paint from an alchemist, we could touch up the blade with it. It has a slight tendency to burst into flames, but it looks damned impressive—"

Before Excalibur could start shrieking, Henry raised his hand. Focusing on the sword helped him not think too much about Mattie. "Alfie, you don't get it. This thing is...it's too big for us. People get killed." Henry paused, trying to forget Brother Pierre bleeding in the snow. "The smartest thing to do is find a likely candidate, collect a big, fat reward, and then spend our money someplace warm. I hear Narbonne is nice."

He glanced at Mattie, and saw her expression clouding up. "What's the problem? You think there's an angle here, too?"

"No! No. I just thought...that...you'd *use* Excalibur. To stop Geoffrey. Establish justice. Fight for the oppressed and downtrodden."

Valdemar grinned. "Oppressed and downtrodden? That's us, honey."

Well, well. I'm not the only one you disappoint, clearly.

"Stop it!" After an hour of the sword's remarks and Henry's responses, the others didn't even look up from their food when he told Excalibur to shut up.

"Listen, young lady." Alfie rapped the table, looking stern. "Our boy Henry has been kidnapped, beaten, sent north across the sea in the dead of winter, braved the

Chapel Perilous, found the sword of King Arthur, survived a massacre, fought a knight, and escaped from bondage, all to bring this weapon to its rightful owner. I think he's gone a bit above and beyond, and so should you."

"Amen, brother," Valdemar shoveled stewed onions into his maw.

Mattie looked stricken. "You're right. I didn't think. Henry, I'm sorry, I should have been congratulating you, and instead I—"

"It's okay. Don't worry." Just the same, Henry felt a pang of regret. When she'd thought he was some kind of Galahad, the way she'd smiled—

"Good. Now that we're all friends again," Alfie rubbed his hands, "just how big do you think this reward might be?"

* * * *

"Where are you staying?"

"With the goliards—you know, the students."

Henry was walking back with Mattie. Now he stopped short. "You're staying in the student rooms? Are you crazy? Don't you know—"

Mattie laughed. "Oh, relax, Mr. Virtue. They wouldn't hurt me in a million years. See?"

She pointed behind them. Henry turned to see they'd collected a retinue of a dozen goliards. All of them had the look of dog-steady devotion he'd seen on Brissac's face when the knight was taking orders from Geoffrey. A thought struggled to the surface of Henry's mind, but before he could seize it, Mattie waved, and the students cheered.

"Well, I guess you didn't need me to walk you back at all."

Mattie laughed and took his arm. "You're right, I didn't need you to. I just wanted you to. Isn't that better?"

Henry tried to answer, but his tongue seemed to be tripping over itself. At least Excalibur wasn't saying anything...in fact, it had gone strangely quiet for the last hour or so.

"Um…okay. Why the disguise? Why aren't you using it now? Who are you?"

"One, in Paris I wore a disguise because men can do things that women can't. Two, I'm not using one now because I can't…get away with it anymore." She blushed and then glared at Henry, who carefully kept his eyes straight ahead. "And three, that's for me to know and you to find out. Maybe."

Suddenly, the plaza was full of bird whistles—fake ones. Henry could see at least five students whistling furiously. Mattie grabbed his hand and pulled him down an alley, as a troop of soldiers entered the square.

They were Aquitaines in rose and lavender livery—and quite dapper they were, with bits of gold trim. Handsome too, Henry noticed, before Mattie shoved him into a doorway. He couldn't be sure, but it looked like they all had their own teeth.

The alley was a dead end, and Henry started getting nervous. Mattie put her finger on his lips—*shut up!*—and peeked cautiously around the corner.

"Who did you piss off?" asked Henry.

"I didn't do anything wrong."

"That's not an answer."

"Shh, I want to hear this."

The lead trooper marched onto the platform. "Listen up, boys!" he yelled. "When that Maid of yours shows again, you hold her. The queen wants a chat with that one."

"What one?" yelled a minstrel in the back of the crowd.

"Goliard, please," snapped the trooper. "Five six, chestnut hair, terrible fashion sense? Twenty *dixaines* for her whereabouts, and two gold *écus* for her in the flesh— and unharmed, you rough trade." He was greeted with jeers from the crowd. Unfazed, he held up his hand. "Any man who refuses to cooperate will be subject to a withering *balada* that will permanently diminish his reputation. And you know I can do it." The crowd fell silent, and Henry shook his head, bewildered. The Aquitaines were clearly a breed apart.

The troopers dispersed through the crowd, questioning students and minstrels at random. Henry turned to Mattie.

"What did you do!?" he whispered furiously.

"I spoke Truth to Power."

"Shot your mouth off, you mean."

"Don't argue, just tell me if those soldiers get close."

Henry peered around the corner. The troopers were circling through the square, getting nearer. He looked back, and saw Mattie scraping away frantically at the door.

"What are you trying to do?"

"Pick the lock. All I need is a lathe, an adze, and two cross-mitre saws—"

"That's not a lock, it's a bolt plate. You 'pick it' with a sledge hammer."

Excalibur shifted in its scabbard. *Bad company makes bad luck.*

"And another county heard from."

Maybe you should let yourself be captured. That troop captain has broad shoulders. And excellent posture. Kingly, even.

"Personally, I don't think a king should know quite so much about clothes, but, hey—"

The troopers were getting nearer. Henry could hear them just outside the alley. "Otho, Clovis, you take the left side. Merulis, you—"

Henry pulled Mattie's hands away, stuck his eating knife in the crack between the door and the lintel, and pushed up. He thanked St. Nick as he felt the knife catch on the bolt inside, and heaved two-handed. He heard the thud as the bolt fell to the floor behind the door. Henry grabbed Mattie and pushed inside to a dark alcove just as the troopers entered the alley.

"Quick!" And before Henry knew what was happening, Mattie was kissing him.

It wasn't Henry's first kiss. But it was certainly his most

serious. No matter what the troubadours said, bells didn't chime and birds didn't sing. It was more real, more…Henry's breath caught in his chest. His eyes closed. His nose was filled with the roses of Mattie's perfume. All he could feel were Mattie's lips, her hands on the back of his neck—

He could feel her smiling.

"Oh, Clovis, look at the lovebirds!"

"Otho, leave them alone."

"But one of them could be—"

"Sure, she snuck into the house and opened it up just so we could catch her kissing. Now come on, Monsieur Peepers. We have to find her before—" And the troopers were gone.

Slowly, Mattie broke away. Henry opened his eyes. He didn't know what to say. They just stood for a moment, looking at each other. Smiling.

"Out of my way. Now!" It was Prince Geoffrey's voice.

"Which alley was it?" There was the sound of boots, and they were getting closer.

And Mattie's hand was on Henry's chest, as she shoved him back into the building and stepped out into the alley.

"Here I am, cousin."

Henry's jaw dropped. *Cousin?*

Geoffrey stopped, casual, at the head of a dozen soldiers. He stared at Mattie, arms crossed. Henry grimaced. Now that the two were facing each other, it was obvious. It should have been obvious months ago. Mattie was a Plantagenet. She had the look, the smarts, the insane self-confidence—

"No need to be so formal, dearest. Come along."

Now is the time, Henry. Draw me.

Henry stood frozen, stiff as a block of wood.

What are you waiting for? Draw me!

Henry inched his hand toward the sword as the memory of Glastonbury ran through his mind. The feel of Excalibur in his head, the cold touch of the sword moving his body, thinking his thoughts…the blood—

"Don't dawdle, beloved. We have a wedding to plan."

"Wedding?" "Beloved?" "WE?"

DRAW ME! shrieked Excalibur.

"No," yelled Henry. But it came out as a whisper. And then Mattie was gone with Geoffrey's soldiers.

17. THE QUEEN OF THE COURT OF LOVE

"What was I supposed to do?"

Valdemar shrugged. "I'm not arguing. Royals are dangerous."

Alfie put a hand on Henry's shoulder. "Don't worry, laddie. Mattie was a princess, and now she'll be an empress. Top of her field before she's twenty."

"She'll be married to Geoffrey."

"Better than sweeping out the Cellars every night. Job security *and* perks. Meanwhile, you need to focus."

Henry stared down at the table. He couldn't get over the guilty feeling that every troubadour and goliard in the tavern was looking at him—

"Henri de Sanbruc."

Henry raised his head. They *were* looking at him. Because he was surrounded by the Queen's Guards, swords drawn.

"Come with us."

* * * *

"Well, at least you don't smell. Much." Eleanor of Aquitaine, Rose of the World, Light of Chivalry, Queen of the Court of Love, hobbled past Henry, took her withered hand off the trooper's arm, and sank stiffly onto her padded seat.

If anyone in Paris had told Henry that he would have an audience with the most famously beautiful woman since Helen of Troy, his mouth would have dried up. He'd have been covered in a cold sweat, and his knees would have trembled beneath him. It would never have occurred to him that the Queen of England and Aquitaine had been famed for her beauty for half a century, and there had probably been a little wear and tear over the years. And that, when he finally met her, he'd have been relieved and disappointed at the same time, and even a little sorry for her because she used a cane.

But now Henry was just scared. Scared to be facing another Plantagenet, scared to be exposed…and glad that he was scared. Because the moment the fear stopped, shame would take its place. Excalibur was silent, a dead weight on his hip, as if it knew that nothing it said could be worse than what Henry was saying to himself.

But if Henry's heart was pounding at his ribs, at least his mind was clear, and all he saw was an old woman with a shock of thick, silver hair, and eyes like a hawk's. She ran them over Henry as if studying a farm animal she might buy, taking in the clothes, the tonsure, the sword. Henry felt a sense of *déja vù*—how many Plantagenets had stared at him like that by now?

"So you are the young man my goddaughter spoke of. You don't look special."

"No, Your Majesty."

"Mattie thought you were. She's a romantic, that one. But sharp. It's a dangerous combination."

"Tell me about it."

A smile raced across Eleanor's lips and vanished. "Who are you, Henry of the lost village of Sanbruc?"

"I—you know of Sanbruc, Majesty?"

"I know everything my children do. They are my

responsibility."

"Majesty, I…I am nothing. I was a thief, and a cheat. Now I'm not even that. Even a thief must be true to his friends, and I was not."

Eleanor took a preserved apple from a dish. "You mean because you didn't leap out and start hacking away at the soldiers who outnumbered you twenty to one?"

"But I…I had a…"

"Silence." Eleanor turned to the trooper. "Leave us." The trooper exited, and Eleanor turned back to Henry. "Yes, I know about the sword." She pointed. "That's it?"

"Yes."

"Hm." Eleanor stared at the fruit for a moment, rolling it about with the tips of her fingers. "Had you attacked my son Geoffrey, in the middle of his men, when he was ready, you would be dead, magic sword or no. My John is a killer, and Richard is a legend. But Geoffrey…my son Geoffrey is dangerous." She might have been talking about the price of beef, instead of her three monstrous sons. "As you get older…if you get older…you'll find there is a difference between what you should do, and what you can do."

Eleanor took a knife from her table and cut a slice from the apple. "For instance, when my goddaughter fled to me, because my son Geoffrey coveted her lands and sought her hand in marriage, I should have protected her by spiriting her away to some land where the Plantagenets have no power. Rome, say…Instead, I gave her disguises, and secret bodyguards, and as much freedom and joy as I could before Geoffrey found her and took her." The queen finished the apple, and stuck the knife, quivering, into the tabletop. Then she stood, and walked to the window.

"I'm old, child. I don't want to die locked up in another castle—or watching my body as my head bounces down the steps. But Mathilde is a dear girl, and I want her to be happy. Will you help me?"

For the first time, the fear and shame left him, and what he felt was joy. "Yes, your majesty. With all my heart."

Eleanor smiled at him. "There's a good boy. Now tell Ranulf he can come in and mull me some wine." She sat back on her throne, rubbing her arms through her robe. "I do so love a man in livery."

18. DOWNTOWN WITH WIGLAF

Geoffrey rode out with a bird on his wrist and a leech at his side.

"That's Raymond of Toulouse. He's hosting the wedding."

Henry, Alfie, and Valdemar watched the procession from the top of a ten-foot stone block. The Count of Toulouse was tall and hunched, with black hair and a pallor that reminded Henry of some of his least favorite dungeons. The two nobles were preceded by a half-dozen of Geoffrey's knights, and followed by the real muscle—a squad of thirty mercenaries armed with short swords and arbalests.

"Hawking with an imperial eagle," said Alfie. "Cheeky bastard."

Geoffrey had already moved Mattie out of the city, sending her up the Gironde river by boat to Raymond's castle at Toulouse. Now the question was how to follow her, spring her from Toulouse, and head to the southern coast, where Eleanor planned to shelter from Geoffrey under the protection of the Viscount of Narbonne.

They scrambled back down after the procession turned the corner.

"What do you think?"

Alfie shook his head. "This town is shut tighter than a reeve's purse."

"What about the Salt Gate?" Valdemar swished wine through his teeth and spat it on the flagstones.

"You mean the gate next to Geoffrey's palace? The one with all the holes for the boiling oil?"

Alfie took the wineskin from Valdemar. "We could hide you in a wagon, under hay. Or in a wine barrel."

"Too easy. Geoffrey knows I'm here, somehow. Otherwise he wouldn't be going to all this trouble."

Alfie nodded. "Aye."

Valdemar took another swig. "So what's your plan, Aristotle?"

Henry waited for a moment to see if Excalibur would chime in, but there was nothing. The sword had been silent ever since that day in the alley. No sarcasm, no advice—nothing more than a lump of iron in a leather case. Henry sighed and looked around.

They were in the city's Roman ruins, the Tutelles, and once again, something tugged at Henry's memory. Something about the columns, the way they were arranged. And about a monk who was standing a few yards away.

Henry stood. "Get ready." He walked out across the pavement, weaving through the pillars, which, now that he had seen them from a height, were definitely laid out as a labyrinth.

He stopped at a fruit stand, then a wine seller, then a peddler of honey candy. The monk stayed put, measuring a column with a straight edge and a sighting tube, and making notes in a writing tablet. The columns' shadows followed the sun, edging over diagrams carved in the pavement. The monk's robe was white and black, his tonsure wide, his buckle carved in the shape of a scroll. Henry grinned. *Let's see if I guessed right.*

"I am a stranger, going to the East," said Henry.

The monk jumped and caught his breath. "Oh. Really?"

Not too encouraging. Still—"For the sake of my mother as well as your own, I ask for aid on the square." Henry waited for the monk to complete the formula Wulfgar had taught him.

Instead, the monk fumbled with his sighting tube. "Do you mean this square? Or the market square by St. André's church?"

Oh well, it had been worth a try. Henry turned to go.

"Wait! That blade—You came from the West? How far west?"

"Who wants to know?"

The monk stood a little straighter. "Wiglaf, the cousin of Wulfgar. Have you any word from the Chapel Perilous?"

Henry's eyes narrowed. Brother Wiglaf was short and pale; between the beaked nose, the wide eyes, and the constant blinking, he looked more like an owl after a night on the town than a relative of the burly Wulfgar. But not every Northman could be a giant, cryptic killer monk.

"Wulfgar is well. He told me to expect help on my way to Constantinople."

"Really. Well, tell me all about it. What's happened? Where are you going? Are you carrying anything important?"

Henry opened his mouth, then shut it again. *I don't need two thousand years as the sword of heroes to smell a rat.* "No, just some letters to friends. Well, take care."

Suddenly the monk was Brother Cooperative from the town of St. Eager. "Look, I can help! Whatever you need! That's my specialty, in fact." The monk bowed, then spread his arms and declaimed, "Brother Wiglaf, monk of St. André, at your service. Indulgences and pardons, letters composed, sums resolved, dogma clarified."

Henry said nothing. Wiglaf started to sweat.

"Right, right, you probably don't need any dogma clarified. Not that you're not concerned about the state of your soul, obviously you're a nice young man, but who has time for it in all this modern hustle and bustle?" He fumbled with his *tabula* and looked up again. "I'm also quite good with codes and ciphers. No? Surveying? Languages? Alchemy? Maps—"

Henry fought to conceal a little start. A map of the town might help them get out, but the last thing he wanted was this character figuring out their plans.

"No."

"But—"

"No. Thank you."

Valdemar loomed up behind Henry, and Wiglaf's mouth shut with a snap. He bowed himself away.

"Who was that?" asked Alfie.

"Nobody, I guess," said Henry. "All right. Let's go with the barrel."

* * * *

That night, after he had rolled his gear into his saddle-bags, he turned to the sword leaning against a chair.

"Excalibur." Henry cleared his throat and waited. "Excalibur." Nothing. "Excalibur!" Was there a shimmer of light around the scabbard? Never mind.

"Look." Henry sat down on the bed. "I'm going to save Mattie, just like you wanted." He waited for a response, then continued. "I can't do it alone. I need your help. If I don't make it, Mattie will have to marry Geoffrey. That really makes her a damsel in distress. The kind you like to rescue, right?"

Still nothing. Henry tried to swallow his worry, and failed. No matter what, he had to try. But if the sword didn't help—Was that a sparkle, a faint glow around the hilt?

"Don't do it for me. Do it for her." Henry held his breath. Slowly, the glow increased, as if the spirit of the sword was returning from some far country.

You want me to help you, Henry? You want to rescue the Princess?

"Yes."

Then kneel.

"You're kidding."

Kneel, or leave me.

Henry knelt.

Until I pass from your possession, you shall serve me in all things. Your arm shall be mine. Heart and mind, body and bone, blood and sinew. Swear it on your soul.

The room seemed filled with a silvery light. A cold wind blew through the open shutters. Henry's blood roared in his ears; his mouth was dry. "I...swear it."

Then go to sleep. We leave tomorrow. And everything was quiet again.

Despite his vow to obey, Henry didn't think he'd get much sleep at all.

* * * *

The next day, Valdemar drove the wagon to the rendezvous, while Henry examined the barrel in which he would be hiding...the one that was currently half-filled with salt cod.

"You couldn't find clean ones?"

Alfie shrugged. "What do they keep in barrels? Wine and fish. You can drown in the wine, if you want. Or hide in a sack of grain and wait for some guard to stick a pitchfork in you. Your choice."

The sun was just clearing the horizon, and the line of wagons waiting to leave by the West Gate already snaked around the corner of the cathedral of St. André, out of sight of the guards. They joined the end of the line, and Henry dumped the rest of the fish. He was counting on the market-day crowds (and now, the smell of the fish) to keep Geoffrey's new guards from spending too much time with the wagon.

"Well, maybe it doesn't matter. How can they really recognize me anyway?"

"Look at the gate, laddie."

Henry squinted around the corner. There was a squad of Geoffrey's men at the gate. Even in the dawn light,

Henry could pick out the features of Brissac's Paris buddy...the one who'd noticed the crest on the fake Charlemagne sword. "Jesu. How did Geoffrey know to bring him here? I've been in town less than a week!"

"Easy enough to guess the ports you'd reach from Southampton. Geoffrey's probably got the other knights in La Rochelle, Brest, and Calais. Maybe some of Brissac's men in the Cinque Ports too, just in case."

"Clever." Henry rubbed his face. "I hate clever."

Fear not, whispered Excalibur in his head. *I shall not compel you to confront them. I shall allow you to sneak past, undetected. This time.*

"Oh. Well, that makes things easier."

Yes. I pushed you too quickly before. Baby steps. Don't worry, we'll have you defying an army in no time.

"Great." Henry tried to put the prediction out of his mind. He poked dubiously at the barrels, and then heard a clamor by the gate. Looking up, he saw the knight running toward them, trailed by a dozen soldiers. "Valdemar! Get us out of here!"

"HEE-YAH!" Valdemar snapped the reins and the wagon lurched into motion, rattling down the cobblestones.

They turned a corner, and another, a third, then the wagon jolted to a halt. "Dead end."

Henry leaped off the cart. Valdemar had taken a bad turn. They were stuck in a dead end formed by the rear of the church and an old fortification that towered black above them. There was no room to turn the cart around, and the guards were streaming in—

"Come with me if you want to live!"

A door opened in the wall. Brother Wiglaf beckoned to them. Henry looked at Valdemar and then at Alfie, who shrugged and shinnied off the cart faster than a rat down a drainpipe. "Any port, laddie."

They followed Alfie through the tiny door. Wiglaf bolted it shut, then lit a lamp and led them down a winding staircase. Behind and above them, Henry heard shouting, curses, and then the THUD, THUD, THUD of a battering ram.

"Where are we going?" Henry had to yell above the sound of the ram. Dust trickled out from between the building stones with each blow.

"Down," yelled Wiglaf. "Down and out!"

The stairs wound deeper and deeper, four turns, six. At seven, the building blocks disappeared, replaced by solid rock. At nine, the stone was crusted with nitre and salt; at ten, water shimmered on the steps, and everyone pressed hard against the walls to keep from slipping.

Stone and water. Just like home.

"Don't get too comfortable. I'd like to see daylight again, if you don't mind."

All Nature is drawn to its proper elements. What are yours? Lead and fool's gold?

"Hah-hah."

The staircase ended in an arch. In the flickering lamplight, Henry could just make out the words *Voyez le Royaume des Morts* scratched into the stone. He turned on Wiglaf.

"'Behold the Kingdom of the Dead'?"

"Are you going to pay attention to every carving you see? This goes from here to St. Émilion, and it will take you under the city walls. Trust me."

"Trust you!? Wh—"

Alfie nudged him. "That door won't hold forever."

Henry shrugged him off. "What's the toll for this wonderful favor you're doing?"

Wiglaf looked around, panicky, then looked Henry straight in the eye. "Let me go with you."

I don't trust him.

"Really? Why ever not?" Henry gritted his teeth. It was a terrible thing to be trapped underground, relying on someone who was as convincing as a brass *écu*.

And then, faint, but growing louder, Henry could hear

a clatter above them.

"Laddie—"

"Shorty—"

Henry—

Oh well, if something went wrong, Valdemar could always rip Wiglaf's arm off. Henry turned to the monk. "Let's go."

Wiglaf held the lamp high. "This way." They followed him into the Kingdom of the Dead.

After a hundred paces or so, Alfie broke the silence with a cough. "Not that bad, really. Reminds me of Basingstoke."

It was a town, deep underground. The low stone ceiling hung over a road, with the granite fronts of buildings poking out of the earth on the left and right. At the far edge of the lamp's light, the passage curved away to the left.

Wiglaf nodded. "This is the old settlement, called by the Romans Burdigala."

A few hundred paces later, the passage widened out, and the ceiling rose higher. *SPQR,* the motto of the Empire, was carved onto some of the larger buildings. After passing three or four of them, Henry felt sure the insignias had been chiseled over something else. At the fifth one, he stopped for a moment. The remnant of a pattern—lines and curves, moving in parallel—peeked out from underneath the letters. *A labyrinth?*

"What did they call it before the Romans?"

Wiglaf looked puzzled. "Before?"

"Never mind." He looked at the buildings, so square, so straight, so unlike anything he had seen masons build himself, and sighed.

What ails you now?

"Mysteries I don't have time to solve. Thanks to you."

Were it not for me, you would never even have known of this place.

"Fine, fine."

When we are done, you can return to this muck and root through it to your heart's content.

Before Henry could reply, there was a grunt of fear from behind. He spun around to see Valdemar staring into one of the buildings, his face slack with horror.

Henry looked inside. Dozens of skulls stared back at him in silence, perched on mountains of bones.

Alfie nudged him. "They're all like that. I checked."

"It's just storage, Vee." Henry patted Valdemar on the back. "Think of them as relics."

"I don't want to think of them at all," said Valdemar.

"That's fine, too. Come on."

You are calmer than I expected.

"I had to go through this once to get you, didn't I? And I was alone then."

Indeed.

They walked on for an hour or more. The sound of pursuit behind them got quieter, then louder again. The road was a single course that twisted and doubled back on itself like a labyrinth.

Until it split into three.

"Okay. Wait…" Wiglaf raised his hand, and they stopped. Three alleys faced them, three paths with nothing to distinguish one from another.

"Which way do we go?" asked Henry.

"Well. Uh."

"You know the right way, don't you?"

"Absolutely. It's just that…uh…according to my research, the passage shouldn't split here."

"According to your *research?*" Henry's mouth went dry. "You've never been down here before?"

"A true scholar can extrapolate the entire universe from Aristotle." Wiglaf coughed. "In theory."

Alfie tugged at Henry's tunic. "I can hear them coming, laddie."

"In theory." Henry grabbed Wiglaf by the robe. "*IN THEORY!?*" Behind and above them, the sound of footsteps was getting louder and nearer.

Be calm. A true warrior saves his rage for the battle.

"Don't worry, don't worry, I have a map!" Wiglaf dug in his robe and unrolled a parchment scroll with a flourish.

They gathered around. Henry studied the map, closed his eyes, opened them again. The map stayed the same—nothing more than a big circle divided into three parts labeled *Asia, Africa,* and *Europa.*

I've changed my mind, said Excalibur. *If we kill him now, we can save future travelers from being led astray in the Underworld.*

"So…Where are we? Under the big letter E?"

"Let me think." Wiglaf began to mutter to himself. "They know about these caves in St. Émilion, they use them for their wineries, but I discovered that they reached all the way here, to Bordeaux. There are entrances at the Tutelles, and under the cathedral, smugglers must use it, and the Romans used it for their legionaries—"

"So?"

"I don't know. I'm just thinking!"

"If we get lost down here, we'll eat *you* first. You know that, right?"

"I can't concentrate while you're making threats!"

Henry could hear dozens of footsteps now; Geoffrey had to be close.

Henry squinted in the lamp light. The dirt in the right and middle passages was flat, but the dust on the left-hand side looked as though it had been disturbed recently.

"All right, a dozen footprints can't be wrong." He turned to Wiglaf. "You want to come with us? Brush the dust and tracks away from the other entrances, and then you can follow." They left Wiglaf and entered the third tunnel.

Darkness all around. The only way to measure time or distance was by footfall—Henry counted a hundred steps, then five hundred, and kept going. The farther they went, the more nerve-wracking it became. Were they on the right track? Had Wiglaf betrayed them? Where was that tonsured weasel, anyway? Were the walls getting more narrow? The darkness was like dust, getting in his eyes and nose—

"STOP!"

They stopped. Henry ran his hand farther along the wall. Yeah. It was a break.

"What is it, Henry?"

"It's another passage." Henry sighed. "Alfie, make us a light."

Alfie struck a spark with his flint and raised a sliver of tinder. Henry studied the two tunnels, but this time, there wasn't enough dirt to hold footprints.

"Damn it, damn, damn—"

"Henry—"

"Wait!" Just before the tunnel wall had ended, he'd felt something different. Something carved.

Henry grabbed Alfie's arm and raised it high. In the flickering light, he saw the labyrinth carved on the wall, and a line in the archaic Latin he'd seen everywhere in the Chapel Perilous: *For strangers from the West*. Below it were columns of text, each with a different heading: *Ut Urbis Burdigala. Ut Vinea Ausoniensis. Ut flumen Garumna.* Below each heading were more words.

"'Three empty doors, then at the cross, turn left—'" Alfie laughed. "It's a *periplos*, laddie."

"What?"

"Directions! Where are we going?"

"'*Vinea*' is vineyards. That sounds like St. Émilion to me."

"Let's go."

"Wait a moment." Henry scrambled in his pouch and pulled out his writing tablet and stylus. Scraping the stylus over the tablet, he covered the wooden rod with wax and held it over Alfie's tiny flame. Once it caught fire, Henry held his improvised candle overhead and they jogged forward.

* * * *

Henry's stylus was sputtering down to its last inch when they made their way out of Very Downtown Bordeaux. Ahead of them, the cavern ceiling rose thirty feet to a hole that allowed in a beam of sunlight, and the dry stone floor ended in the rush of an underground river: wide, black, and very, very cold.

Beware. It was in just such a flood that Sir Bragomant lost the sword of his fathers.

"Don't give me any ideas."

Alfie pointed upstream. "See it, laddie? We've got a bridge."

The bridge sent a shiver of recognition down Henry's spine. It was a narrow stone span without seams or joints, so long it seemed impossible that it could stand without supports, and so smooth that it looked like it had just grown over the river. Like the branch of a tree. Like the bridge of the Chapel Perilous.

Valdemar went first. Then Alfie. On the other side, Alfie walked into the sunbeam and stared up. "It's the way out, laddie!" he shouted. "There's stairs."

"What are you waiting for?" Henry shouted back. Alfie and Valdemar scrambled up the stairs and out of sight. Then Henry stepped onto the bridge himself.

He looked down for an instant. It was a mistake. What he had assumed was a wide river was a whirlpool, a giant pit sucking in water from all sides and leading down into darkness. A thin beam of sunlight struck the water as it fell, and fell, and fell—

A crossbow bolt flew out of the darkness, nicking him on the ear. More bolts followed, clicking on the stone around him.

"Don't move, Henry."

Geoffrey stepped out of the darkness, followed by Hauptmann, Brissac…and Wiglaf. Henry cursed.

"You've taken what doesn't belong to you, Henry. I'll have it back now."

He could double for Mordred, this one. A thousand years have I spent in the earth, and the fashion in villainy has changed not at all.

It was the damned crossbows that gave Geoffrey the edge. Even Hauptmann could hit a penny on a moonlit night, and someone like Haer (there he was, on the left flank, crossbow cocked) could take him down with a single bolt. Henry choked back a whimper.

Take the offensive, Henry!

"What?"

Don't argue! Take the offensive!

"How?"

"My spies have told me of your charade, Henry. Playing at madness won't help you."

Take the offensive. Slowly, Henry drew Excalibur, holding it up in the air. Geoffrey gasped as he saw the sword for the first time, then recovered.

"Are you going to fight me, boy?" Geoffrey smiled gently. "That *would* be a change for you, wouldn't it?" The prince drew his own sword and stepped forward.

"You take hostages, Geoff. I remember that." Despite his best effort, Henry's voice shook a little. But maybe that was okay. Sometimes it let people know you were serious.

Slowly, Henry extended his hand and held Excalibur out over the black, quick-flowing water. Over the pit.

Henry, what are you doing?

"Don't joggle my arm," Henry muttered. "We don't want any accidents."

You promised! You SWORE!

"I'm taking the offensive." Henry turned to Wiglaf. "How deep is the water, pig?"

"I...I don't know. Vitruvius tells us underground rivers may be both deep and swift, and lead to caverns that are infinite in depth."

Henry turned to Geoffrey. "Drop your crossbows and swords. Let me leave, or Excalibur takes a permanent swim."

Geoffrey smiled, and stayed put.

"I'll do it!"

The prince shook his head, still smiling. "No, I don't think so." He leaned on his bastard sword and spoke to Henry as easily as to an old friend. "You see, boy, Excalibur is Power. And no man surrenders Power freely."

Do not release me, Henry.

Henry licked his lips. If he dropped Excalibur…The burden would be gone, off his shoulders once and for all. No more voices in his head. No more constant nagging. No more freezing or starving on the road. No more ghosts.

What about Mattie? *No. Not a problem.* He'd find some way to free her without Excalibur. In fact, it would probably be easier without a hunk of ill-tempered steel looking over his shoulder. He'd gotten this far on his wits. He didn't need a magic sword.

But if he was going to do it, he had to do it now, before Excalibur zapped him, or took him over, or tried some other devilish trick. He loosened his grip—

Henry, don't be foolish. You need me for this quest. Henry—

The sword's voice was growing desperate. How long would it last, anyway? At the bottom of a chasm, forgotten in the darkness? Year after year, century after century, with no light, no sky, no friendly voices, nothing but the taste of cave water, and the feel of cavern mud as it silted up over you, burying you forever…Would he hear Excalibur's voice behind him as he left?

Henry sighed. Geoffrey's smile became a grin. Henry let his arm drop to his side, still gripping Excalibur.

"Okay, so how do I escape, steely-pants?"

Kneel down next to the water.

Geoffrey's smile faded as Henry followed the sword's directions. "What are you doing, Henry?"

Dip me in the water, and don't let go.

Henry touched Excalibur's point to the water.

Geoffrey snapped. "I've called your bluff, boy. Don't play with me."

DON'T LET GO.

The power rose from the earth, into the sword, and then out into the water. He felt a surge of force that almost twisted him off his feet—but it was nothing compared to the wall of actual water that rose out of the river and slammed into Geoffrey's party. In an instant, they were on their backs, washed right and left across the stone shelf, blades ungripped and crossbows flying.

Henry hot-footed it across the bridge, up the stairs, and into the sunlight.

19. ON THE ROAD

"Don't focus on the armor; focus on the ensemble as a whole."

Alfie and Valdemar posed in front of Henry, decked out in their finest princess-rescuing gear. They were hidden in a vineyard that was already green with new leaves, rummaging through the supplies they'd been able to buy (mostly) in St. Émilion.

"A pitchfork, huh?" Henry tried to sound enthusiastic.

"Don't knock the pitchfork, lad. Your standard-issue pitchfork has been the weapon of choice for peasant uprisings since the Servile Wars. You don't want to be on the other end of it. And that breastplate Valdemar's wearing, that's pure Toledo steel."

"Really?" Henry glanced at Valdemar, whose eyes avoided his. Another Valdemar original, apparently.

Still, the sunlight filtering through the leaves made the armor look almost respectable, and Henry would take any help he could get. Eleanor had given him some gold, most of which had gone to the horses and equipment; she'd even named a few people who might be sympathetic. But she hadn't given him soldiers, or a warrant, or a plan, or anything that Geoffrey might use against her. And Henry still didn't know what Excalibur had planned for him.

Of course he was grateful (and, frankly, astonished) that Alfie and Valdemar wanted to help—it wasn't as if Mattie were actually part of their crew. But they had no idea what the Plantagenets were really like. And Alfie, at least, should be wintering in Marseille, not suiting up for a commando expedition—

"Don't worry, lad. It's simple. We just sneak up behind Geoffrey and hit him on the head."

Valdemar nodded. "Never fails."

Henry smiled gamely.

That night, Henry had first watch. He stared into the flames.

Henry.

So Excalibur was finally speaking to him again. "Hey. How are you?"

I am well. Are your friends asleep?

"Yeah."

Are you currently holding me over a deep, black river?

"No."

Good.

Henry had never been staked out over an anthill, but that's what it felt like—as if bugs were crawling over every inch of his body, from his hair to his eyes to his belly to his—"HEY!"

Frantically he tore off his breeks and leggings, and dancing around like a naked madman, he cursed and slapped at himself until he tripped over a branch and hit the ground. After a moment, he sat up. The creepy-crawly feeling was gone. His skin was clear. Still twitching, he gathered up his clothes.

If you even hint at breaking your oath to me again, far, far worse awaits you.

"Gotcha."

Now, pack your things and saddle your horse. We are leaving for Toulouse.

"But—"

Those two men are an evil influence on you. Along the way, we shall collect companions of a more suitable nature.

Before the sun rose the next morning, Henry and Excalibur were far to the south. Henry tried not to think about ditching Alfie and Valdemar. It wasn't like he had a choice, after all. And besides, he'd make sure they got a piece of the action. If he lived.

* * * *

The wedding was set for Toulouse-le-Château, Raymond's castle south of the actual city of Toulouse. Royal weddings usually took place in September, so the guests could have the widest choice of fruits and meats. And then there was the preparation—the clothes, the tapestries, the announcements. The needlework alone could take months. But with a bride like Mattie, Henry suspected Geoffrey might try to nail things down as soon as possible. He rode as fast as he dared along the muddy, treacherous spring roads.

Aside from a few caustic comments about his horsemanship, Excalibur stayed quiet. Henry wasn't fooled. He didn't know what the sword was planning, but it wouldn't be fun. Henry tried to focus on the rescue. First, he'd need a map of the Chateau. Maybe there were tunnels. Or he could scale the walls somehow. Or use a disguise. He wished Alfie were with him. Or Valdemar. Or anybody, really, except for the crotchety piece of iron he was stuck with.

That night, he stayed at an inn some twenty miles up the river from Bordeaux. He slid Excalibur under the bed, waiting for an extended lecture, a command, a scolding. Nothing. The minutes, then the hours, slid by in utter silence. That night he slept very badly.

The next day, the roads had dried a little, and they made better time. About midday, they arrived at a nameless stream flowing north into the Garonne. In late summer it was probably no more than an easily forded brook, but now it was swollen with snow-melt. Henry trotted up and down, looking for a crossing, and finally found a bridge about a mile south. He had dismounted and was preparing to lead his horse across, when he heard the *clop-clop* of horseshoes on wood. A knight had ridden out onto the bridge.

"None shall pass."

Henry sighed and turned his horse around. The next idiot-free bridge was probably miles upstream—

No.

Excalibur froze, sending Henry sprawling. Once again, the sword and his leg were rooted to the ground.

"This…isn't…HELPING!"

He is a knight. We are at a crossing. You swore an oath.

"How is this going to help us rescue Mattie?"

If you break your oath, I will turn on you. That's how.

"I can't rescue her if I'm dead!"

You wield Excalibur. What could possibly go wrong?

"Does 'it sounded like three knights' ring a b-"

But Excalibur had already threaded ghostly tendrils through Henry's arms and legs. He swallowed his own beginning scream as he felt himself stepping back toward the bridge, away from his horse, and turning to face the knight—who was not happy, apparently.

"What knave disputes the crossroads?" cried the knight. "What rogue and peasant slave dares stand against Sir Percy of East Dulwich? Art thou prepared for battle?"

Good-looking, this one.

Yeah, he was. Tall, big-shouldered. Blond, too. Between the fair complexion, the pointy nose, and the spiky, jet-black armor, Henry thought Sir Percy looked like a large, courtly hedgehog—but he was just the kind of jerk the girls went for.

"Like 'em big and stupid, do you?"

As opposed to small and snide, yes. Perhaps I shall let this Percy defeat you, and make him king.

And now Percy was ten feet away, and there was nowhere to run. Excalibur rose in Henry's hand, and

Henry's gorge rose in his throat.

"Ah-ha! A horseless knight! Fear not, I know the Code."

"Code?"

The Code of Chivalry, you dunce.

The knight jumped off his charger, dropped his lance, and drew his sword. It was considerate, but Henry couldn't help noticing that Sir Percy was still in full armor, just a tad more protection than the wool cloak Henry was wearing.

Now pay close attention. Arthur called this "The Full Merlin." We feint high, and then slice through his armor, letting it drop to the ground. If he continues to fight, then he is a man of valor, and we grant him mercy—

The knight approached. Once more, Henry felt the surge of strength, giving power to his legs, his hips, his arms. Once more, Excalibur was behind his eyes, a ghost of points and edges and cold, sharp metal. He feinted and struck at the joints of the armor—

—and Excalibur bounced straight off with an enormous CLANG.

The shock reverberated through Henry's body like a cathedral bell, rattling his teeth and shaking his bones. Sir Percy looked rattled too, but his armor was unscathed.

"What the hell?"

What sorcery is this? His breastplate should be in pieces!

"Should be!? SHOULD BE!?"

Sir Percy looked spooked. "To whom speak you, my enemy? You cannot frighten me with your tricks!" The knight raised his sword—

Henry's brain shifted into overdrive. *Right, Miss High and Mighty,* thought Henry. *You asked for it.* "Beware, Sir Percy! My sword is cursed, and forces me to fight unarmored and horseless! Flee! Flee! Lest, as victor, it attach itself to thee!"

Sir Percy reared back in his tracks. "Whoa! I mean— Cursed, you say?"

CURSED!? You DARE call me cursed!?

"Aye, noble knight! See how I struggle!" Excalibur chose this moment to clamp onto Henry's leg, sending him tripping across the road.

Knave! Recreant! Impudent wretch!

"Even now the weapon seeks my blood and yours!" Henry hopped in front of Sir Percy, fighting to retain his balance.

"Yeah, cursed swords are nasty like that." Sir Percy was trying to sound sympathetic, but his smile was a grimace of pure fear.

Henry stumbled closer to Percy. The knight backed up frantically. "Why, what are you doing, Sir Percy?"

Percy backed up even farther. "Oh, just giving you a little more, uh, breathing room. That's it."

One hop, two, and Henry was panting in Percy's face. "But sir, don't go—"

"Can't talk. Sorry. Lots of tourneys. You know how it is, joust, joust, joust. But, uh, good luck with the whole curse thing. I'll send you a priest. Do a little exorcism. You'd like that, wouldn't you? Ta-ta for now!" Percy scrambled to remount his horse.

Vile, despicable—Bide a moment. His armor is adamant.

"You mean 'steel?'"

Aye. Neither iron nor bronze, but the Damascene adamant. Very well, then. Problem solved. Onward.

A hop—*that's called a 'balaestra' for future reference,* noted the sword—a lunge, and they were back at Sir Percy. Attack number one, and his saddle straps were severed. Attack number two, and his bridle was gone as well, and his horse was galloping down the road from a swat to its rump.

"You have sought single combat, Percy of Dulwich," bellowed a voice that was at once Henry's and Excalibur's. "You shall have it."

A feint to the belly, a feint to the head—and now Sir Percy was two knights at once in Henry's eyes: One, a flesh-and-blood jerk in armor; the other, a skeleton, an artist's sketch of joints and leverage points and weak spots, where blood and bone became irrelevant, and all that mattered were angles of attack and defense, distance and openings and footwork.

With a fancy triple pass, Henry lunged and recovered. Sir Percy stood there a moment, and then gaped like a fish as his armor slid off his body and fell to the floor like a puzzle shaken to bits. He had clearly purchased his knightly undergarments in Bordeaux—they were embroidered with roses and valentines.

That is your first lesson. Keep your underwear clean and simple. You never know when you'll have an accident.

Henry had to give Percy credit—he didn't hesitate. To hit the bridge knees first and beg for mercy was for Percy the work of an instant. "Spare me, good knight. I yield!"

Henry opened his mouth to answer, then staggered with relief as he felt Excalibur retreat from his mind. In an instant, he was a civilian again. He grabbed the bridge's rail and stood tall, breathing in great gasps of air.

Will you just leave him there to grovel on his knees?

Henry glanced at Sir Percy. "He does it well. I'll give him that." Henry waved at Percy to stand. "It's all right. No harm done."

Percy bounded to his feet. "And my horse and armor, noble warrior? Do you wish them as spoils of battle?"

"Well, that armor didn't do you much good, did it? Keep it, keep it."

Percy's face was one big smile. "What is your name, noble knight, that I may herald your prowess—and mercy—to the countryside?" He was very accommodating, now that his hearts and flowers were blowing in the wind.

"I…"

Oh, go on. You deserve that much, at least. You have kept your word so far.

"No. Um…don't you think it's better Geoffrey doesn't know about us?"

I…hadn't thought of that. Very well.

"Who are you talking to, Sir Knight?"

"I…uh…no one. Old head wound. Got it on Crusade. Sometimes I mutter. Sometimes I ramble on about cursed swords. Just ignore it."

"That whole cursed sword thing. It was all a ruse, to buy you time! Brilliant!"

"Yes, I'm clever that way. Now, if you'll excuse me…" Henry took the reins of his horse and pushed past Sir Percy. Percy followed.

"Long have I sought a knight worthy of my steel, worthy of my loyalty. You are such a man."

You're right. He IS stupid.

"I will follow you to the ends of the earth, to the far reaches of the world, even to Death's kingdom itself!"

Henry grinned. "Really? Terrific! Because that's where we're going!"

Sir Percy's enthusiasm faltered for a moment. "Oh. Because that's just sort of a figure of spee—" He caught his breath and squared his shoulders. "Never mind. You and I shall confront Hell's minions, shoulder to shoulder!"

You had to give Sir Percy credit. For all he knew, Henry really was going on some magical doomed voyage—after all, the knight had swallowed the cursed-sword story fast enough—and yet Percy still stepped up. Oh, well. Henry got on tip-toe and put his hand on Percy's shoulder.

"Look, Percy, that's a very generous offer, but—"

Accept it.

"But he'll just—"

A true knight has retainers, accepts fealty, and both leads and follows.

"I'm not a—"

You have sworn. DO IT.

"I…uh, the Muttering Knight…accept your fealty. Is there anything we have to do—" But the knight was already on his knees in the mud again, groveling into Henry's palms. Clearly, Percy was comfortable playing to his strengths.

This was going to be a long trip.

20. THE MUTTERING KNIGHT

WAKE UP.

Henry crawled back to consciousness and looked around the clearing. It was pitch black.

Just before Matins. Time to start training.

"The sun isn't up yet."

A knight must be ready for battle at all times, not just in the afternoon after a nap and a light snack.

"Okay. Just give me a minute…" Henry snuggled into the bedroll, let his eyes close—

WAKE UP. WAKE UP. WAKE UP. Trumpets blared. A choir sang. A bright light shone. A bell rang in his ears.

Henry heaved himself to a sitting position. "I hate you."

This will be easier for both of us if you simply accept that I am in charge. NOW GET UP!

Henry stood. Between the frosty air and the refrozen ground on which he'd been sleeping, his entire body was one big knot.

Draw me and hold me out, parallel to the ground.

Henry pulled out Excalibur and held her outstretched. For a moment, everything was normal. Then, instant by instant, Henry felt the sword grow heavier, until it was like holding a boulder up with one hand, and his shoulder felt like it was being wrenched from its socket.

Keep still. Don't move.

Henry stood like a statue, gasping through clenched teeth, sweat pouring down his face. He couldn't hold it much longer. He was going to lose it—

Enough.

And Excalibur was light again.

That was the weight of a normal sword, as it feels after an hour of battle: no more than three pounds, yet a dead weight to the untrained hand. In combat, a knight will wield that weight and more for hours on end, lightly as a feather. You were able to hold it up for a count of fifteen.

Henry sagged against a tree, breathing.

What, no smart remarks? No clever quips? Now stand with your feet perpendicular, your lead leg out, your knees flexed, your sword arm bent at the elbow. It's time for drills.

* * * *

"Allow me, My Lord." Sir Percy bustled around the camp, rebuilding the fire, fetching water from the stream, while Henry sat against the tree, exhausted.

For two hours Excalibur had led him through footwork drills, sometimes weighing one pound, sometimes thirty, sometimes three. Back and forth, back and forth, counter cut, counter cut, attack, and parry.

And this is just the beginning! sang Excalibur. *Soon we'll have armor conditioning, lunge sprints, and eye-hand drills. Those are fun.*

"Terrific." If Excalibur had been a person, Henry was certain she'd be rubbing her hands in glee right now.

Maybe the pell-quintain, if we have time. And you'll spar with Sir Percy. Nothing trumps a live opponent.

"You really are a cursed sword," muttered Henry.

What?

"Nothing."

By the time they neared the next town, Henry had recovered just enough to sit up straight in the saddle. Sir Percy rode behind him, as befit a loyal vassal. But as they came in sight of the walls of St. Medard, Percy cantered up beside him.

"Allow me, My Lord. I shall precede you into the town and arrange for treatment as befits your prowess."

Barely conscious, Henry nodded, and Percy galloped into town. But as Henry trotted toward the town gates, the word "befit" trickled through his swamp of exhaustion.

"Oh, no!" He nudged his horse into a gallop and pounded into the town square, but it was already too late.

Henry entered the square just as Percy was wheeling his charger on two legs, drawing a crowd. "Hear me, good people! Behold the greatest knight of our age! Who defeated me in single combat! Horseless and without armor! A mere boy! A stripling! Whose prowess is without peer! Behold, the Muttering Knight!"

"NO!"

He takes his vassal duties seriously. Well done, that man.

"A knight errant, fighting for the right! Here is he to Right Wrongs, to Vanquish Evil, to Mete Justice! Ask and ye shall receive! Seek and ye shall find! Bring him thy quests, and tell him thy injustices!" The offer of free meting perked up the townspeople, who turned to appraise Henry's evil-vanquishing potential.

Henry rubbed his eyes. "He's just ruined our cover."

Yes. But his declamation is first rate.

Percy and the townspeople finished their conference. A little old lady walked up to Henry.

"*Bonjour, grandmère.* What can I—"

"How much do you weigh?"

"Uh, ten stone, but—"

She grabbed his bicep, then turned back to Percy. "I don't like this sword arm. Where's the muscle?"

"Madame, he severed my armor from my very body. Behold the cuts." Percy started to point.

"Yeah, yeah, whatever." She turned back to Henry. "I'll give him one cup of cider, and not a drop more."

Henry yanked his arm away. "Hey, Grannie, keep your

damned cider—"

We shall do this. You need questing practice.

"We *have* a quest, remember? Mattie—"

We have some time. And you will do her no good untrained.

The old lady stared wide-eyed at Henry. "He talks to himself? Is he crazy?"

Percy stepped in. "Madame, it is a wound he received on Crusade—"

The old lady waved Percy off. "No, no, I like it. You want a little crazy in your knights. Stiffens 'em up." She turned to Percy. "Okay, he gets a full lunch. But that's it. Who's next?" The other townspeople gathered around Henry.

"But—"

And don't forget to jot down your thoughts about each adventure. It's never too soon to start gathering material for the troubadours.

* * * *

Notes from the Questing Diary of Sir Henry, the Muttering Knight

Day One.
Town: Saint-Medard d'Eyrans.

Quest: Cat up a tree.

Supplicant: Old Lady Goncourt.

Result: One dead tree, one vicious cat, one scratched face.

Reward: One bowl of onion soup, one slice of onion bread, one onion for dessert.

Stupid Comment From the Sword That Is Ruining My Life: There are no small quests, only small warriors.

Training Exercise Number Three: *Vault onto a horse using a lance. Note to self—wear groin armor.*

Day Five.
Town: Beautiran.

Quest: Tame the Wild Horse of Charpentier, so that Charpentier can use it to plow the back forty.

Supplicant: Giles Charpentier, Europe's least trustworthy serf.

Result: One sprained back, one bruised wrist, one harsh tongue-lashing, one war horse returned with apologies to the Chevalier de Tourenne, who has been looking for it for two months.

Reward: The sight of the Chevalier de Tourenne kicking the backside of Giles Charpentier from Beautiran to Ayguemorte-les-Graves.

Stupid Comment From the Sword That Is Ruining My Life: You of all people should recognize a thief when you see one.

Original Training Exercise Number Nine: *Turn somersault in full armor.*

New Training Exercise Number Nine: *Stand up in full armor.*

Day Seven—

And again. And again. Keep on until I say stop.

"What's the point of this?"

One hand rested on his hip. The other twirled Excalibur, over and under, making fancy passes and figure eights.

First, it is good exercise. My weight shall increase every day—

"Oh, great—"

—until you are able to manage this with a normal sword.

"And why?"

Who loses a fight?

"The one who dies first."

No. The one who gives up. Imagine this—you are challenged by a genuine swordsman who sees an easy victory. He draws. You draw. And then you add a flourish. Using only one hand, you show complete control of a bastard sword, even a two-handed sword. And now, perhaps, your opponent is discouraged. Before his name was known, Arthur did this many times to discourage unworthy opponents.

"Oh." Winning without fighting. Excalibur was making sense. Henry frowned. That couldn't be right.

Day Nine.

Town: Preignac.

Quest: Rescue the kidnapped Minstrel of Preignac.

Supplicant: Edwina daughter of Ralf, who needs to lay off the honeyed fruit slices and troubadour chansons and get out more often.

Result: One massive headache, one set of nerves scraped raw, and the realization that the kidnapping of the Minstrel of Preignac, AKA Tin-Ear Ralf, AKA Tone-Deaf Ralf, AKA Ralf the Curse, was probably instigated by his fellow citizens.

Reward: The undying gratitude of the fair Edwina, carefully and tactfully transferred to Sir Percy.

Stupid Comment from the Sword That Is Ruining My Life: She seems very nice. You could do worse.

Training Exercise Number Seventeen: *Sparring with Sir Percy. Delayed on account of groveling. Note to self: explain to Sir Percy the concept of "self-esteem."*

Day Thirty.

Quest: Dispatch the Robbers of the Secret Cave.

Supplicant: The lord mayor of Meilhan-sur-Garonne.

Result—

It was early morning. The mist blew cold and wet through the clearing. The secret cave wasn't much of a secret: The remains of a dozen meals were scattered at the cave mouth, and the smell told Henry that the robbers hadn't gone very far into the woods when nature called.

The robbers would probably be back soon. Henry, Percy, and Ralf the minstrel waited in the clearing. Percy was sharpening his sword on a rock. Ralf was just sitting, getting ready to record the details of the battle for a *chanson*, presumably. Not that it mattered to Henry. He hadn't wanted Ralf along; the lord-mayor had insisted that they take Ralf with them. Henry suspected the mayor was more interested in Ralf's exit than in the exit of the robbers.

Not that the rest of the town felt that way. The robbers were clearly not the jolly, Robin Hood kind of robber, but the other, un-jolly kind: bad men who took from the poor and kept for themselves. They were the kind of thugs Henry knew pretty well, lordless knights, ex-mercenaries, predators…one step lower than the Brissacs of this world, the sort of free swords Geoffrey would hire for his dirty work and then wash his hands of when they'd finished. Dangerous men.

Henry wished he had something to occupy his time. This would be his first pitched battle, and he felt as weak and cold as a snail out of its shell. He had considered begging off, but he hadn't thought of any graceful way to turn it down. And with Excalibur attached to him like a barnacle, he couldn't run away. His mouth was dry. He wanted to go to the bathroom like nobody's business.

"This is the greatest moment," said Percy. "Just before the battle. The heart pounds, fear lies on brow and bicep, and you know your courage is—"

"Shut up."

"Oh. Sorry. You want to prepare yourself. I understand."

"We can have a song while we wait," said Ralf. He whipped out his lute, and without tuning, began to sing. "Oh, golden leaves on golden trees, in the glade were glistening, merrily, merrily—"

"Enough." "Enough." *Enough.*

It wasn't often that Henry, Percy, and Excalibur all agreed, but Ralf's singing was like that. It brought people together.

"Did anyone ever suggest that you tune the lute, first?"

"Hey. That's a great idea! Thanks!"

Henry took stock of Ralf. Edwina's dad was as withered as Alfie, with a huge nose and the spark of crazy enthusiasm that Henry was coming to know and dread from his encounters with Brissac, Geoffrey, Percy,

Mattie...sweet St. Dismas, had the whole world gone mad? Was Henry the last sane person in Christendom?

"So, Ralf. What did you do before you became a...ahem...minstrel?"

"I was a goldsmith, my boy. Rings, brooches, cunning little figurines and book-covers. 'If it's a Ralf, it's pure gold!'"

"You were a goldsmith. A member of the guild? Established?"

"Oh, sure, apprentice to journeyman to master smith, that was me. The only one in Preignac, too. Folks came from miles around."

Henry felt his jaw starting to clench. "So I guess all that wealth, safety, and respect just got to be too much, huh?"

"Boring, lad, boring! Now your life, that's how it's meant to be lived! Adventure! Excitement! Zest! I wrote a song about it." He pulled out his lute. "In the golden spring we lightly sing, and joy's gold crown is beckoning, and—"

"Okay, terrific. Maybe later."

When they come, do not fight me.

"Why should I? You're just the one who got me into this."

If you want to live, raise me, challenge them, and charge. From the minute we entered this camp, I knew these men. We shall take them. Do not fear.

Hoof beats.

As they'd planned, Henry stood on a small rise in the middle of the clearing. Percy took position on Henry's left. Henry drew Excalibur and wished he were wearing more than a small helm and a mail shirt. But even after a month of training, the weight of full armor would have dropped him like a stone. Better to stay mobile and trust in Excalibur. At least, that's what Excalibur had said, and it had sounded good at the time.

The training had helped a little, but mostly it had taught Henry just enough to realize how lucky he had been so far.

There had to be a way out of this—

Remember. Anticipate your opponent. Know what he will do and get there first. Take the initiative.

The robbers entered the glade. There were six of them, on horseback. They were filthy. They wore bits and pieces of armor, and their horses were half-starved. But they were big, and they looked like they knew what they were doing.

"Surrender, thieves, and you will not be harmed!" Once again, it was Excalibur in his throat and lungs, making a challenge with his voice.

The lead horseman stared for a moment, and then laughed. "Thank God and St. Mike! I haven't heard a good joke since we tortured that priest." He put his hand on his sword. Henry took a deep breath—

NOW.

Excalibur filled Henry as he leaped from the stone toward the horses. Head down, sword out, he could feel the dangerous areas above, those spaces where swords could slash or spears could bite. Excalibur was out, slashing—a nick here, a cut there, upsetting the horses, throwing the riders off balance. Getting first blood on sword arms, taking the initiative, moving faster than they expected because he had almost no armor—

And in an instant he was through the press, leaving chaos behind him. The horses whinnied in terror, biting and kicking at each other. One of the robbers was down, thrown from his horse and unconscious. Three others struggled for control of their beasts. Two had dismounted and now closed on Sir Percy.

"Ralf!"

The minstrel was already at the horses, waving his hands, yelling, and keeping them panicked. Maybe he wasn't less than useless. Henry ran back to Percy. One of the robbers was behind Percy, raising a broad sword.

With Excalibur's vision, Henry could see how the robber had exposed himself with his attempt at a head-cut. Henry brought Excalibur up from below. A blow with the flat of the blade, and the robber dropped the sword. Another with the pommel, and he was down.

Henry turned back to Ralf and the robbers. One had managed to dismount and two were in their stirrups. Henry ran for the one about to attack Ralf and managed to bring out Excalibur just in time to keep Ralf from being carved into minstrel nuggets.

"Run for the horses!" panted Henry. Ralf turned to stampede the horses that were left as Henry faced the robber on his feet. The robber backed away, his sword out. Henry met his eyes—the robber was afraid. Afraid of him. Henry beat at the sword, shattered it, and turned back to the clearing. Behind him, he heard the sounds of the robber fleeing into the woods.

When he arrived, he saw the last two robbers down on their knees before Sir Percy and Ralf.

Congratulations, Henry. You've won.

21. A MEMBER OF THE WEDDING

The townsfolk cheered as they rode into the square, four robbers trailing behind them. One had fled, and Percy had killed the one who'd bragged about torturing priests.

Percy had been matter-of-fact. "What's one hater, more or less?" Henry thought about asking Percy how many men he'd killed, and then changed his mind. Percy might remember all of them in gory detail. Or worse, he might not even know the answer. It was a good reminder—no matter how friendly or goofy, Percy was a killer.

But now the sun was shining, and the people were cheering. The people were cheering...him. There was Old Lady Goncourt. She was waving. And Edwina. And the Chevalier de Tourenne, and Marcabru the innkeeper, and—Henry felt as though he should look behind him to see the person they were really cheering for.

Not too shabby, is it?

"What?"

The hero's reward.

"Gold? Jewels?"

No, you, you...ninny. The REAL hero's reward.

"Right. Which would be..."

The love of the people. Honestly, why do I even bother?

159

Cautiously, Henry raised a hand and waved back. The crowd went wild. "I could get used to this." And from Excalibur there were no more words…just a radiating sense of smug satisfaction.

* * * *

The party lasted into the night. The innkeeper even uncorked the good wine. At first, the crowd had wanted Henry to tell the story. But after a while, he let Sir Percy take over and wandered outside. He sat down on a barrel and stared up at the sky.

Why aren't you inside?

"I needed some air." Henry sipped from his mug and leaned against the wall. "Besides, it's Percy they really want. He looks like a hero. You said so yourself."

What if I did? This is your party. You deserve it. Percy is your vassal.

Ralf's cracked voice quavered from inside. Faintly, Henry could hear, "gold, mighty, golden, sword, gleaming…" Then the crowd roared and Ralf shut up. Henry took another sip.

"I'm…afraid, maybe."

Yes. Parties are fearsome things.

"No. It's like…it's like borrowing something. If they say I'm a hero, and I agree, then I have to be one. And I'm not."

Really. And you are the expert on heroism.

"I know I'm not. When the Young King's knights came to my village, they killed everyone. My parents. My brothers and sisters. They burned it to the ground. I lived because I ran like a hare and hid in a cave."

Henry leaned back and looked up at the sky. It was clear, and cold, and full of stars.

Henry.

Henry looked down, to see a woman facing him, an apparition, slender and pale, with silver lips and silver eyes.

In this guise, Arthur knew me as the Lady of the Lake.

"You're beautiful."

160

She reached out—her touch was the faintest breeze on his forehead. *I have seen more than a thousand years of battle, so I speak as an expert in bloodshed. There is nothing a child can do, but live.*

Henry buried his face in his hands. Somewhere behind his eyes, the tears welled up and pushed their way out despite the best he could do. Excalibur waited patiently, until the sobbing slowed and finally stopped.

Finally, Henry stood up. "I'm sorry." He looked up at the moon and sighed. "I'm glad Mattie wasn't here to see that."

I don't think she would have minded, said Excalibur. *Go inside. You paid for your party.*

* * * *

"It's the sword." Alfie threw a six, a six, and a four.

"Of course it's the sword," said Valdemar, watching the game. Alfie's opponent hesitated, his hand over the coins. Valdemar gave him a look, and the hesitation stopped. Valdemar switched to Frisian. "It's worth a fortune."

Alfie replied in the same dialect. "No, that's not it." He rolled back his sleeves and turned his hands palms-up to the other players. *See, no tricks.* Then he gathered the dice and cast them again. "He's changed. He's talking like a knight. Politics, princesses, refusing help...You know what happens to the tall poppies."

Valdemar nodded. "They get chopped down."

The dice rolled to the next player in the circle. He picked them up, studied them, and threw. One, two, and two. The player cursed and added to the pot.

Valdemar spit thoughtfully into a nearby manger. "Then what do we do?"

Alfie sighed. "We get that thing away from him. For his own good."

* * * *

Right Trusty and Well-Beloved Cousin,
Your Presence Is Requested,

At the Seat of Our Faithful Vassal,
Raymond of Toulouse,
On the Feast of St. Maximinius,
To Celebrate Our Wedding to the Princess of Navarre.
RSVP With Your Meal Preference—Boar, Pheasant, or
Venison.

"And behold," Percy pointed to the second scroll of the invitation, "The service is to be performed by Pierre, Bishop of Chartres. They say he married five Crusader princes on the walls of Jerusalem in the middle of a battle and received a vision of St. Julian the Aeropagite, all in one afternoon. Plus he's XII-and-Nought for conversions. How did you get these, My Lord?"

Five miles from the chateau, and they'd already passed dozens of wagons, carts, and pack trains headed for the castle. The wedding was going to be huge, all right, an Event with a capital E. "The Chevalier de Tourenne didn't want to pay for a wedding present, so he gave me the scroll."

Henry hoped the size and confusion would help him sneak in unrecognized. Even with the invitation, he'd take all the help he could get. Ever since Meilhan, Sir Percy had bragged to anyone who'd listen about his service to the Muttering Knight. Henry had finally gotten him to turn down the volume, but they'd still attracted much more attention than Henry wanted. They'd heard the Muttering Knight mentioned on the road four or five times in the last few days; fortunately, accurate descriptions hadn't traveled as far...yet.

Percy studied the invitation. "It says there shall be tourneys, as well."

"You want to get back in the saddle?"

"The ladies love a jouster, My Lord."

"That really works?"

Percy nodded. "Better than troubadours. Knock a man off his horse, you've got company that evening."

"Huh. I'll have to think about that."

Oh, for shame. Have you no decency? None at all? What of chastity?

"I haven't even done anything yet, Your Sanctimoniousness. Relax." They were coming to the final turn in the road. Henry stopped. "Remember, we've left the Muttering Knight behind. When we get to the castle, you're Sir Percy, and I'm your loyal squire."

Percy looked unhappy. "It's not Chivalry, My Lord. A true knight is forthright in all things. Besides, I should be your shield man. If the ladies know you're the MK, you could be knocking them down like ninepins."

"Focus, Perce. We're here for the princess."

Sir Percy stared hard at Henry, and grinned. "Thou hast been smitten, My Lord. I can tell."

Henry turned away. "Look, there's the castle."

And there it was. The road had opened out to a ferry crossing on the river. And on the other side, Toulouse-le-Chateau. It was big, no question—dozens of towers, and curtain walls eighty feet high. The guests were already ferrying across the river and streaming into the castle, which was hung with banners of red and gold, blue and silver—the colors of England and France...the Plantagenet Empire. To the east of the castle, a village of tents, pavilions, and tourney fields had been set up, and if you squinted hard, you could just make out knights on horseback training with dummies, partners, and equipment. And once Geoffrey arrived, the encampment would grow even bigger.

"It'll stink like a sewer come Monday," said Henry.

"But until then, a brave sight, My Lord."

Why can't you get into the spirit for once?

"Yeah, yeah. Let's grab a boat."

As they rowed across and then disembarked, Henry had to admit that it *was* a "brave sight"—pennons and banners fluttering in the breeze, bright colors shining, the smells of wine and beer, roasted meat, even horses and iron and charcoal from the smithies, people shouting, hugging, singing—and some of his fellow street rats practicing their trade, certainly…They stepped out of the boat and headed toward the tents and pavilions of the tourney field.

Finding a good spot for their tent wasn't easy. Most of the high ground had already been snapped up by the early birds; other plots had squads of bad-tempered, well-armed vassals, who were reserving them for the earls and barons powerful enough to afford that kind of treatment. Finally, they set up camp near the dank, but unclaimed, mud of the river's edge.

Next on Henry's list was talking to Mattie. Finding her wouldn't be a problem—Geoffrey would have made sure she was stuck in the castle, instead of out seeing the sights—but talking to her might be. Usually only family members, vassals, or servants would get near a princess so close to her wedding day. No knight would get within ten feet of her without guards; nobles had a nasty habit of kidnapping landowning brides for ransom or a wedding of their own. Henry tried not to think of how much Mattie—Princess Mathilde—was worth. A duchy, at least. Thousands of *livres*. And she had been running around free on the streets of Paris and Bordeaux. No question, the Plantagenets were insane.

But if he *were* a servant, he might have a chance. He pictured himself, just one more peach-fuzzed menial, strolling through the palace grounds. Only one problem with that picture.

I am the problem here. No servant would bear a sword.

"Well, no kidding. What if Percy—"

"I'm sorry, Lord. No kidding what?"

Sir Percy may not bear me.

"I thought you liked him."

Only three of the knights of the Round Table could find the Grail, even though they were all good men and true. Not all knights may wield Excalibur. If Percy were the man to wield me, he would already be doing so, and you would be free to go.

164

Henry turned away from Percy. He smiled and whispered, "Are you saying I'm better than Percy?"

Excalibur sighed. Once again, Henry was impressed by how Excalibur could pull off that trick, considering that the sword had no lips, lungs, or teeth. *Find us a hill, an outcrop of the living rock. Draw me, and thrust into the stone. I shall remain embedded, as you found me, until you return.*

Henry shook his head, stunned. "Stick you into the bedrock."

Yes.

Henry felt the fury building in him. "Like the bedrock in Bordeaux? Or under Southampton? Or in those hills I had to cross, in the dead of winter, back in Sussex?"

Yes, exactly.

"I could have walked away any time, and you—"

And I would be no closer to Constantinople.

A small crowd had gathered to stare at the muttering manservant. Sir Percy got in their faces. "Well? What ailest thou? Hast thou not seen a Crusader veteran before?" The crowd dispersed, whispering:

"Jesu, you'd think every village idiot in the West went on Crusade."

"Why not? Crusaders are all nuts anyway."

"Hey, watch it. My cousin went on Crusade for your sake."

"Yeah? Who asked him to?"

Henry wasn't finished. "We're going to have a long talk about this—"

Yes, yes, yes, I'm dishonest and you're perfect. Now leave me in the rock and find the princess.

"I don't know…a big magic sword sticking out of a rock at Geoffrey's wedding. You think someone might notice?"

Then what would you do?

"Errrr…" Henry thought furiously for a moment. "When is a sword not a sword?"

I hate riddles.

"When is a sword—"

All right, I don't know, when IS a sword not a sword?

"When it's a gift."

* * * *

Count Raymond of Toulouse, aristocrat, power broker, collector of antique weapons, stared gloomily at his prize possession—the sword of Charlemagne.

"Of course it's a fraud, old man. I had my agent on the rack two hours after he sent it to me. You've traveled all the way from Bourdeaux to tell me that?"

The old Welshman shut his mouth with a snap. Raymond nodded in satisfaction and continued. "Now, do you have anything else to tell me? Anything useful?"

"We might know where there is a real sword of the Nine, My Lord. If you're willing to trade for it."

* * * *

After Percy found a suitable wooden case, Henry left him guarding their camp while he went to scout the castle. Although there was a forest of tents and pavilions outside the castle walls, the castle's main courtyard was definitely the hub of the action, and there was a huge crowd milling over the drawbridge and trying to get in.

I don't like this case. It pinches my forte.

"Two thousand years in a rock was okay, but a linen-lined case pinches you?"

Once in the rock, I sleep the sleep of ages. And besides, this case smells of pig glue.

"You don't even have a nose!"

Henry shifted Excalibur's case to his other shoulder, drifted to one side and tried to look servile. There were a couple of pikemen on guard at the portcullis in Geoffrey's livery, but they didn't seem to be scrutinizing the people too closely: peasants, townsfolk, peddlers with packs, shabby monks offering to write letters or read documents.

Inside, the courtyard was packed with carts and booths and people exchanging news, gossip, and insults. Henry scanned the high walls, and spotted what he was looking for: a small, thick wooden door on the wall to the right of the inner bailey's main gate. It was a one-man doorway into the central courtyard, an entrance for the castle's servants. After a few minutes, a heavyset cook lugged a spit of beef to the door. Henry grabbed the end of the spit and helped him inside.

The kitchen was a huge open space, half belowground, with slit windows letting in the light from above. Henry and the cook struggled the meat down the stairs and onto a spit in the fireplace. The cook wiped his forehead and then stared at Henry.

"Who are you?"

"You're welcome for the help," said Henry.

"No sass from kids," said the cook. "Who are you?"

"I'm Henri, servant to the Chevalier de Tourenne. The Chevalier sent me with this as a wedding gift for the Prince." Henry opened the case.

The cook grunted. "Huh. Not exactly Durendal, is it? Where's the jewels and gold inlay?"

How DARE he—

"Family heirloom," said Henry quickly.

The cook shrugged. "His funeral. Anyway, you want to see the Master Chamberlain with that thing. I'll send someone with you. Then you can get back to your lord."

Henry smiled and looked embarrassed. "Would you mind if I stuck around for a bit? The Chevalier's in a bad mood. Time away is time well spent."

For the first time, the cook seemed sympathetic. "One of those, is he? All right. You can stay if you help out. I'm Ulric, you can call me 'sir.' That's Stephanie, Segolène, Pierre, Wulf." Henry nodded and waved. Ulric handed him a bunch of carrots and knife. "Start chopping, son."

In the next three hours, Henry learned a lot about making a *cassoulet*, and almost as much about the Chateau's servant politics. Once he mentioned that he and the Chevalier had visited Bordeaux and England, the conversation moved quickly, because everyone was starved for news. He had to resist the temptation to do all the talking, and tried instead to steer the conversation toward the nobles who were in residence at the castle.

"Oh, yeah, we've got both princes here already," said Wulf.

"Princes?"

"The Plantagenets. Prince Geoffrey is quite courteous; we've naught to say against him," said Segolène primly.

John, apparently, was as charming to the servants as he had been to Henry. But they didn't mind much, because he spent most of his time in the central keep with Princess Mathilde, who was apparently insane.

"She told me yesterday to 'subvert the dominant paradigm,'" said Segolène. "When I asked her what it was, she said I had to 'deconstruct my false consciousness.' I think she's eaten bad mushrooms."

Pierre disagreed. "No, no, she's under a spell. There's that Granny Maudrey who lives down by the river, it's her doing."

Stephanie had the final answer. "I hear she snuck into the university lectures in Paris. That's the problem. It's overheated her brain."

The kitchen came to the general agreement that Prince Geoffrey would have a difficult household on his hands, with an overheated wife and an empire to conquer. Henry imagined Mattie listening to this conversation, and stifled a smile. "When did she tell you this? Did she come down here herself?"

The kitchen folks shared a look. "We take her food up to her," said Pierre. "She eats in her rooms."

"And we get the lecture," said Stephanie. "She calls it 'fighting cultural hegemony.'"

"It's not fair," burst out Segolène. "Bad enough we have all this extra work for the wedding, but we have to listen to a sermon, too?"

"That's enough," said Ulric. "No one here speaks ill of their betters. Especially not royalty, and especially not

Plantagenets."

Henry shrugged. "I don't think I have a hegemony. I could take her the food." There was no way he could get Mattie out right now, but at least he could find out where she was, and let her know he was here.

Ulric looked dubious. "I don't know. We've got no livery for you. If you make a mistake in the presence of the princess, it's trouble for the rest of us."

Henry fought to keep the anxiety from showing on his face. "I understand, sir. I was just looking for a reason to stick around."

Ulric looked guilty—clearly, he'd had a few bad masters of his own, and was sympathizing with Henry against the mythical Chevalier.

"He can have my shirt, Ulric," said Wulf, "if it means I'm not doing it."

Ulric nodded. "All right, then."

Twenty minutes later, Henry was wearing Count Raymond's livery and helping Pierre carry a big covered platter through a series of courtyards. The platter had holes cut out to hold the different bowls and plates, but it was heavy as death, and Henry suddenly understood why even the women in the kitchen had wider shoulders than he did.

If you'd gotten a lighter case, or simply wrapped me in cloth, you wouldn't have this problem.

"Will you *please* be quiet?"

"What was that?"

Henry bit down on his tongue.

In between pauses to catch his breath, Henry made a mental map of the territory. The castle was ring within ring of walled courtyards—baileys—each with its own heavy gates. Some baileys had their own shops and residences, little stone-encircled neighborhoods. The construction was meant to keep out invading armies, but Henry soon came to the dismal conclusion that it would do a pretty good job of keeping out a young thief as well. If Mattie was in the central keep, surrounded by walls and baileys—

"Is this the only way to the keep, Pierre?" he asked. "Through all the gates and courtyards?"

"It's fastest. When it's dry, anyway. Here, let's switch off." Pierre set the tray down and they stretched for a moment. "If it's raining or snowing, you can go through the walls—there are passages through."

Great. Then all Henry would have to do would be to confront guard after guard on their way out. At least it would be easier moving around as a liveried servant. Henry had tipped Wulf a couple of *dixaines* so that he could keep the shirt, no questions asked. Wulf and Ulric probably figured he wanted it to make a break from his "evil master." In a way, they were right. Kind of.

They passed through one more portcullis and approached the keep, a round black tower that rose over the surrounding walls and flew the pennons of the Plantagenets and the House of Rouergue. The front gate was big, intimidating, and guarded. They passed it by and went to a servants' entrance. "Remember," said Pierre, "Take the weight with your knees on the stairs."

They hiked up the winding servants' staircase. Sixty feet up, they reached the top floor, an antechamber guarded by soldiers in Geoffrey's personal livery.

"Dinner for the princess and her ladies," bawled Pierre. Henry just panted and tried not to sweat too much. A soldier opened the antechamber's one door, and Pierre and Henry stepped through.

"The rooms of a princess," whispered Pierre. "Not as exciting as you thought, eh, boy?"

It was true enough. In the back of his mind, Henry had expected something with lots of lace, jewels, and gorgeous ladies-in-waiting. But the ladies-in-waiting had clearly been waiting for twenty or thirty years, and they were spending the time doing needlepoint. The room itself was big, bare, and gloomy.

A pair of lap dogs smelled the food and started to yap

around the platter.

"Is that you, Pierre?" A woman in white came out of the solarium, a book clutched under her arm. "Have you thought about controlling the means of production, like we talked about—"

She saw Henry and stopped. It was Mattie...*no, it's Mathilde, now,* thought Henry. His breath caught in his chest. There was no longer any question that she was a princess. Even in her day robe, she just...glowed. Beneath the joy of seeing her again, Henry felt a pang. *She's a princess. What am I doing here?*

The silence stretched for a moment. "So, who's the new guy?" asked the princess.

Pierre prodded Henry, who recovered his wits after a moment and bowed. "I am Henri, servant of the Chevalier de Tourenne, an' it please you, Highness."

"Sure, why not. One feudal oppressor's the same as another." She turned to Pierre. "You ready for your political philosophy quiz, Pierre?"

Pierre gave a sickly grin. "Actually, Your Highness, I was thinking that you might want to work on Henri's, uh, consciousness. He hasn't had any fo—philosophy, and I think I, uh, pulled a muscle while serving my oppressors."

"All right, get out of here, Master Puny, you're excused. Henri can take care of dinner."

Shooting a glance of sympathy in Henry's direction, Pierre bowed out.

"Soup's on, girls," yelled Mathilde. The ladies in waiting dropped their knitting and swooped down on the tray like a flock of vultures, scooping up stew and bread and meats. While they were occupied, Mathilde tugged on Henry's sleeve and drifted toward a far window. Henry followed. For a moment, they were out of sight behind a pillar, and Mattie kissed him hard. But before he could even respond, they were in plain view again, and Mattie was suddenly a chaste three feet away, leaving Henry shaken and breathless.

"What are you doing here, you goof?" she asked.

"Gee, it's nice to see you too," said Henry. "Hey, don't thank me for trying to rescue you. We wouldn't want to break your ingratitude streak."

"'Rescue'? Are you nuts?"

"I have a magic sword. And a vassal."

"Very nice. Will you be able to take down Geoffrey's army and Raymond's, not to mention crazy Uncle John?"

"Oh, thank God."

Mattie frowned. "For what?"

"That I'm not the only one who thinks your Uncle John is crazy. I was afraid I'd say something and offend you."

Mattie laughed. "Oh, that's no secret. It's just when you give the crazy prince a sword that things get scary." She glanced out the window for a moment. "I love Grandma Eleanor to death. But when you think about my uncles, you have to wonder about her parenting skills. I mean, Uncle John, Uncle Geoff, Uncle Richard…and my Uncle Henry was no bargain either, by all accounts."

"They're…they're not really your uncles, right? I mean, you're—"

Mattie shuddered. "Oh, God, no. *Ick.* It's just courtesy titles. But Eleanor treats me as her ward, and I'm a vassal of King Philip, who's a cousin of—well, it gets complicated."

"Still…ick."

Mathilde sighed. "Yeah."

Henry looked over at the ladies in waiting. Two of them were snarling over a braised rib, and none of the others seemed inclined to lift their heads from the *cassoulet*. He should get the recipe…"Still preaching the revolution, I see."

"Not really. But I found that if you talk long enough about something no one else cares about, they pretty much ignore you. And that's how we can have this cozy chat."

Henry looked at her in admiration. "You're good."

"I'm a Plantagenet. Now, will you do something for me?"

"What?"

"Will you get out of here before Uncle Geoff finds you?"

"But what about you?"

"Oooh!" She almost stamped her foot. "Forget about me! Henry, you've got the most powerful weapon in Europe, and Uncle Geoff wants it so badly he can taste it. It's all he talks about. Can you imagine what he'll do if he gets it? He's already conquered everything north of the Loire. Not having the sword, not controlling it yet, is the only thing that's keeping him from going after all of the West, from Ireland to Germany." She stepped back and studied him. "Where is the sword, anyway?"

"In the case. Gift wrapped."

"Clever." She sighed, made sure the ladies were still ignoring them, and turned back to Henry. "So what was your plan?"

"Uh, plan?"

"For escaping. You have an escape plan, right?"

"I didn't even know where they were keeping you. I think I did a good job just getting in to see you, for starters."

Mattie snorted. "Uncle Richard would have had this castle besieged and demanded me for ransom before you'd even pulled Excalibur from its scabbard."

"Well, why don't you get him to rescue you, then? Oh, wait, I know—because he's three thousand miles away and crazy, just like the rest of your family."

"Watch it, gallows-bait." She smiled.

"You're crazy, too," he said.

"Okay. You know what? Anything that distracts Uncle Geoff is a good thing. Two days from now there's a feast at the pavilion by the jousting field. I'll be there from the beginning, mistress of ceremonies, but Geoff and John will be out hunting and they'll show up at sunset—"

"I'll be there. Wear something escape-y."

Mattie nodded. "My finest fleeing outfit. Now get out of here, before the hens get suspicious." She shoved him toward the door. "And remember, if things don't work out, just…go. The sword is more important." Then she kissed his cheek. "But it's great that you tried." She walked back to the ladies in waiting. "Is there any more rabbit? I could eat a whole covey."

22. FOOD FIGHT

Early the next day, Henry spotted Ralf the Minstrel-slash-Goldsmith wandering the grounds, looking for an audience to annoy. Henry ducked out of sight before the hyphenate could spot him. "That's bad."

Why? He's harmless enough.

"Wait for it." And within hours, as he searched and bartered for supplies, Henry heard the Muttering Knight catch up with him, in the rumors of the marketplace:

"Took care of a band of highwaymen, neat as pin."

"And no swagger to him. That's real class. None of that give-me-your-daughter, kiss-my-horse attitude you get from most knights."

"Well, he *sounds* all right. But where's his *chanson?* You can't be a real hero without a *chanson.*"

A minstrel strung his harp and cleared his throat. *"I sing the Knight Who Mutters, a mere youth to some, with golden heart, and flashing sword..."*

"Oops. Spoke too soon, I guess."

Henry's heart sank. Something told him the Muttering Knight was going to be a real problem. He pushed the problem to the back of his mind and laid out his supplies. Food for the road—check. Flint and tinder—check.

Horse—check. Party clothes—check…sort of. Clothes that would truly fit you in at a party like this were handmade by a troupe of family retainers who spent long, cold winters laboring on your behalf in one of your outlying duchies. Henry's stall-boughts might get him through the line, but there was no way they would make him look impressive. Map of the grounds—well, it was supposed to be on an open field. Either he and Mattie could dash for the horse, or they couldn't.

Step One: Grab Mattie. Step Two: Run. It wasn't much of a plan. But what it lacked in potential it made up for in simplicity.

The next afternoon the bells rang out from the castle chapel, and the nobility gathered for the feast. Geoffrey had commanded that the pavilion be laid out on the great tourney field, and it made a brave sight—acres and acres of red and gold tenting above, but open to the sides for the breeze.

The nobles entered family by family, announced by heralds, dressed in their finest. The herald squinted at Henry's invitation, and looked down at him from his dais.

"The Chevalier de Tourenne is a man of many years, with a large mole on his nose. Have you suddenly discovered the Fountain of Youth, Sir Chevalier?"

"I'm his squire, here to carry his sword so that he be not unduly burdened. If that's a problem, why don't you go clear it with Princess Mathilde? I'm sure she'd like to discuss the philosophy of the issue."

The herald's face took on a haunted expression, and he waved Henry through. Henry sauntered around the pavilion.

What are you doing? Why do you waste time?

"I'm casing the joint—er, scouting the battlefield. Haven't you ever done that?"

Indeed. And what have you noticed?

"The servants' entrance. Or exit, in our case. The location of the musicians, the wine, the food."

He had to admit Geoffrey did things up right. The tenting was pierced to let in light; rows of tables ringed the pavilion, with cold dishes on one side and the wine on the other, so guests had to keep walking to have food and drink together—no solitary drunks at Geoffrey's parties. Well, okay, there was one surly looking knight trying to empty a keg...but that was a far cry from the traditional feast, where dozens would go unconscious before the candles burned out. The musicians were Italian, from their dress, and the music was filled with sweet harmonies. There was even a huge wooden floor set up on the grass for dancing. Yeah, if Geoffrey couldn't make the whole emperor thing work, he could definitely find success as a party planner.

Henry maneuvered through the crowds, looking for Mattie. He was blocked for a moment as a line of cooks brought in the highlights of the feast: boars and venison, hares and swans, pies and preserves, and a collection of *sotleties* molded to look like buildings, fish, trees, anything but what they actually were. Finally he spotted Mattie at the far end of the pavilion, surrounded by guards, receiving guests from a raised throne. He joined the line.

"Yes, that silver wine muller is a wonderful gift. I'm sure Prince Geoffrey and I shall use it night and day. Thank you. Yes, of course I remember you, and your lovely little br...boy. Now, darling, please don't grab my hair like that. That's a good boy. Thank you, see you at the wedding. No, there's nothing like a bunch of figs for a wedding present. They're lovely, and they symbolize, uh, God's love. Take care..." she muttered, "...cheapskate."

The line advanced, bringing Henry to the front. He bowed. "I come from the Chevalier de Tourenne, Your Highness, with a message."

Mattie took Henry's hands in hers. "The Chevalier is our most beloved cousin. What has he to say?"

"He wishes you joy and health and many children, Highness," said Henry.

"Terrific." Mattie smiled. Then she whispered, "Get out of here now. Geoff got suspicious when he heard those songs about the Muttering Knight, and he'll be here any moment."

"Then come with me now. Tell your chaperone you're sick."

"I'll meet you at the oaks by the far corner of the field. Now GO!"

Henry stepped down, and Mattie graciously turned to the next guest in line.

Excellent. A chance to call Geoffrey out.

Henry didn't stop his brisk walk to the exit. "No, a chance to rescue the princess, remember?"

You are my servant. Remember that.

"And you swore to help me save Mattie. Remember *that*." He was just a few yards from the exit now.

Yes, yes, I know.

"Henry!" Alfie and Valdemar, dressed as monks, appeared from nowhere.

Henry's jaw sagged down to his chest. "What are you doing here!?"

"We've found a way out of your troubles." Alfie smiled.

"This is a bad time, Alfie."

Valdemar flanked him. "Trust us."

"I've got to go."

Alfie and Valdemar shared a glance. "We thought you'd say that." Alfie's hand snaked out to grip Henry's right thumb and palm in a joint lock, while Valdemar simply grabbed his left arm hard enough to turn it purple.

"We've been thinking, laddie. You haven't been yourself."

"Ignoring a score."

"Wearing armor."

"Gathering vassals."

"It's not your fault, laddie. You're possessed."

"What!?"

WHAT!?

"But fortunately, we've got just the man to help us all out."

"Be gone, foul spirit!"

Henry blinked hard as stale water splashed into his face and dribbled down his collar.

"I cast thee out by any and all of the foul names thou knowest—Old Evil, Satan, Serpent of Ophir; Crooked Tail, Bad Business, the Whisper in Darkness; Lucifer, Tempter, the—"

What is this idiot doing?

The splasher was a short, round fellow in the tonsure of a parish priest, going about his business with an energy and enthusiasm you had to admire.

"This is Father Gillem, my family's confessor." It was Count Raymond. He wore gorgeous clothes and a ten-*dixaine* smile that reminded Henry of a shark his dad had caught once off Point Nerac. The Count draped his hand around the priest's shoulders and nodded amiably at Henry.

"Laddie, I want you to meet our good friend, Count Raymond of Toulouse," said Alfie. "He collects swords."

"—Apollyon, Belial, Father of Lies—" The holy water was now saturating his tunic.

"Ah, the Muttering Knight."

"Abaddon, Asmodeus, Tricky Dick—"

"That's enough, Gillem."

"But—"

"I'm sure he's thoroughly exorcised by now. Aren't you, boy?" Henry nodded. Raymond gave the priest a gentle shove. "Now, run along. We need to discuss some business."

Nonplussed, Gillem wandered away. Raymond turned back to Henry, Alfie, and Valdemar. "My sister's boy. You understand." He rubbed his hands. "And there you are. Exorcised. With a Great Sword, one of the Nine, that you may now relinquish whenever you desire." He smiled again. "Name your price."

You will not sell me to this creature. You will not give me to him. He is an assassin and a plotter. You will not, under any circumstances—

"I know, I know." Henry shrugged out of Valdemar's grip and looked at Raymond. "Your Lordship, with all due respect, the sword is mine in trust. I may not sell it, not to you, nor to anyone."

Alfie hissed in Henry's ear. "Think, Henry! This is a count! He could make you a noble, give you a castle. And he's family with Mattie. He could stop the wedding. He'd go that far. And the worst that happens is someone else deals with Geoffrey, not you. This is a way out."

"I—"

A blast of trumpets cut him short. A second blast, and the heralds formed two lines at the entrance. Geoffrey and John entered the pavilion. Henry felt his guts dissolve in fear.

At last! Our enemies!

"Oh, great. Our enemies." Henry turned to Raymond. "Tell you what, Your Lordship, let me think about your offer and get back to you." Henry smiled and started to inch away. Raymond's eyes flickered from Henry to Geoffrey. Henry could see Raymond's mind working, and it didn't look good. Time to stall. "Actually, Your Lordship, come with me. Let's walk, and talk, and discuss matters. For instance, why don't *you* make *me* an offer, and we'll start from there?"

"No, I think not." Raymond stepped back from Henry, appraising him. "No, I think your first refusal was sincere, young man, and now you seek to gain time. Well, if I cannot buy the sword, I can at least buy some goodwill." Grabbing Henry by the jerkin, he turned toward Geoffrey and John, still some yards off on the far side of the pavilion. "Geoffrey! It's Uncle Raymond! Look what I have!"

"Yikes!" Henry raised his arms and went limp,

slithering out of his tunic like a snake from its skin. Hitting the ground, he rolled away from Raymond, bounced to his feet, and sprinted for the exit.

Slay him! Strike that impudent wretch down where he stands!

"Or not," said Henry as he dodged random dinner guests. The servants were bringing in a line of pastries. He ducked under one tray, swerved around a second. He was nearing the exit—but he wasn't close enough. From both sides of the pavilion, Geoffrey's men-at-arms came at him, and before he could turn, he was encircled in a ring of mercenaries.

"Draw no weapons! Do not strike at him!" yelled Geoffrey, as the circle parted to let him in.

Now we face him. Traitor, murderer, usurper—

Henry felt his hand go to the sword's grip, and Excalibur rise behind his eyes.

"I am unarmed, Henry," said Geoffrey, his hands by his sides. "So are my men." He turned to the mercenaries. "Drop your weapons." The soldiers stood like rocks, astonished. "DROP THEM!" And then there was the thud of first one, then a dozen swords hitting the wooden floor.

Geoffrey turned back to Henry. "I have no sword, Henry. Neither do my troops. We shall not strike you. If you want to leave this circle, Excalibur must draw first blood. On unarmed men."

Henry felt Excalibur's spirit whirl in confusion. "Excalibur…"

I—Henry—He is clever, that one. He knows the Code of Chivalry, and uses it against us. We cannot strike an unarmed opponent, where there is no threat.

"Of *course* there's a threat! We can't stay like this! He'll—"

Yes, yes. It's a stratagem. You esteem yourself clever—defeat it.

"Simon!" Geoffrey pointed to a soldier. "Get us some chairs. This may take a while." The soldier trotted off and the other troopers closed ranks.

Henry's eyes followed Simon as the soldier walked past

the trays of food, past Alfie and Valdemar—Henry smiled. Sometimes you didn't need swords.

"ALFIE!" he yelled. "PIE!"

The first dish to land on Geoffrey's head was a *sotletie* of venison designed to look like a leaping herring. The pie-crust fins disconnected from the main body of the fish and cascaded down the prince's shoulders in a shower of oat flour. This was followed in quick succession by the castle of Poitou rendered in barley sugar and marzipan, and a large roast hare coated in gold leaf.

The nobles and vassals froze in shock. Slowly, ever so slowly, Geoffrey raised a hand to remove an almond-paste battlement from his eyebrow, then a pie-crust dorsal fin from his shoulder. No one said a word. Geoffrey's composure was remarkable, all things considered. Had the assault centered entirely on him, Henry might still have been in trouble. But at that moment, Valdemar's second volley hit. A roasted peacock with its own feathers reattached clipped a noblewoman and two mercenaries on its way toward Prince Geoffrey. The noblewoman's husband took offense to the knight nearest to him, and grabbed a pikefish in verjuice with which to retaliate.

The disturbance began to widen.

A long-simmering disagreement between the Comte du Val d'Aosta and the Duke of Normandy erupted when the Chevalier Sans Peur et Sans Regret, a vassal of the Comte, took the opportunity to hamstring the Duke with a swordfish in aspic. Six of the guests, allied to the Duke by blood or oaths of fealty, decided to wreak vengeance while the wreaking was good, and used a young hart, boiled in milk with almonds and cherries, to subdue the Comte and all his train.

Two mercenaries rushed to Geoffrey's aid, but by now Mattie had encouraged other courtiers to grab plates. The mercenaries went down, victims of a large platter of baked trout in sauce galyntyne, and Henry raced through the gap. Ducking beneath a volley of preserved fruits, he scuttled toward the exit, only to have it blocked by two knights armed with spits full of chickens. He leaped to one side, allowing the knights to meet in combat with four men-at-arms carrying racks of stuffed piglet in cameline sauce.

Twenty-three pottages filled the air, and the conflict became more or less general. Henry hunched down and sprinted for the servants' entrance on the far side of the pavilion. One of the mercenaries leaped toward him, but was sidelined by a blackbird pie to the left temple. Henry barely avoided a grab by the Duke of Orleans, a champion of the joust, who was then knocked unconscious by Sir Locrahin of Brest, wielding a jar of leeks in vinegar. Sir Locrahin himself was laid low by the Bishop of Besançon, who had turned his roast loin of pork into a weapon most fell. Sir Gaymard of Orgeille, who had slain fifty men on the walls of Damascus, was blinded by the Count of Monte Albano with a bowl of green soup of almonds before Gaymard could dash out Henry's brains with the centerpiece—a single boar, roasted on a spit and decorated in almond paste, spun sugar, and preserved plums with scenes from the *Gospel of Mark*.

Ducking the boar, Henry dived on his belly into a spreading pool of cinnamon sauce and slid out of the pavilion. There was his horse. Mattie was standing next to it. It was going to work! They were going to leave! They could be up and—

LOOK OUT!

The sky exploded with stars, and everything went black.

183

23. FUN WITH MASTER WIGLAF

I want a new head, thought Henry as he opened his eyes. *This one hurts too much.*

"Ah, you're awake," said Wiglaf. "Help me with this coil."

The monk looked no worse for his time in the Bordeaux sewers. Henry tried to correct that by grabbing Wiglaf's neck and twisting as hard as possible. It was a mistake. The room spun, and Henry almost threw up.

Wiglaf bent over him, solicitous, with a thin strip of copper wound over and over around his shoulder. Underneath the nausea, Henry was impressed—that much copper was a ransom in farthings, if it were anywhere near as pure as it looked.

"Hmmf. Drink this." Wiglaf held out a bottle. When Henry turned his head away, Wiglaf waggled it. "It's perry. Good for the warm humors." The monk drank from the bottle himself and offered it again. Henry drank, and the taste of pears and wine filled his mouth. After a few swallows, he felt a little better and sat up.

The room was well lit, and big enough for cabinets filled with scrolls and bottles, three or four tables, and at least half a dozen unguessable devices; they ranged from a wooden box draped with silk to an iron column topped by an etched bronze disc. The room also had bars on the windows, and a big, thick door—one that opened from the outside.

"Where—"

"The castle's old east tower. Here, take this." Wiglaf handed him a black stone that was unexpectedly smooth and heavy, and then turned to one of the devices.

Henry stood up, and a couple of knives flew from a nearby table straight at him. He ducked in panic; they hit the stone and then stuck there as if they were glued.

"Oh, and don't get it near the iron knives."

Henry shakily handed the lodestone back to Wiglaf, who plucked away the knives and fitted the rock into what looked like a wagon wheel attached to a chain.

"Where's Excalibur?"

"Ahh! This way." Wiglaf led Henry to a booth covered in black cloth. "I just assembled this from a diagram in Alhazen. Look inside."

Henry's first instinct was to shove Wiglaf inside ahead of him, but the scrawny monk seemed so focused on his gadget and so completely oblivious to danger that Henry just walked in.

"Watch the wall on your right!" yelled Wiglaf.

Henry turned. There was the sound of glass sliding on metal, and Henry flinched. An image had appeared on the black wall—a circular, upside-down image of the courtyard of the castle, thirty feet below.

"Can you see it?"

"Uh…it's upside-down," Henry said.

"Oh, right! Sorry about that. There's a lens I have to position…" Once again, the sound of something sliding into place, and now the image was right side up, and perfect to the last detail. Henry smothered a gasp. This wasn't just an image; he could see people walking, and trees bending in the wind. It was like looking into a mirror, but a mirror more clear and perfect than any he'd ever seen.

"Better?"

"Uh…yeah. But I don't see Excalibur."

"Right, it's outside the walls. Hang on, I'll change focus."

Henry grabbed at the wall as the objects in the circle swam, blurred, and slid away to the right. In a moment, the circle revealed the jousting grounds outside the castle. Then the river. Then the pavilion from the wedding feast. Then finally, sticking up from a rock outcrop, there was Excalibur, its hilt gleaming in the sun.

"Damn." The sword was surrounded by guards, of course.

The flap folded up and Wiglaf glanced inside. He held a writing tablet. "Tell me, can you still feel the presence of the sword, even now that it's stuck in the stone?" He waited for an answer, stylus poised.

"I—" Henry thought for a moment, probing his skull like a tongue in an empty tooth socket. Was there a little tug toward the east and the tourney field? A sense of Excalibur out there, waiting for him? "I—" Henry looked away from the image, at Wiglaf's pale, eager face. "Who are you, anyway?"

"'Subject initially unresponsive…'" Wiglaf jotted in his tabula.

Henry pressed a little harder. "You didn't think I believed you were actually a Brother of the Sword, did you? You're not exactly Brotherhood material."

"No need to get nasty."

"You sold me out to Geoffrey!"

"Well, he was about to kill me."

"So who are you? How do you know about the sword?"

Wiglaf put down the writing tablet. "All right, help me with the *probatos automata*, and I'll tell you." He gave Henry the copper coil and walked back to the wheel and lodestone.

"Take the *cupros* and wind it around the wheel, like so."

Henry started winding the copper. After a moment, he turned to Wiglaf. "Still waiting."

"All right. I was just gathering my thoughts." Wiglaf cleared his throat. "Before the Great Flood, there was an island in the West, beyond the Pillars of Hercules. Plato mentions—"

"Who?"

"The teacher of Aristotle. Plato mentions it in his *Timaeus* and *Critias*—"

"His what and his what?"

"Look, if you keep interrupting—"

"All right, all right."

"Anyway, this island, which I have named 'Hesperos,' was bigger than All-Britain, and its lords had more skill and cunning than Solomon and Archimedes put together. They founded colonies throughout Africa and Europa, even as far as Lydia and Phrygia. Then God destroyed it in the Great Flood. Not so much copper on the right."

Henry adjusted the copper strips, and Wiglaf continued. "I'd learned of Hesperos when I was writing my *Treatise on Knightly Prowess*. For—"

"Wait! *You're* Gervasius Florentium?"

Wiglaf, AKA Gervasius, beamed. "You read my book?"

"Yeah. Great stuff." Henry held back another barf. He had conned the greatest prince in Europe on the say-so of a lunatic.

"Ah, the *Treatise*. It's a minor work now, but when I rewrite it in Latin, it will have some real *authoritas*." The monk tied down a few of the copper strips and gave the lodestone a shove. It spun freely on the axle. "It was my first opus. But as I worked on it, time and again I would hear tales of a land in the West, the source of the Nine Swords and of all magic. Home to Prester John. Refuge of the Kings of Babel when they fled there after the fall of their Tower, and took with them a cutting from the Tree of Knowledge. Avalon. The Hesperides. Mag Mell. Elysium. The Fortunate Isles, Annwn, Tir na n'Og—"

"Wait. I *have* heard this tale. It's called Atlantis."

"'Hesperos' is more technically accurate." Gervasius' eyes were beginning to glow with enthusiasm. He'd lost his stammer, and Henry could see crazed certainty practically seeping up through the soles of the man's feet into his brain.

Oh, no, he thought. *Another one.*

Gervasius raised his hand like a university lecturer. "But—and this is a big but—Hesperos was lost beneath the waves millennia ago. So how, I asked myself, could these legends persist, let alone be so specific and agree over a distance as great as that between London and Athens? How?"

Gervasius leaned forward and grabbed Henry by the tunic. "I'll tell you how! Because there are still Hesperans in Europa, Henry, trying to regain their lost dominion!" He raised his arms triumphantly. "THEY are the Brotherhood of the Sword! THEY built the Chapels Perilous in Glastonbury and Bordeaux and Constantinople! THEY got me kicked out of St. Gregory's Young Choirboys Association of Marseilles! And they are even now plotting to TAKE OVER THE WORLD!"

"What, from all the way out there in Glastonbury? With all the snow, and the ice in the chamber pots?"

"Yes! With weapons like Excalibur, they could do it easily!"

"Then why haven't they?"

"Um…"

"And if I were going to take over the world, I'd do it from someplace warmer. Rome sounds good."

Gervasius hesitated. "Yes…Wiglaf never actually mentioned world conquest per se…"

"Wiglaf?"

"The uh, real Wiglaf. I was his secretary for a year, before he left for Constantinople."

"And he told you all their secrets, huh?"

Gervasius coughed and looked embarrassed. "Uh, no. Not as such. There was more, uh, laughing at me, than actual sharing of secrets. But I did see some of his *teknematoi*. That was how I knew, you see. I found a room full of Hesperan devices that he had preserved—a mechanical bird that flew; an unrusting blade that was springy as sinew, but sharp as death; and a bronze head that spoke."

Henry leaned forward, interested despite himself. "The head spoke to you? What did it say?"

Gervasius now looked even more embarrassed, if possible. "It said 'Stop! Thief!'"

Henry burst out laughing. Gervasius smiled and then returned to work—clearing a path between the lodestone machine and a badly stuffed dead sheep that had been placed near the door.

"I tried to build a head of my own, but no matter how many gears I put in, it never worked." Gervasius examined the sheep, and nudged it a few inches to the left. "Anyway, Lord Raymond believes in my work, so the last few weeks have actually been very satisfying. I think you'd enjoy working here, too."

"Oh." *So that's it,* he thought. *Pump me for information, then use it to take control of Excalibur.* "Well, uh, Gervasius—"

"Call me Gerry."

"—Gerry…say, what is this?" He pointed to the lodestone machine, now fully wound about with copper.

"That is my Automatic Shepherd," said Gervasius with pride. "Have you ever rubbed wool onto amber, and then noted that the amber attracted bits of parchment?"

"Uh, I've been busy."

"According to the *Aethiopica* of Marcellus, the Hesperans were able to generate more of this force of attraction by means of a lodestone device like this one. Now, as you can see, I've placed a stuffed sheep here by the door. And of course, parchment is merely dried, cured sheep's skin. If my calculations are correct, once we fire this baby up, it should attract the sheep's skin, and the sheep should fly across the room to the device. Imagine it. Sheep filling the sky! Shepherds' crooks, obsolete! Come on, help me spin the axle."

Dubiously, Henry joined Gervasius by the wagon wheel, and together they began to spin the lodestone, which was surprisingly resistant. After a few minutes, Henry felt heat coming from the copper strips.

"Uh, Gerry—"

"Keep spinning!"

The heat grew. A curl of smoke rose from the device's frame.

"Gerry—"

"Faster!"

The hairs were standing up on the back of Henry's neck. Tiny sparks crept through his tunic. "GERRY!"

A flash of light too bright to look at arced away from the machine. A thunderclap blew Henry to the floor.

When he was able to sit up again, his eyes full of green and purple splotches, the device was gone. Gervasius was stretched out on the floor a dozen feet away, and the door had been blown off its hinges.

Henry got to his feet. He checked Gervasius—the monk was dazed, but alive—and then picked his way past puddles of molten copper and iron, to where the door had been. The stuffed sheep had been blown to bits, and nothing was left but a few scraps of wool. Mixed with the stuffing were the remains of a clay jar Gervasius had apparently left next to the sheep. Henry picked up one of the shards; it read *aqua fortis*—the acid that the royal coiners used to dissolve base metals like iron and lead.

So that's what happens when lightning hits it, thought Henry as he sidled out the door.

The good news was that the workroom hadn't been at a dead end; the corridor ran off in both directions. The bad news was that Henry could already hear footsteps coming up from the stairway to his right. He ran left.

The corridor took a sharp right to another door. Henry pulled it open, and found himself in what must have been Gervasius' storeroom. It was filled with furniture under cloths, more clay jars, and bits of ironwork and brass tubing. The one thing Henry didn't see was a staircase. But there was a door, and the door led into a garderobe.

Oh, I hate this. I really do. The garderobe looked just like the ones he'd used in the Chapel or in the half dozen donjons he'd seen in his travels—just a stone shelf with a wooden bench on top. The bench had holes; you sat on them and did your business. Below the hole was a shaft— usually it led to a dungheap that was mucked out by peasants; sometimes it led straight to the river. The only real question was—were the holes under the bench too narrow for a skinny fugitive?

Henry heaved, and the bench came loose. Underneath were three holes. And they were wide enough. Henry sighed, took off his shoes and tunic and tossed them down the shaft. He'd have to crabwalk down the shaft by pressing his feet to one side and his shoulders to the other; clothes would slip and slide around him. Sucking in his gut, he wiggled into the hole, and pulled the wooden bench back above him.

Twenty feet down a toilet shaft wouldn't be so bad. And if he slipped, at least there would be something at the bottom to cushion his fall.

24. SAME SWORD, NEW STONE

Excalibur jutted up from the rock in the center of a pavilion packed with people, lit by torches and surrounded by guards.

Dressed in a ragged smock and peasant *sabots*, Henry wormed his way through the mob. He needed the outfit for more than a disguise—after his trip through the toilet shaft and out of the (unguarded, thank St. Dismas!) cesspit, Henry's original clothes were good for nothing, and it had taken an hour bathing upriver and a waterskin full of soap before he'd even started to feel clean again.

He was trying to get a better view of Excalibur, but the crowd was enormous. It was democratic, too—everybody was there, from barons to serfs.

"It just appeared—"

"The *Matter of Britain*—"

"—rightwise born king of—"

"—miracle—"

"—Excalibur stone chips! Gitcher Excalibur stone chips! Pieces of the rock Excalibur touched! Only ten *dixaines* a bag!"

Before Henry could get any closer, a squad of soldiers in Plantagenet livery parted the crowd and entered the pavilion. In less than five minutes, they had erected a fine silk tent over the sword, hiding it from view.

The crowd shouted and booed. The guards took two steps forward, hands on their swords, quieting the crowd and clearing a space in front of the tent. Then the tent flaps parted and Geoffrey emerged. Henry oozed his way back into the crowd.

"People of Toulouse!" said Geoffrey. "A miracle has come among us, a sword of kings! Already many knights, brave and true, have tried and failed to draw this sword from the living rock. So that all worthy men of valor may have their chance, I have arranged a special joust!"

The crowd cheered. *Nothing like a free show to keep folks happy,* thought Henry.

"He who wins in the lists may try to draw the sword. He who fails must abandon hope. We begin two days hence, on the feast of my patron, St. Pancratius Martyr, at the hour of Terce. To the winner, the sword!"

Geoffrey extended his arms, and the crowd roared. With that, he walked inside the tent. Satisfied, the crowd dispersed. Henry snuck behind a tree, impressed despite himself. Geoffrey hadn't said anything especially smart or inspiring. But by the end of his tiny speech, he had the crowd eating out of his hand and ready to abandon the greatest attraction in Toulouse just so they could return again in forty-eight hours, on nothing more than his say-so. Maybe Geoffrey did deserve Excalibur...No. Henry shook himself. There was a difference between a *born* leader and a *good* leader. And for all his skill and talent, no one could put the words "Geoffrey" and "good" in the same sentence.

Henry hunkered down behind a tree and waited for the crowd to thin out. After a few minutes, he heard thudding in the brush, and Percy was sitting next to him.

"My Lord, it was all my fault, I—"

"Just the facts, Perce."

Percy sighed. "Lord Raymond had men stationed

outside the feasting tent. When you fled, they followed, and before I could do anything, you were down. Lord Raymond grabbed your sword and ran, but before he could go more than three horse-lengths, he screamed in agony, fell, and the sword flew out of his hands. It was most miraculous, My Lord. It flew through the air and buried itself point first in the living rock."

"It's a magic sword, Perce."

"Well, *duh*."

Henry raised his eyebrows. Sarcasm? From Percy? Was he becoming…human?

"Your comrades-in-arms filled me in. Is it truly Excalibur?"

"Yeah."

"And did you truly take it from the stone?"

"Did I *take* it…yeah, I guess I did."

"And this game with the shells and the pea that I played with Aelfred—are my chances of winning truly one in three?"

"Er…no. Not really."

"I see." Percy was silent, staring out at the crowd.

Henry shifted uncomfortably. "But the magic sword means that I'm no knight. If it hadn't been Excalibur, I'd have been the one on my knees on the bridge when we met. If you want to leave, I understand."

"You're right, you're no knight." Percy picked up a blade of grass and chewed it for a moment. "You're a king."

"Are you cra—"

"You bear Excalibur. I think I'll stick with you for now. My Lord." Percy stood. "Let me know if you need anything."

Henry shut his mouth and shook his head. Percy waved and strolled off.

As night fell, Henry was still waiting for the guards to break their concentration. When he heard the faint rattle of dice, he stood up.

The outside torches were burning low, and the two guards were crouched over their game. Henry left the shelter of the tree and looped wide around the pavilion, passing between the tents of the various knights and knightly service providers—smiths, brewers, vintners, peddlers of armor wax and helm polish—until he was facing the rear of the pavilion from across an empty swathe of grass. When one of the nearby torches guttered out, he walked across to the tent.

Henry could hear voices inside. Even better, the wind had risen, and he could see light from inside the tent—it would be hard for Geoffrey and whoever else was there to see or hear him. He crouched down, gently lifted the bottom of the tent panel, and peered in.

There they were: Excalibur, Geoffrey, and John, a few hench-knights, and good old Brissac. Geoffrey was pacing, and he wasn't happy.

"Remind me, Edmond." Geoffrey stopped in front of Excalibur and drummed his fingers along the hilt. *Don't you touch her!* Henry wanted to scream. He bit his lip instead.

"When the boy came out with the sword, did he tell you where he'd found it?"

Brissac looked miserable. "No, My Lord."

"Did he tell you how he'd retrieved it?"

"No, My Lord."

And now Geoffrey's hand was on Brissac's throat, lifting Brissac from his chair. "Did you think to ask him before you tried to gut him like a fish?"

"NO, LORD! MERCY—"

Geoffrey released him, and Brissac slumped back down. Outside, Henry shuddered. Brissac weighed at least twelve stone, but Geoffrey had lifted him one-handed.

John smirked. "You could try drawing the sword now, dear brother. No one here but us chickens."

"I've already tried, Johnny. Did you expect me to deny it?" Geoffrey smiled. "Of course, if you want your turn, I won't stop you."

John pouted. Geoffrey put his hand on John's shoulder. "Don't worry, Johnny. The right to rule isn't decided by some magic trick. It's determined by blood, brains, and courage."

Well, that cuts John out, thought Henry. *Richard too, probably. I wonder if John even realizes what his brother is saying.*

"My Lord," choked Brissac, rubbing his neck. "I did return afterward. I went down into the cave myself, once I knew the monks no longer maintained a watch."

Geoffrey turned back. "So my faith in you was not utterly misplaced. Continue."

"I saw what we expected to see from the *Book of Four Branches* and the *Scroll of the West*. The armies of the dead, the lake under the hill, the island in the middle."

The Book of Four Branches? The Scroll of the West? Brissac hadn't mentioned any of that to Henry. Nice guy.

"The sword would have been buried at the peak of the hill in the lake. What did you see?"

"At the peak, nothing, My Lord, save for a shallow hole, perhaps a yard wide. But at the base of the hill, by the water, we found these." Brissac dug into his pouch and pulled out a handful of chips and pebbles—remnants of Excalibur's original stone, Henry realized.

Geoffrey examined the chips—held them up to the light, smelled them, tasted one. "Marble. Some of these have flat surfaces…Polished? Carved? Were there many?"

"Aye, My Lord. And more, larger pieces, in the water of the lake."

Geoffrey smiled. "Hah! The sword was in the stone. The stone was in the hollow. Our Henry levered the stone out of its hole and sent it crashing down the hill to shatter on the bedrock of the floor. Well done, that boy." Geoffrey nodded to himself. "Pity we have to kill him. We could use some brains on the team."

Ridiculously, Henry felt pleased by the compliment.

"Why the tourney, brother? It will only provoke the people. If neither of us can draw the sword—"

"The word's spread, Johnny. I've already had twenty different knights come to me, some of them powerful men, demanding a chance to try their luck. You saw the Count try for it—"

"Uncle Raymond!?"

"The man's sixty-two with piles, but he still thinks he has a chance." Geoffrey poured some wine and drank moodily. "And the Archbishop of Paris was here, nagging—which means that Philip already knows."

"Uncle Raymond is our vassal. The sword was found on his land. That makes it ours."

"Didn't you learn anything from Dad, Johnny? It's ours if we can keep it. The crows are circling. If Raymond switches sides and joins Philip, and the Count of Poitou and the Pope all band together, I'll—*we'll* have nothing."

Geoffrey's eyes turned inward for a moment, contemplating something only he could see. Then he stood. "We can't hide this. But we can delay, until we can summon sappers and engineers to remove the sword for us. Until then, we have this tourney. The winners get to try their luck. All we have to do is make sure that the winners of the tourney are not the ones who could possibly succeed at drawing the sword. You remember Lammastide, four, five years ago, when you beat Richard in the joust?"

John grinned. "He was furious. Amazing what the right herbs can do to a horse, and in a day, the steed is good as new."

Brissac gasped. "You would taint a knightly charger? But—"

Geoffrey turned on him. "This isn't a game, Edmond. This is for an empire. Grow up, or I'll find someone to serve me better." Brissac shut his mouth with a snap.

"So. The last question is…where's our young Henry?" Geoffrey strolled around the tent, hands behind his back, thinking.

John shrugged. "Maybe he's gone. Maybe he just

decided the danger was too much for him, and he wanted to be rid of it. Especially after you locked him up with that lunatic Gervasius."

Geoffrey stood still for a moment. "I'd like to believe that. It's possible—he's a peasant, after all." He came to a decision. "No. It's too easy. Keep the guards looking for him. He's still here, and I want him."

John nodded. "Dead or alive."

"No, you idiot." Geoffrey recovered his temper almost immediately. "Johnny, we want him alive. There are too many questions about that sword, and we need answers. Right?"

John looked down at the ground. "Right."

"All right, then." Geoffrey stretched. "I will organize the tourney. Johnny, you stay here with my men and guard the sword. You have the most important job, you know that."

"I know," Johnny mumbled.

"And Edmond—you'll find our little friend."

The meeting broke up soon after. More soldiers crowded into the tent and surrounded the sword. Henry drifted back into the trees before he was spotted, to ponder what he'd heard. Geoffrey was clever, no question. By now, word of the sword had probably spread up and down the river. In less than a week, it would have gone north and south to Paris and Bordeaux. If Geoffrey simply tried to draw the sword in public, and failed, it would cripple his campaign for empire. But if he sat back and let everyone else compete, and fail, and then secretly had stonemasons come and loosen the sword, so he could draw it…

Everyone would have to acknowledge Geoffrey as king, and even his former rivals among the jousting knights would be forced to admit that he had treated them fairly and given them their chance.

There were too many guards around the sword now. Henry knew he had no chance to just steal it back.

Which meant he'd have to enter the tourney.

* * * *

Percy frowned. "I'll do my best, My...I mean, Henry. But just to survive the joust takes years of training."

"We have a day. Unless you think between us we can cut down the two dozen guards they have surrounding the sword."

They were standing in the practice area next to the jousting field where, despite the bright sun and the good wine, the day was looking darker and darker. Geoffrey's men had put up the field practically overnight. It was some hundred yards long. The royal pavilion was at the midway point. Next to the pavilion was the tent that held Excalibur.

"How will we reclaim the sword, My—Henry?"

"There is one possibility." Henry hesitated, afraid that Percy would lose his cool. "And when I tell you this, keep your voice down. Geoffrey and John are going to cheat."

"Big surprise."

"Really?"

"Please. The Plantagenets have been cheating on the tourney circuit for years. No one ever says anything, of course," he added bitterly. "They're the Plantagenets! Oooohhh! Scary!" He raised his hands and rolled his eyes.

Henry smiled. Sir Percy was becoming a human being, after all. "They talked about feeding herbs to the other horses to slow them down."

Percy nodded. "Valerian or chamomile. The knight on a sluggish horse is at the disadvantage."

"Winning knights will have a chance to draw Excalibur—"

"So they will drug the horses of those they think might have a chance."

"Right. Good thinking. So, what about you, Percy? What's your standing?"

Percy looked shamefaced. "Not good. I've yet to win a joust, or even make my name as a warrior. That's why I was on that bridge when we met. I had to build my reputation."

"Does Geoffrey know?"

Percy shrugged. "The world of knights and tourneys isn't big. If he doesn't know himself, his master of heralds does."

"So he'd leave your horse alone, and go after your opponent, especially if it were someone big, some major competitor he thinks might have a chance to draw Excalibur from the rock." Henry stood. "Come on. Let's figure out how to take advantage of this."

An hour later, they began to train. "This is a coronal. Hold it." Percy tossed Henry a lance with a three-pronged tip. Henry caught it—it was like catching a tent pole. He staggered for a moment, and then used the lance to steady himself just in time.

"This is the jousting helm." A helmet the size of a wine keg was next. Henry fitted it onto his head, and was instantly plunged into darkness.

"Now just stand like that for a moment, let me see if I can snug any of my armor onto you." Henry felt a heavy weight draped over his neck, then more on his chest and back. Yet more weight on his legs. His arms. His shoulders.

With a *thump*, he toppled over.

"Yes, I can see we're going to have some challenges here," said Percy. "Strap it all on, and mount up on Pegasus." Like a turtle on its back, Henry struggled to sit up and get to his feet.

"Maybe we should try some riding drills first," said Percy.

Henry detached the helmet, unbuckled the breastplate, and stood. They were in a meadow a few hundred yards upriver of the tourney site, and higher up the valley slope. Henry turned to stare at the guards around Excalibur's tent.

"Perce...those aren't pikemen, guarding the sword?"

Percy squinted. "No, M—Henry. Men at arms, with swords."

Pikemen were effective against cavalry charges, against men on horseback. But men with swords...

Henry turned to Percy. "How's your horse at jumping?"

25. KNIGHTS IN WHITE SATIN

"Tourney day. It makes your heart sing. The bright banners, the brave knights with favors from their ladies. Not that I'll be jousting in this one, of course." Percy tried to keep up a brave front. Henry patted his shoulder.

"There will be others. I promise. And remember, keep Alfie and Valdemar occupied. I don't want them doing anything stupid." Henry glanced at the two of them, standing shamefaced by the corral. "Anything *else* stupid." He nudged Pegasus with his knees, and the charger obediently trotted forward.

It had taken a lot of work, for a plot that had so little chance of success. Percy had modified his armor, dropping secondary bits and pieces to make it light enough for Henry to wear without seeming odd to the spectators. To the casual eye, it would still look like Percy astride the horse—the Dulwich insignia, a big blue badger on a silver field, gleamed proudly in the sun. Percy had also deliberately committed the armorer's cardinal sin: He had secured all the remaining pieces of armor with a single harness strap. Then they had practiced the maneuvers Henry would need to carry out the plan. Now all Henry had to do was convince Geoffrey's master of heralds to match "Sir Percival of Dulwich" against Sir Marlay of Groussey, the best jouster in Normandy.

Pegasus, Percy's stallion, was feisty and hard to control. He knew that he was carrying Henry, not Percy, and he could feel the difference in weight. Henry didn't care. Pegasus didn't have to carry him into battle. He had to do three things right, and if he did, they'd be home free. If not, a long interrogation, followed by a short execution...

The field was packed. Favored guests, in satin and jewels, lounged in the royal box, next to Geoffrey and John...and Mattie. Henry swore to himself. If he succeeded, there would be no way for him to get to her. He took a deep breath. One thing at a time.

He trotted over to the Master of Heralds and, with a bit of effort, raised his lance for attention. "Sir Percy of Dulwich," he shouted past his closed visor, "to contend with Sir Marlay of Groussey on the field of honor."

The Master Herald, a tall, skinny specimen with a face like a haddock, laughed outright. "Oh, really? You think you get to pick and choose whom you fight? You'll take what I say, Sir Knight, and like it." The herald glanced down at his writing tablet. "Besides, Sir Marlay is already spoken for."

Henry's heart started to pound. The whole plan depended on confronting a knight who was guaranteed to be riding a drugged horse. Sir Marlay was the only one who was truly a sure thing. If he was already spoken for—

"AYE! BY ME!" A new knight, tall and perfectly at ease in his armor, stalked up to the herald's podium and leaned in. "Who are you, varlet, to speak in such wise to a brother knight?"

The herald didn't even bother to grin nastily. "I'm the master of heralds and Prince Geoffrey's confessor. That's who."

The new knight took off his helmet, revealing a ridiculously handsome face only a few years older than Henry. The knight's red hair blazed in the sun. When he spoke, his French was tinged with a German accent. "And I am Frederick of Swabia, the Prince's favored guest. I will give my place to this, my honored comrade."

The herald shrugged. "No skin off my *nez*."

The knight turned to Henry and smiled. Henry stammered. "Thanks. I don't know what to—"

Frederick laughed. "No worries. I've fought Sir Marlay before, I'll fight him again. You tyros deserve a chance." He leaned a little closer. "And anyway, don't let Geoffrey's minions get you down. Good luck." Then he patted Pegasus on the neck and vanished into the crowd.

Henry trotted back to his spot in the line. Peasants and townsfolk packed the wooden rails. Peddlers passed through the crowd, selling wine and dried fruit. There was a trumpet call, and the next two jousters entered the ring.

The herald stepped forward. "Behold, Sir Calix of Griyand. Device, three daisies *or* on a field *azure*. Behold, Sir Stefan of Sophia. Device, a shield *ermine* with two horizontal bars, *azure* and *gules*, with three roses *gules* in chief and a lion *or* in a canton *gules*."

Henry was always amazed at the number of jousting enthusiasts—peasants who'd never even be allowed to touch a lance, let alone own one—who could tell you every twist, motto, lozenge, shield, mythical beast, and bar sinister of the heraldry of the knights in each competition. For him, it was just "a shield *blah* with a device *blah* and a *blah* of *blah* and *blahdi-blahdi-blah-blah-blah*."

The knights trotted onto the field, one at either end. A wooden railing ran down the length of the field, and they took up positions, one on each side. The trumpets sounded again, and the crowd fell silent. A third trumpet call, and the knights lowered their lances and charged on either side of the railing, with their lances held to the left, across their bodies, pointed at each other.

They began slowly, but by the time the knights had covered half the distance, they were moving like lightning, and you could feel the hoof beats in your chest, they were so powerful. Henry kept his eyes focused on Stefan, the popular favorite.

And yes...Stefan's horse was beginning to falter, just a little, barely a trace, invisible unless you were looking for it. His stance on the horse shifted, and he spurred it on. But it was no use. Sir Calix's lance hit with the force of a...well, of a knight's lance at the charge, and Sir Stefan went flying.

Percy, hooded and robed so that no one would see him off his horse, nudged Henry. "See? Sir Calix drinks more beer than any twelve monks I know. They practically have to pour him into his armor. But his horse traveled almost twice as far as that of Sir Stefan. The fix is in, My Lord."

Henry nodded and turned back to the field. Sir Calix had gotten off his horse and stalked over to Sir Stefan, with his mace raised. Stefan raised one hand in surrender. Calix turned away and hiked toward Excalibur's pavilion.

Geoffrey had outdone himself on staging and crowd control. There were no onlookers between the field and the sword, so the view of Sir Calix and Excalibur was absolutely clear. Everyone at the joust had a perfect, uninterrupted view of Sir Calix bending down and grasping Excalibur. Of Sir Calix heaving, and grunting with effort. Of Sir Calix heaving again. And then, of Sir Calix practically giving himself a rupture with his third try, and finally, of Sir Calix losing his lunch. His final, muffled "Ooof" echoed across the riverbank, along with the rattle of his armored body hitting the ground. A trio of monks carried him off, still groaning.

The herald turned from Excalibur to face the crowd. "Calix of Griyand has failed to draw the sword from the stone. Bring on the next riders."

This time it was two nobodies from Gascony. Percy had them already sussed as no-hopers, and their performance bore that out when both knights lost control of their steeds and slid from the saddles. They sprang up and whaled with their maces at each other, at their horses, and at nearby fence-posts until the heralds separated them. Clearly, Geoffrey hadn't bothered to waste any valerian or chamomile root on these two.

There was one more joust before Henry was up. The herald stepped forward. "Sir Mercadier de Bainac, against Sir Charles of Brest." Percy gripped Henry's shoulder hard.

"This Mercadier, he's good. As good as Sir Marlay. He was Richard's man before Richard left on Crusade, but some say he's even better than Richard. The best, maybe. I tried to get you a spot against him, but it was taken. Keep your eyes open."

The herald made the announcement, and the two knights rode into the lists. After months living with Excalibur, Henry had enough experience to see that Percy was right—you could see Mercadier's skill in the way he rode, relaxed but controlled, his motions smooth and fluid even under the weight of his armor.

The trumpets sounded. The knights lowered their lances. Their horses moved from a canter, to a gallop, to a charge. Once again, Henry could see the sleepiness, the hesitation in Mercadier's steed—clearly the Plantagenets had agreed with Percy's opinion of who was the better knight.

The knights met, their lances crashing together. Percy and Henry gasped in shock—with his horse almost falling asleep underneath him, Mercadier had stayed mounted.

The knights wheeled and circled for fresh lances. Once again the trumpets, and the charge. Once again, two shattered lances, and Mercadier still astride his horse.

And now the third charge. His horse practically comatose now, Mercadier hunkered down, waiting for the charge. When it came, he caught his enemy's lance on his shield, breaking it, and swept his opponent off the horse with his own lance. Mercadier dismounted, drawing his mace. His opponent drew his as well. In three passes, the other knight was down on the ground, bloody and unconscious. Mercadier turned to the crowd, and raised his hand in victory. The crowd roared, and Mercadier started walking toward Excalibur.

Percy was right—Mercadier was *good*. Could he actually draw Excalibur from the stone? Henry swallowed, his mouth suddenly dry as flax. He glanced at the royal box. Geoffrey looked about as unhappy as Henry felt...Mercadier was bad for both of them.

Henry looked around. The way to Excalibur was clear. Mercadier was the only man on the path. Henry swallowed again. He had planned to carry out the "operation" during the joust, but this looked like the best chance he'd get before Mercadier started tugging on Excalibur.

And now Mercadier was two steps from the stone. He paused for a moment, removing his gauntlets for a better grip.

Now or never.

"HEE-YAH!" Henry spurred on Pegasus, pointing the horse toward Excalibur. At the same time, he tugged on the leather strap binding Percy's armor. The bits and pieces fell off with a clatter, leaving Pegasus with nothing on his back but a youth, a bridle and a saddle—less than half of what the stallion could carry in battle.

Pegasus leaped into action, charging forward, while Henry waved his arms and flailed the reins to get people out of the way. "MOVE IT MOVE IT MOVE IT MOVE IT MOVE IT!"

Onlookers scattered right and left as Pegasus charged uphill toward the magic sword. The guests in the royal box were on their feet now, John stunned, Mattie yelling, Geoffrey furiously pressing through the crowd to get toward Henry.

"Run! Run!"

"He's mad, I tell you! Flee!"

"WAIT YOUR TURN, YOU POXY SARACEN!" This last from another knight who was running after him with a sword.

A dagger flew past his head, and Henry ducked. A gift

courtesy of Geoffrey, who was trying to cut him off from the Excalibur pavilion.

And now Mercadier, ignoring the commotion, was kneeling before the sword, crossing himself in prayer.

Twenty yards. Ten yards. Three yards. ONE—

Henry leaned low out of the saddle, hanging on with one hand, and grabbed for Excalibur. And caught it.

Hello, Henry. What kept you?

Events slowed. Color drained out of the world, leaving only the important things—enemies, weapons, armor— bright and vivid. Henry felt the ghost of the sword enter him again, even as the tug of drawing Excalibur from the stone pulled him off Pegasus and sent him tumbling to the ground.

He and Excalibur were up in a moment. Mercadier stood before him, mouth open, hands empty.

Not a threat, thought Henry and Excalibur, and stalked past Mercadier.

The crowds were running every which way, but there was still some ten yards of open space around the stone. Pegasus stood still, waiting for a rider. Henry wheeled around, searching for—

Geoffrey.

Alone in Excalibur's colorless world, Geoffrey glowed with menace, a long knife in each hand as he sprinted toward Henry.

Henry leaped on Pegasus. "How do I make him rear up?"

Pull back on the reins and give a light kick with the heels. Grip hard with your knees, or you'll fall off.

Pegasus danced, his front hooves flailing. Henry raised Excalibur high. "BEHOLD EXCALIBUR, SWORD OF KINGS!" they yelled together. "A BOY HAS DRAWN IT, A COMMONER AND PEASANT, AS WAS ARTHUR HIMSELF! AS YOU SEEK A KING, STOP THAT MAN!"

Henry pointed Excalibur straight at Geoffrey. The

crowd stopped, and turned, and stared at the prince with an assassin's blade in each hand.

Henry nudged Pegasus. They galloped forward, past Geoffrey, toward the royal pavilion. There was John, standing in their way, his giant claymore in one hand and a grin on his face. John raised his blade—

And Henry leaned down and shattered it with Excalibur, barely breaking stride.

There was Mattie. Henry galloped toward her. She raised her arms, and he grabbed her, lifting her onto the back of Pegasus' saddle. She grabbed him around the chest, and they were away, past the pavilion, past the castle, deep into the woods, on their way to Narbonne.

26. YOU'VE GOT TO LET ME KNOW

"Grandmére! Grandmére!"

"Venez ici, chére!"

Mattie ran into Queen Eleanor's arms, murmuring little Provençal endearments. It was pretty heartwarming, Henry had to admit, even with the Provençal *au*s and *eu*s. Queen Eleanor's men-at-arms were sniffling and wiping their eyes. Otho, who was at least six feet tall and looked like he could crush brick, was blowing into a handkerchief, and now Clovis and Merulis, the two troopers who'd practically carried him one-handed when taking him to see Eleanor the first time, were weeping like fountains and clinging to each other for support.

And now to Constantinople.

"Huh?"

That shall be our reward from the Queen. Safe and speedy passage to Constantinople, on a ship of Her Majesty's choosing.

"Sure of that, are you?"

When gratitude and politics meet, expect rapid results. The last thing any monarch wants at court is a young man with the ancient, magic sword of kings.

"Is that…cynicism I hear?"

Ask King Leodegrance. He gave Arthur a castle, a bride, and a famous table to keep us out of Gameliard.

Before Henry could respond, the Queen spoke.

"Master Henry. Come here."

Henry swallowed and stepped forward. Eleanor stared at him, and once more he had that uncomfortable feeling of being weighed in the balance, found wanting, and then forgiven, all in one moment. The queen had a stare that entered your eyes and came out your backbone.

"So. Did you have fun on your adventure?"

"No, Your Highness. At least, not while people were trying to, you know, kill us."

The queen nodded and peeled another apple. "And after you and my granddaughter fled Toulouse, was that more pleasant?"

Actually, it hadn't been. Henry had spent a lot of time thinking about Mattie in the month before he got to Toulouse-le-Chateau to stop the wedding. But somehow, his dreams of romance had never included a talking sword as chaperone.

In the week it took to get from Toulouse to Narbonne, Henry and Mattie hadn't been alone a single moment. They'd been accompanied morning, noon, and night by a rigid, prissy, stainless-steel governess that couldn't be bribed, never slept, and never, ever closed its eyes. It had been the six most frustrating days of Henry's life. Any time he had moved closer to Mattie—or she to him—his hand would inconveniently freeze on Excalibur's hilt. Or he'd get a little warning jolt. Or the sword would burst into speech with a running commentary on the martial virtues of self-denial.

On the third day, Henry had been so wound up he'd tried to stick Excalibur in a passing boulder, only to receive what felt like a thunderbolt from his hand to his chest, followed by a two-hour lecture on the contemptibility of oath-breakers and the glories of chastity. The shock he could handle, but the fear of another mind-numbing lecture had kept him on the straight and narrow until they reached Narbonne.

And somehow, he knew, Eleanor could tell all this just by looking at him. Queens or swords, old women were scary.

Eleanor leaned in and spoke softly to him. "You couldn't have taken her away quietly, could you?"

"Uh—"

"Now Geoffrey will have to act." She sighed and straightened. When she spoke again, it was clearly for the benefit of the entire court. "So. You have risked your life for us, and done us much service. How shall we reward you, Henry of Sanbruc?"

Constantinople. Constantinople. Constanti—

"I heard you," muttered Henry.

"Excuse me?" asked the queen.

"Your pardon, Majesty. Your Majesty, if I could request any boon of you, I would ask for safe and speedy passage to the city of Constantinople."

"Constantinople!" Mattie gasped. Henry looked away from the shock on her face. He'd told her about Excalibur's quest, but he hadn't mentioned their final destination.

"You're sure? The food isn't nearly as good as people say."

"Majesty, I would never joke about a trip that takes me a thousand miles from home." He glanced at Mattie. "Believe me, I would much rather stay here."

Eleanor and Mattie both caught the look. "I believe you would," said Eleanor. "Constantinople...Good. Maybe you will distract my son."

She stood. "Into each life some rain must fall, my dears. Young man, you've asked for Constantinople. And Constantinople you shall have."

She snapped her fingers. Clovis and Merulis came to her side. "Make the arrangements," she said.

As they helped her past Mattie, she reached out her hand. "Some things can't be helped, my dear." Mattie didn't respond. Eleanor kissed Mattie on the cheek, and left.

Mattie walked up to Henry. "Constantinople?" she said, her voice cracking. "Not even back to Paris, you have to go to Constantinople? When were you going to tell me?"

"Five minutes ago?"

"You…you…"

"Do you think I want to go? I made a promise. If I hadn't promised, you'd be married to Geoffrey by now. Is that what you want?"

"Will marrying him keep you here?"

"No. I made the promise, and I have to keep it."

I'm impressed, Henry. Maybe you are learning, after—

"And you shut up! Just shut up! Give me one damned minute alone, can't you?" Henry unbuckled Excalibur and threw it in the corner.

Mattie stared at him, open-mouthed. "You really do hear it in your head."

Henry sat down and ran his hand through his hair. "I told you I did."

Mattie sat next to him. "I know. I guess I just didn't…think about what that meant." She took his hand. "Is it…is it awful?"

"Yes. No. Not really. Mostly she—Excalibur just comments on things. Smart mouth. Not like you'd know anything about that."

Mattie smiled.

"And she, it, keeps its promises. Excalibur's saved my life, a couple of times at least. But it can get a little…cramped."

Mattie nodded and looked away. "I was wondering, about the trip back."

Henry didn't say anything. Neither did Mattie, for a moment. Then she took a breath, and seemed to come to a conclusion. "I think, that if I had…had someone in my head…I would do almost anything to get back to normal." Gently, she stroked his cheek, and stood up. She turned to

Excalibur, lying in the corner. "You—you better protect him, or I'll hunt you down and beat you into a plowshare. And that's a Princess Promise." And she left.

Henry and Excalibur were alone in the throne room. For a moment, neither spoke. Then—

I like her. At first, I thought her unladylike. But she will make a good queen, some day.

"I'm sorry I lost my temper."

Arthur used me once to win a fight over who had the right to enter a dining-room first. That angered me, if you like. This...I should have given you two more time alone—even if it was just an illusion.

Slowly, Henry buckled on Excalibur. "At the wedding...should I have just left you? Could the right knight have been there?"

Had the right knight been there, Geoffrey would have killed him before he ever had a chance to draw me from the stone. He would have died mysteriously in his sleep, or after a special meal or a delicious sip of wine.

"You're pretty sure."

As I said before, after two thousand years as the sword of heroes, I can smell treachery. No. Constantinople is our best hope. But fear not. I shall protect you, and the Queen's ship shall take us. We're almost finished.

He wished he could be as optimistic. Slowly, he walked out of the room.

* * * *

It isn't easy to catch a couple of scrawny youngsters on horseback. Not when you're a squad of twelve grown men, wearing heavy armor and carrying supplies. A good tracker helps, as does a guess at the quarry's final destination. You also bring a few agile, skinny men on fast horses, as scouts and messengers.

You travel south and east, confidently. You know there are other squads heading north, northwest, even east. And then, on the second day, you find tracks—one horse, carrying two riders. On the third day, you find a path hacked through trees, sharp as if a razor had cut it, and you know that only a remarkable blade could have done this work. And you smile, and send a courier back to your master.

To raise the army.

* * * *

"Well, she's free. Congratulations."

"Got any other bright ideas? Want to sell me to the Pope while you're at it? How about Saladin? I hear the Templars are looking for a few good swords."

"Okay, okay, so maybe Raymond wasn't a perfect prospect—"

"He tried to kill me, Alfie!"

Alfie drained his cup and sighed. "You want me to pay for lunch, is that it?"

"And dinner. And none of that 'plowman's lunch' garbage either. Real food. Meat."

The inn was crowded, even more so than the streets outside. But Alfie raised two fingers to the servant girl, and after a few minutes she came back with three bowls of the pork stew that was the local specialty, and three more cups of wine.

"What is this stuff, anyway?" asked Henry, poking at the lumps in the stew.

"If you have to ask, you don't want to know," said Valdemar. He ladled some stew on a crust of bread and took a giant bite.

Well, fair enough. Henry was savoring the odd feeling of reunion with friends who have disappointed you, and worried you half to death, and totally screwed up—joy, irritation…and finally forgiveness.

Valdemar picked a chunk of marrowbone from the bowl and slurped enthusiastically.

"Is this the new base of operations?" asked Henry.

Valdemar nodded. "Why not? The wine's good, and the girls aren't."

"Look out there," said Alfie, pointing to the boulevard.

"The city's bursting at the seams, lad. That's silver on the hoof." He sipped a little wine, ignoring his food. "You've got Catalans, Aragonese, Moors, Jews—it's wide open. And the heretics—sure, they'll bang on your door at sunrise and ask if you've been Perfected, but—" He rubbed his thumb and fingers together in the ancient, universal sign for money.

Heading back to his rooms at the palace, Henry had to admit that Alfie was right. The city was packed. There were twice as many people on the streets now as there had been in Bordeaux. But not many of them had the rich, arrogant look they used to pray for, back in Paris. There were a lot of people who were clearly wearing their entire fortunes on their backs. Many of them were crowded into the Church of St. Michel. On a hunch, Henry crossed the main square to the Archbishop's Palace, where he saw the same thing—dozens upon dozens of folks in ragged clothes, camped out in the palace courtyard.

Refugees.

"Yeah, I figured. Let's find out why." Henry approached a priest who was handing out small parcels to the refugees.

"Prince Geoffrey, God forgive him." The priest handed a loaf of bread to a mother and three children, and blessed them. "He holds everything north of the Gironde, now, and he destroyed quite a bit to get it."

"But...but he was at a wedding for a month. How has he—"

"Prince Geoffrey is apparently quite good at doing two or three things at once," said the priest, bitterly. "He calls it 'multi-tasking.'"

From the palace, Henry walked to the town's north gate. Dozens of masons crawled over scaffolding, patching and reinforcing the walls. Down at the docks, shipwrights were building barges. The barges didn't look particularly well-made. They were just big wooden boxes that could float.

Aye. Boxes that can float, and be coated with tar, and moored in the center of the harbor, and set on fire. Excalibur was matter of fact. *Someone expects an invasion…and a last stand.*

When Henry got back to his room, he found a note telling him that the ship that would take him to Constantinople had been sighted at the headland, and would probably arrive within a day. He packed—there wasn't much—and went looking for Mattie. But Mattie, and the Queen, and the Viscount of Narbonne were in a closed meeting with the leaders of the commune, the city's government. Henry had a lump in his gut that wouldn't go away.

The Queen's Guard was drilling in the courtyard. They still looked big and trim, but for the first time, they also looked deadly serious. It didn't take long to find out that an armed vanguard had been spotted on the Aude river two days before.

There's no need to worry.

"Huh?"

In a few hours, we'll be on our way to Constantinople.

"Right."

Henry paced through the streets. If Geoffrey attacked Narbonne…Henry could probably take Valdemar with him on the ship, but Alfie was old. How would he take yet another trip, and this one a forced flight by sea? And what about Mattie? Geoffrey wouldn't kill her, she was better off than the townsfolk, but if he conquered Narbonne, the best she could expect was a nunnery. And knowing Geoffrey, it would be a particularly strict, joyless, escape-proof place, too. There were convents that specialized in inconvenient relatives. And if Mattie came along to Constantinople—if she even agreed to come, which was about as likely as Alfie being elected Pope—that would just be one more incentive for Geoffrey to hunt them by sea. Henry might sneak aboard a ship secretly, maybe; there was no way that would be true any more for Princess Mathilde.

*You couldn't rescue her quietly…*Henry gasped. That's what Eleanor had meant. Of course Geoffrey was coming here. He had to. Henry had made him look like an idiot before half of Europe.

As he ran through his unhappy chain of logic, Henry's feet had taken him down to the market square. He paused before a cart selling dried figs and apricots, to pick up something for the trip.

"It's him!"

"It's him! That's the one!"

"I saw him at Meilhan! It's him!"

"He's here! Praise the Blessed Virgin, he's here!"

"The Muttering Knight is here!"

Henry whirled around. He was faced by a small crowd of people that was growing larger by the minute. Some of them were townsfolk; many had the about-to-be-ragged look of new refugees. One of them grabbed his hand. It was old lady Goncourt, the one who'd given him onion soup for getting savaged by her miserable tom cat.

"Will you save us again, Sir Knight?" she asked. Henry blinked, too surprised to even move his hand. Three months ago, she'd called him a snow-faced pipsqueak. Now he was "Sir Knight."

"Uh—"

"Of course he will! He's the Muttering Knight!" This from a burly guy Henry had never seen before, which meant he had a lot of nerve, if you thought about it.

"Hey, comrade, do I know you—"

"He's fought six against one! He helps the helpless and returns stolen property!" Where were they getting this from?

"He saved my dad from the kidnappers!" Yep, there was Edwina.

"I saw him at Toulouse, face to face against Prince John himself!" And there he was, of course. The source of all this great publicity.

"Hello, Percy," said Henry.

"My Lord!" Percy clasped him to his bosom, squeezing the air out of him. "Here he is, my lord and master, the Muttering Knight! He will save us from Prince Geoffrey!"

Henry smiled and waved, feeling like he'd just been kicked by a mule. "Hello, everyone."

The crowd went wild. Henry felt about two feet tall.

* * * *

"Thank St. George I found you, Henry." Percy was stalking through the armor bins of the castle, picking up a greave here, a gauntlet there. "I know we were supposed to meet here, but I confess I didn't know where to look."

"How about at the Viscount's castle?"

"Oh. Yes. Of course, that makes sense." He tossed a substandard foin back in the bin.

"So what happened in Toulouse after we left?"

Percy grinned. "It was chaos. Prince Geoffrey couldn't control a thing. A dozen knights saddled up and rode after you, but they were in heavy armor. The most determined got about three leagues before turning back."

"What about Geoffrey and John?"

Percy turned serious. "Prince Geoffrey assembled all his vassals, provisioned them, and left. At first, everyone said he was heading to Paris. But on my way here, I overtook the vanguard of his forces. He's coming here, and he's summoned knights from every duchy and town that pays him homage. He says he wants to rescue his kidnapped bride."

"He wants the sword."

"He wants both."

"I wish you hadn't said anything to those people, Percy. You know my job is to get Excalibur to Constantinople." Percy looked stricken, but Henry couldn't tell if it was because he was disappointed in Henry or in himself.

"But, but—"

"I don't want to hear it. I'm going to my room."

And what would Geoffrey do to Narbonne when he arrived and couldn't find Excalibur? Henry chewed on that question all evening, staring at the ceiling.

* * * *

The next day dawned clear and cool, with a strong breeze from the East. Perfect sailing weather. Henry heaved his bag over his shoulder and walked down the Rue des Bons Hommes to the quay. The streets were empty, the shops and windows shuttered. On the city walls, the defenders shifted restlessly, waiting.

"You've been pretty quiet," said Henry.

I'd think you would welcome that.

"Just saying."

There was no one at the dock to say good-bye, not that Henry had expected anyone. The ship was waiting. Henry climbed aboard.

"So, Constantinople you going to."

It was Captain Dimiturglu. Henry smiled.

"Yes. And I know the difference between Constantinople and Bordeaux."

You had to hand it to him. Dimiturglu didn't hesitate. He spread his arms wide and hugged Henry like a long-lost brother. "You good boy! Good for to see you! Because Queen of Love asks, we take you fast to Constantinople, no party this time!" He turned to the sailors. "RIGHT, BOYS?" The sailors cheered. Dimiturglu leaned close to Henry.

"Also, you know maybe what happen to my money pouch? I could not find after to leave Bordeaux. I think maybe one of these ship monkeys took it. You see anything?"

Dimiturglu yelled at the crew, and the *Gorgonoki* shifted sail and tacked downstream. The shore surged past, faster than Henry expected. Soon they had rounded the river bend. And there was Geoffrey's army.

Henry gasped. It stretched from the riverbank to the far hills. Rank upon rank of foot soldiers. Peasant bowmen, with long knives and the unstrung bows that doubled as quarterstaffs. Wagon after wagon of timber for siege engines, pulled by teams of draft horses, guarded by tough, determined combat engineers. Mercenaries with crossbows, the iron hand-cranks of which were weapons in themselves. Freebooters, picked out by their outlandish gear and battle flags. And in the vanguard, knights and retainers, each one a separate battle group of armored horse, surrounded by loyal footmen. Even at this distance, you could smell them, a stink of dung, sweat, leather, and spoiled food.

Rank by rank, squad by squad, they sailed past the invaders, a tour by ship of an irresistible force. By midday, they were approaching the rear-guard, and the river mouth was in view.

Henry was on the port side of the ship, staring at the army. Would Geoffrey send some of his force around the city walls by boat? Or would he keep them all for the city walls? Or do both? Or neither, somehow—some completely new tactical coup, courtesy of Geoffrey's Plantagenet-educated military brain?

And if—face it, *when*—he took the city, then what? Tribute? Mercy? Or fire and blood? Henry could taste the answer in his mouth. Mercy at first, while Geoffrey still believed the townsfolk could find him Excalibur. Then, when it became clear that Excalibur was gone...the torch. Especially if John was traveling with him. If Henry had ever seen a firebug, it was John. How would Alfie and Valdemar get out of a burning town?

Dimiturglu came up and slapped him on the back. "So, mouth of river we are. Now, sail we set, and off to Constantinople! You see Greek Isles, first time, yes?"

The defenders would fight valiantly. Percy would be with them. But they'd see the size of the army. The professionals. How long could they hold out? And then a terrible thought came to him. Mattie. What if Mattie joined the front lines? It was just the kind of stunt she would pull. She had that Plantagenet craziness, she thought nothing could harm her. She would sneak past her guard, sneak out of the castle, put on armor, and join the defenders. She had no idea, no clue, no fear. She would die—

"Excalibur."

Yes.

"I swore to take you to Constantinople."

Yes.

"I can't leave. Do whatever you want, yell, scream, lecture, pretend you're stuck in mid-air, stick pins in me, but we're not letting Geoffrey in. I swore, and I'm breaking my promise, I'm sorry, but I can't do anything else."

Henry closed his eyes and tensed up. Going on past form, whatever Excalibur was going to do to him would be a whopper. Illusionary lightning? Fire crawling up his torso? The feel of a sword cutting into his body?

Henry.

Henry clenched his teeth.

You're wrong.

"Huh?"

You didn't swear to bring me to Constantinople. You swore to obey me until we found a suitable bearer.

"Yeah."

Henry. I command you to protect your friends.

Henry turned to Dimiturglu. "Take me back to Narbonne."

Captain Dimi looked at him as though he were a madman. "Crazy, you are? See the army? They go to Narbonne, right now!"

"Yes. Take me back."

Captain Dimi laughed. "No one sails into battle."

In a flash, Excalibur was at Dimiturglu's throat, pressing hard. Henry smiled tight and wide, a direct copy of the smile he'd seen on Prince John's face just before some attempt at violence.

"Take me back. RIGHT NOW."

Dimiturglu looked into Henry's eyes. Without moving, he yelled out to his crew. They scrambled into activity. The boom swung, and the ship turned again, heading back upriver.

"Now, we're going to stay here, you and I, until I reach Narbonne. Then you can go wherever you want, and keep the Queen's fare. Won't that be nice?"

The captain nodded, very, very slowly. Behind his smile, Henry's heart was sinking into his boots. Now *he* was the jerk with the sword.

27. KNIFE IN THE WATER

The trip back was achingly slow, as they tacked against the river's current. The sailors weren't happy. Henry kept Excalibur at Dimi's throat; the moment he relented, he knew, they'd jump him.

Three hours later, they had come within a mile of the city. Rowboats were being launched into the river, a bid by Geoffrey to circle around the walls and invade by water. The docks inside the walls had been torn down, and the wreckage moored in the river as a defense—but that wasn't stopping Geoffrey from trying.

Henry. Until now, you have been fortunate.

"Really?"

You have not had to kill.

"Oh."

But to survive this battle, you may have no choice. Do you understand? Can you do what is needed?

"I'll have to. Won't I?"

Now they were coming level with the city. The army was encamped in front of the walls. How could he get on shore? If they tried to dock, Geoffrey's boats would intercept them. If he swam, he was asking to be shot. *Hmm.*

"Captain, how would you like twenty *livres* from the hand of the Queen herself?"

"For twenty *livres*, you don't need to use sword. What do we do?"

"Sweep those boats from the river, and land me at the docks."

Well done, Henry.

"A moment." As if the sword were not pointing at his throat, Dimiturglu stood and peered over the starboard side, assessing the situation. He turned back to Henry. "Who are you, to promise this?"

"I am the Queen's right hand. I am the sword that rescued her niece, the Princess Mathilde."

"I heard from this. You, that was?"

"Why else was the Queen paying my fare?"

The captain looked at the water again for a moment. "Forty *livres*."

"Thirty. But nothing if the city falls."

"Of course. Yanos! Semikodomir! *Arfootsi nafar! Terentum aures!*"

Dimiturglu must have yelled something about gold, because the sailors dropped their panicked expressions and started to load their crossbows. Henry would have recognized the look of greed anywhere—it was a universal emotion. Like crankiness.

Dimiturglu turned to Henry. "We go for the rowboats. But we have no boat for you. You wait until we finish and dock, or you swim now to shore. You choose."

Henry looked at the river. The *Gorgonoki* was curving around in an arc that encompassed Geoffrey's boats.

"Can you put yourself between me and the rowboats?"

"Yes."

"I'll swim."

"What about sword?"

I do not rust.

"It will be fine."

"Clothes and boots, you to take off. Otherwise, water

soak into them, drag you down."

"Yeah." Already he wasn't liking this idea. But if he waited for Dimiturglu and the crew, he could be here for hours. And, the darker part of his mind admitted, there was no guarantee they'd win, anyhow. "But bring me closer."

"Yah, that can we do. Mikhail, *veni navire!*" The captain rummaged in a locker and pulled out a greasy drawstring bag. "Here. Put in this, keep dry against water."

The ship caught the breeze and swung closer to shore. Henry stripped to his breeches and shoved everything in the bag but Excalibur, which he strapped to his back.

An arrow arched across the deck, embedding itself in the starboard decking. It was followed by another, and then a flight of a dozen more. One of the crew yelled out and grabbed his arm; the others took cover and returned fire.

"Hurry!" yelled the captain. The whistle of arrows grew louder. They lanced into the deck, the mast. Another found its mark and a sailor went down, screaming.

"Thirty *livres!*" yelled Dimiturglu.

"Thirty *livres!*" yelled Henry, and he jumped.

It was fifteen feet down, just long enough to be scary, and the water was bitter cold. Henry bobbed up, gasping for breath, and swam as fast as he could for the shore, twenty yards away. He was under the cover of the ship, which sat between him and Geoffrey's boats, but he didn't know how long that would last. He moved as fast as he could, but the bag bobbed and dragged behind him, and Excalibur hindered his strokes.

Fourteen yards, twelve yards, and still safe. Eight yards, and no arrows. Four yards, and the arrows splashed into the water around him. He dove underwater and swam for the docks as fast as he could. He surfaced underneath the pier as the arrows pocked the river behind him.

Under the pier was a long, dark space made of water, damp wooden beams, barnacles, and seaweed. Henry crawled onto a piling and looked around. On the bad side, they probably knew where he was. On the good side, they couldn't come in after him without running the risk of ambush. But was there a way out?

He clambered along the beam in toward the shore. There wasn't anything as convenient as a stairway through the upper deck, but the beams did continue out past the wharf onto the shore. He'd be exposed for a few moments on the beam, but maybe—He crawled to the end, and peered out. He couldn't see anyone…but his angle of view was lousy. They could be waiting, just above—

Hurry. The longer you wait, the more likely that the archer who saw you will row this way.

"Right."

Wedged on the beam, he pulled on his pants, shirt, and boots, and dropped the bag into the water. He breathed a prayer to St. Dismas and climbed out into the sunlight.

Thank God. The dock was still empty. And then Henry was struck by an unpleasantly responsible thought.

"Maybe I should stay here. To stop the boats from docking."

The time hasn't come for a last stand. You do no one any good if you're shot from the river. Make your way into the city and join the defenders. If nothing else, there will be a certain boost to morale when they see what weapon has joined their defense.

"Think a lot of ourselves, don't we?"

Shut up and run.

A quarter mile through a maze of narrow streets and empty wharves brought them to a small gate in the city's south wall. An arrow whizzed from the sentry post into the dirt a foot from Henry, and he stopped.

"Who goes there?"

"Henry of…of…I am the Muttering Knight!"

"You lie! The Muttering Knight stands with our defenders, wearing the Sign of the Badger!"

Right. That must be Percy being clever, trying to boost morale. Henry muttered to Excalibur. "Time to shine, Miss

Pointy."

I shall gleam to impress.

"Behold, the sword Excalibur! Blade of Kings from the Dawn of Time!" Henry waved Excalibur in the air. It caught the light, gleaming and flashing, glowing even in the bright noonday sun. "I come to stand with the defenders! Who would hinder me must face me in combat!"

The sentinels shared a look. "Okay. Hold on. But if you're lying, you're in big trouble, mister!"

The gates creaked open, and Henry ran in. Behind him, the second sentry slapped the first sentry on the head. "'If you're lying.' He's in big trouble if he's telling the *truth*, you moron."

The streets were deserted, the shops locked and shuttered. Only the churches were open, and running up the main street, Henry saw them filled with priests…waiting.

A squad of old men with buckets ran across the street. Henry yelled. "Where's the fighting?"

The leader looked at him. "Who wants to know?"

Henry raised Excalibur. "The Muttering Knight."

"I thought you were already up there. Take this street north until the Church of St. Sebastian, turn east, and then north again at the big market square. Then you can start killing those bastards."

"Great. What are the buckets for?"

The leader looked at him like he was the village idiot. "Fire."

Henry looked around at the wooden houses, shops, and carts, and shuddered. He nodded at the fire squad and trotted north. Along the way he passed two more fire squads, and provision carts heading for the castle. Say what you would, Queen Eleanor ran a tight battle.

This city cannot be defended.

"What?"

I do not say that the queen cannot win. Only that the city, open to the river, cannot be truly defended. Unless she breaks Geoffrey's forces now, she will have to fall back to the castle eventually.

"Let's keep that to ourselves, shall we?"

As you wish. The queen surely knows it already.

"I wish I didn't."

Heading east on a side street, he heard voices and footsteps. He was about to head forward, expecting another fire squad, when he realized the voices were speaking Norman French, not Provençal. That made them invaders. He hid in a doorway as three men trotted into view. They were young and hard-looking, all in grey, carrying long knives, mason's tools, and greased canvas bags. Their hair was wet.

Firestarters. Draw me.

Henry took a breath. He was alone. No Percy to help him. No rush of attack that would let him react, carried on by events. This time, he would have to challenge someone, by himself, and it was hard. "Can't we—"

If you don't stop them, they'll set fire. What do you think is in those bags? Flint and tinder and tallow. Remember— CONFIDENCE.

Swallowing spit, Henry took a breath and drew Excalibur. Like diving into frozen lake, the sword's power surrounded him and flowed into him. Once again, the weapon squatted behind his eyes and twitched his limbs.

Two gliding steps, and he was in front of the commandoes.

"Surrender," said Henry/Excalibur. "Throw down your knives and your bags, and you will not be harmed."

"And who might you be, young Sir One Against Three?" The leader grinned.

"I am Henry of Sanbruc, and this sword is Excalibur, your death if you resist. This is your only warning."

The commandoes shared a glance. "Then you've saved us much trouble, Master Henry. Our lord would like very much to speak with you." The leader wagged a finger, and the two others spread out, moving to flank.

Move back. Good. And again. Back into the alley so they cannot

*get behind you. Excellent. Now. Brandish me; let them see how
lightly you hold me.*

A circle, a figure eight. Next, the script called for a big
smile and cocky air. Instead—"Please. Surrender. I don't
want to hurt you."

*They will try to crowd you, so our greater reach cannot help. If
you let them, you will lose. Your only hope is to attack first.*

The leader smiled. "Surrender, and you will not be
harmed. Our prince wants you alive." He gestured, and the
commandoes all stepped forward.

It's time. You gave them fair warning. Henry…

Henry licked his lips, and took a step back. The
commandoes moved forward.

HENRY!

He felt paralyzed. He couldn't just attack—

Then the commando on the right moved to grab his
arm. That broke the spell. Henry lashed out. Excalibur
caught the commando's hand. He howled. The backswing
came down on the leader's arm, and Henry moved past
him to swing two-handed at the commando on the left.
That quickly, it was over.

"Are they—"

*Not yet. You must grab their bags and leave NOW. While this
battle rages, do not think. ACT. Do not hesitate, or you will fall,
and Geoffrey will take me. Do you understand?*

"Yes."

Now go.

Henry grabbed the firestarters' gear and ran out of the
alley. He didn't look back.

* * * *

He heard the battle before he saw it—a distant roar.
Another ten minutes, and the noise resolved itself: screams
and yells, the creak of wood under pressure, the sound of
metal on metal. The road twisted to the left, and there it
was.

The North Gates were huge. Invading-army size. The
defenders seemed tiny. Flights of arrows lofted over the

walls, rattling down on shields and helmets. Jutting up above the battlements, Henry could see siege ladders.

There was an enormous crash and the gates burst open, smashed to pieces by a giant wheeled battering ram. The invaders poured in as the defenders shouted in dismay. Henry sprinted forward, Excalibur in his hand and in his bones.

The first wave was of men-at-arms, tough and wiry, with mail shirts, helms, and short swords—soldiers prepared for the nasty, close-quarter fighting of the vanguard. They poured through the rubble, swords out, confronting Eleanor's troops hand-to-hand. Behind them came the van, foot soldiers and pikemen, advancing in good order. The defenders' line held, but they gave ground again, and again, and again.

Henry saw all of this in flashes as he closed with the invaders. To Henry, they were sketches of soldiers, their weaknesses highlighted, and the path he had to follow through them a glowing track. He ran past the Queen's men, Excalibur out and slashing.

Keep moving. You have no armor; you will die if you stand still. Slash and move. Do not engage any one foe. Attack and move, and let the men behind you fight on.

Henry raised Excalibur and shattered one man's sword. And then past that man to the next, with a blow to the helm. And on to the next, a slash to the torso, cleaving the mail, cutting the skin, and now Henry was on the rubble, light on his feet, without the burden of armor, exposed—

Don't think about that. Move.

More attackers were pouring through the broken gates. Henry hacked at a soldier, and saw the attackers were circling him, trying to get behind him—

There's too much space behind you. They could surround you. Back up.

Henry raised Excalibur and yelled. "BEHOLD EXCALIBUR! DEFENDERS TO ME! DEFENDERS!"

Better. Here they come.

The defenders charged forward, yelling, big men in armor that carried the Queen's rose-red favor. They joined shoulder to shield and charged through the wreckage, straight at the invaders, whose line held for a moment, and then broke, retreating back through the gates. The defenders cheered.

Arrows, Henry. Get back. You've broken the assault. Now get some armor.

The Queen's guard pressed around him, cheering and hugging him as they retreated back over the wall.

"I knew you'd be back!" It was Clovis. "Love is the greatest force in the world."

"Where is she?"

"Back at the castle. She wanted to put on armor and fight with us, but someone, uh, persuaded her not to."

Henry stared at the guard. "Clovis. You didn't lock her in her room, did you?"

"No! Never!" He coughed delicately. "It was Otho."

"I had to tie her up, too," said Otho.

"Where's Percy?"

"Here, My Lord." Percy stepped forward, covered in gore. He looked like a different person...a seriously dangerous one. Henry thought of all the times he'd mentally dismissed Percy as a buffoon, and shuddered.

Someone passed Henry a helmet and a leather jerkin sewn with iron rings. Just as he was putting on the helmet, there was a hissing like a thousand chops being fried, and a hail of arrows struck the defenders. Henry crowded under Percy's shield, where he heard the thuds of the arrows striking wood and metal.

"They're coming!" someone yelled, and the invaders charged the gap again.

You have a retainer. Use him.

Henry turned to Percy. "You spot archers and protect me from arrows. You got that?"

"Yes, My Lord!"

This time there were more attackers, moving faster, in

tighter formation. Henry and Excalibur charged their left flank, Percy on his right, while the defenders moved up behind them.

The attackers recognized Henry this time. As he charged forward, they moved away, concentrating their forces against the other defenders. It was like herding sheep. Henry drove the attackers to the left, against the main force of the defenders, which had grown as well. The men on the battlements had now climbed down to help repel the attackers—the town's militia, by the look of them.

Henry hacked and slashed, driving the attackers backward and leftward. But more and more of them poured through. Soon they were flowing past the far end of the defenders' line, and archers were sprinting to take up positions in nearby buildings. Henry spotted Clovis forty yards away, confronting three men. Henry hacked forward until he reached the guard.

"We're being outflanked—"

"We have to fall back to the castle. The main force is there, and we can wait for reinforcements."

"I'll slow them down."

Clovis raised his sword. "To me!" he yelled. "Form to the rear!" The defenders pulled back and gathered together, their shields overlapping.

Henry raced between the defender line and the attackers.

"The next invader to approach meets Excalibur!" he yelled.

Remember the flourish!

Henry waved Excalibur in the air. A low, fearful muttering ran through the attackers' lines. The invading troops slowed, hunkered down, and stopped.

The defenders backed away down one of the narrower streets that led back to the castle. As they streamed away, Henry stood in place, Excalibur raised, Percy on his right. The attackers stood still, unwilling to approach Henry and his sword.

An arrow lanced out of the gathering gloom. Percy caught it on his shield.

Time for a little psychological warfare, thought Henry/Excalibur.

"Where is Geoffrey?" he/it yelled. "Where is that spineless, craven fop? Is he afraid to meet a boy on the field of battle?"

Nothing.

"I'm waiting..."

By now, the last squad of defenders was trickling away behind him.

"Tell your lord, if you see him, that I would have called him coward to his face—but he wasn't here! Tell him I spit on him! Tell him he's the village idiot of Europe's most inbred family!"

Five defenders left. Four.

"And tell Prince Johnny that I'd say the same to him, but I don't speak Moron!"

Three. Two.

"Tell them their daddy's waiting in Hell, and I'm going to send them for a visit!"

One.

"Farewell, and good night!"

Henry and Percy backed away, down the alley.

28. THE SIEGE OF NARBONNE

"I shall slaughter a dozen of Geoffrey's best knights!"

"Three cheers for Sir Laurent! Hip-hip-hoorah!"

Enthusiasm. That's what we like to see.

The crowd cheered and pounded the table. Sir Laurent, a big guy with a beard and a wine belly, nodded to the other nobles and sat back down.

"I shall wear Prince John's guts as a lining for my shield!" This speaker was a tall, skinny knight with black hair and acne.

"Hurrah!"

"Huzzah!"

"Hoorah for Sir Cagris!"

Well said, that man.

Henry turned to Percy. "Is it always like this?"

Percy looked puzzled. "How do you mean, My Lord?"

"When we were invited to a council of war, I thought…I don't know…we'd talk about strategy, or food supplies, or how many enemies there are. Or something."

Either we kill them, or they kill us. Don't make things so complicated.

"Either they kill us, or we kill them." Percy shrugged. "What is there to discuss?"

"Ah. I hadn't thought of it like that."

Henry had gotten his invitation to the war council that morning. Excalibur had been all for it, of course, but Henry expected to be met with either hero-worship à la Percy, or contempt à la Brissac. Instead, Eleanor's allies had greeted him briefly and then gotten back to the important business: drinking and bragging. Apparently, the nobility didn't find magic swords—or strategy—nearly as interesting as promises of colorful violence.

Henry turned back to Percy. "What about reinforcements? Getting allies? How long before Geoffrey's catapults break through our walls?"

"Oh, that. Six days."

Henry's jaw dropped. "Six days? Just like that?"

Percy nodded. "It's a rule of thumb, My Lord. A half day to assemble each engine, and then subtract one day per engine from the sum of ten days, unless the walls and gates be unusually strong, or the catapults special in some way."

You see? That is strategy. Not my province. A sword is all about tactics. And enthusiasm.

Up on the throne, Queen Eleanor clapped politely as the Viscount himself—a short, stocky knight with black hair—swore to use his bare hands when removing her son's head from his shoulders. Henry tried not to think too hard about the implications of that.

"Oh, don't worry, H." Mattie leaned over and rested her head on his shoulder. Henry was sure she did it just to blow his cool. It worked, of course. "Phil is on the way."

"Phil?"

"The King of France. He's borrowed forces from the Pope and the Germans, and he's Uncle Geoff's overlord. He'll spank Geoff hard."

"You're pretty confident."

Mattie shrugged. "If you're royalty, you get used to these things."

"Well, yeah, when you're the one who's safe in the castle."

Mattie's face dropped. "Sometimes you really stink." She turned on her heel and left.

Smooth, Henry, he thought to himself, and rubbed his face. Percy looked tactfully at the ceiling.

Quite the snob, aren't you?

"How can I be a snob? I'm a commoner!"

Exactly.

At the head of the table, a beefy guy in chain mail was vowing unspecified injury to Geoffrey, his knights, his horse, and his "demesnes," whatever they were. Henry went looking for Mattie.

She had gone to her rooms. Otho was on guard, and he told Henry that the Princess had left instructions that she not be disturbed…by Henry, specifically. Henry was forced to leave his apology with Otho. He turned to stare out the slit of a window onto the sea of campfires in the central courtyard.

Go and walk among the people.

"Why?"

You are their refuge and their strength, a very present help in times of trouble.

"I'm a boy with a trick sword."

I am no trick. And to them, you are no boy. This is part of your job, defender.

"But—"

GO.

He took a breath and left the keep. The courtyard was packed with refugees and townspeople. Each fire belonged to some family or guild or charitable association; they were connected by roofed walkways that were meant to protect against arrows and stones. Sometimes it worked.

"Hey, there he is!"

"Yo, Mister Arthur, this way! We got some brandy for ya!"

"Sir Muttering Knight, have you seen my son?"

"Hey, MK, when you gonna kill that son of a Saracen?"

"Way to rub his nose in it, MK!"

"Sir Knight, may I see your sword? Is it real?"

They crowded around, happy to see him, not touching him, but more and more of them, looking at him like he was Arthur, like he could just wave the sword and make everything okay. How could he tell them he was responsible for their situation? Geoffrey was here because he wanted Excalibur and Mattie. Henry had taken both. And he couldn't see any way to stop Geoffrey from hunting him down, wherever he went, except to kill him. Or...

"Henry."

The crowd stepped back. Flanked by Clovis and Otho, the queen approached and held out her hand. Henry bowed, and took it. "Majesty."

"Walk with us."

Walking with the queen, Henry was safe from the crowds—the folks in the bailey bowed, smiled, and kept their distance, unless Eleanor made a point of stopping to talk with someone, which she did every few yards. She would exchange a few words, listen, smile, and move on.

"How do you do it?"

"Do what, child?"

"When I'm by myself, they crowd me till I can't breathe."

"That's simple, dear. I'm speaking to them, listening, being sympathetic. So they're already getting what they want from me. All you would have to do would be to defeat Geoffrey's armies single-handed."

They walked a little farther. When the crowd thinned out, Henry spoke. "Majesty...what's Geoffrey like?"

"Be more specific, dear." A girl ran up with a rag doll that she displayed proudly to the queen. "Yes, sweetheart, that's a lovely dolly."

"Does he keep his promises? When he gets what he wants, is he satisfied?"

Eleanor studied the rag doll carefully, and turned to the little girl. "What's her name, dear?"

The girl smiled. "Catherine."

"Well, I shall see if I have some cloth that would suit her. Would you like that?"

"Yes'm. Thank you." The girl took the doll and skipped back to her mother.

Without looking at Henry, Eleanor spoke again. "None of my sons have ever been satisfied. They are consumed by hunger." She turned to Clovis and Otho. "Leave us." They bowed and moved a few yards away, giving Henry and the queen a little privacy.

"So there's no chance of…giving him something that he wants, so he'll leave."

"Mathilde, you mean?" Her tone was sharp enough to cut glass.

"No! Never! Something else, maybe." Henry glanced down at Excalibur, and the Queen followed his gaze.

"Ah. I understand."

What does she understand? Bribing Geoffrey?

"Yeah."

Eleanor stared at the girl playing with her doll. She stood straight as a knife, her eyes drifting far away. "I had four sons, child. They united to kill their father, my husband. I helped them do it. I urged them to. And my Henry was a great king." The queen paused, remembering. "If you and your sword had never been, if Mathilde had never been born, Geoffrey would still be here, laying siege. We are Plantagenets. We cannot stop."

An icy hand touched the back of Henry's neck. What he remembered of his own parents was two soft, wide people who smelled of fish and woodsmoke, and hugged a lot. He tried to imagine a mother who urged you to kill your father. He couldn't.

The silence lengthened. Finally, Eleanor smiled and patted Henry on the arm. "So no, dear. I don't think giving Geoffrey…whatever he wants…would make him go away. But thank you for thinking of it."

"So…uh, begging Your Majesty's pardon…is it true? Is

King Philip coming?"

"Yes. Whether he will fight for us or for Geoffrey remains to be seen."

"And he'll be here soon?"

"We hope so. Within the week."

"What happens tomorrow? Will they attack?"

She stared at him for a moment. "You really are just a...you really have no experience, do you? I'd forgotten."

Forgotten that I'm just a peasant, you mean, thought Henry.

The queen smiled sadly. "Of course they will, dear. Of course they will."

* * * *

The sun hadn't risen yet. The strange, flat gray before dawn lay over the castle and the town. The air was chill and wet, the stones of the battlement freezing cold. Spears and helmets, shields and swords, all were slick with dew.

Henry stood with the defenders on the battlements of the castle, looking down on the invading army. Geoffrey's men had clearly worked through the night. The siege towers hulked against the sky. The catapults (trebuchets, actually—Percy had been drilling him on military names) were being hauled into place.

"You the kid with the sword?" The speaker was a short, wide man with a thick yellow beard and enough scars to make him look like a quilt.

"Uh, yeah."

"Etienne, the Viscount's marshal. You ever been in a fight like this?"

"Uh, at the gates. That's about it. And I was at that, uh, war council last night."

"Yeah, that must have been a big help. You see where your buddy is?" He pointed to a wad of men on a tower fifty yards north. Percy stood with them. "They're pole men. Stay with them. Do what you're told. If somebody comes over the top they can't handle, stick your sword in. Think you can do it?"

Henry nodded. He felt cold and small with the special

weakness that comes from rising in the hours before dawn. "I have a choice?"

"Funny. I hate funny."

"You're not the first person to tell me that."

"Get going, kid." The marshal jogged away.

"Have you done one of these, Excalibur?"

A siege defense? Of course. I remember once, on the wall at Luguvallium—

"What's going to happen?"

The archers and catapults will begin. Then the towers will move close to the walls, under cover of the arrows and stones. Geoffrey's men will climb up inside the towers and try to take our battlements, while we try to destroy the towers and throw things down at the troops on the ground. It's quite simple, really.

As Henry hiked to the tower, the sun cleared the hills, and the war started.

The first flight of arrows struck while Henry was still twenty yards from the tower. He dived to the floor. The arrows whistled overhead for what felt like minutes, flickering against the pale blue sky, so thick it was like a wall of wood and noise moving quickly just above his nose.

Staying low, Henry turned over and crawled forward on his knees and arms. Every now and then an arrow would come in low and shatter against the stone, its pieces ricocheting behind the merlons.

After he had crawled about ten yards, the volley ended. He got to his feet in a crouch, and dashed from merlon to merlon until he reached the tower. Percy pulled him up. "That will wake you up, eh, My Lord?"

The men in the tower were foot soldiers, wide and hard, some of them almost as young as he was. Many had polearms, ten- or twelve-foot long spears with complicated heads that could be used to jab at an enemy or dislodge a siege ladder. All of them had short swords, for up-close fighting if the polearms failed. They smiled when they saw him, and then turned back to watch the invaders.

Thump. Thump. Thump.

Ah. The ram is at work.

Henry bent over the wall, to see Geoffrey's battering ram hammering at the wood and iron front gates. The ram soldiers heaved the thing forward while locking their shields above their heads—the defenders' rocks and arrows bounced off.

Then a cascade of liquid fire spattered down the castle walls to land on the battering ram and its soldiers. Faintly, Henry heard screams, and saw the soldiers flee from the burning ram and roll on the ground in a frantic effort to douse the flames on their own bodies.

"Greek fire," said Percy. "A filthy thing. I didn't know we had any."

"I think...I think it was in the gear I took from the firestarters," said Henry. "I gave it to the Queen. She must have decided to use it." He felt sick.

"Oh. Well...any weapon in a melee, I always say." Percy patted Henry's shoulder.

"Look out!"

Henry and Percy ducked behind a merlon as a second volley of arrows flew at the tower. This time, the arrows kept coming, and so did a trio of siege towers.

The siege towers were sixty feet high and covered in hardened leather. From Percy's lectures, Henry knew there was a wide ladder inside each, protected by the leather from arrows, stones, and hooks. Because the inside ladder was built up from a base, it didn't have to lean against the castle wall, and it couldn't just be tossed from the wall like an ordinary ladder.

"Here they come—"

The siege towers rolled closer. At the top was a ten-foot opening. Henry could see inside the first one to the men waiting on the inside ladder, getting ready to leap onto the castle walls. Some of them raised crossbows—

"Get down!"

Henry and Percy ducked behind a merlon, dodging the

flight of crossbow bolts from the siege tower. There was a crunch as the siege tower connected with the castle wall, and the invaders leapt onto the battlements.

Ah. You see? The invaders have made it onto the battlements the only way they could, by attacking at many points at once, and using a volley of arrows to stop the defenders from bringing their polearms up in time. Now it will be hand to hand all along the east wall. Draw me!

Henry did. This time, he welcomed the cold rush as Excalibur entered his nerves and muscles; it meant he might live. Once again, the unimportant details drained out of his vision, leaving only what was significant to the sword—posture and motion, leverage and position.

The invaders pushed in from the siege towers, man over man, surging against the defenders. The crush was intense. Henry couldn't move. All of Excalibur's magic was useless—there was no room to lift an arm, let alone swing a sword. Instead, it was a shoving match, and Henry was carried along by the tide, unable to keep his feet while surrounded by bigger men. Every now and then, a space would open up—someone had gone down beneath the press of bodies, or fallen victim to a dagger, the only weapon that could still be used in the scrum. He heard screams as the crowd forced men over the side, to fall to the bricks below.

And then the crush thinned out. The invaders had spread along the battlements and were fighting hand-to-hand with the defenders. Prompted by Excalibur, Henry whirled and smashed the two swords that had been coming for him. The soldiers backed away, looking for weapons. Henry stalked forward.

Keep moving, keep—

"What does it look like I'm doing?"

Touchy.

"Could we focus, please?" Henry ran forward, looking for Percy.

One   soldier,   three   soldiers,   two   soldiers,

Henry/Excalibur marched forward, shattering their armor and weapons, letting the defenders retake the battlements they cleared, the Henry part of the pair trying hard not to think about men wounded and bleeding behind them.

The crowd in front of them parted, revealing one of Geoffrey's men, a knight, forcing the defenders back. He was big, and fast, and—

—efficient.

One defender came at the big knight, and got a bastard sword in the guts. The sword kept moving to cleave the armor of a second defender, and then to cave in the helmet of a third who had tried to sneak up behind the knight. A fourth man went down, a fifth, and the knight showed no sign of slowing.

At last, a foe worthy of us! Attack!

"Are you *crazy?*"

And then it didn't matter, because the knight spotted Henry and Excalibur and charged.

Henry couldn't believe it. Fifty pounds of armor and a hand-and-a-half sword, and the knight moved as quickly as Henry did, jinking past others to seek him out. It was terrifying.

Do not fear. He has a weakness.

"What?"

When I find it, I'll let you know.

And then the big knight was on Henry. The hand-and-a-half came up from below, a move that almost no man could make with a sword that big, but the knight handled it like a thrust with an assassin's dagger. Henry leaped back. Then the knight was hacking from right and left, the strikes lightning-quick. Even with Excalibur's speed, Henry was barely able to parry in time, let alone attack.

Time after time, Henry tried Excalibur's stock in trade—shattering the knight's sword and slicing open the armor. But somehow the sword was never quite where Henry expected, or Excalibur wasn't at quite the right angle. Now Henry was getting tired, and the knight seemed fresh as sunshine.

"Excalibur…"

I'm working on it.

Then they heard it—the *crunch, crunch* of more siege towers hitting the wall. A ramp fell between Henry and the knight, separating them, as a wave of new soldiers poured out along the battlements. The knight screamed in frustration as the crush of attackers pushed him away from Henry.

Thank you, St. Dismas! thought Henry. He saw Percy at the East Tower, and ran toward him.

"A sharp set-to, My Lord." Percy grinned at him, already covered in gore. Henry raised his hand and saw that he was bloody, too. *Whose blood*—He quashed that line of thought. If he stopped to think about it—

More.

Another wave. Henry and Percy stood back to back. Each attacker seemed outlined in red and yellow, his weaknesses highlighted by Excalibur. Blades and armor shattered, guards fell, and opponents wheeled away, clutching their sides or chests or legs, to be replaced by others. Almost unnoticeable in the rising sun, Excalibur began to glow.

And then the invaders turned and ran for the towers, leaping onto the ladders, fleeing the battlements. The walls were clear. Henry turned to face the other soldiers, and raised Excalibur. They cheered.

"We did it, My Lord! We did it!" Percy grabbed him in a bloody, sweaty bear hug. Henry grinned.

"Wait a moment." Henry looked over Percy's shoulder. Rolling up to the walls was another siege tower, not like the others.

"Percy, do you see it?"

"Aye."

It was a huge pillar, gleaming red in the sun. No ladders, no grappling hooks, no catapults, no troops.

Henry rubbed his forehead. It looked familiar. Where

had he seen it before—the Chapel Perilous? It had that weird simplicity—

"What's that, My Lord?" Percy pointed to the thing's base. "A giant wheel?"

Henry looked down. A huge wheel, sheathed in red metal. Surrounding a lump of black metal.

Copper and loadstone.

A loud *CLANK* filled the air. Then another. Henry turned. A dozen men, wearing leather tunics and leather hats, were working a giant treadmill connected to the wheel by a vast chain that was slowly accelerating.

Percy peered over the wall. "Milord. Over there, by the ditch in front of the castle. Do you see it?"

"Yes." A squad of men pelted away from the wall.

"I feel...strange, Milord." Percy took off his helmet. His hair rose on end and waved in the breeze.

"Oh, God." Henry spun around to face the defenders. "GET DOWN! GET DOWN!" he yelled.

The men stared at him.

"NOW!"

Then the lightning struck.

The world flashed white, and the thunder rolled. It died away, and Henry clutched at the stones, trying to hear past the roaring, try to see past the blue dazzle in his eyes.

He waggled his fingers. All there. His teeth, his heart, his fingernails—the lightning machine had missed.

Henry turned back to the wall. Gervasius' machine was in pieces, just a crater surrounded be dazed men in leather tunics. He smiled. The monk's workmanship was as good ever. Maybe things would be all right—

A deep, tooth-rattling groan rumbled through the wall, and suddenly the Narbonnese were screaming. They knew something that Henry didn't, and they were all scrambling for the stairwells and the ladders. The rush threatened to become a panic. Henry leaped onto the merlon and held up Excalibur.

"LISTEN UP! YOU'RE MEN, NOT SHEEP! THE

NEXT GUY THAT SHOVES HIS WAY TO A LADDER BITES STEEL!"

The defenders stood still.

"Bites steel"?

"Go with it," Henry muttered. "All right. One at a time, down the ladder, single file...or chop-chop!"

The defenders started to climb down. Another groan echoed through the wall, and they started to move even faster, but in good order. Henry turned to Percy. "What's happening?"

Percy looked around, sweat on his forehead. "The lightning must have blown a hole under the castle wall. That sound is the stones, settling. Any moment now, this wall will collapse."

Another groan, this time followed by a shudder that ran straight through Henry's bones. There were still a dozen men waiting to get down the ladder. Henry eyed the crowd. There must be room for one teenaged-sized soldier to get down RIGHT NOW—

You are the defender. You wait until everyone else is down.

"I hate you." He hustled people down the ladder. "HURRY! HURRY! MOVE YOUR ASSIZES!"

"LOOK!"

Everyone turned. Behind them, the wall was swaying back and forth. There was something terrible about seeing a mass of stone that big, built solid as eternity, waving like a tall weed in a meadow.

The last few people were waiting for the ladder. "GO! GO!" Henry yelled, shoving them forward. Then, with a sound like a million avalanches, the wall came apart.

First, it sagged in the middle like a giant U. Then, in an instant, the depression deepened by twenty feet, sending a shock through the battlements that knocked Henry and Percy off their feet and sent the ladder falling backward through the air.

Percy got hold of a merlon's edge and grabbed Henry before he tumbled off the battlement. Now the wall's destruction was speeding up, huge building blocks tumbling off the wall, and the devastation spreading faster and faster from both sides of the original break. In a heartbeat, the disintegration was just a few feet away and leaping toward them.

"RUN!" Henry and Percy turned and pounded south along the wall.

"Where's the next ladder down?"

"It's the stairway in the north gate tower!" shouted Percy.

Thirty yards away. Henry sprinted like he was running from some mark through the streets of the Latin Quarter. The thunder of falling stone was constant now, an earthquake waterfall. The cracks were getting closer and closer.

Percy was dropping behind. "Lose the armor!" Henry yelled. Percy whipped off his helmet and shield fast enough, but he had no time to pause and take off his mail. "Breathe deeper and push with your calves!" Percy got a few more yards—and then he tripped and went sprawling.

Whimpering with fear, Henry dithered for a moment and then turned back. He helped Percy up. The void was leaping behind them now as they raced forward. The gate tower was in view. It was closer—

The wall came apart underneath them. With his last bit of momentum, Henry leaped for the tower doorway, and he and Percy smashed into the doorframe. Their legs dangling over emptiness, they hauled themselves into the tower.

Wheezing like Alfie on a cold morning, Henry stood in the doorway and turned to look at the wreck. Between their tower and the next, a hundred yards away, there was now nothing but dust and air. The sheer drop started just inches from Henry's feet; it was as though he were standing on emptiness, looking down from the sky. He closed his eyes as a spasm of vertigo whirled through him.

Percy's hand on his shoulder brought him back.

"Hurry, Lord. We have to join the defenders on the ground. Geoffrey's men will be coming through any second."

Together they clattered down the spiral staircase, hands spread out to the walls for balance, skidding occasionally on the worn stone steps. From outside they could hear shouts and the clash of metal on metal.

The stairwell opened out into the huge archway that housed the gate and portcullis. Beyond was the main courtyard, hazed in dust and lanced by sunbeams. Through the murk, Henry could already see the dim outlines of soldiers struggling. He drew Excalibur and stalked forward. Percy followed.

The courtyard was a ruin. Boulders and paving stones the height of a man were scattered dozens of yards in every direction. Blood slicked the ground, coating the rubble and mixing with mud. The courtyard's own cobblestones had been shattered here and there by the force of the impact. Dust hung in the air, making Henry's eyes water; the sharp, dry particles made him sneeze and gag. Sunlight came down in beams and shafts, making the yard seem like a cathedral—until you saw the bodies of the people who'd been hit by the stones.

The gap was huge. Too big to be called a hole, it was more like the absence of wall. At the base, rubble rose up in a wide, steep hill, ten feet high. Beyond that was the city, and the siege engines, and the army.

It was the end of things.

Henry heard a loud crash, and then another. At first, he saw nothing. Then, like the snout of a hedgehog poking out of its burrow, the edge of a wide wooden deck appeared at the crest of the hill of rubble. It was followed by another. Soon, wooden decks covered the top slopes of the hill, providing sure footing to the invaders.

Henry turned to Percy. "We're scattered. Go through the north courtyard, gather up all the defenders you can find, and make for the inner gate. I'll take the south."

Percy nodded and they split up. Henry stalked past the boulders and the wreckage, holding up his sword. "GO TO THE INNER GATE! GO TO THE INNER GATE!" He passed ten or twelve soldiers whom he pointed back to the gate of the inner courtyard, but no more. The collapse of the wall must have killed hundreds. At least he didn't see any townspeople among the dead—they had been moved to the inner courtyards and the keep that morning. Of course, if the siege lasted much longer, hunger and disease would take care of that.

Crash. Crash. Henry weaved in and out of the rubble, looking for more soldiers. *Crash.* He peered out from behind a boulder. The decking was halfway down the inner slope now. *Crash.*

One more round—finding people in the wreckage was like walking a maze. You couldn't be certain if you'd been to a particular area before. He turned left and saw a flicker of movement back near the north tower, by the rubble that had been the east wall. He saw the rose and lavender of the Queen's colors. It was right in front of the hill of rubble.

Henry glanced at the decking. It was getting closer to the ground. He could see the heads of the invaders rising a little above the crest of the hill. There wasn't any time to help; he had to get back to the gate—

Henry took a deep breath, tucked in his head and ran to the gap. The soldier waving was Valdemar.

"Valdemar! What are you doing he—"

"Just shut up and help."

Valdemar's leg had been hurt. Henry couldn't tell how badly, but Valdemar couldn't walk on it. As Henry stooped down and got Valdemar's arm around his shoulders, the wooden decks hit the ground of the courtyard.

Henry glanced up at the hill top. For a moment, he could see nothing but sky. Then he heard the neighing of horses, the slow clop-clop of their hooves striking wood and trotting forward.

Valdemar cursed. "Get out of here, Henry. Drop me and go."

"Don't be an ass."

"I can play dead. But they'll cut you to pieces, just to make sure."

Clop-clop. Clop-clop.

The horses crested the hill and stood out the top. The knights surveyed their new conquest in a perfect row, outlined by the sky. There was no time or place left to run. Henry eased Valdemar to the ground.

"Have a seat. I need my hands free."

One boy against a line of knights on horse. Terrific. He drew Excalibur.

"Any suggestions?"

I can cleave stone.

"Yeah. So?"

I can bring down this hill, and the knights upon it. But it will be hard, and you must do it now. Step forward—

Henry took a breath and stepped forward to the base of the hill. He held up Excalibur. As he did, he felt a rush, a surge of power come up from the ground, a tidal wave of force. His own lightning machine—it was excruciating, like being stung by a thousand bees. His head screamed; his teeth became pinwheels of agony. He could barely hold on to the sword. He smelled burning hair. Smoke rose from his shoes.

Now! Bring me down with all your might on the stones!

Henry did. A thunderbolt blew him backward. For a moment, he was spinning through the air. The sky was above him, to one side, below him, and then the paving stones slammed into him and drove his breath away. He rolled onto his back and stared at the sky, his mind blank.

"Henry. Henry. Get up, boy." Valdemar was shaking him.

Henry sat up. For a moment, he couldn't remember a thing—where he was, who he was. Then his thoughts returned to him. He stood. He ran a hand over his head, and came away with a mass of burned hair and some blood. His hands were blackened. Where was Excalibur? He spotted it a few yards away. He ran as fast as he could—a crippled half trot. Everything hurt. When he picked up the sword, it seemed perfect—untouched, gleaming, still sharp. But it was silent...like the best ordinary sword in the world. He sheathed it.

"Look what you did, boy."

Henry looked up. The hill was gone. It was a plain, strewn with more rubble, and with knights crawling off dead horses. From behind them came a sound, faint at first...people yelling.

Soldiers yelling.

Soldiers charging.

All around them, the defenders were running, weapons out, charging the unhorsed knights. They were pushing them out. They were winning. Henry raised his hands.

"THAT'S IT! THAT'S IT! WE'RE WINNING—"

The first arrow took him high in the chest. At first he felt no pain, just a sudden, intense pressure. The second arrow was lower, right in the center. It knocked him back.

"Where—" *had it come from?* He couldn't finish the sentence. The pain rushed in. His chest was paralyzed; he couldn't breathe. The agony spread through his body. For the first time in his life, he thought—

—*i am dying*—

29. ONE FOR THE ROUND TABLE

Everything was white. White curtains, white bedspread, a white gown. Maybe he was in Heaven. Then the pain hit. This had to be The Other Place. His eyes closed.

He was back in Sanbruc. Poppa was showing him how to build a coracle. "You see, Aimeric, you seal it good and tight with the pitch, eh? Then the *mare*, she don't get in. You take her out, you catch the fish. In the summer, you dive for the *huitres*, maybe find a pearl or two. Sometime, you look sharp, amber washes up. Brother Ambrose don't teach you that, I guess. Useful things."

"No, Poppa. But I like the stories."

"That's in order, little one." Poppa looked up. Henry followed his stare. There were ships on the water. They were beautiful. The big sails were red, with golden lions on them.

Henry. Wake up, Henry.

Poppa stood slowly and picked up his fishing spear. He turned to Henry. "Go find your sisters. Take them back to Uncle Bleys." Poppa looked scared. But Poppa was never scared—

His eyes opened.

"Look! He's awake!" Mattie leaned over him, smiling.

Behind her, he could see Alfie and Valdemar. He smiled. Something was wrapped around his chest. He couldn't breathe.

"How are you, boy? How do you feel?" Alfie grabbed his hand, for the first time Henry could remember—it felt like warm leather. He tried to speak. "Alfie…" And then he slipped away, down into the dark.

He was in the abbot's office. The evidence of his crimes was spread out before him on the abbot's desk—the scrolls he'd taken from the library, the wedge he'd used to close the door to his cell and ensure some privacy, Brother Louis' record of his absences from Mass.

"I just wanted to read the *chansons*, father. I've never read things like that before."

"You don't read for pleasure, boy. You read for the glory of God," said Father Jean. "You have broken the Rule of Obedience. Hand me the rod, and take off your shirt."

Wake up, Henry.

He was hiding in the woods. He could see the fire on the thatched roofs. He could see the men on horses as they rode through the village. He could see the swords—

WAKE UP.

It was night. Moonlight coated the white walls, the chairs, the tables. Mattie was asleep in a corner. Alfie and Valdemar were stretched out on benches. He tried to sit up, but something wrapped his chest and side. The pain came then. Henry felt himself slipping away—

Stay with me, Henry. We have decisions to make.

Henry struggled to breathe. After a few moments, he felt the pain recede a little. He sat up carefully and looked down at himself. He was wrapped in linens, mostly around his chest and belly.

Get up, and put on your shoes. There are things you must see.

"Can't…it…wait?"

No. I'm sorry.

Slowly, Henry got to his feet. The floor seemed to sway

back and forth, like the deck of a ship.

Put me on. I shall lend you strength.

Clinging to the bedframe, Henry reached for Excalibur and buckled it on. The pain in his joints ebbed as the sword's cool power rose up from the ground. The wounds, the ache, the fever were still there, but he could stand and walk again, even if he was slow and stiff.

He laced up his boots and put on his tunic and cloak. Stepping into the corridor, he saw his room was guarded, but he raised his finger to his lips, and the guards nodded and sat back down.

"How long have I been out?"

A night and a day and a night.

They made their way upstairs, to a trap door that led to the roof. Henry paused to catch his breath, and then climbed out.

"Where are we?"

The central keep. Can you see?

Henry squinted. The castle and the town were outlined in torchlight. The outer courtyard was a sea of campfires. "Geoffrey's invested the main courtyard."

Yes.

Henry felt his heart sink. "What happened? Geoffrey's army...it's almost double."

You see the campfires of the armies of Raymond of Toulouse, and King Philip of France.

"He stabbed us in the back. There's a shocker."

Not yet. They are still negotiating, Philip, Geoffrey, and the Queen. But in the end—

"Geoffrey wins."

Yes.

Henry sagged against the battlement and sank down to sit cross-legged on the floor. "How long before they come for me?"

I am a sword, not a diplomat. What I know is from the speech of your friends in your room as you slept. But soon; there is no reason for any of them to delay.

"Well, we can run away, I guess. And once I heal, we can come back for Geoffrey."

Excalibur hesitated for a moment. *Of course. And we shall sweep him from his throne.*

Henry rubbed his face. "What aren't you telling me?"

Nothing. I…just wanted to keep you informed.

Henry nodded. "Okay. Whatever you say." He shifted position, and a sick, metallic pain broke through Excalibur's influence. Henry looked down. His bandages were oozing a yellow fluid. "My shoulder, my belly…"

I'm not an expert on healing wounds, just causing them—

"Excalibur."

The chirurgeons here are not the monks of Glastonbury. Your injuries have become infected.

"How long do I have?"

I saw Sir Gawain, wounded full sore, rise from his couch and defeat the Black Knight—

"Stop it."

Excalibur hesitated for a moment. *A week. Perhaps a little more.*

"Can't you do anything?"

I am doing what I can. You stand, you walk.

"For now. Right?" Excalibur didn't reply. "What happens…after?"

If I am left masterless on the ground, anyone could take me. You must not let that happen. Even if you stick me back into stone, that will be something. Make Sir Percival responsible for returning me— Oh. You meant what happens to you.

"No. That was it." Henry's sigh threatened to turn into a sob. "Can't you do *anything?*" Despite his best efforts, his voice broke and he leaned back. He realized that tears were leaking down his face. It wasn't *fair*. He'd never wanted a sword. He'd just wanted to stay in Paris, hang with Alfie and Mattie and the others, read, eat, steal…

I…I am sorry, Henry. This burden should never have been yours.

"Yeah."

Despite everything, you have done your best. I am proud of you.

Henry smiled and wiped his nose. "A compliment. Great. Now I know I'm dying."

It is true. You have grown in ways I never expected. I promise, I shall not look at a…a…whatever you are in the same way again.

"Then at least I did something right."

I cannot tell when you are joking.

"Neither can I, sometimes."

Slowly, Henry got to his feet. The wave of fear and sorrow had passed over him, leaving him tired but clear. The feelings were still there, waiting, but for right now…

"So why did you bring me up here? Just to remind me to stick you in bedrock?"

You asked what I could do. For you I can do nothing. But there is still something you can do.

"For the Round Table?"

Yes. If you like, for the Round Table.

"Go ahead. I'm all ears."

* * * *

Percy was dreaming of a *hareem* of beautiful Saracen maidens when Henry shook him awake. "Come on, Percy. We've got work to do."

In the beginning, Percy had sometimes doubted his decision to swear loyalty to Henry. The man (let's face it, the boy) had all the panache of a rabid weasel; sometimes he got a *shifty* look in his eyes, which was the last thing you wanted to see in someone who was standing next to you in battle; and over time it had become distressingly clear that he was afflicted with madness, which was forgivable in a knight, and intelligence, which wasn't.

But there had been moments when Percy saw another Henry looking out of those eyes. A prince. Maybe even a king. He saw it when Henry had spared his life, and again when Henry had admitted his humble origins and the nature of his sword. Over time, that other Henry had spoken to Percy more and more often.

Now, in the dead of night, in this castle hallway silvered

by the moon, that Henry glared out of eyes resting in a skull of a face, whose features had been hollowed out by pain and illness. And Percy could no more disobey than he could give up breathing.

From Henry's room they went down to the main hall of the keep, where dozens of the Queen's knights slept with the dogs on the straw floor. Quietly, Percy and Henry discussed which knights they would use for the mission. After they had chosen ten, Percy woke them up in silence, and they drifted down to the gates.

As they walked, Percy saw the knights staring at Henry like he was some hero out of legend, a Lancelot or a Roland. Everyone had seen that sword strike into the rubble, had seen the hill collapse, and seen Henry fall, stricken by arrows. It was the kind of story that *didn't* grow in the telling; it was big enough already. As usual, Henry seemed entirely unaware of the effect he was having on the warriors around him.

The sentries at the main gates were serious and determined. Fortunately, there was a smaller gate, farther along the wall, that had been hidden behind barrels of salted fish for the townspeople. They used that, and within minutes they were mingling with the crowds in the broken outer court.

"Where are their stables?" asked Henry. One of the men—Clovis—pointed out of the courtyard and then right. "On the south side, by the stream. Water for the horses." Henry nodded.

The horses hadn't been that necessary in the Battle of Narbonne, and Geoffrey had stabled them far down the wide Boulevard St. Jacques, hundreds of yards from the front lines. Percy and Henry and the men walked casually down the oddly empty street, as if they were just a bunch of men returning from a late night at the tavern, and not about to ride, and kill.

It was in the stables, saddling the horses, that the reality of what they were doing sank in. Even in Dulwich, Percy had had an armiger and a smith for his serious battles. Tonight, the knights were their own squires and stable lads and armorers. Tonight there would be no heralds, no chivalry, no ransom. No second chances. Tonight was the real thing.

Finally, they were mounted, a dozen lightly armored men on fast, steady horses.

Henry stared at them from his hollow eyes. "Gentlemen, this is a stupid stunt. I've got nothing to lose, but if any of you want to change your minds, do it now."

"Save the speeches." It was Clovis.

"All right. Remember, yell and shout—" Henry stopped as a spasm of coughing overtook him. Percy reached out, but Henry waved him off. "Make a lot of noise. People have to see us charge, they have to know we're not assassins trying to stab Geoffrey from behind. But if we're loud and we challenge him to a melee, or I challenge him to single combat, then he can't run or back down or have his mercenaries shoot us with crossbows. Right?" Henry turned to Percy.

Percy smiled, embarrassed. "Well, that's the theory. At least, he can't do that with Count Raymond and his brother and the other nobles watching."

Henry straightened his back. "If I die, who will take my sword?"

Percy swallowed. "I will, My Lord." Henry stared at him, and Percy spoke again. "I will, Henry."

"Will you use it?"

"No, Henry."

"No. No matter what. Instead, you will run, you will flee, to the Cathedral of St. Just, and before the altar, you will ram it point-first into the foundation. Swear it."

"I swear, on my soul."

Henry looked around. "If Percy dies, who will take my sword?"

Clovis answered. "I will. I swear, I will take it to the cathedral, and I will bury it in the living rock."

Around the circle, they all swore. When Otho, the last one, had given his promise, Henry nodded and nudged his horse out of the stables. The others followed.

Henry hadn't been on a horse since the flight from Toulouse with Mattie, and he had never ridden a horse into battle. Toulouse had been a big mess, but it hadn't been a battle, not really. Now he felt the strike of the horse's hooves in his wounds; each jolt was agony, cushioned partly by Excalibur. "Remind me about the defenses."

Percy nodded. "Prince Geoffrey has knocked down the nearby houses to create an open space around his camp, one that is easy to guard. In that space, we will meet his sentries. If we pass them, we are in the outer ring of his camp, where the mercenaries and engineers are sleeping. They are gathered in ranks and files, so we can ride between the rows without trampling them."

Henry smiled. "Percy, you're beginning to think like a human being, and not a knight. You'll have to watch that." Percy blushed.

"If they wake, they may fire on us, so that we face arrows both before and behind. If we live, then in the center, on a rise opposite the main towers of the castle, is Geoffrey's pavilion. It is watched at all times by his personal guard, but I doubt they will expect a charge of horses in the middle of the night. We ride over his pavilion, slashing and challenging him to single combat—"

"—and if we're lucky, our horses trample him to death before he can take me up on it." Henry muttered this last low enough so that only Percy could hear it.

By now, they had emerged on the boulevard. Ahead of them, at the end of the road, the camps of Geoffrey and Raymond were lit by torches. "Give me everything you have," Henry muttered.

I will, said Excalibur.

The night became brighter to Henry, every detail picked out as if by torchlight. The pain receded, replaced by the cold certainty of the sword. He nudged his horse with his heels, and they started forward.

In the first block, they moved from a walk to a trot. By the second block, they were in full gallop. And now they were coming up on the sentries and the guard posts. Henry leaned forward as Excalibur had taught him, his legs taking his weight. He drew Excalibur and waved it above his head.

"CHARGE!" he yelled, as they galloped through the outer perimeter. Guards were shouting and bells were being rung. The whole camp was waking up. There was a hiss and a thump, and a horse went down, an arrow poking from its hindquarters. More hisses, more yells, and the soldiers were scrambling like ants in a mound that's just been kicked.

To your right, five mercenaries with crossbows. Charge them and they'll scatter.

"I hear you," said Henry, and the mercenaries fled.

Wheel your horse, scatter their friends, and continue the charge forward.

Henry's horse whinnied, pranced, and came down hard with her hooves. The other mercenaries scrambled for their breeches and weapons.

Ahead of you, a squad of pikemen are forming to break your charge. Disperse them before they fix their polearms.

They raced toward the pikemen and rode over them, shattering the spears. And now forward again, regaining momentum. Arrows flew past them. They leaped over a ditch, and a hurdle, and now they were in the inner camp. Ahead of them, up the slope, were the tents of the princes, glowing with firelight, bristling with guards.

Percy's horse whinnied in pain and went down. Then Clovis's horse, and Otho's. Henry jumped off his and looked down. Geoffrey's engineers had dug little holes in the earth, just big enough to trap a horse's foot and break its leg.

Don't stop. Keep moving. A knife in the back is dishonorable, but surprise is part of war. Surprise him. Charge.

Henry pelted up the slope. His breath caught. For a moment, Excalibur's power faded. Underneath the energy and the fear, Henry could feel the fatigue and pain the sword was keeping from him.

I am still weak from the siege. Cleaving stone isn't easy.

"Now you tell me."

Now the soldiers were coming down the slope at them. Henry shattered a pike, and a two-handed sword. A soldier went down, his chain mail in tatters. Henry stood in one place and let the soldiers run toward him, taking them as they came, letting them tumble past clutching arms and legs. The fatigue returned, and the pain. This time, they didn't leave. Henry glanced down for a moment. Blood was dripping out from underneath his mail shirt.

Finally, the soldiers stopped coming down. The rest of Geoffrey's men stood, waiting for him on the top of the hill. Henry marched up, trying to hide the shakiness in his arms and legs. Percy and the others followed.

Henry, do it now. I cannot help much longer.

There were four giant tents. They charged the first, cutting it down. Empty. The second. And then the tent flaps of the last two whipped open. There was John, and Brissac. And Raymond, staring at him without any shame.

And Geoffrey.

"We had an appointment in Paris, I think," said the prince. He brought up his bastard sword and attacked.

He swung one-handed, and the force of the blow as it hit Excalibur knocked Henry back a full yard. Then Geoffrey came again, and again. Some warriors are strong, and some are fast, and some are precise; Geoffrey was all three. Now he was chopping at Henry's hands, now at his torso, aiming for his injured shoulder. In a heartbeat, Geoffrey had taken the initiative, and it was all Henry could do to hold on.

This is the knight we fought on the battlements. The good one.

"No kidding."

Henry's blood seeped down his arm onto his sword hand, making the grip slippery. He could hear his breath rattling in his chest, in between parrying Geoffrey's attacks. He couldn't hold on much longer.

Henry leaped back. They circled each other. Henry caught a glimpse of the other knights—Brisssac, John, Raymond. Their faces were slack, their jaws hanging.

They are amazed that you still live, fighting against this prince.

"Yeah…" Henry grinned, and ducked under Geoffrey's next blow. He faced Raymond. "It's the sword, My Lords. It's magic. If it can do this for me, imagine what it will do for Geoffrey!"

Geoffrey came at him again, nicking him in the arm. For a moment, they were corps-a-corps. "Playing them against me. Clever lad."

Geoffrey sprang back, flourished his sword and circled. Without looking at Raymond or John, he said, "We have sworn oaths. You know what happens to oath-breakers."

There was a roaring in Henry's ears. Something was wrong with his eyes, too—the torch flames doubled and went out of focus. Where was Geoffrey? Henry spun and found himself facing the prince. Geoffrey spun his blade so the flat of it faced Henry. With a casual twist, he batted Excalibur out of Henry's hand.

Henry took a step. And another. Then he fell to his knees, a puppet without strings. He no longer had the strength even to move his fingers. Color returned to the world, and noise, and pain. The pain was terrible, a fierce stabbing in his chest and side, a fever, a throbbing in his arms and head. It hurt to breathe.

Geoffrey put his foot on Excalibur. "This blade is mine. Does anyone disagree?" He gazed at John, at Raymond. They said nothing. Geoffrey looked down at Henry.

"What say you, Master Henri? Don't you agree that this sword is mine? Don't you apologize for stealing it from me, and putting me to all this trouble?"

Faint and far away, Henry heard Excalibur. *Do not yield! Do not yield!*

Geoffrey turned. "Brissac, bring out my bride." Brissac entered the tent, and came out holding Mattie by the arm. Geoffrey took her casually, but Henry could see that even without an armored glove, his grip was strong enough to draw blood. With one hand, he forced Mattie to her knees.

"Mathilde, you need to see this. It is an...object lesson...in obedience. The disobedient never come to any good. Isn't that right, Henri?"

It was a tableau—Geoffrey with a sword in one hand, Mattie in the other, Excalibur under his boot. Mattie was shrieking, but all the voices seemed very far away. The only thing that was clear in Henry's mind was that Geoffrey had Mattie. Geoffrey had Alfie and Valdemar and Percy and the men who had come with him. Geoffrey had Excalibur.

Henry, don't leave. Not now. Stay here! I order you to—

The darkness welled up. "Yes," said Henry. "Yes."

His eyes closed. It was good to sleep.

30. THE EMPEROR OF THE WEST

This time, there were no dreams. When he opened his eyes, it was to a broad waking in clear daylight. But he could not remember much, and it didn't seem to matter. He was bandaged in clean white linen, without a speck of dirt or blood.

He sat up, slowly. His head swam. It was hard to move; it felt like every joint had been coated with rust. He felt old, and he knew he shouldn't.

He stood, and felt shackles on his feet. Just the word "shackles" sounded strange. He repeated it to himself several times.

The curtains were thin and white. He pulled them back.

He was in a cage. It was a carriage with bars, a circus cart. There was a door, but it was locked.

There had been a time, he knew, when he could have opened that lock. He just needed a…a…*a lathe, an adze, and two cross-mitre saws*…no. That wasn't right. A sledge-hammer? No. It didn't matter anyway. When he touched the lock with his right hand, it felt numb, as if the hand were a block of wood. He should have been holding something in that hand, but it was gone.

It was cold and damp. The sky was a bright, blank gray.

That wasn't right either. The sky should have been blue, the weather warm. Trees. Instead, a barren plain, dotted with flat pools reflecting the sky, and the smell of seaweed.

"So, Henry, we're awake."

He turned too quickly, and lost his balance. He grabbed onto the bars to keep from falling back onto his bed. The voice was familiar, and he knew in his head that this man was dangerous. But he couldn't summon any fear, and the man seemed friendly enough. He was all in white, white hose, white tunic, a silver coronet.

The man put a key in the lock. "We're not going to do anything foolish, are we?"

That's right, he thought. *My name is Henry.* "No."

The man smiled and entered. "Good. Sit down. Let me see your wounds."

Henry sat on the bed and the man...Geoffrey. Yes. Geoffrey unwrapped the bandages with a professional gentleness. Underneath were two deep arrow wounds, and assorted other cuts and gashes, all clean and stitched.

Geoffrey nodded. "Mmmm. This will sting a bit. Don't worry." He opened a small flask, and a sharp, winey reek filled the room. He poured some of the contents on a cloth and daubed Henry's wounds. It did sting, but after a moment, the pain faded and the liquid dried away. Geoffrey started to rewrap the dressing. "The Saracens distill this liquor from new wine. *Al-ghawl*, they call it. It will get you drunk quickly, if you're willing to burn the lining off your mouth. But wounds bathed in it seldom rot, and it can arrest the spread of gangrene and blood poisoning if you apply it soon enough. My brother wrote of it from the Holy Land. It was the only thing I asked of him—that he send back reports of new discoveries. He didn't see the significance, of course. Now, if it had to do with horses, or poetry..." Geoffrey retied the last bandage. "You'd also be amazed at the power of boiled water and clean bandages. I'm making them all standard for my army. Plague and camp-fever will be a thing of the past."

Henry frowned. He knew a response was expected, but the words swam away from him. It didn't seem terribly important.

Geoffrey studied Henry, his eyes searching, like…like a man buying a horse. "What do you think of that?" He waited a moment. There was no response from Henry.

Geoffrey sighed. "All right. You don't remember, clearly, but we've had this discussion before, on several occasions. I have no more time to spare, Henry, so we'll try a little experiment to jog your wits. Do you understand? Just nod your head."

Henry did.

"Good. I'm going to show you something. Whatever happens, you may not touch it. Do you understand?" Another nod. Geoffrey smiled. "Come along." He unshackled Henry's legs and left the cart. Henry followed.

"Where are we?"

"The Camargue. They had a hard winter and a scant spring. And now the summer is passing, but no better. Ah well, it's all part of the new empire. We'll see what we can do to help."

Henry frowned. The words "help" and "Geoffrey" didn't fit together somehow. Another fact. Also not important.

With Henry at his heels, Geoffrey strolled through the camp. It was vast, a city on foot and horseback— thousands of men, wagons, horses. At the center was a big tent, ringed with guards. They walked in.

Inside, it was an austere headquarters—maps and almanacs, writing tablets, scrolls, armor, a meeting table. And by the bed, a box. Geoffrey reached in, and pulled out a sword.

Excalibur…

It was like falling from a height back into your own body. He was himself again, his memories, his feelings. Grief welled up inside him, sharp as a knife, sour as vinegar. He fell to his knees.

"Excalibur…"

His head was buried in his hands, and hot tears dripped through his fingers. He remembered everything, and it *hurt*.

"Interesting." Geoffrey sheathed Excalibur, replaced it in the box, and locked the lid. "I take it you are…returned?"

Henry nodded.

"Can you hear the sword? Is it speaking to you?"

Henry opened his mouth to answer, then stopped himself. Geoffrey smiled. "No matter. It speaks to me, and that's enough." Geoffrey's eyes were wintery, and Henry noticed streaks of pure white in his hair and beard. His smile was thin and taut as a strangling cord—not the charming grin Henry remembered from their first meeting, but the dried corpse of one, the skeleton of a smile. For a moment, he looked—

"What does she say?"

The horrible grin grew wider. "Oh, that would be telling." He led Henry out of the tent.

They stopped at an armorer's booth. More relaxed— *now that Excalibur is back in the box?*—Geoffrey picked up a dagger and let fly, straight into the trunk of a dead tree that was clearly being used as target practice by his men. "Do you know how long it's been since our fight at Narbonne?"

Henry didn't respond.

"Three months. Between your wounds, and the toll Excalibur took of you, you were very close to death. I could have let you die."

"Should I thank you?"

Geoffrey smiled his old, glorious smile. "Ah, that's the Henry I remember. No, you were an experiment. To my knowledge, you are the first man to bear one of the Great Swords, lose it, and survive the loss. Your physical wounds healed weeks ago, but your spirit wandered. I had to see what happened. Killing you would have been a crime against Philosophy."

"What about my friends?"

"I have not harmed them."

A faint warning bell rang in Henry's mind, shunted to one side by an image of—

"Mattie, what about—"

"Her real name is Berengaria, and you will not speak it." Geoffrey smiled coldly at Henry's reaction. "Ah, she didn't tell you."

"No."

"Well, no matter. In a little while, she will have the royal wedding that is her birthright. Your conduct has made it more difficult, but I have already annulled one marriage for her sake. She shall still be Queen."

Three months. Geoffrey had sent him to Glastonbury in October. Narbonne was in May. It was August, then. He'd missed his name day. In Paris, the rains had just begun, turning the dirt roads to mud. The Worm had closed the windows of his "scriptorium" against the damp. Alfie and Valdemar would be running "The Relic Game" or "The Honest Turk" on the pilgrims at the Cathedral of Notre Dame, before they all fled back to their villages.

And he was a special prisoner in an army camp, touring the swamps and mountains. One of—how many?—who had held a legendary sword, had wielded it in battle. Had lost it. Had lived. That didn't feel like him. It was like another life, separate and cut off. *He had drawn the sword from the stone.*

They passed a squad of archers, practicing with enormously tall bows. "English longbows. They can pierce armor, you know. Superior to the crossbow, but it takes more training. They will break cavalry for me."

Beyond the bowmen were pikemen, practicing in formation with their polearms. "It's called the hedgehog. Another way to shift the balance from knights to footmen." Geoffrey stopped and studied them for a while. "They're mercenaries, too. You see where I'm going with this?"

"No."

"A professional army. A world where no one stands between the people and their emperor. No knights taking what isn't theirs, no petty squabbles laying waste to villages and fields. That should appeal to you."

Henry chewed on that. He'd spent so much time hating knights...but it didn't matter if their replacement was just as bad, a lunatic killer with a sense of entitlement.

Geoffrey continued. "You have been given a rare privilege, Henry. You will be present at the birth of a new order." A clerk approached them, bowed to Geoffrey, and handed him a scroll. Geoffrey read it. "Well done. And right on time."

"What is it?"

"Not yet."

They passed a cooking fire, with men gathered around a spit. Geoffrey reached in and grabbed two pieces of roast fowl. The men nodded at Geoffrey; he nodded back, bit into one bird, and gave Henry the other.

"Pretty casual for an emperor. Shouldn't they be kneeling or something?"

"The more respect you demand, the less you receive. The more you give, the more is returned to you. When it's time, they know their place." He pointed to a pair of rocks, and they sat.

Once Henry smelled the bird, he was suddenly ravenous, and he tore into the flesh. For a few minutes, there were no sounds but chewing and swallowing.

"Be careful," said Geoffrey. "That's the first solid food you've had in a while." He smiled again. "I remember saying something like that to you back in Paris."

"I was your prisoner then, too."

"And what can we learn from that?"

Henry shrugged and focused on the bird. It was tough, and marinated in wine and rosemary. Pigeon, maybe? Whatever it was, it was delicious. "Emperor. How's that working out for you?"

"My reach is longer than my father's was. I control the Empire of the West, from Ireland to the Rhine."

"Isn't Richard king of England? And Philip is king of France, and Raymond count of Toulouse—"

"They serve me, now. And come October, they shall swear fealty at my imperial coronation."

Henry nodded, but didn't stop chewing. "I don't see Richard coming all the way back from the Holy Land just to kneel in front of you."

"My brother will be gone for some time, particularly if he travels through Austria on his way back. By the time he does return, he will have no one to take his cause. He hasn't been England's most popular king."

"Hate to break it to you, Geoff, but none of you Plantagenets are that popular. Except for your Da. And you killed him."

Geoffrey's eyes grew dark for a moment, and then he smiled. "That's where you come in, Henry. You're for the common man, aren't you?" Geoffrey broke the bones of his bird and sucked off the last bits of flesh. "Think of the implications of a true empire. Safety for the common man. No more Sanbrucs. No more needless destruction. No more saboteurs sneaking in under the cover of night and spraying Greek fire about the place—I thrashed Johnny for that, by the way. A return to the days of the Caesars. Peace and order from Hadrian's Wall to the Appian Way. The flourishing of learning, medicine—the kind of healing that saved your life. You can help make that happen."

"How?"

Geoffrey stood and clapped his hands. Brissac appeared. "Soon, Henry. An emperor has much to do. Until we meet again."

Brissac took Henry back. As they walked to the cage, Henry studied him. The knight had aged years since Henry had seen him in Toulouse—he was gaunt, and there was gray in the black of his hair and mustache. The vicious self-righteousness was gone, too, replaced by…what?

"So, how are things, Eddy? Good to be on the winning side, I guess."

Henry braced himself for an offhand blow, but the only response was a one-word answer. "Yes."

"Geoffrey made you a duke or a baron yet? I'd guess he'd be scattering rewards right and left by now."

"No."

They arrived at the cart. Brissac opened it and helped Henry in. After he locked the door again, Brissac remained for a moment. "At Glastonbury, you could have killed me."

"Uh…yeah."

Brissac stared at him for a moment, and then left.

31. HARD SELL

The next few weeks were strange and dull at the same time. The camp traveled regularly. When it did, units of Geoffrey's army would disappear for several days, only to reappear later, sometimes bloody.

Brissac let Henry out for meals and exercise; otherwise, Henry stayed in the cage. It was a schedule that gave him plenty of time to think, but parts of him were still lost to time and injury. Feelings would well up in a flash and disappear again, leaving him numb, staring out across the woods or fields; sometimes his memory fled, and he was nothing but a blank, staring through the bars. At first, the lightest effort tired him—the first meeting with Geoffrey and Brissac had exhausted him, and he fell asleep as soon as he sat down. He cried easily.

Instead of thinking about what had happened, Henry found himself focused on the present: How much farther he could walk that day without exhausting himself. The taste of food. Fighting those moments when fatigue would hit him out of nowhere, putting him to sleep in the middle of the day.

Worse than everything was the nagging feeling that he was incomplete—that his arm was missing something, that he had somehow lost a piece of his body as vital as a hand or a foot. Sometimes the feeling would come in the middle of the night, and that was bad: Memory had an open door then, and Henry would relive Glastonbury and Narbonne and Toulouse until dawn.

From the guards' gossip, Henry slowly built up a picture of the world outside the camp. Mathilde was in Paris, but no one could tell him if she was still supposed to marry Geoffrey, or go to a nunnery, or teach Natural Philosophy as Christendom's only beautiful, crazy female lecturer. Narbonne had fallen without any more bloodshed, so Henry could only hope that Alfie and Valdemar and Percy were all right.

And there were rebellions. Even with the fealty of the King of France and the Count of Toulouse, Geoffrey's domain was not docile—small revolts seemed to break out regularly, led by local squires, dukes, and knights who fancied taking a crack at the new emperor. Geoffrey would leave with a squad or two, put down the rebels, and return.

In a weird sort of way, Henry's captivity was comfortable. He felt like he was fathoms beneath the waves, with no need to struggle anymore.

The first sign that things had changed was when Brissac woke him at dawn. For the past two weeks, squires and pageboys had been guarding him, and none of them had even bothered to get him up for meals.

Brissac shook him awake, backed by two men-at-arms.

"Put this on." Brissac tossed Henry a dressing gown. "Move."

"What…"

"The Emperor will tell you. *Allez.*"

They took him to a tent next to Geoffrey's headquarters. Inside was a barber, a tub of hot water, and a pile of clothing. They made Henry strip and bathe. He expected the usual insults a naked man gets from those who are still clothed, but Brissac and his troopers stayed silent. Once Henry was wearing breeks again, the barber shaved him close and lopped off his pony-tail.

Then they dressed him. Fine linen hose, rich cloak, soft boots, even a few rings—and a tunic with an insignia he had never seen before: *Or*, a sword rising from a stone, on a field *gules*. *Or* and *gules:* gold and crimson, the colors of the Plantagenets.

They led him into Geoffrey's tent. Geoffrey was surrounded by knights, staring at a table full of maps. He looked up as they entered.

"Stop. Step away from him." Brissac and the others stepped back, and Geoffrey scrutinized Henry in his new clothes. "All right. Where are his weapons?"

"My Lord, we can't give a prisoner—"

"If this is to work, they must see him as a knight. Give him a sword and dagger—stop making faces, Edmond, you can give him practice weapons." Geoffrey took Henry's chin in his hand and moved Henry's head right and left. "I don't like the shave. It's too good, not common enough. Next time, tell the barber to be a little less meticulous." Then Geoffrey focused on Henry himself. "How's your Breton, boy? Can they still understand you in Armorica?"

"Sure," Henry shrugged. "I can ask for directions and buy a drink."

"Today, you ride with me." Geoffrey turned to the box that held Excalibur. He looked into Henry's eyes, grinning his skeleton grin. Then he took out the sword and buckled it on. A shiver worked its way up the back of Henry's neck.

The sun was still low when they mounted their horses. It was a full company, dressed for a formal occasion. The bannerets were up, the soldiers in their finest livery, the knights in their shiniest armor. They rode in formation up the high road to the town of Vannes, and galloped through the front gate as befitted an embassy from an emperor.

Once they were through the gate and circling the town square, Geoffrey jerked right and left with his thumb.

Detachments broke off and rode through the town. Within minutes, the people of Vannes started to gather.

As they waited, Henry studied Geoffrey. The casual, almost relaxed air Geoffrey had had in the past was gone. He was strung tight as a harp.

Half an hour later, everyone was in the square, ordered by rank, from the lord mayor down to the children of the streetsweepers. Brissac rode close and held up a clenched fist—*they're all here*. Geoffrey nodded, and nudged his charger into the center of the square.

"I am Geoffrey Plantagenet. Your emperor." A murmur ran through the crowd. One or two people made as if to kneel. Geoffrey waved at them. "No. I do not accept your obeisance. Stand."

He pitched his voice higher and louder. "When a duke moves against me, that is simply rebellion. I execute him and move on. But when my people move against me— when they whisper against my right to kingship, when they murmur against Excalibur—that is *treason*."

He wheeled his horse around the square. "Evil tongues spread slander. Evil minds breed lies. Evil hearts desire pride and rebellion. Behold the sword of kings, Excalibur!"

Geoffrey drew the sword from its sheathe and held it high. It shone in the sunlight, and the crowd gasped. Henry stifled a moan; seeing Excalibur unsheathed was like being punched in the heart.

Henry stared at the sword and at Geoffrey. For a moment, it was as if he, Henry, held Excalibur again. He could decode Geoffrey's grip on the sword, read every intention in his body. Geoffrey wanted to kill someone. He was looking for a target. He wanted an example. He was going to run forward and kill—

"NO!" Henry leaped between Geoffrey and the lord mayor, who was paralyzed with fear, his eyes bulging wide. "I HAVE SEEN THE SWORD OF KINGS!"

Geoffrey froze, the veins standing out on his neck and forehead. Henry continued in a rush. "I saw Prince

Geoffrey pull the sword of kings from the stone myself! He is the true king!" He turned to the crowd, spread his arms, and then knelt in front of Geoffrey.

Slowly, terribly slowly, Geoffrey unclenched. He smiled down at Henry, and spoke quietly. "Oh, well done, boy. How did you ever guess that's what I wanted?" He held the point of Excalibur an inch from Henry's eyes. "Now get up, and tell your people what I want them to do."

Henry stood and faced the crowd. "Bow down. Bow down to your lord, the Emperor of the West." They stood, uncertain, looking to the lord mayor. Henry clenched his teeth, grabbed the Mayor's collar, and forced him to the ground, where they both groveled, their faces in the dirt.

"Very good," said Geoffrey. He dismounted and pointed Excalibur at a two-story building that bulked over the other buildings in the square. "Your town hall." He stalked toward the building, sword out. The crowd parted for him. "You don't need it." Geoffrey lifted up Excalibur and brought it down on the thick stone walls.

The building collapsed.

Dust and air shot outward, coating everyone in a thick layer of dirt, but no stones or wood moved even an inch toward the crowd. In an instant, the hall was nothing but a pile of rubble. Henry clenched his fists. Using the sword that way had nearly fried him; Geoffrey had done it as casually as swatting a fly.

Now Geoffrey turned to the crowd. "No longer are you 'Vannes.' Now, you are called 'St. Louis,' after the patron saint of loyalty and oaths. No longer shall you have a mayor or a council or a charter of liberties. You shall be ruled by my regent, until such time as you beg my pardon and I grant it."

He sheathed Excalibur and remounted his horse. "Slanderers in your midst have murmured about Excalibur, about how I found it, proved myself worthy, won the sword, and won to kingship. I am your Emperor. I will not lower myself to dispute lies, like some clerk in a debate.

Instead, I give you the Muttering Knight, Sir Henry of Sanbruc, who has held the sword Excalibur, who was there when I drew it, and who knows the truth!"

Geoffrey nudged his horse closer to Henry. "You've just saved a lot of lives. That will be your service to me from now on." He tossed Henry a parchment scroll. Henry unrolled it, and saw a long speech in Breton.

"You will have many towns and villages to convince. Edmond will help you with your mission." Geoffrey bent down to speak more quietly. "And remember, Henry, when your job becomes a sentence; when the taste of dead hopes threatens to choke you; when it seems that you cannot tell the same story even one more time…remember that each commoner you convince is one who will live a long and comfortable life, thanks to you." He smiled. "Starting with your old Welshman, and the freak who made your swords."

Henry stared up at him.

Geoffrey nodded. "As I said, I haven't harmed them. Yet." He straightened up and wheeled his horse through the gates, accompanied by his personal guard. Brissac remained, with his mercenaries.

Henry stared at the crowd. They stared back. Henry started to read the scroll. "I am Henry of the Lost Village of Sanbruc…I saw Geoffrey Plantagenet, in Glastonbury, pull the sword from the stone…"

He tasted ashes on his tongue. Maybe it was from the rubble of the hall.

32. PUBLIC RELATIONS

"...and thus he found the sword, and carried it forth out of the Chapel Perilous. This I saw with mine own eyes, I, Henry of Sanbruc, called also the Knight Who Mutters."

Henry stepped down from the dais and let the guards clear a path for him through the townspeople. There was one thing to be said for a lie: The more you told it, the easier it became. He adjusted his clothes—scarlet and miniver, with gold accents and plenty of jewelry—and walked to the inn at the far side of the square. As always, he walked straight ahead, not lingering, not looking at anyone. The guards fell in behind, their pikes gleaming. The *bourgeois* stared after him, ragged and thin. He could feel their eyes on the back of his neck.

Inside, the Swiss had already cleared a place at the boards for him to eat in privacy, if he wished. Instead, he turned to Hauptmann and said, "I'll eat in my room." Hauptmann nodded, and Henry went upstairs.

A book lay on the table in his private room. Henry picked it up—Aristotle's *Politics*, just as he'd asked. He had long since stopped being impressed by the value of the books, or the fact that whatever volume he requested, Geoffrey sent him by fast horse. As bribes went, it was as subtle as offering wine to a drunkard, and as effective.

He shrugged off his tunic, lit a couple of oil lamps, and tried not to think of the day, or of what he'd have to do tomorrow. Taking occasional careful bites from the roast chicken the innkeeper had sent up, he opened the book and began to read.

Henry had reached the Master's examination of polities with mixed constitutions when the door opened and Brissac entered. The knight sat down opposite him, saying nothing. Henry closed the book and put down his table knife. He waited for Brissac to speak.

Henry knew this might take a while. Since joining Henry on the Propaganda Tour, Brissac had become even more dour and withdrawn than before. He no longer gambled or chased tavern girls. To the mercenaries who knew his battle record, this indicated iron self-control. To Henry, it suggested that something was eating deep into whatever Brissac used for a soul, and it made him nervous. The only thing more unpleasant than a smug Brissac would be a Brissac with issues that he would inevitably try to work out on others.

The hour-candle burned down. The fire hissed in the grate. Finally, Henry turned away from Brissac and reached again for the book.

The knight spoke. "Are you happy now?"

Henry turned over the question in his mind. What was Brissac getting at? Was he serious, sarcastic, bitter? How should Henry respond?

"Why not?"

"Yes." Brissac stood, and paced around the room. He flipped through a stack of books, examined the remains of Henry's dinner, sniffed the wine. "Your wants are satisfied, and so are you."

"And people aren't getting killed. That's always good, I think."

Brissac swigged moodily from Henry's wine cup. "There are more important things than just staying alive."

"Easy to say, when you're the one holding the sword."

Brissac lifted his head and stared at Henry. For the first time, Henry got the feeling that Brissac was actually looking at *him*, instead of at something playing out in his own mind. And Brissac's sword was on his belt.

Finally, Brissac stood. "Yes. It is easy to say." He left the room.

Henry shivered for a moment, and let out a long, pent-up breath. *Normans. Crazy, just crazy.* He climbed into bed. Tomorrow they had a long ride, and another town to save. At least, that's how he was determined to look at it.

As usual, they set off a little after dawn. Geoffrey had left a list of a dozen or more towns and villages deemed insufficiently loyal, where Henry was to expound upon the glory of Geoffrey, his successful quest for Excalibur, and the futility of opposing him.

They traveled in style, Henry, Brissac, and the Swiss. Gold gleamed on their fingers. Gems winked from their scabbards and hilts. Geoffrey's new device, a sword rising from a stone, flew on banners above them. They were followed by a full camp train, crewed by a team of cooks, reeves, manciples, and castellans from one of Geoffrey's estates.

At the crossroads to Dionne, they passed a long line of gallows carrying Geoffrey's insignia. The dead men were strung up with the names of their crimes tied around their feet: *Treason. Poaching. Stealing bread.* Henry opened his Aristotle to the chapter on oligarchies.

About midmorning, the camp train slowed to a halt. Henry jumped off the wagon and walked to the head of the train.

A few yards ahead, the Swiss were pushing people to one side and clearing a path. Brissac looked down at Henry impassively. "We've run into a train of refugees," he said. "It will take a while to clear the trash off the road so we can pass."

"Why not give them some food to—"

"If we do, they'll swarm the wagons." Brissac turned back to the mercenaries.

Henry opened his mouth, closed it, and returned to his wagon. A few minutes later, they rode past the other train. Henry kept his eyes on his book.

When they arrived in Anbal, half the town was left. The eastern walls had been torn down. All the houses east of the main street and south of the church had been destroyed, leaving a plain of rubble and shattered timbers, as though a giant had carelessly stepped on that neighborhood and then moved on. The townsfolk wandered through the wreckage like ghosts, trying to salvage what they could from their homes. Henry looked down at his natty scarlet tunic and felt sick. Why linger here? What more could Geoffrey do to these people?

He could wipe out the whole town, and all the people in it. He could kill Valdemar and Alfie. Henry got a grip and stepped off the cart.

The Swiss took over the inn, tossing the other guests out into the night. The next day, Brissac and the Swiss gathered the *bourgeois* into the town square to hear Henry's speech.

It was hot and muggy. Thick clouds towered over the town walls. Henry opened his collar, but it was too little, too late—he was drenched in sweat from his braies on out. As Brissac walked beside him past the townspeople, Henry heard a voice.

"...of course it's not the *real* Muttering Knight."

He hesitated, but only for a moment. Then he continued on to the platform. He turned around to face the crowd—the skinny, ragged crowd. He opened his mouth. "I...I am..."

Then he closed his mouth again. He walked off the platform, through the crowd, and into the tavern. He went up to his room and shut the door.

He expected Brissac to throw open the door and yank him downstairs, but no one came. After a while, he fell asleep in the hot, close air of the room.

When he woke up, it was late at night. Opening the door, he saw an empty, unguarded hallway. He walked down the stairs to the common room.

It was all but empty, just Brissac, a cup, and a dozen jugs. Brissac stared at him and then drained his cup. Cautiously, Henry sat down opposite. Brissac handed him another cup and poured. They drank, and Brissac filled their cups again. And again.

"When you kill somebody, do you go for the chest, or the head?" So this was pub-talk among the knightly classes. At least with the goliards, you could get some dirty Latin drinking songs.

"I try not to kill people," said Henry. "If I have, it's by accident."

Brissac laughed. "That's because you're not Geoffrey." Brissac leaned in. "He's good at killing people. Very good. Better than I am."

"I'll bet."

"And he's possessed." This was followed by another swig of wine.

"Really? Tell me more."

But Brissac wasn't listening. "You think Geoffrey made me guard you now because I let you escape before? As a punishment?"

"Well—" Brissac wasn't as stupid as he looked, apparently. That's exactly what Henry thought.

Brissac gulped the dregs at the bottom of his cup and poured more wine. "Who do you think sent in all those...those vultures with Greek fire? John? He can't even *build* a fire. It was Geoffrey." Brissac paused to study Henry's reaction, then continued. "He knew there was an escape tunnel under the wall, see? All we had to do was set fire to the supporting beams, and when they burned away the wall would collapse. So he didn't want to waste any time. Break the castle, grab the sword, go. And burn the town, the whole town, mothers and children...just so it wouldn't *get in the way.*" The knight grinned, wide and sloppy. "But I ordered the Greek fire destroyed that morning, poured it into the river. The stuff that remained was just smatterings, here and there."

Brissac emptied his cup again. "It's a filthy thing, Greek fire. Burns forever, water doesn't put it out, it sticks to your skin..." He swallowed, poured again. "There's no honor in it. It's no weapon...for a true king. And that was *before*. Now, there's a devil in him...he's so much worse..."

Brissac trailed off, staring into the middle distance. For a moment, Henry thought Brissac had passed out with his eyes open—it took years of practice to do it, but Brissac looked like he'd put in the drinking time. Then the knight spoke again.

"You," he said to Henry. "You make me laugh. Thinking you'd protect people. Thinking you could keep 'em alive if they kept their heads down. If they *behaved.* As if anything you do matters to Geoffrey. As if he won't kill them all if he wants to. *When* he wants to. Just because he can. You're a joke. A monkey he's tormenting. Your friends, you think they're still alive? They're in the ground. Rotting." Brissac's eyes closed. In a moment, his head was on the table.

Slowly, Henry stood and looked around. The inn door was open. He looked at his tunic, his rings.

Properly pawned, they'd take him far.

33. THE WILD MAN OF MEILHAN

Meilhan was in ruins.

The walls were broken. Burned timbers and cracked stones marked the lots where houses had stood. Henry rode along the track of mud and rocks that had been the main street and listened to the wind blow across the wreckage.

He came to the main square. This was where Old Lady Goncourt had offered him a bowl of onion soup to get her cat. It was rubble now. The tavern was a pile of charred beams. That's where the party had been, after they'd beaten those robbers.

Well, what could he do about it? *I'm open to suggestions,* he thought.

He heard something move in the rubble to his right. He looked—nothing. Maybe it was a bird, or a rat. Henry swallowed. He'd eaten rat before, when he'd gotten hungry enough. It might be rat stew tonight.

He quartered the town. Here and there a building stood, its doors ripped open, its shutters smashed. Again he heard the scuttling. He rode to the town's main well. It was choked with rocks and dirt. The scuttling came back, closer this time. Henry's hand went to his sword. His

285

practice sword. His useless hunk of metal. It was probably a good idea to stop wandering and find a place where he could set up camp and get his back to a wall. He turned his horse to the church.

It was as ruined as the rest of the town. The roof and windows were gone, though most of the walls still stood. Henry led his horse inside and tethered her to a doorpost.

The altar remained, but the furniture and fittings were gone. Henry walked to an open hole that had once held a window. The floor underneath it was coated with a skin of lead and colored glass. The church must have burned, and the window's materials had melted in the fire and cooled on the church floor.

The wind started to bite. It was cold, and night was falling. Henry built a fire. It took a while. Dry wood and kindling were hard to find, and he had to make sparks by striking a flint against the flat of his sword. He imagined what Excalibur would have said if he'd tried that with her. Heh. *You dare use the Sword of Kings as a striking stone?* Henry smiled.

Finally, he had a fire burning against the church wall. He fed the horse the last of the oats. It was the fall, and the grass was going. If he couldn't find more food for the horse, he'd have to sell it. He couldn't eat the poor thing. He'd grown fond of it, and besides, he didn't have a sharp knife to butcher it with.

Then, over the crackling of the fire, he heard the scuttling again. This time it was nearer and louder. It could have been a rat. It could have been the slap of leather against stone. Something was out there in the dark. Henry stood.

And then the sound changed to a howl.

It was an awful thing, like a wolf from Hell. It raised the hairs on Henry's neck and sent his hand to his sword—maybe it was a practice sword, but it was all he had.

He stepped away from the fire so that it was behind

him, illuminating the church. The howling was from outside. He thought about staying where he was, by the fire, but he had to sleep some time. And when he did…it was no choice at all, really.

He stepped outside. The moon was bright and almost full. The howls filled the air. Now it was all around, in front, behind. Henry took another step out into the square.

"Show yourself!"

"AAAIIIYEEEEEE!!"

A big black shape flew out of nowhere, knocking him to the ground and screaming. He had a glimpse of beard and hair and big arms. Then he spun underneath the thing, knocking it off, and leaped to his feet, his sword out.

It growled, drew a sword, and came for him.

The wild man knew what he was doing. He struck at Henry's head, his head again, his chest. He moved like a knight, like his sword was light as air. Without Excalibur, Henry was holding nothing more than a lump of iron, while another one whizzed at his head. He tried to move, to stay on the balls of his feet, to keep his sword up and threatening the stranger. But the power that he'd felt with Excalibur, the knowledge deep in his bones, was gone; every move felt slow, clunky, filled with effort. He was going to lose.

No. Henry forced himself to focus, to remember Excalibur's lessons. It wasn't about stopping the blade. It was about anticipating where the blade would be, forcing it there, taking the initiative—

There was a ringing crash, and the stranger's sword smashed point-first into the mud, forced there by Henry's blade. Henry's next stroke was a blunt sword to the stranger's temple. With the faintest of "oofs," the wild man fell to the ground.

Henry picked up the stranger's sword. It was long and sharp, in excellent shape. It looked familiar. Carved on the hilt was a crude sketch—if you were charitable, you'd say it looked a little like a spastic badger. Henry kneeled down. It was hard to tell in the moonlight, but under the hair, under the beard…It was Percy.

It was easier than Henry expected to drag Percy back inside—the knight had lost a lot of weight. Henry laid him out by the fire and covered him with the blanket. He kept Percy as warm as he could, checking his breathing. When the sun came up, he boiled the last of his dried beef into soup and shook Percy awake.

"Where—"

"Drink it."

Percy grabbed at the cup as if he hadn't eaten for days. *He probably hasn't,* thought Henry. Percy finished the soup, put down the cup and stared at him.

"Are you going to go crazy again?" asked Henry. "Are you going to jump me?"

"I…I…" Percy's face worked under his beard for a moment. Then he raised his hands to his face and started to sob.

To Henry, Percy had always been big, dumb, and invulnerable. What was he supposed to do now? Hug him? Look away? He waited uncomfortably, pretending that Percy wasn't crying.

It was hard to find out what had happened, at first. Percy was half-starved and weepy. It was hard to keep him on the subject.

"We followed you. We saw you fight Geoffrey, wounded and sick as you were, and almost defeat him."

"Almost defeat him?" Geoffrey cleaned my clepsydra. Maybe Percy's still off his rocker.

"Then you fell. And we resolved to fight on. But Geoffrey took Excalibur, and he could not be stopped. He needed no troops. He shattered our blades and then advanced upon us like Death himself."

"How…how many…did he kill?"

"Five…of ours."

"What?"

"When he came to kill us, he paused for a moment,

Excalibur held high. His face twisted, as if he were suffering a fit. Then he shrieked, and charged like a whirlwind. He killed five of us and then, before his lieutenants could stop him, he killed two of his own in his frenzy."

He is possessed, Brissac had said. Henry forced the thought away.

"I tried to reach the princess, but a pikeman swung at me, and I knew no more." Percy was calmer now. He took another gulp from the cup. "When I awoke, the battle was over. Raymond ruled in Narbonne for Geoffrey. I was one of dozens of wounded men left over from the battle. No one marked me, nor cared who I had been or what I had done. Except the Princess."

Oh, no. Henry's heart sank.

"She was determined to fight on. She escaped from Geoffrey and fled with a small retinue, including your friends from Paris."

Henry's jaw dropped. "Alfie and Valdemar joined Mattie to be rebels?"

"Geoffrey has taxed the land into famine. If the people don't poach, or hold back their harvests, they starve. But if they do, Geoffrey hangs them as lawbreakers and rebels. And the Princess is very persuasive."

Well yeah, but still—What had she said to them? What could she have promised? The mind boggled. "I'm going to have a serious talk with them."

"We lived as rebels in the woods. We made our stand here." Percy looked around. "We lost. Aelfred and Valdemar the Valiant were taken prisoner to Paris. The Princess is in a convent there as well, and is to be wed to Geoffrey as soon as he is crowned emperor."

"Valdemar the Valiant?" Blessed St. Dismas. And then, cold as ice—*Alfie won't survive.*

"How did you escape?"

Percy looked away. "I tried to die in battle, Lord! I really tried! But Geoffrey just beat me down again, and…and left me…" His face screwed into a knot, and he started to cry again.

Henry put a hand on Percy's shoulder. "It's okay, Perce. Really. I know you did your best." Percy snuffled and nodded. "Now I need you to do one more thing for me. Can you remember when this battle took place? How many days ago? It's important."

Percy tried to gather his scattered wits. "Two weeks ago…I think. It's hazy…"

Two weeks ago. The day after Henry had left Brissac face down in the tavern. *They're still alive!*

Geoffrey had lied to him. Of course he had. Why hadn't Henry seen it? And then Geoffrey really *had* taken Mattie and Alfie and Valdemar prisoners. But he had left Percy.

It was an invitation: *Come visit scenic Paris. See the sights. Take the bait.*

Henry glanced at the two swords, his own blunted practice sword and Percy's deadly earnest weapon. From a distance, you couldn't tell them apart.

He'd take the bait. And so would Geoffrey.

34. HOME AGAIN, HOME AGAIN

Did you sleep well, Your Majesty?

Geoffrey skinned back his lips in a smile. "Excellently, madam. The apparition of my dead father that you sent me last night was most amusing. And yourself?"

Swords do not sleep. We wait, and watch for the moment. The moment to strike.

Geoffrey did not look up from his work—reckoning the troops he would need to secure Paris for his coronation and subsequent wedding. Most especially, he did not look behind him. He knew what he would see: a beautiful woman with silver eyes, who was somehow more frightening than the worst of nightmares. But you didn't grow to manhood as a Plantagenet by losing a battle. Any battle.

"It would seem to me you have had plenty of opportunity to strike in the last few months. There was the Count of Picardy, the lords of Toulon and Marais, that little town in Alsace—what was its name? And—"

You have defiled me. I shall not forget. I shall not forgive.

"I have your power, madam. I don't need your forgiveness."

Indeed?

The pain that shot through him was appalling. It was a lightning bolt roaring through his nerves and joints, but unlike a lightning bolt, it didn't stop, but went on, and on—

Clenching his teeth, Geoffrey stood and faced the Lady and the Sword. Staring straight into the eyes of the Lady, he shoved his hand through the apparition's chest, drew Excalibur from its sheath, and slammed it against the wall, again and again.

"Is that it? Is that all you have?"

The pain stopped. *No. That is merely a taste of what I will—*

"Listen closely, my blade. From this moment on, each time you move against me, each time you try to thwart my will, an innocent will suffer. Do you understand me?"

There was silence.

"Say 'yes,' or by nightfall you will be hilt-deep in the intestines of a child." Geoffrey waited. Finally—

Yes.

"Excellent. I like my utensils well-behaved."

Geoffrey left the bed chamber and stalked down stairs. With each step, his mood improved. After all, the gifts had been arriving for days, all suitably lavish and gem-encrusted. Philip, Raymond, and the nobility of a dozen tiny German principalities were already in attendance. The Pope himself was riding up from Rome for the coronation—that had taken a lot of work. John had sailed in from England, abusing the castle staff until Geoffrey had found some compliant demoiselles to distract him. He had cleaned up that rat's nest called the University of Paris, locking up the "students" for the duration of the coronation. And to top it all off, he'd just gotten word that Leopold of Austria had committed to giving big brother Richard a suitable reception on his way back from the Crusades. Things were going well. Now all he had to do was check on his bait.

* * * *

"How do I look?"

"Very convincing."

"I want to try that trick where you mix vinegar and soap on your skin and it looks like boils."

"You look fine. Don't overdo it."

"Well, how about the pilgrim drop? You said you'd teach me the pilgrim drop."

"That's just what we need. A holy hermit who cheats pilgrims of their life savings."

Percy pouted. "I want to shave."

"Show me a holy hermit who shaves, and I'll show you a holy hermit who isn't giving it a hundred and ten percent."

"But it *itches*."

"Well, you're the one who grew it. If you hadn't let yourself go, I would never have gotten the idea. Now, babble and drool like we practiced."

Traveling back to Paris had proven to be as difficult as Henry had feared. Geoffrey had made refugee life hard for him before; now that the entire land was organized, it was almost impossible. Every big city had a dozen companies stationed in the surrounding countryside on the lookout for rebels and bandits and people who had looked at Geoffrey the wrong way. Each watch-post had a scribe who carried with him a book of lists of those wanted by the Emperor, with descriptions, sketches, and once or twice even a nice Italian portrait. Of course, all the male portraits tended to look like St. John, and all the female portraits like Mary Magdalene, but still…an "Alpha" for effort on Geoffrey's part.

The good news was that the book was thick. There were clearly a lot of people Geoffrey didn't like. So, as often as not, the sentries just waved people past, rather than hold up traffic for another hour.

Or maybe, thought Henry darkly, *Geoff just wants us to get to Paris quickly so he can deal with me himself.* Whatever the reason, the lack of scrutiny was good luck: While Percy was perfectly all right when it came to the real thing, he was terrible at *faking* crazy.

"I didn't 'let myself go,'" said Percy. "Madness is expected of the knight whose lord dies or forsakes him. Sir Lancelot went mad. Sir Bedivere ate bark and howled at the moon. Sir Palomides wrote chain letters. It's tradition!"

"I *forsook* you?"

"If the greave fits—"

"Shut up and drool."

After passing four checkpoints on the way north, they were coming up on the fifth and final one, the entrance to Paris. They weren't the only ones. Geoffrey's upcoming coronation had attracted thousands of travelers to the city, despite the lateness of the year. Henry noticed, to his satisfaction, that there were dozens of other unwashed holy men entering the gates, often with novices of their own. At this rate, they'd just be two more sacred, smelly drops in the ocean.

The crowds that had shuffled their way north were now compacted into a line of travelers, waiting before the gates for the chance to enter. The guards had divided the line into travelers and freight, an innovation that kept the manure off your boots, mostly. It had the Plantagenet touch—something clever that made life easier, without decreasing Geoffrey's power one bit. And the troop of Benedictines in front of them were prettier than a bunch of horse's rear ends. Almost.

Soldiers walked down the line, asking questions.

"Name?"

"Roger the Hermit, plus one," replied Henry promptly.

The soldier stared at them dubiously. "We've got all the filthy beggars we need right now. Maybe your master could come back in fifty years?"

Henry ignored the sniggers from the Benedictines. "But your honor, my master is of exceeding holiness! He passes miracles all the time!"

"Entertainment, eh? Why didn't you say so? What's his

line?"

"Speaking in tongues."

"*Brek-ek-ek-ex! Brek-ek-ek-ex! Ko-kwax! Ko-kwax!*" babbled Percy obligingly. Maybe he was getting the hang of this after all.

The soldier sighed. "That might play in the sticks, kid, but this is Paris. He got anything else up his sleeve?"

"Uh…healings?"

The soldier's expression cleared. "Now that's always good for a *dixaine* or two. My cousin, he's got the leprosy—"

"Master Roger healed a blind puppy last week. We're trying to work our way up. Got any sick goats?"

* * * *

Coming back to Paris was like coming home, even in the fall, under dead leaves and gray skies. But as he led "Master Roger's" palfrey through the streets, Henry could see that things had changed.

There were two cities now. The first was a festive Paris, preparing for a coronation. The streets were filled with minstrels, jongleurs, pardoners, preachers, and students. The great family palaces of the nobility, from the Tour St. Louis to the Chateau du Capet, were decked out in Geoffrey's colors of crimson and gold. The lions of England were everywhere, and the crowds in the streets were all wearing little sprigs of the broom plant, the *planta genesta* that had been the symbol of Geoffrey's grandfather, founder of the line. That was obviously the Paris that Percy saw. His eyes were big as saucers, and his mouth was just one big drool reservoir. This was Paris with a capital "P" to him, his first time in the Big Crêpe.

But underneath, Henry saw a darker city. Looking past the wealthy visitors, Henry could see hunger in the eyes of the Parisians. Their cheekbones stood out more than they had a year ago. Buildings that he remembered decorated with gold leaf and mullioned windows now stood naked to the October wind, the expensive glass replaced by bare wooden shutters. And the great citadel of the Louvre loomed over everything in a way he'd never noticed before.

"Where now?" asked Percy. "Er, I mean, *veeblefetzer! Potrzebie!*"

"We're going to try to find out what's happening."

"Ah," nodded Percy, knowingly. "We're going to 'case' the 'joint.'"

"Uh, yeah."

* * * *

Something is wrong.

Henry sat in the shadow of Notre Dame, waiting for Percy, watching the scene. The crowd was thick. A lot of them were pilgrims, but more than a hundred were workmen. Even with the nave, apse, and great glass windows in place, the cathedral wouldn't be finished for years, and the transepts were still nothing more than stones and scaffolding. Masons carved blocks on the ground or perched high in the air, raising great stones in place for the cathedral's walls and buttresses. Then there were the carpenters, preparing stands and barriers for the coronation ceremony, and the peddlers hawking wine and herb fritters.

Something is wrong.

In his mind's eye, Henry traced a route from the river through the building areas and into the cathedral itself. There was more than one way in, of course. The area around the cathedral was a maze of giant stones, wooden frames, vats and pits, and there were no guards: An ashlar or foundation stone might be worth a *livre* of silver to the master builder of a cathedral, but how would you steal it? And who would buy it from you if you did?

Once inside the building area, someone small and fast could climb the scaffold, get in through the great open gaps that would one day be the side wings of the church, and clamber down into the nave. But getting that close would be a problem on coronation day. Even though he was taller and heavier than he'd been a year ago, Henry knew he couldn't pass for a mason, even an apprentice. And the island would be crawling with Geoffrey's men.

Something is wrong.

Henry was missing something. He knew it, but couldn't figure out what. Percy came out of the cathedral, waving a small burlap sack. "Knuckle of St. Gustaf, knuckle of St. Wulstan, and the big toe of St. Eleutherius of Nicomedia. This is a collector's item! There are only three in existence!"

"St. Eleutherius had three big toes?"

"No, of course not. One of them is from when he was a kid. I need some reliquaries to hold them."

Henry sighed and pointed to a relic shop on the north side of the plaza. Percy scampered off. Henry stared at the crowds. The whole city was clamped tight. There were guards and checkpoints. But he and Percy had practically strolled onto the island. There wasn't a man at arms in sight. And according to the rogues' marks on the walls nearby, the Cellars, the most underground (literally!) criminal slum of a tavern in the entire city, was open for business. Something was very, very wrong.

"*Ave, frater!*"

Henry looked up. It was Pete the Worm, freelance librarian—and looking very well. The hollows in his cheeks had filled out, and he had a nice, new robe.

"*Ave, fra!* How—"

The Worm took his arm. "Walk with me, brother." They strolled toward the bridge. "Are you alone? Did you come back with anyone?"

"I—" Henry shut his mouth and looked around. Half the "workmen" had dropped their tools and drawn swords.

"THERE HE IS!"

The Worm was gone in a flash, dashing around the rear of the church. At least a dozen men closed in from the south, east, and west. They blocked Henry's way to the

Pont l'Evecque; the only way clear was the river. He sprinted to the shore and dove in.

The river was filthy. For some reason, it was warmer than he'd expected, which kind of made things worse, considering the garbage he saw floating in the water near him. Ferries and river boats rowed past, raising wakes that made it hard to see. He tried to keep the water out of his eyes and mouth as he swam for the Right Bank.

The current was sweeping him along the length of the island. If he didn't get to the shore quickly, it would carry him underneath the bridge and near all those wonderful sentries—he kicked harder.

It would carry him under the bridge…and out of sight, if only for a few moments. *Oh, I have a really dumb idea*, he thought. Kicking just enough to stay above water, he stopped paddling with his arms and instead got busy unknotting his cloak.

An arrow flickered past him, then another. He dived deep into the filthy water and used the moment to unknot his boots. As he was untying the left boot, he hit one of the bridge's stone columns with a thud, and grabbed hold. He raised his head out of the water. The bridge's arch was low overhead, and he was out of sight of Geoffrey's men. As fast as he could, he pulled off his cloak, boots and hose, tied them together, and tossed them back into the water. He watched them float away, out from under the bridge, one bundle surrounded by the rest of the river traffic.

Henry crossed his fingers—maybe Geoffrey's men would believe it for long enough. Time for the second part of the plan. He was under one of the lower arches near the shore, too low for most boats. He inched his way along the west face of the column, paddling when the footholds gave out, until he reached the bridge's central arch.

Here the current was faster and the small boats and ferries drifted past, one or two at a time. Henry dug one of the last *dixaines* from his coin pouch and stuck the silver penny in his mouth. The first boat was an open barge—no place to hide. The second was a ferry full of honest burghers. Now Henry was getting nervous. If the soldiers had been fooled at all by his little bundle of clothes, they would still have figured it out by now and would soon be coming back to the bridge. Time was running out.

A third boat drifted toward him, a barge full of rubbish and rags. He swam out to meet it and hauled himself on board.

THWACK! The broom hit him square on the shoulders, the twigs biting him on his ears and neck. THWACK!

"HELP! BRIGANDS!"

The old lady wasn't little; she looked like she could tear Henry in two or three—and her yelling wasn't helping either. As fast as he could, Henry spit the *dixaine* onto the deck. "My last penny, *grandmère*, if you take me down the river."

The yelling stopped. The barge-lady grabbed the coin and looked out at the river, where one or two arrows still fell in the water around Henry's clothing. "They want you for murder?"

"No, *grandmère*."

She nodded. "Right, then. Get under those bundles, cover yourself, and stay still until we reach St. Marcel."

The barge drifted out from under the bridge. Henry tensed, but no arrows came. They floated down the Seine, past the Île St. Louis. The barge-lady turned to him and opened her bag. "You want an onion?"

35. OLD FRIENDS

"I failed you. I should have been on guard against such treachery, but I was too busy looking for relics." Percy's voice dripped with self-disgust.

"Time for that later." Henry toweled his hair and put on the new clothes Percy had gotten for him. "Geoffrey knows we're here, so we have to get Alfie and Valdemar now."

"But how?"

Henry shrugged. "I know a guy."

"I see," said Percy. "This man, does he know what we need to know?"

"Yes," said Henry.

"Will we do 'good *gendarme*, bad *gendarme*'? Can I be the bad *gendarme*?"

"We can both be the bad *gendarme*."

* * * *

From the hilltop of Montmartre, the city was spread out below them in the night: the Cathedral of Notre Dame, surrounded on all sides by the campfires of throngs of pilgrims awaiting the coronation; to one side the dark mass of the Louvre, hulking over the city and lit by torches; to the other, the Latin Quarter and its rat's nest of churches, lecture halls, monasteries and back alleys, illuminated only by the bright harvest moon.

"Is the rope really necessary?"

"Silence, traitor." Percy probed with his dagger, and the Worm subsided with a hiss of pain. Henry smothered a pang of guilt. Not so long ago, he'd been the one tied up, playing where's-the-knife with a grinning killer.

"What do you think, Perce?"

Percy turned his attention from the Worm for a moment. "Not good, My Lord. Geoffrey has troops on all the bridges leading to the City Island, and we know he has spies in the crowds of pilgrims."

"Sound about right, Petronius?"

The Worm muttered something.

"I'm sorry. What was that? I didn't hear you."

The Worm sighed. "I said 'yes.'"

"Here's the fifty-*livre* question. Are Alfie and Valdemar still alive?"

"As far as I know. Geoffrey swept up all your old Paris gang and keeps them caged in the Louvre."

"And someone fingered them all, I'm guessing."

The Worm sighed. "Come on, *fra*, you know the score. All Geoffrey had to do was haul in a few to get the names of a few more and then a few more. I didn't turn in Alfie, I swear."

"Has he moved them?"

The Worm shrugged. "How should I know?"

Percy raised his knife.

"Really!" screamed the Worm. "I don't know! I couldn't!"

Henry waved Percy off. The knight was starting to enjoy the whole thing a little too much, anyway. "Why hasn't he killed them all yet?"

"The pope's coming for the ceremony, so he's been making a big show of mercy."

After the coronation would be a different matter, of course. "How do we get in and free them?"

"But—"

Henry raised a hand. "Ah, ah—no objections. And please, assume that you're coming with us."

Percy leaned in. "Shall I toss him down the hill, Lord?"

"That's his choice."

The Worm looked from one to the other. "I've done business with five of the regular guards. Two of them are on the fourth watch, right before dawn. They're your best bets, Renard and Fouquet—"

* * * *

Swimming a river through a hail of arrows, being dragged behind a horse to a darkling castle—this was getting all too familiar. Henry swallowed his gorge and reminded himself that this time it was different. This time, he had a plan.

Frankly, he would have preferred a big, magic sword.

Percy leaned back. "Lord, as a knight, I approve of rescuing prisoners from a castle. I mean, it's what I do. But if we're going to stop Geoffrey, shouldn't we do that first, instead of tipping our hand even more—"

"If I'm to get Excalibur back, we'll need Alfie and Valdemar. Trust me." *And I won't let them die. But no way I'm going to let Percy get all knightly on me.*

"Right." Percy trotted to the front gate and yelled upward. "Hola, the castle! A prisoner for the emperor!" There was nothing but silence—which was to be expected in the middle of the night. In fact, the longer it took, the happier Henry would be. Slow sentries, tired sentries, few sentries…He started to count, getting to *fifty plantagenet* before a small door opened in the thick wood of the gate and a soldier peered out. "We've got enough prisoners. Come back in July!" Henry heard sniggering behind the door.

Percy nodded. "Sure, I'll just let this Muttering Knight fellow walk, why should I bother you?"

The guard's eyes widened. "Bide a moment." There was a clanking of iron, and the door swung wide.

"Dismount and enter with the prisoner."

Percy got off the horse and shoved Henry ahead of him into the castle. The guard studied him, and Henry stared back arrogantly, doing his best to look like a legendary rebel. The guard was short, with red hair. This would be Renard—one of the Worm's favorites. He'd try to grab a cut of Percy's reward, but he'd have to split it with someone.

Renard nodded. "Aye, that could be him. Wait here." He locked the door again and left them standing in the darkened courtyard of the gatehouse.

"Now what?" said Percy, quietly.

"Pray," said Henry. It wasn't that bad, really. They had at least a fifty-fifty chance. If Renard came back with his watch captain and a squad, or even Geoffrey himself, they were doomed, no question. But if he ran true to the Worm's description, he would come back with Fouquet, the castle bailiff—it being the middle of the night and all—and they'd try to stiff Percy. And then it was possible, just possible, that they'd all go down to the dungeons together, just the four of them.

"There they are!" Henry sagged with relief. Renard was back with Fouquet, a grizzled man shaped like a wine barrel. Fouquet studied Henry and started to grin. "Aye, that might be him."

Percy stepped forward on cue. "Where's my money?"

Fouquet raised a thick, stubby finger in response. "Reward's to be paid after the outlaw's identity is confirmed, and he is genuinely in custody."

"Well, let's take him to the cells, then," Percy growled.

Fouquet nodded. Henry breathed a sigh of relief— Fouquet could easily have decided to summon Geoffrey and more guards. They walked through the door and down the stairs to the dungeons.

The corridor was narrow, and Renard's torch filled it with smoke. Henry walked ahead, shoved by Renard, his hands tied. He tried to commit the path to memory, so he could reverse it when necessary—past a courtyard on their left; through a great hall filled with rotted straw, sleeping troops, and long tables; down a spiral staircase and out into a lower courtyard near the Seine—he could smell the stink of the river.

Percy jogged up close, whispering in his ear. "The main hall with the retainers will be trouble, Lord." Henry nodded, eyes front.

Then back into the walls, and down another staircase. And down. And down, and down. The walls were dank now, slick with scum and river water. The torch's flame faded down to a blue and orange nub in the close air.

Finally Renard and Fouquet stopped in front of a blackened oak door, the top half of which was fitted with iron bars. Henry looked through and saw a giant room, barely lit by the moon shining through an air shaft, filled with ragged men chained to the walls. Percy turned to Renard. "That's it? You keep them all here with the rats?" He wasn't keeping his voice down; inside, some of the inmates stirred awake. Henry peered through the shadows. In the back—was that Alfie?

Renard laughed. "They're not knights, man. They're thieves and outlaws. No one will ransom them." He grabbed his key-ring as more of the prisoners stood up. Henry searched through the crowd. They'd only have the one chance…time to wake them up.

"I'm not going in there!" Henry yelled, loud as he could. "I'm the Muttering Knight!"

His voice echoed across the stones, waking the prisoners. A roar of prisoners' voices came back, in Breton, in French, in Latin.

In Welsh.

It was Alfie, there in the back, and Valdemar. The next instant, Percy knocked Henry to the floor.

"Shut up, you!" growled Percy, maybe a little too much in character. Henry glared up, hiding his smile. Underneath him, he felt the long knife Percy had dropped in passing.

Alfie and Valdemar were standing, tugging at their chains. Henry caught their eyes. *That's it, you gallows-birds. Get ready.*

Renard pulled out a ring of keys and opened the door. "There's a set of chains at the back."

"With locks," chimed in Fouquet. "You don't need a blacksmith, a forge, or anything."

Percy nodded. "Very advanced."

They hustled to the back, the inmates awake and shouting on both sides. Renard turned to Percy. "Give him here and we'll lock him in."

A glance flickered between Henry and Percy. Henry's falsely knotted ropes dropped to the ground. His knife came out in time with Percy's sword. He went for Fouquet as Percy went for Renard.

But Fouquet was ready for him, and caught him by the knife hand with surprising strength. The bailiff wrestled him, trying to lever his arm up behind his back, while Henry tried to go limp and roll with Fouquet's leverage. Whipping out in front of Fouquet once more, Henry swept his foot behind the bailiff's, and they both dropped to the cell's stinking mud floor.

Now all the prisoners were awake and yelling.

"Let me out, boy!"

"Let us out! We're innocent!"

"I have gold!"

Henry heaved against the bailiff's bulk. They thrashed for a moment, and parted just in time for Percy to rap Fouquet hard on the skull with his sword pommel. Fouquet rolled off, stunned and groaning. Renard was already unconscious against the wall.

Henry grabbed the keys off Fouquet and unlocked Alfie and Valdemar.

"Henry." Alfie grabbed him and hugged. Henry smiled and hugged back, even though you could tell Alfie had been a while in a cell without plumbing.

"Took you long enough," said Valdemar, rubbing his

wrists.

"Nice to see you too."

Alfie leaned in. "Free the rest, laddie."

Henry looked around. "I don't know, Alf, we need to leave fast and—"

"For God's sake, boy!"

Something huge crashed far above them, the sound of metal against stone. Henry turned to Fouquet, who laughed at him from the ground.

"You didn't think we just let you in, did we? That's the king's men coming for you."

Henry turned to Percy. "Unlock them all."

"But—"

Henry ran to the center of the cell. "You want to be free?" he yelled. "You're going to have to fight for it!"

One sword, one knife, and thirty starving prisoners, they stumbled up the stairs as fast they could. The ones who'd been held longest drifted toward the back.

"Where do they keep the swords in a place like this?" Henry asked Percy.

A voice came from behind. "In the armory."

Henry turned. Brissac stared at him from among the other prisoners, gray and ragged as a wolf in March. "Captivity. My reward for not sticking a knife in your back. Thank you for that."

Henry swallowed. "Any time."

Percy interrupted. "Can we get there from here?"

"Aye. But—" Brissac held up his hand. In the pause that followed, the sounds of footsteps echoed down the hall from the far doorway. "I think they're between us and it."

"Is there any other way out?"

Brissac shook his head. "The emp—Geoffrey is in residence. Every gate is locked."

Henry leaned close and spoke low. "What about every wall?" He turned to Alfie. "Alfie, can you still hang from a rope?"

Alfie got a noble, constipated look on his face. "Don't bother about me, laddie. Go on. It was a good try—"

"Don't go soft on me, old man. I have a plan, and I need you. Now, can you hang?"

Alfie grinned. "Tie me in a knot if I can't."

"Right." Henry turned to the other prisoners. "I freed you. If you have any honor, you'll follow me. But I warn you, if Geoffrey finds out you joined me, he will hunt you down personally."

Brissac laughed hollowly. "'If'? Try 'when.'"

The other prisoners stared at Henry. In a minute, they were gone, leaving only Alfie and Valdemar, Percy and— *sweet Jesu!*—Brissac.

Henry turned to Brissac. "We want a wall with a catwalk, overlooking houses on the other side...or at least something soft. And any spare rope, if we can find it."

Brissac nodded. "This way."

As they hustled up the corridor, Percy gasped. "Oh, I get it! The prisoners will distract the guards—"

"Right."

"You didn't *want* them to come with us! You wanted them to be a diversion! That really *is* dishonorable." He frowned. "And not in a good way."

Henry sighed. "I know. Should we go back?"

They were outside now, in a small courtyard under the stars. Percy glanced back. From behind them came the far-off sounds of yelling and steel. "No. I guess not."

Brissac led them through a series of stables and carters' sheds, which had the rope they needed, and some barrel staves for makeshift weapons. Valdemar started right away, making climbing knots in the rope. Brissac pointed toward a gate in the far wall. "Through there. The courtyard beyond has a flight of stairs that leads up to the battlements."

Henry smothered a smile. They might actually get away with this. He led the way to the gate, his heart rising with every step. Then, just a few yards from the gate, he heard the faint jingle of chain mail, and low voices echoing on stone. He stopped them and peered around the gateway into the courtyard.

The guards stood between them and escape—a squad of ten led by a knight, some still buckling on swords and armor, but enough to take them all down even if they'd had weapons. Henry's crew stared at him, waiting for him to come up with an answer. Henry shivered, because he had one. A really, really crazy one. Well, if knights were as sword-crazy as they seemed to be, it should work. And if it didn't, then his plan for Geoffrey wouldn't work either. Better to know now…

He tossed his knife to Brissac. "Alfie, Valdemar—make for the stairs when you see your chance. Take the rope with you. Percy, give me your scabbard." Percy moved to unbuckle the whole affair. Henry raised his hand. "Keep the sword. Just the scabbard, please." Henry took it and strapped it on.

"Let's go." He stepped out into the courtyard, not bothering to look back.

It was frosty cold. He straightened his tunic as he walked forward, throwing back his mind to the time with Excalibur, trying to remember how it felt, to be a…a vehicle for the sword.

And then he was face to face with the knight.

"I am the king's man. Yield." The knight was Percy's age, with a patchy beard and unscarred face. A kid.

Henry looked dead into his eyes. "I am the Muttering Knight. Yield to me." He grinned the lunatic killer's grin he had stolen from John. It was all he had. He felt light and empty, a shadow without strength.

"The Muttering Knight? The rebel?" The knight drew his sword. "Don't you have a magic sword?"

But the knight's *en garde* opened a door in Henry's mind. Now he remembered a time with the sword, when a warrior's stance had been etched into his flesh and bone.

Rooted to the earth. Light on the balls of the feet. Legs bent and right arm extended. The blade heavy but easy to move, a fearful engine, perfectly balanced.

He grinned wider and slowly, ever so slowly, drew an invisible blade from the scabbard. He held up his right hand, fist perfectly cupped around an invisible hilt, every muscle revealing the weight of a sword that wasn't there.

"This is my blade, magic and invisible."

The young knight grinned nervously. "Is this a joke?"

Henry just smiled.

"Are you mad?"

"Come find out."

The knight licked his lips and looked back at his squad. "There's no honor in fighting a lunatic…"

Around them Henry could hear the scuttle of feet on stone—Alfie and the others pattering through the shadows, making the most of his distraction. Henry edged right, putting himself between the stairway and the hesitating knight. One foot up, then the other, he slowly climbed the stairs backwards, his imaginary sword extended, as the rest of the crew raced above him to the parapets.

"They're going over the wall!" shouted one of the guards. That broke the spell. The young knight charged ahead, closing the gap that had opened between him and Henry.

"My turn, now." Brissac's hand was on Henry's shoulder, shoving him back up the steps. Percy's sword in hand, Brissac shoved himself between Henry and the knight. With two swings, the knight's sword clattered down the steps and away. "Go on, before they raise the alarm."

At the catwalk, Valdemar had looped the rope around a merlon and draped it down the outside wall. He was lowering Alfie, slow and steady, to a wagon that was drawn up to the wall, one of a line of carts waiting for the gates to open at sunrise.

As Henry joined the others on the catwalk, the castle's

bells began to ring out. His bladder started to loosen. "Faster is better, Vee."

Valdemar grunted. "Lower him yourself, why don't you?"

"Percy, you're next."

"But, My Lord—"

"Just go."

Percy grabbed the rope and clambered down as Brissac arrived. "None of them wanted to rush me, but they'll come at us from the towers in a few moments. Archers too, probably. Here." Brissac shoved a new sword in his belt, and handed Percy's sword to Henry. "Nice bluff, boy."

"Wait till you see what I have planned for Geoffrey. I'm going to fake him out of his codpiece."

"I'd like to see that."

"Help us get out alive, and I'll show you the real sword of kings."

An arrow whistled overhead, a taste of things to come. Valdemar shoved Henry to the rope. "Your turn."

Henry grabbed the rope and kicked off from the wall. Valdemar had knotted it well, every five feet. Then he was down, the sides of his fingers raw from the friction of the rope. He looked around. Alfie and Percy waved to him from behind one of the supply wagons. In minutes they were joined by Brissac and Valdemar. Crouching low, they ran into the darkness of the alleys and away.

36. THE WRONG SWORD

The bells rang at dawn. The noise echoed across the city, from St. Marcel to St. Lazare, scattering birds into the air, sending rats scuttling back into their nests, waking pilgrims and Parisians alike. The nobles, with their knights and troops, had been awake and waiting since the third watch. The gates of the family palaces opened wide, and the retinues rode out along broad, muddy avenues through suburban farmland toward the heart of Paris, the Ile de la Cité, and the cathedral where their emperor would be crowned. With nothing better to do, the students and slackers of the *universitatis* lined the processional boulevard of St. Michel to watch the free show, grabbing the best spots before the town's merchants and craftsmen could even wake up to make a try.

Soldiers dotted the intersections along the Boulevard St. Germain, the Rue St. Jacque, and the Rue du Temple. They patrolled in squads through the mucky alleys of the Latin Quarter and stood guard over the guild houses on the Rue du Bourgeois. Their livery was fancy, but they were not: blank-faced Swiss mercenaries, Teutons with the hard stares and red crosses of ex-Crusaders, twitchy Angevins who were loyal only to the Plantagenets.

By the time the sun rose fully over the eastern Marais, the retinues of the nobles had entered the city. First came the heads of the households, in their finest robes, riding war horses. Then came the house's vassal knights, in order of rank or favor, and the ladies of the house, on horseback or in sedan chair, surrounded by men-at-arms. The knights rode their best horses; the noblewomen wore their wealth on their necks and fingers and gowns. Today was a coronation—a chance to impress, to socialize, to make marriages and other business deals.

From the roof of the inn, Henry watched the nobles advance up the Boul' Miche. He was wearing the knightly tunic Geoffrey had forced on him. It had been cleaned by a fuller, its rips and holes carefully mended. He was sick of it, the sword and stone insignia, the whole stupid show, but this would be the last day he'd ever wear it...one way or another. He wore a sword on his hip, and in a small leather pouch he carried one of the two reasons he'd rescued Alfie from prison: a clay pot sealed with wax and inscribed with alchemical symbols.

"Let's have a look at the sword, lad," said Alfie. Henry drew it. It was an odd weapon, but so obviously precious that it had cost their last gold pieces from the Charlemagne score. Henry turned it over in the sunlight.

"Vee's a genius. How did he do it?"

"The Worm had a book. From his brother, he said. And it seems one of Valdemar's strikers is a Saracen."

The blade was as long as a man's arm, flexible and bright, with patterns on the steel like oil on water, and an edge sharper than a razor. Gems studded its hilt and pommel. It was beautiful. It was light, too, maybe half the weight of a knightly sword—and without Excalibur, every ounce was important. For what Henry had planned, it was perfect.

"It's a different kind of steel. How will it take to the treatment?" Alfie was worried about the stuff in the pot. So was Henry—"the treatment" was as nasty and dangerous as wearing a snake for a bracelet. Just being near the stuff gave Henry the shivers. They kept it in clay because it ate through wood, and they had tested it twice on steel before they decided to use it.

Henry shrugged. "I'm sure it will last long enough."

"I don't like it, lad. In a good cheat, the mark comes to you and suspects nothing. Geoffrey's waiting for you."

Brissac hawked and spit over the edge of the roof. "For what it's worth, I still have some friends in Geoffrey's retinue. They say he's gotten worse. Crazier." He was dressed as a Swiss mercenary, down to the crossbow and mail shirt.

Henry nodded. "I'll bet Excalibur is making his life interesting."

Brissac smiled. "We should help the man. Take it off his hands."

"It's time." Henry held out his hand to Alfie, who gave him a monk's robe. He draped it over his clothes and pulled the hood over his freshly tonsured scalp. "Where's Percy?"

"With Princess Mathilde's retinue. Geoffrey has been too distracted to pay close attention to her men-at-arms."

Alfie fussed with Henry's robe. "And Valdemar is downstairs with the Worm."

Henry turned to the stairs. "Let's go."

They climbed down the stairs and out on to the street. The crowds were already thick, and the invitees to the coronation paraded past in good order. Valdemar was waiting, one hand clamped tight to the Worm's shoulder.

"Pete, where's this brother of yours?"

The Worm pointed down the road at a band of monks progressing toward them, chanting. "There. They've been given the honor of singing the coronation mass."

"You kept your mouth shut?"

The book thief looked offended. "Of course!" He licked his lips. "But I told him you'd make a gift. A copy of Avicenna."

"After. I'll pay him directly, if you don't mind."

"Fine. Now let me go."

"Valdemar is going to stay with you until after the coronation. Vee, what will you do if something goes wrong?"

"Burn his books."

"No! For Christ's sake, Henry—"

"Sorry, can't talk. That's my retinue." Henry pushed through the crowds and joined the monks. One of them looked up.

"Henry! There you are!"

Henry whimpered in terror. It was Gervasius, the mad monk.

"I knew it was you! As soon as Pete started talking about swords and alchemy, I knew it was you!" Gervasius—or Gerry, or Wiglaf, or whatever name he was using now—seemed unharmed by his lightning machine. Maybe being crazy was its own form of unbreakable armor.

"Shut up!" Henry whispered fiercely. "Don't—"

"It's okay!" Brother Gerry whispered. He winked elaborately. "I understand about secrets!"

Wait a minute. "You're the Worm—You're Petronius' brother?" But of course he was. He had to be. The height, the complexion, the nose—

"You mean Pete? Of course. He loaned out my first manuscript."

Naturally. The apple didn't fall far from the tree in the Florentium family.

The sky was clear, and the sun was bright on red banners and cloth of gold. The onlookers were cheering like mad, and after a moment, Henry saw why: Geoffrey had stationed men throughout the procession who scattered pennies into the crowd. It was clever. Too clever—it was hardly the work of a desperate, easily fooled madman.

Henry shrugged off the fear and concentrated on

walking in step with the other monks. It was harder than it looked, and the manure left by the nobles' horses didn't make it easier—no pedestrian lane here. But at least Brother Gerry was quiet now, and the route wasn't long— from the Rue Cujas up the boulevard to the island was less than a mile. Before Henry knew it, he could smell the Seine, Notre Dame was looming ahead of them on their right, and they were facing the guards on the bridge. The sentries were Swiss mercenaries, guarding the way with pikes.

The one on the left was Hauptmann.

Henry's breath caught. If Hauptmann spotted him, it could all end here. The band of monks got closer. Hauptmann stared at them, made eye contact with one or two, then looked directly at Henry. Henry felt all his luck draining away.

Then Hauptmann nodded to the other sergeant, and the Swiss stepped aside. Henry snuck a peak at Hauptmann as he walked past. The mercenary looked exactly as he had before. Just a soldier doing his job.

They walked over the bridge and joined the huge crowd in front of the cathedral, waiting for the coronation. Here Geoffrey had put another bright crowd-control idea in place—everyone was separated. Monks were with monks, townsfolk with townsfolk, knights with knights. Mercenaries patrolled the borders. It was tidy and impressive, and if Henry wanted to take a look around, he'd stick out like a pork roast in Lent.

Henry turned to Gervasius. "When do we go inside?"

The monk smiled. "The Holy Father is inside already. We enter next, and then Geoffrey will enter, the nobility will follow, and the pope will crown him emperor. Quite an event, eh? And we'll have a terrific view from the gallery on the second floor."

Henry fought to keep the smile on his face. "The second floor? The gallery?" High above the action, with no way to get down? How was he supposed to reach Geoffrey from the gallery? Would he have to run down the packed stairwell past a dozen monks and twice that many armed killers before he even got to the altar? *Maybe if I just wave hard enough, Geoffrey will see me and ask me to come on down.*

Gerry nodded. "Of course. It's not like we're knights or anything. But don't worry, you'll be able to see everything, even better than the nobles on the floor. Oh, the bell is ringing. Time for us to enter." The monks got to their feet, singing, and walked out to the processional avenue. Facing hard stares from the patrolling mercenaries, Henry rose and followed.

Rope. If he had some rope, he could climb down…The monks filed toward the entrance, passing row after row of nobles and knights. Every few feet they would stop to chant an *Ave Maria*, and then continue. Henry looked around frantically. If Percy was around—There! He was on horseback, in the front rank of what had to be Mattie's retainers.

The monks stopped again for a hallelujah break. Henry tried to catch Percy's eye without being too obvious. It wasn't easy. Eye contact—nothing. A little wave—zip. Finally Henry pulled down his hood, and Percy figured out who he was. Percy's whole face lit up like a puppy with a new bone, and Henry had to make frantic little "shushing" gestures. Finally, Percy seemed to figure it out and nodded. Next, Henry tried to pantomime "rope," twisting his hands, miming a hangman's noose, even pointing to the rope of his monk's belt. Percy just looked more and more puzzled.

Finally, Henry pointed to the sedan chair. *Get Mattie.* Percy understood that and wheeled his horse around, but as he did, the procession started up again, and Henry was forced to enter the church.

It wasn't the first time Henry had been in Notre Dame, of course, but no matter how many times he entered, it still stopped his heart—the vast walls of colored light that were the stained glass windows; the great rose window above all, illuminated by the sun, glowing in the darkness; the pillars that marched down both sides of the nave and reached high above, leading to the glory of the altar…even for someone like him, who liked to keep Mother Church at a distance, it was a reminder that there were bigger things in the world than Henry of Sanbruc…or Excalibur, for that matter.

But not today.

They marched down the southern side aisle, toward the winding stairs that would lead up to the gallery. Henry looked right and left, but Geoffrey's men at arms were on either side, marking the way for the monks. Waiting until it seemed that the mercenaries weren't looking, Henry wandered into a side chapel. In a heartbeat, a soldier was at his elbow, pointing toward the stairs. Geoffrey might be evil, but you had to admire his organizational skills.

Henry trudged up the circular stairwell with the monks and out onto the gallery. The soldier shut the door behind him.

"Wasn't I right?" asked Gervasius. "About the view, I mean."

"You're right, Gerry," said Henry. "It is a great view." *For a dead end.* They hung halfway between floor and ceiling, flanked by the pillars, the arches of the roof vaulting far above. The gallery was a full thirty feet above the floor, not even counting the distance to the altar itself, which was dozens of yards farther east, beyond the church's transept.

A full thirty feet. Henry fingered the rope around his waist. Four feet, at most. But it was strong and clingy and flexible, and there were more than a dozen monks here with him. Maybe Gerry could help. If he wanted to.

Henry turned to the monk. "Where do you stand, Gerry?"

"What do you mean?"

"Do you care who gets your knowledge? Is it all right with you if it's Geoffrey and Raymond?"

"Of course not."

Henry blinked.

Gervasius grimaced. "The man won't fund anything except automatic shepherds now! Do you know how hard it is to find loadstones? And we both know that the shepherding aspect of the machine is fundamentally flawed. All it does is destroy castles!" He sighed. "I can admit it. A philosopher learns from his mistakes. That's why I took refuge with the Benedictines."

Henry fought the urge to smile. "I need to get down there, fast."

Gerry brightened. "I have a device, a *pneumo*—"

"I need your belt," Henry cut in quickly. "And those of your brothers."

Henry had forgotten about the vow of obedience that you took as a monk; he hadn't taken his own that seriously, after all. But these monks were hardcore, and they obviously saw something in Gerry that Henry hadn't. Gervasius lifted his hand, and they turned to him. He took off his own rope belt and handed it to Henry, and the others lined up to do the same, singing the whole time. It was impressive.

"You'll need some help with the knots," said Gerry.

While the monks tied their belts together, Henry carefully took out the clay pot and broke the wax seal. Inside was a greased-leather pouch, submerged in a pool of water. Henry put a glove on his left hand and lifted out the pouch. Alfie's instructions had been very clear. Whatever happened, he was to keep the pouch away from his naked skin. It carried a lump of white wax that, in a weak and adulterated form, was one of the ingredients of Greek fire. But in its pure form, according to Alfie's alchemist friend, there was no "Greek" about it; it was the philosopher's mercury, nothing more or less than the solidified element of fire itself. Henry was to pierce the pouch with the blade the instant before he confronted Geoffrey, smear the wax up and down, and pray that it worked as they said it would.

Cheers and hosannas rose from the church entrance. Henry bent over the gallery rail, craning for a look. It was Geoffrey making his entrance. Henry scanned the prince's face for any signs of incipient madness. There was still time to call it all off—

No. He couldn't tell; Geoffrey was too far away. Either he would believe the grift, or he wouldn't. Henry studied the rope. The knots looked good. Carefully, he placed the pouch back in the pot and checked the knots. Solid. He turned to Gervasius. "I'll need a loop for my foot. Can you lower me down?"

"Sure. But are you sure you don't want to try the *pneu*—"

"And I'll need to get Geoffrey's attention. Can you stop the singing for a moment when I'm on the balcony?"

"We can do better than that. Get ready."

"Uh—"

"Trust us."

Henry tied one end of the rope around the closest pillar, and fit the last loop of the rope around his foot. Still singing, the monks lined up along the rope and grabbed it like a band of old men playing tug-of-war. Whispering a prayer to the Virgin Mary, Henry picked up the pouch, and pierced it with the sword. The glowing wax spread up and down the blade, shining coldly in the gloom of the cathedral like the full moon on a clear winter night. There was a faint hiss as the wax met the air. It was as impressive as it was dangerous. Someone less skeptical than Henry might easily think it was magical. Clinging to the pillar, Henry climbed onto the gallery railing and turned to Gerry.

"Now," he said.

Gerry raised a hand. The monks turned upward, as if aiming their voices at a particular spot on the ceiling. All at once, they stopped chanting the *Ave Maria* and sang one word.

"MURDERER!"

It echoed through the cathedral. It seemed to come from everywhere at once. The procession stopped. Henry could see the knights and nobles looking around to see where the sound was coming from. Gerry leaned in and pointed. "Pitch your voice toward that arch and speak from your gut—it will carry throughout the cathedral."

Henry nodded. "LOOK UP, DUKE OF BRITTANY!" All the eyes down below turned up. "YOU SAY YOU HAVE THE SWORD OF KINGS. I SAY IT IS FALSE, AND SO ARE YOU."

There. Geoffrey saw him. They locked eyes. Even though Geoffrey was dozens of yards away, Henry felt his bowels drop into his boots, but he matched Geoffrey's grin with his own. Through a rigid smile, he muttered "now," and the monks lowered him to the floor.

The singing had stopped. There was dead silence. Geoffrey stood in front of the altar, dressed in silk and ermine, a gold chain on his neck...and Excalibur in his hand. Henry walked toward him. Each step echoed. Henry drew his sword. In the darkness of the cathedral, Excalibur and Henry's fake gleamed together with a pale, unnatural fire.

"I've been waiting for you, Henry," said Geoffrey. The streaks of white in his hair were wider, and he was grinning like a death's head. Henry met Geoffrey's eyes and knew then that Brissac was wrong. Geoffrey wasn't mad, not any more—he was as far beyond madness now as the sun is beyond fire. Had Excalibur done all that? Or had it always been in Geoffrey, waiting to come out? Henry's life depended on the answer.

Geoffrey raised his hand and turned to the waiting nobles. "You see this poor child. He helped me find Excalibur, but then went mad. Now he imagines himself a knight. Take him, but treat him gently."

Before anyone could move, Henry raised his sword and shouted. "I AM THE MUTTERING KNIGHT! I

WIELD THE SWORD OF DAVID, GOD'S ANOINTED! COME AND FACE ME, PRETENDER!"

There was a wave of confused motion, but no one in the crowd stepped forward to take Henry. Geoffrey's face darkened. He turned again to the nobles and knights. "You want to see the blood of innocents? So be it."

Out of the corner of his eye, Henry saw a priest in vestments—the bishop of Paris, probably—race to the front, ready to stop bloodshed in a holy place. But he disappeared into the crowd, his voice muffled by Percy's hand. So Percy was good for something, anyway.

Staring into Geoffrey's eyes, Henry wanted to run. If he couldn't make Geoffrey believe his sword was magic, was one of the Nine, he was a dead man. But to make Geoffrey believe, Henry would have to act as though he himself believed, as though his sword really were magic. He couldn't merely defend; he would have to attack. If he could attack, if he could survive the first few passes, that might be enough to convince Geoffrey.

As he had at the prison, Henry tried to remember what it felt like to wield Excalibur. It was easier this time, with a real sword in his hands. He lowered his sword, point toward Geoffrey, took a deep breath—

—and Geoffrey charged.

Excalibur was everywhere, at Henry's head, his guts, his legs. Henry had grown a few inches over the past year, but Geoffrey still had the reach on him, and he used it relentlessly, forcing Henry back down the long central aisle. Henry gave ground and gave ground, fighting to keep his balance and not be overwhelmed. But if Geoffrey had been deadly with a bastard sword, with Excalibur he was…supernal. He moved so fast Henry couldn't even see the blade—every block, every parry was based on guesswork and hope. His only advantage was the memory of Excalibur fighting in his muscles and joints, keeping him centered, his legs bent, his wrist straight.

"You're still standing," said Geoffrey. "So that really is

a magic sword." He wasn't even breathing hard.

Yes! Somewhere beneath the terror, Henry's heart leaped. Geoffrey couldn't believe Henry was fighting on his own. He believed that Henry's sword was real. Henry grinned and flourished the weapon in a figure eight, Excalibur-style. "Come find out, old man."

"Now we end it."

Geoffrey swung at Henry's head. Henry moved to block, but even faster, Geoffrey changed the attack, and Excalibur was humming toward Henry's unprotected side. This time, Henry could see the blow coming, but he couldn't move fast enough. He was going to die—

Geoffrey's face twisted. He groaned and faltered, giving Henry the moment he needed to parry. Sparks flew, and Henry jumped back.

"What's the matter, Geoff?" Henry twirled his sword again. "Touch of gout?"

Geoffrey snarled and lunged. Once again, Henry was at the center of the whirlwind. But he could see Geoffrey's face—the prince was in agony. Excalibur was fighting her master.

Henry leaped away from a cut that would have disemboweled him if it had been two inches closer. Staggering in pain, Geoffrey was still a better fighter. Geoffrey attacked again, hacking and slashing, until they stood *corps-à-corps*.

"Give up, boy."

"I don't think so, Geoff," said Henry. "My sword's better. You see, it doesn't talk back."

You don't know despair until you see hope. Henry saw it in Geoffrey's face and knew what would happen next. Geoffrey shoved him back and bored in with a spiral that sent "David's sword" clattering across the floor. Geoffrey dropped Excalibur and leaped for the other blade.

In a moment that seemed to stretch forever, Henry reached down for Excalibur. He touched its hilt. His hand closed around it, and the sword's spirit moved—

So. What kept you?

Henry and Geoffrey stood facing each other. Geoffrey stared at the sword in his hand. He waved it once, twice. "No magic." He looked Henry in the eye. "Clever lad."

His standards for "clever" are obviously low.

"You—"

No time!

The scimitar sliced toward Henry's head in a blur. Henry ducked, parried Geoffrey's backslash, and hopped out of range. Excalibur was light in his hands, and once again he felt the sword's power rising.

Geoffrey lunged twice at his head, then whirled at his chest. Henry ducked. The world lost its color; he could feel the sword's cold ghost seeping into his skull.

"Stay out of my head!"

You do not command me!

"Right back at you!"

Geoffrey pressed him relentlessly. In his hands, the razor-sharp blade seemed to slice the air itself in pieces.

But you need me!

"Not that much!"

Geoffrey caught Henry on the left cheek, just below the eye, and drew a line of fire to Henry's nose.

Very well.

Henry's vision cleared. The presence behind his eyes faded. But Excalibur still felt light. His arms and legs felt strong. He could sense Geoffrey's stance—there was a slight imbalance, favoring the prince's right leg over his left—he knew what to do.

There. You have my power. Now finish it!

Henry attacked, catching Geoffrey's sword mid-blade with Excalibur. Sparks showered down on them, skittering across the floor of the cathedral. Henry chopped at Geoffrey's head, throwing off Geoffrey's rhythm, putting him on the defensive.

They traded blows, cut, parry, riposte, their attacks carrying them up and down the nave. Henry's body ran with sweat under the showy tunic. Blood ran from the slash on his cheek, and another, longer one on his torso. Geoffrey's attack was so fast and Valdemar's damned blade was so sharp that Henry hadn't even felt the cut at first. Now it burned with the remnants of the chemical fire on Geoffrey's sword, and the blood was trickling into Henry's braies.

Damned Valdemar. He didn't have to be *that* good.

Without Excalibur, Geoffrey was breathing easy— easier than Henry. He was unwounded, he moved light as a bird, and he fought with a terrible joy.

"I owe you, Henry! You brought me magic, and now you've brought me freedom!"

Henry ducked Geoffrey's attack. A few stray hairs drifted to the floor, severed by Damascus steel. The crowd *oohed* and *aahed* at the nearness of the cut. *Glad you're enjoying the show,* thought Henry.

"Once you're dead, I might not even torture your friends!"

"You're a giver, Geoff!" Henry pointed Excalibur and lunged. Geoffrey parried easily and riposted, forcing Henry to scramble to recover. "Shatter his sword already!" Henry muttered to Excalibur.

What do you think I've been trying to do!? That cursed prince knows me to well. He turns the blade so I cannot catch it.

"I'm bleeding. We don't have a lot of time here."

"You're losing, Henry." Geoffrey attacked, was parried. "Yield, and…oh, hell, boy, we both know I'll kill you, no matter what. Never mind." Geoffrey grinned, and cut at him again. And again.

Geoffrey forced him relentlessly down the aisle, past the Archbishop, past the assembled noble families, past Mattie, who was gripping Percy's hand with whitened knuckles, rigid as a statue. Henry beat uselessly at Geoffrey's attack. He felt like screaming. He had practiced, he had come all this way, Geoffrey had fallen for the scheme, he had Excalibur—and Geoffrey was still beating him. Was toying with him. It wasn't *fair*.

If you are about to die, shove me into the foundation stone of the cathedral. Geoffrey shall not move me from it, and I shall stand as a testament against his rule.

"Yeah. You give up too easily, you know that?"

Then what are you waiting for? KILL HIM!

Henry screamed and leaped. Geoffrey grinned and raised his blade—strong, confident, with the sword's edge turned just slightly toward Henry.

There it is.

Excalibur sang with certainty. The swords met with a metal shriek. There was a sound like a bell cracking, and more sparks.

And Geoffrey staggered back, staring at his broken sword. The crowd gasped.

Tell him to yield.

"Do I have to?"

Believe me, I am sorry, but…yes.

"Geoffrey Plantagenet, tyrant and usurper, yield!"

Geoffrey looked up. His face was slack. The focus, the driving, terrifying Plantagenet craziness, was gone. For the first time, he looked like an ordinary man, one who had been caught out by bad news that he didn't quite believe. His mouth worked. "I…" Maybe it was over. Maybe—

Then, like wine filling a skin, Henry saw the pride return. Geoffrey stood straight, and smiled. "I think…not." He leaped at Henry, the broken sword seeking Henry's face.

Henry's hand twitched. Excalibur rose. Geoffrey caught the sword square in his chest.

Henry's arm cramped with the sudden weight, and Geoffrey's eyes locked with Henry's. Henry saw the light blaze brightly for a moment, and then go out. Geoffrey sagged against Henry, and then fell to the floor, dead.

Henry looked down stupidly at himself. He was covered in Geoffrey's blood and his own. He wanted to vomit. He wanted to sleep. He wanted to—

Stay awake, Henry. Stay alert.

"Wha—"

You have killed their prince. Maybe they'll kneel, maybe they'll charge. We don't know.

"How about I run?"

Then they will definitely charge.

"Oh."

You always have a plan. Didn't you plan for this?

"I didn't expect to get this far."

The noise of the assembled crowd grew louder and louder. It was starting to sound distinctly less happy.

Do something quickly, Henry. Left alone, crowds go to the bad.

"What should I do?" The nobles had hitched up their sword belts. Henry saw a few determined expressions he didn't like at all.

Raise me high. Claim the throne for yourself.

"You're kidding!"

Why not? You're better than that thing you killed.

The mob inched closer.

"Did you actually compliment me? Are you sure you're Excalibur?"

Henry...

One knight had drawn his sword. Another did it. And another.

Henry licked his lips. At least he had to make sure that no one got Excalibur. The sword's suggestion made sense now—stick it in the bedrock of Notre Dame, and no one would chip away sacred ground to get it. He raised Excalibur, and aimed it point first at the floor. The knights were all around him.

"GOD SAVE HENRY OF SANBRUC!"

Mattie's voice rang out through the cathedral. Henry turned, and the crowds parted to let her through, with a little help from Percy, who shoved away a couple of knights who didn't move on their own. She walked toward him, one hand on Percy's arm, dressed all in white, with a silver crown. Henry's mouth went dry, and his heart punched at his ribs. She was the most beautiful thing he had ever seen.

"Kneel, Henry."

Henry knelt. Without looking away, Mattie held out her hand. "Guillaume. Your shirt." One of the knights who had looked ready to kill Henry stripped off his tunic and handed it to Mattie.

And all the knights with drawn swords knelt, too, bowing their heads.

Oh, clever girl. She IS a princess, that one.

Mattie held her hand out.

What are you waiting for, idiot? Give me to her!

Slowly, Henry presented Excalibur to Mattie. She wiped it clean of her uncle's blood as casually as polishing a piece of silverware. Then she grabbed it by the hilt, and held it over Henry's head.

"Henry of Sanbruc, you have served us well. Take from our hands your knighthood. By St. Louis and St. Charles, we grant you the right to bear arms and to mete justice, to raise troops and to hold land. We bind you to our service, to the order of chivalry and the code of arms. Protect the weak, defend the helpless, confound the wicked." She struck him lightly on both shoulders with the sword. "Rise, Sir Henry."

Henry staggered to his feet. Percy gave him the thumbs up. Mattie smiled, kissed him lightly on both cheeks and handed him Excalibur. "You have a way out of here?" she said quietly.

It took him a minute to understand. "Brissac's waiting with the Swiss. If you can get me outside—"

"Right. Take my hand. Smile. Wave to all the pretty people."

She lifted his hand and turned him to face the guests.

"THREE CHEERS!" yelled Percy. "HIP, HIP— HURRAH! HIP, HIP—"

The cheering echoed from the pillars and the walls. It couldn't be true, but Henry thought he could see everyone he'd met in the crowd—Alfie and Vee, Wulfgar and Madame Goncourt, Edwina and Ralf and Ulric...he shook his head.

They walked smoothly down the nave, nodding to the crowd.

"Berengaria?" murmured Henry, out of the corner of his mouth.

"Oh, like you wouldn't have changed it, too."

The doors of the cathedral opened, and they walked into sunlight.

37. UNDER NEW MANAGEMENT

Mostly, people had wanted a party, and they got one.

King Philip made sure of it. A good party makes everything right. So minstrels and jugglers filled the streets, the students and criminals were roaring drunk on the Left Bank, and even the nuns of St. Agnes were ready to party like it was 999. And Henry, Alfie, and Valdemar had passes to the hot-ticket event of the post-Geoffrey season: the Park Royal.

Despite the lateness of the year, Philip had decreed a giant festival area in the fields outside the city's western wall. Bonfires of specially seasoned oak burned hot with very little smoke, turning the late October weather back into September. Tiny oil lamps with horn casings studded the trees. Tents and pavilions were everywhere, some private, some open for business: wine, food, entertainment.

Henry, Alfie, and Valdemar were walking up the main avenue to the royal enclosure, dressed in their finest, courtesy of the Houses of Plantagenet and Capet. They'd even had baths.

"Put on your hat. It cost sixty *dixaines*."

"I look like a damned Italian courtier," said Valdemar.

"That's the style." Henry looked around at the crowds. He hadn't realized just how many people had attended the coronation that wasn't. Most of them were here in the park, and the babble of different languages was incredible. In just a few steps, he'd heard Swabian, Frisian, Milanese, and something he was sure was Greek.

"Lots of nobles, too," said Alfie.

"What?"

"I'm just saying, lad—fat pickings if we want them. That fellow yonder, with all those spearmen, he's a Hohen-something. Rich as Midas they are, and they dabble in alchemy. We could—"

Back to your old ways, eh?

"That's enough out of you," muttered Henry.

Well, it won't matter soon. Are you sure he'll be at the Royal Pavilion?

"I checked three times. You're not the only one who wants this hand-off."

It was the one benefit of the coronation that Henry hadn't considered—where you had a gathering of royalty, you might actually have someone Excalibur considered worthy. And they were meeting him tonight. By tomorrow, he'd be a free man. Goodbye, insanely dangerous journey to Constantinople. Hello, soft Parisian bedspread. Goodbye, evil Plantagenet emperor. Hello, smart, beautiful Plantagenet princess. Henry grinned like an idiot.

The Royal Pavilion spread out in front of them. Philip knew how to put on a show—there were yards of silk, hundreds of torches, music, guards. This was clearly the place to be.

Henry turned to Alfie. "If someone catches a hand on their purse, I don't know you."

"But they're the oppressing class—"

"And no puking on people's shoes. Valdemar, I'm looking at you."

Valdemar muttered something nasty in Flemish.

I give them two hours, tops. Let's cut their throats now, and save ourselves the embarrassment of having to do it later.

"And another county heard from. Thank you all for your support. Shall we go in?"

The guards opened the gate, and they entered. Inside, it was a blaze of light. Musicians were doing something classy with strings, and pages circulated with trays of food and wine cups. Henry looked for a central dining table, until he saw guests just reach out and pick food off the trays.

"It's all the rage in Rome."

Henry turned. The man had strong features, with black hair and eyes. And a crown.

"Your Majesty." Henry bowed. He didn't have to look up to know that, with the instinct of true street rats, Alfie and Valdemar had already peeled off and scuttled for cover.

Not a bad bow. A little stiff, perhaps—

King Philip of France extended a suave, well-manicured hand. "Rise, Sir Henry. I see my tailors did good work for you."

"Yes, Majesty. The new clothes were much appreciated, as were the rooms at the Palais."

Henry tried to study Mattie's new guardian without staring. He was handsome, Henry noted with displeasure. And tall. Too tall, really. Who did he think he was?

Now THERE is a king.

"Why not go with him, then?"

Too cunning, too bigoted. My true bearer must possess a certain innocence.

"No mind of his own, you mean?"

But this one is a monarch nonetheless.

"Were you addressing me, Sir Henry?"

"No, Majesty. I'm sorry. Muttering is an affliction of mine—"

"So I hear. As is the sword you bear."

How dare he! Some puppy of a prince, with no more than thirty winters behind him—

Henry winced.

Philip noticed. "I see the stories are true." He gestured, and a servant brought them wine. "You know, many who did not see your final battle refuse to believe you fought Geoffrey at all. Some say he was trampled by a horse."

"I wish it were so, Your Majesty."

Philip raised an eyebrow. "This was your first time in combat?"

"No, Majesty. But it was the first time I…looked into his eyes."

Philip nodded. "Indeed. Well, you offered him mercy. He refused."

I said as much! But would you listen to me? No—

"But that is not the issue, is it? It is the act itself." Philip put a hand on his shoulder. "I felt the same way. No one retains his innocence outside of Eden, Sir Henry. You'll feel better soon enough."

"Thank you, Majesty."

Philip paused for a moment, and studied Henry. "Tell me, Henry…if I asked you for your sword, would you give it to me?"

Excalibur shrieked. Henry ignored it, and tried to frame his answer carefully. Very, very carefully. "I hope that you would not, Majesty. For your own sake. It did no good at all to its…previous owner."

The king nodded. "Yes. We noticed. But you're not drooling or screaming at phantoms. Are you stronger than a Plantagenet?"

Hah. You're about as strong as a custard. Tell him that.

"No, Majesty. I am just…more humble. And less likely to commit atrocities. Excalibur frowns on them, you see."

Philip sipped his wine. "It dictates policy, does it?"

"It expects to have a say, Majesty."

"That must have infuriated Geoffrey."

"I hope so, Majesty." They shared a smile. Philip's smile made him look dark and interesting; Henry smothered a pang of jealousy as big as the Louvre.

"Majesty?"

"Yes?"

"Princess Mathilde...how is she? I haven't spoken to her since the cathedral."

Philip nodded to the dais. "There she is. You can ask her yourself."

"No, that's all right—"

"Well, she has asked to see you. So stop by any time. I'll tell her chaperone to allow you an audience." Philip clapped him on the shoulder and left.

"'Chaperone.' Nice. Letting me know where I stand."

Well, you did steal her once. If it is any consolation, your feelings are in the best tradition of knightly—

"No. It's not. Where's Percy?" Henry stalked through the pavilion. Percy had promised to get the low-down on Excalibur's hot prospect—some princeling they had spotted a few days before at one of the tourneys Philip had organized. Excalibur had seen the kid win joust after joust and offer mercy to his vanquished foes; naturally, the sword had fallen for him point over pommel. But he'd jousted in cheap, no-name armor (a mark of modesty that had sealed the deal as far as Excalibur was concerned) and so they'd set Percy on the trail of the Unknown Knight.

"You're a joust groupie, you know that?"

You can tell more about a man by his lance than you can by his speech.

Henry took a chair near the wine kegs and grabbed a cup. He had walked to the party from the Royal Palace, and his wounds hurt. "Is it my imagination, or are people staring?"

Yes, they are. Some are trying to gauge your worth as a foe in tourney; others wonder whether they can take me from you; still others are certain they can, but doubt they can do it honorably, now that you are wounded. Do not worry. By tomorrow, you will no longer be worth their consideration.

"Well, thank you. It's nice to know I was so important to your plans."

Honestly, there is no pleasing you. I was trying to cheer you up.

"As soon as I give this knight a certain magic sword, I'll be so happy I'll need a purge."

Well, that goes double for me. Triple! In fact, I'll—

"Wait. Hold that insult." Henry spotted Percy and raised a hand. Percy came over.

"What's the word?"

"Good. His name is Frederick. He's a German, a prince in Bavaria—"

Henry glanced down at Excalibur. "The Alps. Fighting the storms, testing yourself against the elements. You'll like that."

Although one must guard one's edge against snow and sleet—

"—and naught but good is spoken of him, and although young, he is said to be deeply learned."

"Yeah?"

"He can read."

I won't hold that against him. Arthur himself was able to sign his name.

"He should be here soon. But I have a message from the princess."

"Yeah?" Henry swallowed. His Adam's apple felt as big as a melon.

"She wants you to meet her behind the kitchen, and to stop standing around like a...well, like something I can't repeat." Percy frowned. "I didn't think princesses knew words like that."

"You'll have to get used to it if you want to continue in her service."

"But—But I thought that I would...I would follow you."

"Percy, by tomorrow I won't have Excalibur. Why on Earth would you want to follow me?"

Percy crossed his arms and looked stubborn. "Sword or no, you still have a Destiny."

"God, I hope not." Henry smiled to take out some of the sting, but Percy's face had set like stale dough. He settled for clapping Percy's shoulder and heading for the kitchen.

The kitchen was an open area with fire pits and tables packed with cooks and servants. Henry pushed through it and spotted a single figure in white near the far edge of the pavilion.

Henry put his hand on Excalibur's grip. "I'd like a little privacy."

I promise to…look away until you draw me again.

"Thank you."

Mattie waved. He ran to her and kissed her. For a long time. No one stopped them.

It was *wonderful.*

After what felt like forever, Mattie pulled her head back and said, "That answers my first question."

"What?"

"You *do* like me."

"Uh…yeah."

"Is Percy right? You've found someone for the sword?"

"We might even make the switch tonight."

"But that's great! You don't have to go East. You can stay here…with me."

"Uh, yeah." *Smooth. I'm a regular Abelard.*

They kissed again, and were just getting down to their third kiss when someone hissed at them from across the field.

"Ignore it," said Henry.

"But it's Percy. He looks serious."

"He always looks—"

"Henry…"

"All right, all right. But don't go anywhere."

"I promise."

Henry grabbed Percy. "This had better be the best news in Paris."

"Prince Frederick has arrived."

At last! At last! sang Excalibur.

"Let's go then."

Inside, guests had gathered around the new arrivals, a small band of nobles in their best velvet who were presenting gifts to King Philip.

"Oranges, I think, pepper, and...what's that, Percy?"

"I believe it's silk, My Lord."

"Fancy."

He is a true prince, who understands the nobility of gifts and hospitality.

Henry glanced down at Excalibur. "How do you want to do this? Just introduce ourselves and hand you over?"

Speed is best.

"Right." Henry took a breath and stepped forward—

Henry.

"What?"

In Glastonbury, when you let Brissac live...

"Yes?"

I knew you would be worthy. I thought I should tell you, before we part.

After a moment, Percy leaned forward. "Are you all right, My Lord?"

Henry blinked hard a few times and wiped his nose. "Fine. Fine." He dabbed at his eyes. "Which one is he?"

"The tall one with the red hair."

"Wait—I think..."

Henry walked closer. Tall, red-haired, wide-shouldered—"Frederick of Swabia!?"

The prince's eyes widened. "Tyro!"

"It's Henry. Henry of Sanbruc."

"*You're* Henry of Sanbruc?" Frederick's hand whipped out and engulfed Henry's in a bone-crushing shake. "I should have known! I've been trying to find you since we arrived in Paris! Here I give my spot to a tyro, and he turns out to be the greatest warrior in Paris!"

Hmm...he doesn't seem to have as much judgment and wisdom as I expected. Oh well.

"We're actually on our way to Calais to sail home. But I

insisted we stop here before we went, so I'd have a chance to meet you—"

Please, in the few minutes we have left, don't disappoint the boy and do something ignoble.

"—and this is my Uncle Raymond, the Prince Regent."

Raymond?

"Well, well, Sir Henry. A pleasure to see you again."

There he was, Raymond of Toulouse, predatory as ever, from his sleek black hair to his pointed shoes. Henry swallowed. "So, you're a regent now. Congratulations."

Raymond shrugged. "An honor bestowed by the late emperor, and not contested." He glanced at Frederick, who was making friends with the wine steward, and then turned back to Henry. "And besides, I *am* the boy's uncle, or cousin, depending on how one reckons consanguinity. Grandfather, too, I think. So it's all in the family." Raymond gazed contentedly at Frederick, who had now gathered a small army of admirers, from knights down to serving boys, and was telling them of exploits in the Alps. "Such a nice boy. So trusting."

Henry kept the smile fixed on his face. He made small talk for a few minutes, and then left the Swabians with Percy. Raymond was describing new methods of torture he had developed for the Toulouse courts of justice.

Henry—

"I know—"

After two thousand years as the sword of heroes—

"I know!"

If you simply give me to Frederick, Raymond will have me away from him in a day.

"You can't be sure of that. You gave him a big old jolt last time."

Frederick needs someone older and wiser. Or at least someone nastier and sneakier. Someone to guide him in my use, so that he will not succumb to the wiles of his uncle.

"There has to be somebody else who's worthy, someone without the uncle problems."

I've been looking since we arrived in Paris. Don't you think I would have told you if I'd found anyone else?

"No. There is somebody. There has to be. You're too picky, that's the problem."

It won't be long. A month, a single tourney season at the most. Frederick is a much more worthy candidate than you were. He'll pick up the basics in a snap.

"Sir Henry!" It was Percy. "The prince's party is leaving for Calais. He wants to say goodbye."

Well? Hop to it. Calais is waiting.

Henry sighed. "Percy, tell Frederick to wait. I...feel like some travel. Have you ever been to Calais?"

Percy grinned. "I'd love to!" He dashed off.

See how easy that was?

"I hate you. Hate, hate, hate, hate, hate."

You're just saying that.

"No, I'm serious." Henry grabbed his cloak and started to look for Alfie and...*oh, blessed St. Nick, what am I going to tell Mattie?* He ground his teeth in frustration.

You like me. Admit it.

"Be. Quiet."

They stepped out of the pavilion. Ahead of them, the moon shone silver on the road to Calais. The prince's horses whickered in the darkness, and the night air was cool and smelled of adventure. Henry hitched up his belt and sighed.

This was going to *reek.*

ABOUT THE AUTHOR

Ted Rabinowitz writes ad copy and speculative fiction, two entirely different kinds of imaginative literature. He lives in the northeastern United States, is a graduate of a few prestigious institutions of higher education, and knows the difference between a claymore and a pike.

www.ingramcontent.com/pod-product-compliance
Lightning Source LLC
Chambersburg PA
CBHW020243200626
46816CB00001BA/106